P9-EDL-342

*Echoes
from the
Macabre*

Daphne du Maurier

Echoes from the Macabre

Selected Stories

DOUBLEDAY & COMPANY, INC., GARDEN CITY, NEW YORK

Copyright © 1952, 1959, 1970, 1971, 1976 by Daphne du Maurier
All Rights Reserved
Printed in the United States of America

Contents

Don't Look Now

"Don't look now," John said to his wife, "but there are a couple of old girls two tables away who are trying to hypnotise me."

Laura, quick on cue, made an elaborate pretence of yawning, then tilted her head as though searching the skies for a non-existent aeroplane.

"Right behind you," he added. "That's why you can't turn round at once—it would be much too obvious."

Laura played the oldest trick in the world and dropped her napkin, then bent to scrabble for it under her feet, sending a shooting glance over her left shoulder as she straightened once again. She sucked in her cheeks, the first tell-tale sign of suppressed hysteria, and lowered her head.

"They're not old girls at all," she said. "They're male twins in drag."

Her voice broke ominously, the prelude to uncontrolled laughter, and John quickly poured some more chianti into her glass.

"Pretend to choke," he said, "then they won't notice. You know what it is—they're criminals doing the sights of Europe, changing sex at each stop. Twin sisters here on Torcello. Twin brothers to-morrow in Venice, or even tonight, parading arm-in-arm across the Piazza San Marco. Just a matter of switching clothes and wigs."

"Jewel thieves or murderers?" asked Laura.

"Oh, murderers, definitely. But why, I ask myself, have they picked on me?"

The waiter made a diversion by bringing coffee and bearing away the fruit, which gave Laura time to banish hysteria and regain control.

"I can't think," she said, "why we didn't notice them when we arrived. They stand out to high heaven. One couldn't fail."

"That gang of Americans masked them," said John, "and the bearded man with a monocle who looked like a spy. It wasn't until they all went just now that I saw the twins. Oh God, the one with the shock of white hair has got her eye on me again."

Laura took the powder compact from her bag and held it in front of her face, the mirror acting as a reflector.

"I think it's me they're looking at, not you," she said. "Thank heaven I left my pearls with the manager at the hotel." She paused, dabbing the sides of her nose with powder. "The thing is," she said after a moment, "we've got them wrong. They're neither murderers nor thieves. They're a couple of pathetic old retired schoolmistresses on holiday, who've saved up all their lives to visit Venice. They come from some place with a name like Walabanga in Australia. And they're called Tilly and Tiny."

Her voice, for the first time since they had come away, took on the old bubbling quality he loved, and the worried frown between her brows had vanished. At last, he thought, at last she's beginning to get over it. If I can keep this going, if we can pick up the familiar routine of jokes shared on holiday and at home, the ridiculous fantasies about people at other tables, or staying in the hotel, or wandering in art galleries and churches, then everything will fall into place, life will become as it was before, the wound will heal, she will forget.

"You know," said Laura, "that really was a very good lunch. I did enjoy it."

Thank God, he thought, thank God . . . Then he leant forward, speaking low in a conspirator's whisper. "One of them is going to the loo," he said. "Do you suppose he, or she, is going to change her wig?"

"Don't say anything," Laura murmured. "I'll follow her and find out. She may have a suitcase tucked away there, and she's going to switch clothes."

She began to hum under her breath, the signal, to her husband, of content. The ghost was temporarily laid, and all because of the familiar holiday game, abandoned too long, and now, through mere chance, blissfully recaptured.

"Is she on her way?" asked Laura.

"About to pass our table now," he told her.

Seen on her own, the woman was not so remarkable. Tall, angular, aquiline features, with the close-cropped hair which was fashionably called an Eton crop, he seemed to remember, in his mother's day, and about her person the stamp of that particular generation. She would be in her middle sixties, he supposed, the masculine shirt with collar and tie, sports jacket, grey tweed skirt coming to mid-calf. Grey stockings and laced black shoes. He had seen the type on golf courses and at dog shows—invariably showing not sporting breeds but pugs—and if you came across them at a party in somebody's house they were quicker on the draw with a cigarette lighter than he was himself, a mere male, with pocket matches. The general belief that they kept house with a more feminine, fluffy companion was not always true. Frequently they boasted, and adored, a golfing husband. No, the striking point about this particular individual was that there were two of them. Identical twins cast in the same mould. The only difference was that the other one had whiter hair.

"Supposing," murmured Laura, "when I find myself in the *toilette* beside her she starts to strip?"

"Depends on what is revealed," John answered. "If she's hermaphrodite, make a bolt for it. She might have a hypodermic syringe concealed and want to knock you out before you reached the door."

Laura sucked in her cheeks once more and began to shake. Then, squaring her shoulders, she rose to her feet. "I simply must not laugh," she said, "and whatever you do, don't look at me when I come back, especially if we come out together." She picked up her bag and strolled self-consciously away from the table in pursuit of her prey.

John poured the dregs of the chianti into his glass and lit a cigarette. The sun blazed down upon the little garden of the restaurant. The Americans had left, and the monocled man, and the family party at the far end. All was peace. The identical twin was sitting back in her chair with her eyes closed. Thank heaven, he thought, for this moment at any rate, when relaxation was possible, and Laura had been launched upon her foolish, harmless game. The holiday could yet turn into the cure she needed, blotting out, if only temporarily, the numb despair that had seized her since the child died.

"She'll get over it," the doctor said. "They all get over it, in time. And you have the boy."

"I know," John had said, "but the girl meant everything. She always did, right from the start, I don't know why. I suppose it was the difference in age. A boy of school age, and a tough one at that, is someone in his own right. Not a baby of five. Laura literally adored her. Johnnie and I were nowhere."

"Give her time," repeated the doctor, "give her time. And anyway, you're both young still. There'll be others. Another daughter."

So easy to talk . . . How replace the life of a loved lost child with a dream? He knew Laura too well. Another child, another girl, would have her own qualities, a separate identity, she might even induce hostility because of this very fact. A usurper in the cradle, in the cot, that had been Christine's. A chubby, flaxen replica of Johnnie, not the little waxen dark-haired sprite that had gone.

He looked up, over his glass of wine, and the woman was staring at him again. It was not the casual, idle glance of someone at a nearby table, waiting for her companion to return, but something deeper, more intent, the prominent, light blue eyes oddly penetrating, giving him a sudden feeling of discomfort. Damn the woman! All right, bloody stare, if you must. Two can play at that game. He blew a cloud of cigarette smoke into the air and smiled at her, he hoped offensively. She did not register. The blue eyes continued to hold his, so that he was obliged to look away himself, extinguish his cigarette, glance over his shoulder for the waiter and call for the bill. Settling for this, and fumbling with the change, with a few casual remarks about the excellence of the meal, brought composure, but a prickly feeling on his scalp remained, and an odd sensation of unease. Then it went, as abruptly as it had started, and stealing a furtive glance at the other table he saw that her eyes were closed again, and she was sleeping, or dozing, as she had done before. The waiter disappeared. All was still.

Laura, he thought, glancing at his watch, is being a hell of a time. Ten minutes at least. Something to tease her about, anyway. He began to plan the form the joke would take. How the old dolly had stripped to her smalls, suggesting that Laura should do likewise. And then the manager had burst in upon them both, exclaiming in horror, the reputation of the restaurant damaged, the hint that unpleasant consequences might follow unless . . . The whole exercise turning out to be a plant, an exercise in blackmail. He and Laura and the twins taken in a police launch back to Venice for questioning. Quarter of an hour . . . Oh, come on, come on . . .

There was a crunch of feet on the gravel, Laura's twin walked slowly past, alone. She crossed over to her table and stood there a moment, her tall, angular figure interposing itself between John and her sister. She was saying something, but he couldn't catch the words. What was the accent, though—Scottish? Then she bent, offering an arm to the seated twin, and they moved away together across the garden to the break in the little hedge beyond, the twin who had stared at John leaning on her sister's arm. Here was the difference again. She was not quite so tall, and she stooped more —perhaps she was arthritic. They disappeared out of sight, and John, becoming impatient, got up and was about to walk back into the hotel when Laura emerged.

"Well, I must say, you took your time," he began, and then stopped, because of the expression on her face.

"What's the matter, what's happened?" he asked.

He could tell at once there was something wrong. Almost as if she were in a state of shock. She blundered towards the table he had just vacated and sat down. He drew up a chair beside her, taking her hand.

"Darling, what it is? Tell me—are you ill?"

She shook her head, and then turned and looked at him. The dazed expression he had noticed at first had given way to one of dawning confidence, almost of exaltation.

"It's quite wonderful," she said slowly, "the most wonderful thing that could possibly be. You see, she isn't dead, she's still with us. That's why they kept staring at us, those two sisters. They could see Christine."

Oh God, he thought. It's what I've been dreading. She's going off her head. What do I do? How do I cope?

"Laura, sweet," he began, forcing a smile, "look, shall we go? I've paid the bill, we can go and look at the cathedral and stroll around, and then it will be time to take off in that launch again for Venice."

She wasn't listening, or at any rate the words didn't penetrate.

"John, love," she said, "I've got to tell you what happened. I followed her, as we planned, into the *toilette* place. She was combing her hair and I went into the loo, and then came out and washed my hands in the basin. She was washing hers in the next basin. Suddenly she turned and said to me, in a strong Scots accent, 'Don't be unhappy any more. My sister has seen your little girl. She was sitting between you and your husband, laughing.' Darling, I thought I was going to faint. I nearly did. Luckily, there was a chair, and I sat down, and the woman bent over me and patted my head. I'm not sure of her exact words, but she said something about the moment of truth and joy being as sharp as a sword, but not to be afraid, all was well, but the sister's vision had been so strong they knew I had to be told, and that Christine wanted it. Oh John, don't look like that. I swear I'm not making it up, this is what she told me, it's all true."

The desperate urgency in her voice made his heart sicken. He had to play along with her, agree, soothe, do anything to bring back some sense of calm.

"Laura, darling, of course I believe you," he said, "only it's a sort of shock, and I'm upset because you're upset . . ."

"But I'm not upset," she interrupted. "I'm happy, so happy that I can't put the feeling into words. You know what it's been like all these weeks, at home and everywhere we've been on holiday, though I tried to hide it from you. Now it's lifted, because I know, I just know, that the woman was right. Oh Lord, how awful of me, but I've forgotten their name—she did tell me. You see, the thing is that she's a retired doctor, they come from Edinburgh, and the one who saw Christine went blind a few years ago. Although she's studied the occult all her life and been very psychic, it's only since going blind that she has really seen things, like a medium. They've had the most wonderful experiences. But to describe Christine as the blind one did to her sister, even down to the little blue-and-white dress with the puff sleeves that she wore at her birthday party, and to say she was smiling happily . . . Oh, darling, it's made me so happy I think I'm going to cry."

No hysteria. Nothing wild. She took a tissue from her bag and blew her nose, smiling at him. "I'm all right, you see, you don't have to worry. Neither of us need worry about anything any more. Give me a cigarette."

He took one from his packet and lighted it for her. She sounded normal, herself again. She wasn't trembling. And if this sudden belief was going to keep her happy he couldn't possibly begrudge it. But . . . but . . . he wished, all the same, it hadn't happened. There was something uncanny about thought-reading, about telepathy. Scientists couldn't account for it, nobody could, and this is what must have happened just now between Laura and the sisters. So the one who had been staring at him was blind. That accounted for the fixed gaze. Which somehow was unpleasant in itself, creepy. Oh hell, he thought, I wish we hadn't come here for lunch. Just chance, a flick of a coin between this, Torcello, and driving to Padua, and we had to choose Torcello.

"You didn't arrange to meet them again or anything, did you?" he asked, trying to sound casual.

"No darling, why should I?" Laura answered. "I mean, there was nothing more they could tell me. The sister had had her wonderful vision, and that was that. Anyway, they're moving on. Funnily enough, it's rather like our original game. They *are* going round the world before returning to Scotland. Only I said Australia, didn't I? The old dears . . . Anything less like murderers and jewel thieves."

She had quite recovered. She stood up and looked about her. "Come on," she said. "Having come to Torcello we must see the cathedral."

They made their way from the restaurant across the open piazza, where the stalls had been set up with scarves and trinkets and postcards, and so along the path to the cathedral. One of the ferryboats had just decanted a crowd of sightseers, many of whom had already found their way into Santa Maria Assunta. Laura, undaunted, asked her husband for the guidebook, and, as had always been her custom in happier days, started to walk slowly through the cathedral, studying mosaics, columns, panels from left to right, while John, less interested, because of his concern at what had just happened, followed close behind, keeping a weather eye alert for the twin sisters. There was no sign of them. Perhaps they had gone into the church of Santa Fosca close by. A sudden encounter would be embarrassing, quite apart from the effect it might have upon Laura. But the anonymous, shuffling tourists, intent upon culture, could not harm her, although from his own point of view they made artistic appreciation impossible. He could not concentrate, the cold clear beauty of what he saw left him untouched, and when Laura touched his sleeve, pointing to the mosaic of the Virgin and Child standing above the frieze of the Apostles, he nodded in sympathy yet saw nothing, the long, sad face of the Virgin infinitely remote, and turning on sudden impulse stared back over the heads of the tourists towards the door, where frescoes of the blessed and the damned gave themselves to judgement.

The twins were standing there, the blind one still holding on to her sister's arm, her sightless eyes fixed firmly upon him. He felt himself held, unable to move, and an impending sense of doom, of tragedy, came upon him. His whole being sagged, as it were, in apathy, and he thought, "This is the end, there is no escape, no future." Then both sisters turned and went out of the cathedral and the sensation vanished, leaving indignation in its wake, and rising anger. How dare those two old fools practise their mediumistic tricks on him? It was fraudulent, unhealthy; this was probably the way they lived, touring the world making everyone they met uncomfortable. Give them half a chance and they would have got money out of Laura—anything.

He felt her tugging at his sleeve again. "Isn't she beautiful? So happy, so serene."

"Who? What?" he asked.

"The Madonna," she answered. "She has a magic quality. It goes right through to one. Don't you feel it too?"

"I suppose so. I don't know. There are too many people around."

She looked up at him, astonished. "What's that got to do with it? How funny you are. Well, all right, let's get away from them. I want to buy some postcards anyway."

Disappointed, she sensed his lack of interest, and began to thread her way through the crowd of tourists to the door.

"Come on," he said abruptly, once they were outside, "there's plenty of time for postcards, let's explore a bit," and he struck off from the path, which would have taken them back to the centre where the little houses were, and the stalls, and the drifting crowd of people, to a narrow way amongst uncultivated ground, beyond which he could see a sort of cutting, or canal. The sight of water, limpid, pale, was a soothing contrast to the fierce sun above their heads.

"I don't think this leads anywhere much," said Laura. "It's a bit muddy, too, one can't sit. Besides, there are more things the guidebook says we ought to see."

"Oh, forget the book," he said impatiently, and, pulling her down beside him on the bank above the cutting, put his arms round her.

"It's the wrong time of day for sightseeing. Look, there's a rat swimming there the other side."

He picked up a stone and threw it in the water, and the animal sank, or somehow disappeared, and nothing was left but bubbles.

"Don't," said Laura. "It's cruel, poor thing," and then suddenly, putting her hand on his knee, "Do you think Christine is sitting here beside us?"

He did not answer at once. What was there to say? Would it be like this forever?

"I expect so," he said slowly, "if you feel she is."

The point was, remembering Christine before the onset of the fatal meningitis, she would have been running along the bank excitedly, throwing off her shoes, wanting to paddle, giving Laura a fit of apprehension. "Sweetheart, take care, come back . . ."

"The woman said she was looking so happy, sitting beside us, smiling," said Laura. She got up, brushing her dress, her mood changed to restlessness. "Come on, let's go back," she said.

He followed her with a sinking heart. He knew she did not really want to buy postcards or see what remained to be seen; she wanted to go in search of the women again, not necessarily to talk, just to be near them. When they came to the open place by the stalls he noticed that the crowd of tourists had thinned, there were only a few stragglers left, and the sisters were not amongst them. They must have joined the main body who had come to Torcello by the ferry service. A wave of relief seized him.

"Look, there's a mass of postcards at the second stall," he said quickly, "and some eye-catching head scarves. Let me buy you a head scarf."

"Darling, I've so many!" she protested. "Don't waste your lire."

"It isn't a waste. I'm in a buying mood. What about a basket? You know we never have enough baskets. Or some lace. How about lace?"

She allowed herself, laughing, to be dragged to the stall. While he rumpled through the goods spread out before them, and chatted up the smiling woman who was selling her wares, his ferociously bad Italian making her smile the more, he knew it would give the body of tourists more time to walk to the landing stage and catch the ferry service, and the twin sisters would be out of sight and out of their life.

"Never," said Laura, some twenty minutes later, "has so much junk been piled into so small a basket," her bubbling laugh reassuring him that all was well, he needn't worry any more, the evil hour had passed. The launch from the Cipriani that had brought them from Venice was waiting by the landing stage. The passengers who had arrived with them, the Americans, the man with the monocle, were already assembled. Earlier, before setting out, he had thought the price for lunch and transport, there and back, decidedly steep. Now he grudged none of it, except that the outing to Torcello itself had been one of the major errors of this particular holiday in Venice. They stepped down into the launch, finding a place in the open, and the boat chugged away down the canal and into the lagoon. The ordinary ferry had gone before, steaming towards Murano, while their own craft headed past San Francesco del Deserto and so back direct to Venice.

He put his arm around her once more, holding her close, and this time she responded, smiling up at him, her head on his shoulder.

"It's been a lovely day," she said. "I shall never forget it, never. You know, darling, now at last I can begin to enjoy our holiday."

He wanted to shout with relief. It's going to be all right, he decided, let her believe what she likes, it doesn't matter, it makes her happy. The beauty of Venice rose before them, sharply outlined against the glowing sky, and there was still so much to see, wandering there together, that might now be perfect because of her change of mood, the shadow having lifted, and aloud he began to discuss the evening to come, where they would dine—not the restaurant they usually went to, near the Fenice theatre, but somewhere different, somewhere new.

"Yes, but it must be cheap," she said, falling in with his mood, "because we've already spent so much today."

Their hotel by the Grand Canal had a welcoming, comforting air. The clerk smiled as he handed over their key. The bedroom was familiar, like home, with Laura's things arranged neatly on the dressing table but with it the little festive atmosphere of strangeness, of excitement, that only a holiday bedroom brings. This is ours for the moment, but no more. While we are in it we bring it life. When we have gone it no longer exists, it fades into anonymity. He turned on both taps in the bathroom, the water gushing into the bath, the steam rising. "Now," he thought afterwards, "now at last is the moment to make love," and he went back into the bedroom, and she understood, and opened her arms and smiled. Such blessed relief after all those weeks of restraint.

"The thing is," she said later, fixing her earrings before the looking glass, "I'm not really terribly hungry. Shall we just be dull and eat in the dining room here?"

"God, no!" he exclaimed. "With all those rather dreary couples at the other tables? I'm ravenous. I'm also gay. I want to get rather sloshed."

"Not bright lights and music, surely?"

"No, no . . . some small, dark, intimate cave, rather sinister, full of lovers with other people's wives."

"H'm," sniffed Laura, "we all know what *that* means. You'll spot some Italian lovely of sixteen and smirk at her through dinner, while I'm stuck high and dry with a beastly man's broad back."

They went out laughing into the warm soft night, and the magic was about them everywhere. "Let's walk," he said, "let's walk and work up an appetite for our gigantic meal," and inevitably they found themselves by the Molo and the lapping gondolas dancing upon the water, the lights everywhere blending with the darkness. There were other couples strolling for the same sake of aimless enjoyment, backwards, forwards, purposeless, and the inevitable sailors in groups, noisy, gesticulating, and dark-eyed girls whispering, clicking on high heels.

"The trouble is," said Laura, "walking in Venice becomes compulsive once you start. Just over the next bridge, you say, and then the next one beckons. I'm sure there are no restaurants down here, we're almost at those public gardens where they hold the Biennale. Let's turn back. I know there's a restaurant somewhere near the church of San Zaccaria, there's a little alleyway leading to it."

"Tell you what," said John, "if we go down here by the Arsenal, and cross that bridge at the end and head left, we'll come upon San Zaccaria from the other side. We did it the other morning."

"Yes, but it was daylight then. We may lose our way, it's not very well lit."

"Don't fuss. I have an instinct for these things."

They turned down the Fondamenta dell'Arsenale and crossed the little bridge short of the Arsenal itself, and so on past the church of San Martino. There were two canals ahead, one bearing right, the other left, with narrow streets beside them. John hesitated. Which one was it they had walked beside the day before?

"You see," protested Laura, "we shall be lost, just as I said."

"Nonsense," replied John firmly. "It's the left-hand one, I remember the little bridge."

The canal was narrow, the houses on either side seemed to close in upon it, and in the daytime, with the sun's reflection on the water and the windows of the houses open, bedding upon the balconies, a canary singing in a cage, there had been an impression of warmth, of secluded shelter. Now, ill-lit, almost in darkness, the windows of the houses shuttered, the water dank, the scene appeared altogether different, neglected, poor, and the long narrow boats moored to the slippery steps of cellar entrances looked like coffins.

"I swear I don't remember this bridge," said Laura, pausing, and holding on to the rail, "and I don't like the look of that alleyway beyond."

"There's a lamp halfway up," John told her. "I know exactly where we are, not far from the Greek quarter."

They crossed the bridge, and were about to plunge into the alleyway when they heard the cry. It came, surely, from one of the houses on the opposite side, but which one it was impossible to say. With the shutters closed each one of them seemed dead. They turned, and stared in the direction from which the sound had come.

"What was it?" whispered Laura.

"Some drunk or other," said John briefly. "Come on."

Less like a drunk than someone being strangled, and the choking cry suppressed as the grip held firm.

"We ought to call the police," said Laura.

"Oh, for heaven's sake," said John. Where did she think she was—Piccadilly?

"Well, I'm off, it's sinister," she replied, and began to hurry away up the twisting alleyway. John hesitated, his eye caught by a small figure which suddenly crept from a cellar entrance below one of the opposite houses, and then jumped into a narrow boat below. It was a child, a little girl—she couldn't have been more than five or six—wearing a short coat over her minute skirt, a pixie hood covering her head. There were four boats moored, line upon line, and she proceeded to jump from one to the other with surprising agility, intent, it would seem, upon escape. Once her foot slipped and he caught his breath, for she was within a few feet of the water, losing balance; then she recovered, and hopped onto the furthest boat. Bending, she tugged at the rope, which had the effect of swinging the boat's after-end across the canal, almost touching the opposite side and another cellar entrance, about thirty feet from the spot where John stood watching her. Then the child jumped again, landing upon the cellar steps, and vanished into the house, the boat swinging back into mid-canal behind her. The whole episode could not have taken more than four minutes. Then he heard the quick patter of feet. Laura had returned. She had seen none of it for which he felt unspeakably thankful. The sight of a child, a little girl, in what must have been near danger, her fear that the scene he had just witnessed was in some way a sequel to the alarming cry, might have had a disastrous effect on her overwrought nerves.

"What are you doing?" she called. "I daren't go on without you. The wretched alley branches in two directions."

"Sorry," he told her. "I'm coming."

He took her arm and they walked briskly along the alley, John with an apparent confidence he did not possess.

"There were no more cries, were there?" she asked.

"No," he said, "no, nothing. I tell you, it was some drunk."

The alley led to a deserted *campo* behind a church, not a church he knew, and he led the way across, along another street and over a further bridge.

"Wait a minute," he said. "I think we take this right-hand turning. It will lead us into the Greek quarter—the church of San Giorgio is somewhere over there."

She did not answer. She was beginning to lose faith. The place was like a maze. They might circle round and round forever, and then find themselves back again, near the bridge where they had heard the cry. Doggedly he led her on, and then surprisingly, with relief, he saw people walking in the lighted street ahead, there was a spire of a church, the surroundings became familiar.

"There, I told you," he said. "That's San Zaccaria, we've found it all right. Your restaurant can't be far away."

And anyway, there would be other restaurants, somewhere to eat, at least here was the cheering glitter of lights, of movement, canals beside which people walked, the atmosphere of tourism. The letters "Ristorante," in blue lights, shone like a beacon down a left-hand alley.

"Is this your place?" he asked.

"God knows," she said. "Who cares? Let's feed there anyway."

And so into the sudden blast of heated air and hum of voices, the smell of pasta, wine, waiters, jostling customers, laughter. "For two? This way, please." Why, he thought, was one's British nationality always so obvious? A cramped little table and an enormous menu scribbled in an indecipherable mauve biro, with the waiter hovering, expecting the order forthwith.

"Two very large camparis, with soda," John said. *"Then* we'll study the menu."

He was not going to be rushed. He handed the bill of fare to Laura and looked about him. Mostly Italians—that meant the food would be good. Then he saw them. At the opposite side of the room. The twin sisters. They must have come into the restaurant hard upon Laura's and his own arrival, for they were only now sitting down, shedding their coats, the waiter hovering beside the table. John was seized with the irrational thought that this was no coincidence. The sisters had noticed them both, in the street outside, and had followed them in. Why, in the name of hell, should they have picked on this particular spot, in the whole of Venice, unless . . . unless Laura herself, at Torcello, had suggested a further encounter, or the sister had suggested it to her? A small restaurant near the church of San Zaccaria, we go there sometimes for dinner. It was Laura, before the walk, who had mentioned San Zaccaria . . .

She was still intent upon the menu, she had not seen the sisters, but any moment now she would have chosen what she wanted to eat, and then she would raise her head and look across the room. If only the drinks would come. If only the waiter would bring the drinks, it would give Laura something to do.

"You know, I was thinking," he said quickly, "we really ought to go to the garage tomorrow and get the car, and do that drive to Padua. We could lunch in Padua, see the cathedral and touch St. Anthony's tomb and look at the Giotto frescoes, and come back by the way of those various villas along the Brenta that the guide-book cracks up."

It was no use, though. She was looking up, across the restaurant, and she gave a little gasp of surprise. It was genuine. He could swear it was genuine.

"Look," she said, "how extraordinary! How really amazing!"

"What?" he said sharply.

"Why, there they are. My wonderful old twins. They've seen us, what's more. They're staring this way." She waved her hand, radiant, delighted. The sister she had spoken to at Torcello bowed and smiled. False old bitch, he thought. I know they followed us.

"Oh, darling, I must go and speak to them," she said impulsively, "just to tell them how happy I've been all day, thanks to them."

"Oh, for heaven's sake!" he said. "Look, here are the drinks. And we haven't ordered yet. Surely you can wait until later, until we've eaten?"

"I won't be a moment," she said, "and anyway I want scampi, nothing first. I told you I wasn't hungry."

She got up, and, brushing past the waiter with the drinks, crossed the room. She might have been greeting the loved friends of years. He watched her bend over the table and shake them both by the hand, and because there was a vacant chair at their table she drew it up and sat down, talking, smiling. Nor did the sisters seem surprised, at least not the one she knew, who nodded and talked back, while the blind sister remained impassive.

"All right," thought John savagely, "then I *will* get sloshed," and he proceeded to down his Campari and soda and order another, while he pointed out something quite unintelligible on the menu as his own choice, but remembered scampi for Laura. "And a bottle of Soave," he added, "with ice."

The evening was ruined anyway. What was to have been an intimate, happy celebration would now be heavy-laden with spiritualistic visions, poor little dead Christine sharing the table with them, which was so damned stupid when in earthly life she would have been tucked up hours ago in bed. The bitter taste of the Campari suited his mood of sudden self-pity, and all the while he watched the group at the table in the opposite corner, Laura apparently listening while the more active sister held forth and the blind one sat silent, her formidable sightless eyes turned in his direction.

"She's phoney," he thought, "she's not blind at all. They're both of them frauds, and they could be males in drag after all, just as we pretended at Torcello, and they're after Laura."

He began on his second Campari and soda. The two drinks, taken on an empty stomach, had an instant effect. Vision became blurred. And still Laura went on sitting at the other table, putting in a question now and again, while the active sister talked. The waiter appeared with the scampi, and a companion beside him to serve John's own order, which was totally unrecognisable, heaped with a livid sauce.

"The signora does not come?" enquired the first waiter, and John shook his head grimly, pointing an unsteady finger across the room.

"Tell the signora," he said carefully, "her scampi will get cold."

He stared down at the offering placed before him, and prodded it delicately with a fork. The pallid sauce dissolved, revealing two enormous slices, rounds, of what appeared to be boiled pork, bedecked with garlic. He forked a portion to his mouth and chewed, and yes, it was pork, steamy, rich, the spicy sauce having turned it curiously sweet. He laid down his fork, pushing the plate away, and became aware of Laura, returning across the room and sitting beside him. She did not say anything, which was just as well, he thought, because he was too near nausea to answer. It wasn't just the drink, but reaction from the whole nightmare day. She began to eat her scampi, still not uttering. She did not seem to notice he was not eating. The waiter, hovering at his elbow, anxious, seemed aware that John's choice was somehow an error, and discreetly removed the plate. "Bring me a green salad," murmured John, and even then Laura did not register surprise, or, as she might have done in more normal circumstances, accuse him of having had too much to drink. Finally, when she had finished her scampi and was sipping her wine, which John had waved away, to nibble at his salad in small mouthfuls like a sick rabbit, she began to speak.

"Darling," she said, "I know you won't believe it, and it's rather frightening in a way, but after they left the restaurant in Torcello the sisters went to the cathedral, as we did, although we didn't see them in the crowd, and the blind one had another vision. She said Christine was trying to tell her something about us, that we should be in danger if we stayed in Venice. Christine wanted us to go away as soon as possible."

So that's it, he thought. They think they can run our lives for us. This is to be our problem from henceforth. Do we eat? Do we get up? Do we go to bed? We must get in touch with the twin sisters. They will direct us.

"Well?" she said. "Why don't you say something?"

"Because," he answered, "you are perfectly right, I don't believe it. Quite frankly, I judge your old sisters as being a couple of freaks, if nothing else. They're obviously unbalanced, and I'm sorry if this hurts you, but the fact is they've found a sucker in you."

"You're being unfair," said Laura. "They are genuine, I know it. I just know it. They were completely sincere in what they said."

"All right. Granted. They're sincere. But that doesn't make them well-balanced. Honestly, darling, you meet that old girl for ten minutes in a loo, she tells you she sees Christine sitting beside us—well, anyone with a gift for telepathy could read your unconscious mind in an instant—and then, pleased with her success, as any old psychic expert would be, she flings a further mood of ecstasy and wants to boot us out of Venice. Well, I'm sorry, but to hell with it."

The room was no longer reeling. Anger had sobered him. If it would not put Laura to shame he would get up and cross to their table, and tell the old fools where they got off.

"I knew you would take it like this," said Laura unhappily. "I told them you would. They said not to worry. As long as we left Venice tomorrow everything would come all right."

"Oh, for God's sake," said John. He changed his mind, and poured himself a glass of wine.

"After all," Laura went on, "we have really seen the cream of Venice. I don't mind going on somewhere else. And if we stayed —I know it sounds silly, but I should have a nasty nagging sort of feeling inside me, and I should keep thinking of darling Christine being unhappy and trying to tell us to go."

"Right," said John with ominous calm, "that settles it. Go we will. I suggest we clear off to the hotel straight away and warn the reception we're leaving in the morning. Have you had enough to eat?"

"Oh, dear," sighed Laura, "don't take it like that. Look, why not come over and meet them, and then they can explain about the vision to you? Perhaps you would take it seriously then. Especially as you are the one it most concerns. Christine is more worried over you than me. And the extraordinary thing is that the blind sister says you're psychic and don't know it. You are somehow *en rapport* with the unknown, and I'm not."

"Well, that's final," said John. "I'm psychic, am I? Fine. My psychic intuition tells me to get out of this restaurant now, at once, and we can decide what we do about leaving Venice when we are back at the hotel."

He signalled to the waiter for the bill and they waited for it, not speaking to each other, Laura unhappy, fiddling with her bag, while John, glancing furtively at the twins' table, noticed that they were tucking into plates piled high with spaghetti, in very un-psychic fashion. The bill disposed of, John pushed back his chair.

"Right. Are you ready?" he asked.

"I'm going to say goodbye to them first," said Laura, her mouth set sulkily, reminding him instantly, with a pang, of their poor lost child.

"Just as you like," he replied, and walked ahead of her out of the restaurant, without a backward glance.

The soft humidity of the evening, so pleasant to walk about in earlier, had turned to rain. The strolling tourists had melted away. One or two people hurried by under umbrellas. This is what the inhabitants who live here see, he thought. This is the true life. Empty streets by night, and the dank stillness of a stagnant canal beneath shuttered houses. The rest is a bright façade put on for show, glittering by sunlight.

Laura joined him and they walked away together in silence, and emerging presently behind the ducal palace came out into the Piazza San Marco. The rain was heavy now, and they sought shelter with the few remaining stragglers under the colonnades. The orchestras had packed up for the evening. The tables were bare. Chairs had been turned upside down.

The experts are right, he thought. Venice is sinking. The whole city is slowly dying. One day the tourists will travel here by boat to peer down into the waters, and they will see pillars and columns and marble far, far beneath them, slime and mud uncovering for brief moments a lost underworld of stone. Their heels made a ringing sound on the pavement and the rain splashed from the gutterings above. A fine ending to an evening that had started with brave hope, with innocence.

When they came to their hotel Laura made straight for the lift, and John turned to the desk to ask the night porter for the key. The man handed him a telegram at the same time. John stared at it a moment. Laura was already in the lift. Then he opened the envelope and read the message. It was from the headmaster of Johnnie's preparatory school.

Johnnie under observation suspected
appendicitis in city hospital here.
No cause for alarm but surgeon thought wise
advise you.

Charles Hill

He read the message twice, then walked slowly towards the lift where Laura was waiting for him. He gave her the telegram. "This came when we were out," he said. "Not awfully good news." He pressed the lift button as she read the telegram. The lift stopped at the second floor, and they got out.

"Well, this decides it, doesn't it?" she said. "Here is the proof. We have to leave Venice because we're going home. It's Johnnie who's in danger, not us. This is what Christine was trying to tell the twins."

The first thing John did the following morning was to put a call through to the headmaster at the preparatory school. Then he gave notice of their departure to the reception manager, and they packed while they waited for the call. Neither of them referred to the events of the preceding day, it was not necessary. John knew the arrival of the telegram and the foreboding of danger from the sisters was coincidence, nothing more, but it was pointless to start an argument about it. Laura was convinced otherwise, but intuitively she knew it was best to keep her feelings to herself. During breakfast they discussed ways and means of getting home. It should be possible to get themselves, and the car, on to the special car train that ran from Milan through to Calais, since it was early in the season. In any event, the headmaster had said there was no urgency.

The call from England came while John was in the bathroom. Laura answered it. He came into the bedroom a few minutes later. She was still speaking, but he could tell from the expression in her eyes that she was anxious.

"It's Mrs. Hill," she said. "Mr. Hill is in class. She says they reported from the hospital that Johnnie had a restless night and the surgeon may have to operate, but he doesn't want to unless it's absolutely necessary. They've taken X-rays and the appendix is in a tricky position, it's not awfully straightforward."

"Here, give it to me," he said.

The soothing but slightly guarded voice of the headmaster's wife came down the receiver. "I'm so sorry this may spoil your plans," she said, "but both Charles and I felt you ought to be told, and that you might feel rather easier if you were on the spot. Johnnie is very plucky, but of course he has some fever. That isn't unusual, the surgeon says, in the circumstances. Sometimes an appendix can get displaced, it appears, and this makes it more complicated. He's going to decide about operating this evening."

"Yes, of course, we quite understand," said John.

"Please do tell your wife not to worry too much," she went on. "The hospital is excellent, a very nice staff, and we have every confidence in the surgeon."

"Yes," said John, "yes," and then broke off because Laura was making gestures beside him.

"If we can't get the car on the train, I can fly," she said. "They're sure to be able to find me a seat on a plane. Then at least one of us would be there this evening."

He nodded agreement. "Thank you so much, Mrs. Hill," he said, "we'll manage to get back all right. Yes, I'm sure Johnnie is in good hands. Thank your husband for us. Goodbye."

He replaced the receiver and looked round him at the tumbled beds, suitcases on the floor, tissue paper strewn. Baskets, maps, books, coats, everything they had brought with them in the car. "Oh God," he said, "what a bloody mess. All this junk." The telephone rang again. It was the hall porter to say he had succeeded in booking a sleeper for them both, and a place for the car, on the following night.

"Look," said Laura, who had seized the telephone, "could you book one seat on the midday plane from Venice to London today, for me? It's imperative one of us gets home this evening. My husband could follow with the car tomorrow."

"Here, hang on," interrupted John. "No need for panic stations. Surely twenty-four hours wouldn't make all that difference?"

Anxiety had drained the colour from her face. She turned to him, distraught.

"It mightn't to you, but it does to me," she said. "I've lost one child, I'm not going to lose another."

"All right, darling, all right . . ." He put his hand out to her but she brushed it off, impatiently, and continued giving directions to the porter. He turned back to his packing. No use saying anything. Better for it to be as she wished. They could, of course, both go by air, and then when all was well, and Johnnie better, he could come back and fetch the car, driving home through France as they had come. Rather a sweat, though, and the hell of an expense. Bad enough Laura going by air and himself with the car on the train from Milan.

"We could, if you like, both fly," he began tentatively, explaining the sudden idea, but she would have none of it. "That really *would* be absurd," she said impatiently. "As long as I'm there this evening, and you follow by train, it's all that matters. Besides, we shall need the car, going backwards and forwards to the hospital. And our luggage. We couldn't go off and just leave all this here."

No, he saw her point. A silly idea. It was only—well, he was as worried about Johnnie as she was, though he wasn't going to say so.

"I'm going downstairs to stand over the porter," said Laura. "They always make more effort if one is actually on the spot. Everything I want tonight is packed. I shall only need my overnight case. You can bring everything else in the car." She hadn't been out of the bedroom five minutes before the telephone rang. It was Laura. "Darling," she said, "it couldn't have worked out better. The porter has got me on a charter flight that leaves Venice in less than an hour. A special motor launch takes the party direct from San Marco in about ten minutes. Some passenger on the charter flight cancelled. I shall be at Gatwick in less than four hours."

"I'll be down right away," he told her.

He joined her by the reception desk. She no longer looked anxious and drawn, but full of purpose. She was on her way. He kept wishing they were going together. He couldn't bear to stay on in Venice after she had gone, but the thought of driving to Milan, spending a dreary night in a hotel there alone, the endless dragging day which would follow, and the long hours in the train the next night, filled him with intolerable depression, quite apart from the anxiety about Johnnie. They walked along to the San Marco landing stage, the Molo bright and glittering after the rain, a little breeze blowing, the postcards and scarves and tourist souvenirs fluttering on the stalls, the tourists themselves out in force, strolling, contented, the happy day before them.

"I'll ring you tonight from Milan," he told her. "The Hills will give you a bed, I suppose. And if you're at the hospital they'll let me have the latest news. That must be your charter party. You're welcome to them!"

The passengers descending from the landing stage down into the waiting launch were carrying hand luggage with Union Jack tags upon them. They were mostly middle-aged, with what appeared to be two Methodist ministers in charge. One of them advanced towards Laura, holding out his hand, showing a gleaming row of dentures when he smiled. "You must be the lady joining us for the homeward flight," he said. "Welcome aboard, and to the Union of Fellowship. We are all delighted to make your acquaintance. Sorry we hadn't a seat for hubby too."

Laura turned swiftly and kissed John, a tremor at the corner of her mouth betraying inward laughter. "Do you think they'll break into hymns?" she whispered. "Take care of yourself, hubby. Call me tonight."

The pilot sounded a curious little toot upon his horn, and in a moment Laura had climbed down the steps into the launch and was standing amongst the crowd of passengers, waving her hand, her scarlet coat a gay patch of colour amongst the more sober suiting of her companions. The launch tooted again and moved away from the landing stage, and he stood there watching it, a sense of immense loss filling his heart. Then he turned and walked away, back to the hotel, the bright day all about him desolate, unseen.

There was nothing, he thought, as he looked about him presently in the hotel bedroom, so melancholy as a vacated room, especially when the recent signs of occupation were still visible about him. Laura's suitcases on the bed, a second coat she had left behind. Traces of powder on the dressing table. A tissue, with a lipstick smear, thrown in the wastepaper basket. Even an old toothpaste tube squeezed dry, lying on the glass shelf above the washbasin. Sounds of the heedless traffic on the Grand Canal came as always from the open window, but Laura wasn't there any more to listen to it, or to watch from the small balcony. The pleasure had gone. Feeling had gone.

John finished packing, and leaving all the baggage ready to be

collected he went downstairs to pay the bill. The reception clerk
was welcoming new arrivals. People were sitting on the terrace
overlooking the Grand Canal reading newspapers, the pleasant
day waiting to be planned.

John decided to have an early lunch, here on the hotel terrace,
on familiar ground, and then have the porter carry the baggage to
one of the ferries that steamed direct between San Marco and the
Porta Roma, where the car was garaged. The fiasco meal of the
night before had left him empty, and he was ready for the trolley
of hors d'œuvres when they brought it to him, around midday.
Even here, though, there was change. The headwaiter, their espe-
cial friend, was off duty, and the table where they usually sat was
occupied by new arrivals, a honeymoon couple, he told himself
sourly, observing the gaiety, the smiles, while he had been shown
to a small single table behind a tub of flowers.

"She's airborne now," John thought, "she's on her way," and he
tried to picture Laura seated between the Methodist ministers,
telling them, no doubt, about Johnnie ill in hospital, and heaven
knows what else besides. Well, the twin sisters anyway could rest
in psychic peace. Their wishes would have been fulfilled.

Lunch over, there was no point in lingering with a cup of coffee
on the terrace. His desire was to get away as soon as possible,
fetch the car, and be en route for Milan. He made his farewells at
the reception desk, and, escorted by a porter who had piled his
baggage on to a wheeled trolley, made his way once more to the
landing stage of San Marco. As he stepped onto the steam ferry,
his luggage heaped beside him, a crowd of jostling people all
about him, he had one momentary pang to be leaving Venice.
When, if ever, he wondered, would they come again? Next year
. . . in three years . . . Glimpsed first on honeymoon, nearly ten
years ago, and then a second visit, *en passant,* before a cruise, and
now this last abortive ten days that had ended so abruptly.

The water glittered in the sunshine, buildings shone, tourists in
dark glasses paraded up and down the rapidly receding Molo, already the terrace of their hotel was out of sight as the ferry
churned its way up the Grand Canal. So many impressions to
seize and hold, familiar loved façades, balconies, windows, water
lapping the cellar steps of decaying palaces, the little red house
where d'Annunzio lived, with its garden—our house, Laura called
it, pretending it was theirs—and too soon the ferry would be turn-

ing left on the direct route to the Piazzale Roma, so missing the best of the Canal, the Rialto, the further palaces.

Another ferry was heading downstream to pass them, filled with passengers, and for a brief foolish moment he wished he could change places, be amongst the happy tourists bound for Venice and all he had left behind him. Then he saw her. Laura, in her scarlet coat, the twin sisters by her side, the active sister with her hand on Laura's arm, talking earnestly, and Laura herself, her hair blowing in the wind, gesticulating, on her face a look of distress. He stared, astounded, too astonished to shout, to wave, and anyway they would never have heard or seen him, for his own ferry had already passed and was heading in the opposite direction.

What the hell had happened? There must have been a holdup with the charter flight and it had never taken off, but in that case why had Laura not telephoned him at the hotel? And what were those damned sisters doing? Had she run into them at the airport? Was it coincidence? And why did she look so anxious? He could think of no explanation. Perhaps the flight had been cancelled. Laura, of course, would go straight to the hotel, expecting to find him there, intending, doubtless, to drive with him after all to Milan and take the train the following night. What a blasted mix-up. The only thing to do was to telephone the hotel immediately his ferry reached the Piazzale Roma and tell her to wait—he would return and fetch her. As for the damned interfering sisters, they could get stuffed.

The usual stampede ensued when the ferry arrived at the landing stage. He had to find a porter to collect his baggage, and then wait while he discovered a telephone. The fiddling with change, the hunt for the number, delayed him still more. He succeeded at last in getting through, and luckily the reception clerk he knew was still at the desk.

"Look, there's been some frightful muddle," he began, and explained how Laura was even now on her way back to the hotel— he had seen her with two friends on one of the ferry services. Would the reception clerk explain and tell her to wait? He would be back by the next available service to collect her. "In any event, detain her," he said. "I'll be as quick as I can." The reception clerk understood perfectly, and John rang off.

Thank heaven Laura hadn't turned up before he had put

through his call, or they would have told her he was on his way to Milan. The porter was still waiting with the baggage, and it seemed simplest to walk with him to the garage, hand everything over to the chap in charge of the office there and ask him to keep it for an hour, when he would be returning with his wife to pick up the car. Then he went back to the landing station to await the next ferry to Venice. The minutes dragged, and he kept wondering all the time what had gone wrong at the airport and why in heaven's name Laura hadn't telephoned. No use conjecturing. She would tell him the whole story at the hotel. One thing was certain: he would not allow Laura and himself to be saddled with the sisters and become involved with their affairs. He could imagine Laura saying that they also had missed a flight, and could they have a lift to Milan?

Finally the ferry chugged alongside the landing stage and he stepped aboard. What an anticlimax, thrashing back past the familiar sights to which he had bidden a nostalgic farewell such a short while ago! He didn't even look about him this time, he was so intent on reaching his destination. In San Marco there were more people than ever, the afternoon crowds walking shoulder to shoulder, every one of them on pleasure bent.

He came to the hotel and pushed his way through the swing door, expecting to see Laura, and possibly the sisters, waiting in the lounge to the left of the entrance. She was not there. He went to the desk. The reception clerk he had spoken to on the telephone was standing there, talking to the manager.

"Has my wife arrived?" John asked.

"No, sir, not yet."

"What an extraordinary thing. Are you sure?"

"Absolutely certain, sir. I have been here ever since you telephoned me at a quarter of two. I have not left the desk."

"I just don't understand it. She was on one of the vaporettos passing by the Accademia. She would have landed at San Marco about five minutes later and come on here."

The clerk seemed nonplussed. "I don't know what to say. The signora was with friends, did you say?"

"Yes. Well, acquaintances. Two ladies we had met at Torcello yesterday. I was astonished to see her with them on the vaporetto, and of course I assumed that the flight had been cancelled, and she had somehow met up with them at the airport and decided to return here with them, to catch me before I left."

Oh hell, what was Laura doing? It was after three. A matter of moments from San Marco landing stage to the hotel.

"Perhaps the signora went with her friends to their hotel instead. Do you know where they are staying?"

"No," said John, "I haven't the slightest idea. What's more, I don't even know the names of the two ladies. They were sisters, twins, in fact—looked exactly alike. But anyway, why go to their hotel and not here?"

The swing door opened but it wasn't Laura. Two people staying in the hotel.

The manager broke into the conversation. "I tell you what I will do," he said. "I will telephone the airport and check about the flight. Then at least we will get somewhere." He smiled apologetically. It was not usual for arrangements to go wrong.

"Yes, do that," said John. "We may as well know what happened there."

He lit a cigarette and began to pace up and down the entrance hall. What a bloody mix-up. And how unlike Laura, who knew he would be setting off for Milan directly after lunch—indeed, for all she knew he might have gone before. But surely, in that case, she would have telephoned at once, on arrival at the airport, had the flight been cancelled? The manager was ages telephoning, he had to be put through on some other line, and his Italian was too rapid for John to follow the conversation. Finally he replaced the receiver.

"It is more mysterious than ever, sir," he said. "The charter flight was not delayed, it took off on schedule with a full complement of passengers. As far as they could tell me, there was no hitch. The signora must simply have changed her mind." His smile was more apologetic than ever.

"Changed her mind," John repeated. "But why on earth should she do that? She was so anxious to be home tonight."

The manager shrugged. "You know how ladies can be, sir," he said. "Your wife may have thought that after all she would prefer to take the train to Milan with you. I do assure you, though, that the charter party was most respectable, and it was a Caravelle aircraft, perfectly safe."

"Yes, yes," said John impatiently, "I don't blame your arrangements in the slightest. I just can't understand what induced her to change her mind, unless it was meeting with these two ladies."

The manager was silent. He could not think of anything to say. The reception clerk was equally concerned. "Is it possible," he ventured, "that you made a mistake, and it was not the signora that you saw on the vaporetto?"

"Oh no," replied John, "it was my wife, I assure you. She was wearing her red coat, she was hatless, just as she left here. I saw her as plainly as I can see you. I would swear to it in a court of law."

"It is unfortunate," said the manager, "that we do not know the name of the two ladies, or the hotel where they were staying. You say you met these ladies at Torcello yesterday?"

"Yes . . . but only briefly. They weren't staying there. At least, I am certain they were not. We saw them at dinner in Venice later, as it happens."

"Excuse me . . ." Guests were arriving with luggage to check in, the clerk was obliged to attend to them. John turned in desperation to the manager. "Do you think it would be any good telephoning the hotel in Torcello in case the people there knew the name of the ladies, or where they were staying in Venice?"

"We can try," replied the manager. "It is a small hope, but we can try."

John resumed his anxious pacing, all the while watching the swing door, hoping, praying, that he would catch sight of the red coat and Laura would enter. Once again there followed what seemed an interminable telephone conversation between the manager and someone at the hotel in Torcello.

"Tell them two sisters," said John, "two elderly ladies dressed in grey, both exactly alike. One lady was blind," he added. The manager nodded. He was obviously giving a detailed description. Yet when he hung up he shook his head. "The manager at Torcello says he remembers the two ladies well," he told John, "but they were only there for lunch. He never learnt their names."

"Well, that's that. There's nothing to do now but wait."

John lit his third cigarette and went out on to the terrace, to resume his pacing there. He stared out across the canal, searching the heads of the people on passing steamers, motorboats, even drifting gondolas. The minutes ticked by on his watch, and there was no sign of Laura. A terrible foreboding nagged at him that somehow this was prearranged, that Laura had never intended to catch the aircraft, that last night in the restaurant she had made an assignation with the sisters. Oh God, he thought, that's impossible, I'm going paranoiac . . . Yet why, why? No, more likely the encounter at the airport was fortuitous, and for some incredible reason they had persuaded Laura not to board the aircraft, even prevented her from doing so, trotting out one of their psychic visions, that the aircraft would crash, that she must return with them to Venice. And Laura, in her sensitive state, felt they must be right, swallowed it all without question.

But granted all these possibilities, why had she not come to the hotel? What was she doing? Four o'clock, half-past four, the sun no longer dappling the water. He went back to the reception desk.

"I just can't hang around," he said. "Even if she does turn up, we shall never make Milan this evening. I might see her walking with these ladies, in the Piazza San Marco, anywhere. If she arrives while I'm out, will you explain?"

The clerk was full of concern, "Indeed, yes," he said. "It is very worrying for you, sir. Would it perhaps be prudent if we booked you in here tonight?"

John gestured, helplessly. "Perhaps, yes, I don't know. Maybe . . ."

He went out of the swing door and began to walk towards the Piazza San Marco. He looked into every shop up and down the colonnades, crossed the piazza a dozen times, threaded his way between the tables in front of Florian's, in front of Quadri's, knowing that Laura's red coat and the distinctive appearance of the twin sisters could easily be spotted, even amongst this milling crowd, but there was no sign of them. He joined the crowd of shoppers in the Merceria, shoulder to shoulder with idlers, thrusters, window-gazers, knowing instinctively that it was useless, they wouldn't be here. Why should Laura have deliberately missed her flight to return to Venice for such a purpose? And even if she had done so, for some reason beyond his imagining, she would surely have come first to the hotel to find him.

The only thing left to him was to try to track down the sisters. Their hotel could be anywhere amongst the hundreds of hotels and pensions scattered through Venice, or even across the other side at the Zattere, or farther again on the Guidecca. These last possibilities seemed remote. More likely they were staying in a small hotel or pension somewhere near San Zaccaria handy to the restaurant where they had dined last night. The blind one would surely not go far afield in the evening. He had been a fool not to have thought of this before, and he turned back and walked quickly away from the brightly lighted shopping district towards the narrower, more cramped quarter where they had dined last evening. He found the restaurant without difficulty, but they were not yet open for dinner, and the waiter preparing tables was not the one who had served them. John asked to see the *padrone,* and the waiter disappeared to the back regions, returning after a moment or two with the somewhat dishevelled-looking proprietor in shirt sleeves, caught in a slack moment, not in full tenue.

"I had dinner here last night," John explained. "There were two ladies sitting at that table there in the corner." He pointed to it.

"You wish to book that table for this evening?" asked the proprietor.

"No," said John. "No, there were two ladies there last night, two sisters, due sorelle, twins, gemelle"—what was the right word for twins?—"Do you remember? Two ladies, sorelle vecchie . . ."

"Ah," said the man, "si, si, signore, la povera signorina." He put his hands to his eyes to feign blindness. "Yes, I remember."

"Do you know their names?" asked John. "Where they were staying? I am very anxious to trace them."

The proprietor spread out his hands in a gesture of regret. "I am ver' sorry, signore, I do not know the names of the signorine, they have been here once, twice, perhaps for dinner, they do not say where they were staying. Perhaps if you come again tonight they might be here? Would you like to book a table?"

He pointed around him, suggesting a whole choice of tables that might appeal to a prospective diner, but John shook his head.

"Thank you, no. I may be dining elsewhere. I am sorry to have troubled you. If the signorine should come . . ." he paused, "possibly I may return later," he added. "I am not sure."

The proprietor bowed, and walked with him to the entrance. "In Venice the whole world meets," he said smiling. "It is possible the signore will find his friends tonight. Arrivederci, signore."

Friends? John walked out into the street. More likely kidnappers . . . Anxiety had turned to fear, to panic. Something had gone terribly wrong. Those women had got hold of Laura, played upon her suggestibility, induced her to go with them, either to their hotel or elsewhere. Should he find the Consulate? Where was it? What would he say when he got there? He began walking without purpose, finding himself as they had done the night before, in streets he did not know, and suddenly came upon a tall building with the word "Questura" above it. This is it, he thought. I don't care, something has happened, I'm going inside. There were a number of police in uniform coming and going, the place at any rate was active, and, addressing himself to one of them behind a glass partition, he asked if there was anyone who spoke English. The man pointed to a flight of stairs and John went up, entering a door on the right where he saw that another couple were sitting, waiting, and with relief he recognised them as fellow countrymen, tourists, obviously a man and his wife, in some sort of predicament.

"Come and sit down," said the man. "We've waited half an hour but they can't be much longer. What a country! They wouldn't leave us like this at home."

John took the proffered cigarette and found a chair beside him.

"What's your trouble?" he asked.

"My wife had her handbag pinched in one of those shops in the Merceria," said the man. "She simply put it down one moment to look at something, and you'd hardly credit it, the next moment it had gone. I say it was a sneak thief, she insists it was the girl behind the counter. But who's to say? These Ities are all alike. Anyway, I'm certain we shan't get it back. What have you lost?"

"Suitcase stolen," John lied rapidly. "Had some important papers in it."

How could he say he had lost his wife? He couldn't even begin . . .

The man nodded in sympathy. "As I said, these Ities are all alike. Old Musso knew how to deal with them. Too many Communists around these days. The trouble is, they're not going to bother with our troubles much, not with this murderer at large. They're all out looking for him."

"Murderer? What murderer?" asked John.

"Don't tell me you've not heard about it?" The man stared at him in surprise. "Venice has talked of nothing else. It's been in all the papers, on the radio, and even in the English papers. A grizzly business. One woman found with her throat slit last week—a tourist too—and some old chap discovered with the same sort of knife wound this morning. They seem to think it must be a maniac, because there doesn't seem to be any motive. Nasty thing to happen in Venice in the tourist season."

"My wife and I never bother with the newspapers when we're on holiday," said John. "And we're neither of us much given to gossip in the hotel."

"Very wise of you," laughed the man. "It might have spoilt your holiday, especially if your wife is nervous. Oh well, we're off tomorrow anyway. Can't say we mind, do we, dear?" He turned to his wife. "Venice had gone downhill since we were here last. And now this loss of the handbag really is the limit."

The door of the inner room opened, and a senior police officer asked John's companion and his wife to pass through.

"I bet we don't get any satisfaction," murmured the tourist, winking at John, and he and his wife went into the inner room. The door closed behind them. John stubbed out his cigarette and lighted another. A strange feeling of unreality possessed him. He asked himself what he was doing here, what was the use of it? Laura was no longer in Venice but had disappeared, perhaps forever, with those diabolical sisters. She would never be traced. And just as the two of them had made up a fantastic story about the twins, when they first spotted them in Torcello, so, with nightmare logic, the fiction would have basis in fact; the women were in reality disguised crooks, men with criminal intent who lured unsuspecting persons to some appalling fate. They might even be the murderers for whom the police sought. Who would ever suspect two elderly women of respectable appearance, living quietly in some second-rate pension or hotel? He stubbed out his cigarette, unfinished.

"This," he thought, "is really the start of paranoia. This is the way people go off their heads." He glanced at his watch. It was half-past six. Better pack this in, this futile quest here in police headquarters, and keep to the single link of sanity remaining. Return to the hotel, put a call through to the prep school in England, and ask about the latest news of Johnnie. He had not thought about poor Johnnie since sighting Laura on the vaporetto.

Too late, though. The inner door opened, the couple were ushered out.

"Usual claptrap," said the husband sotto voce to John. "They'll do what they can. Not much hope. So many foreigners in Venice, all of 'em thieves! The locals all above reproach. Wouldn't pay 'em to steal from customers. Well, I wish you better luck."

He nodded, his wife smiled and bowed, and they had gone. John followed the police officer into the inner room.

Formalities began. Name, address, passport. Length of stay in Venice, etc., etc. Then the questions, and John, the sweat beginning to appear on his forehead, launched into his interminable story. The first encounter with the sisters, the meeting at the restaurant, Laura's state of suggestibility because of the death of their child, the telegram about Johnnie, the decision to take the chartered flight, her departure, and her sudden inexplicable return. When he had finished he felt as exhausted as if he had driven three hundred miles nonstop after a severe bout of flu. His interrogator spoke excellent English with a strong Italian accent.

"You say," he began, "that your wife was suffering the aftereffects of shock. This had been noticeable during your stay here in Venice."

"Well, yes," John replied, "she had really been quite ill. The holiday didn't seem to be doing her much good. It was only when she met these two women at Torcello yesterday that her mood changed. The strain seemed to have gone. She was ready, I suppose, to snatch at every straw, and this belief that our little girl was watching over her had somehow restored her to what appeared normality."

"It would be natural," said the police officer, "in the circumstances. But no doubt the telegram last night was a further shock to you both."

"Indeed, yes. That was the reason we decided to return home."

"No argument between you? No difference of opinion?"

"None. We were in complete agreement. My one regret was that I could not go with my wife on this charter flight."

The police officer nodded. "It could well be that your wife had a sudden attack of amnesia, and meeting the two ladies served as a link, she clung to them for support. You have described them with great accuracy, and I think they should not be too difficult to trace. Meanwhile, I suggest you should return to your hotel, and we will get in touch with you as soon as we have news."

At least, John thought, they believed his story. They did not consider him a crank who had made the whole thing up and was merely wasting their time.

"You appreciate," he said, "I am extremely anxious. These women may have some criminal design upon my wife. One has heard of such things . . ."

The police officer smiled for the first time. "Please don't concern yourself," he said. "I am sure there will be some satisfactory explanation."

All very well, thought John, but in heaven's name, what?

"I'm sorry," he said, "to have taken up so much of your time. Especially as I gather the police have their hands full hunting down a murderer who is still at large."

He spoke deliberately. No harm in letting the fellow know that for all any of them could tell there might be some connection between Laura's disappearance and this other hideous affair.

"Ah, that," said the police officer, rising to his feet. "We hope to have the murderer under lock and key very soon."

His tone of confidence was reassuring. Murderers, missing wives, lost handbags were all under control. They shook hands, and John was ushered out of the door and so downstairs. Perhaps, he thought, as he walked slowly back to the hotel, the fellow was right. Laura had suffered a sudden attack of amnesia, and the sisters happened to be at the airport and had brought her back to Venice, to their own hotel, because Laura couldn't remember where she and John had been staying. Perhaps they were even now trying to track down his hotel. Anyway, he could do nothing more. The police had everything in hand, and, please God, would come up with the solution. All he wanted to do right now was to collapse upon a bed with a stiff whisky, and then put through a call to Johnnie's school.

The page took him up in the lift to a modest room on the fourth floor at the rear of the hotel. Bare, impersonal, the shutters closed, with a smell of cooking wafting up from a courtyard down below.

"Ask them to send me up a double whisky, will you?" he said to the boy. "And a ginger ale," and when he was alone he plunged his face under the cold tap in the washbasin, relieved to find that the minute portion of visitor's soap afforded some measure of comfort. He flung off his shoes, hung his coat over the back of a chair and threw himself down on the bed. Somebody's radio was blasting forth an old popular song, now several seasons out-of-date, that had been one of Laura's favourites a couple of years ago. "I love you, Baby . . ." He reached for the telephone, and asked the exchange to put through the call to England. Then he closed his eyes, and all the while the insistent voice persisted, "I love you, Baby . . . I can't get you out of my mind."

Presently there was a tap at the door. It was the waiter with his drink. Too little ice, such meagre comfort, but what desperate need. He gulped it down without a ginger ale, and in a few moments the ever-nagging pain was eased, numbed, bringing, if only momentarily, a sense of calm. The telephone rang, and now, he thought, bracing himself for ultimate disaster, the final shock, Johnnie probably dying, or already dead. In which case nothing remained. Let Venice be engulfed . . .

The exchange told him that the connection had been made, and in a moment he heard the voice of Mrs. Hill at the other end of the line. They must have warned her that the call came from Venice, for she knew instantly who was speaking.

"Hullo?" she said. "Oh, I am so glad you rang. All is well. Johnnie has had his operation, the surgeon decided to do it at midday rather than wait, and it was completely successful. Johnnie is going to be all right. So you don't have to worry any more, and will have a peaceful night."

"Thank God," he answered.

"I know," she said, "we are all so relieved. Now I'll get off the line and you can speak to your wife."

John sat up on the bed, stunned. What the hell did she mean? Then he heard Laura's voice, cool and clear.

"Darling? Darling, are you there?"

He could not answer. He felt the hand holding the receiver go clammy cold with sweat. "I'm here," he whispered.

"It's not a very good line," she said, "but never mind. As Mrs. Hill told you, all is well. Such a nice surgeon, and a very sweet Sister on Johnnie's floor, and I really am happy about the way it's turned out. I came straight down here after landing at Gatwick— the flight O.K., by the way, but such a funny crowd, it'll make you hysterical when I tell you about them—and I went to the hospital, and Johnnie was coming round. Very dopey, of course, but so pleased to see me. And the Hills are being wonderful, I've got their spare room, and it's only a short taxi drive into the town and the hospital. I shall go to bed as soon as we've had dinner, because I'm a bit fagged, what with the flight and the anxiety. How was the drive to Milan? And where are you staying?"

John did not recognize the voice that answered as his own. It was the automatic response of some computer.

"I'm not in Milan," he said. "I'm still in Venice."

"Still in Venice? What on earth for? Wouldn't the car start?"

"I can't explain," he said. "There was a stupid sort of mix-up . . ."

He felt suddenly so exhausted that he nearly dropped the receiver, and, shame upon shame, he could feel tears pricking behind his eyes.

"What sort of mix-up?" Her voice was suspicious, almost hostile. "You weren't in a crash?"

"No . . . no . . . nothing like that."

A moment's silence, and then she said, "Your voice sounds very slurred. Don't tell me you went and got pissed."

Oh Christ . . . If she only knew! He was probably going to pass out any moment, but not from the whisky.

"I thought," he said slowly, "I thought I saw you, in a vaporetto, with those two sisters."

What was the point of going on? It was hopeless trying to explain.

"How could you have seen me with the sisters?" she said. "You knew I'd gone to the airport. Really, darling, you are an idiot. You seem to have got those two poor old dears on the brain. I hope you didn't say anything to Mrs. Hill just now."

"No."

"Well, what are you going to do? You'll catch the train at Milan tomorrow, won't you?"

"Yes, of course," he told her.

"I still don't understand what kept you in Venice," she said. "It all sounds a bit odd to me. However . . . thank God Johnnie is going to be all right and I'm here."

"Yes," he said, "yes."

He could hear the distant boom-boom sound of a gong from the headmaster's hall.

"You had better go," he said. "My regards to the Hills, and my love to Johnnie."

"Well, take care of yourself, darling, and for goodness' sake don't miss the train tomorrow, and drive carefully."

The telephone clicked and she had gone. He poured the remaining drop of whisky into his empty glass, and sousing it with ginger ale drank it down at a gulp. He got up, and crossing the room threw open the shutters and leant out of the window. He felt lightheaded. His sense of relief, enormous, overwhelming, was somehow tempered with a curious feeling of unreality, almost as though the voice speaking from England had not been Laura's after all but a fake, and she was still in Venice, hidden in some furtive pension with the two sisters.

The point was, he *had* seen all three of them on the vaporetto. It was not another woman in a red coat. The women *had* been there, with Laura. So what was the explanation? That he was going off his head? Or something more sinister? The sisters, possessing psychic powers of formidable strength, had seen him as their two ferries had passed, and in some inexplicable fashion had made him believe Laura was with them. But why, and to what end? No, it didn't make sense. The only explanation was that he had been mistaken, the whole episode an hallucination. In which case he needed psychoanalysis, just as Johnnie had needed a surgeon.

And what did he do now? Go downstairs and tell the management he had been at fault and had just spoken to his wife, who had arrived in England safe and sound from her charter flight? He put on his shoes and ran his fingers through his hair. He glanced at his watch. It was ten minutes to eight. If he nipped into the bar and had a quick drink it would be easier to face the manager and admit what had happened. Then, perhaps, they would get in touch with the police. Profuse apologies all round for putting everyone to enormous trouble.

He made his way to the ground floor and went straight to the bar, feeling self-conscious, a marked man, half-imagining everyone would look at him, thinking, "There's the fellow with the missing wife." Luckily the bar was full and there wasn't a face he knew. Even the chap behind the bar was an underling who hadn't served him before. He downed his whisky and glanced over his shoulder to the reception hall. The desk was momentarily empty. He could see the manager's back framed in the doorway of an inner room, talking to someone within. On impulse, coward-like, he crossed the hall and passed through the swing door to the street outside.

"I'll have some dinner," he decided, "and then go back and face them. I'll feel more like it once I've some food inside me."

He went to the restaurant nearby where he and Laura had dined once or twice. Nothing mattered any more, because she was safe. The nightmare lay behind him. He could enjoy his dinner, despite her absence, and think of her sitting down with the Hills to a dull, quiet evening, early to bed, and on the following morning going to the hospital to sit with Johnnie. Johnnie was safe, too. No more worries, only the awkward explanations and apologies to the manager at the hotel.

There was a pleasant anonymity sitting down at a corner table alone in the little restaurant, ordering vitello alla Marsala and half a bottle of Merlot. He took his time, enjoying his food but eating in a kind of haze, a sense of unreality still with him, while the conversation of his nearest neighbours had the same soothing effect as background music.

When they rose and left, he saw by the clock on the wall that it was nearly half-past nine. No use delaying matters any further. He drank his coffee, lighted a cigarette and paid his bill. After all, he thought, as he walked back to the hotel, the manager would be greatly relieved to know that all was well.

When he pushed through the swing door, the first thing he noticed was a man in police uniform, standing talking to the manager at the desk. The reception clerk was there too. They turned as John approached, the manager's face lighted up with relief.

"Eccolo!" he exclaimed. "I was certain the signore would not be far away. Things are moving, signore. The two ladies have been traced, and they very kindly agreed to accompany the police to the Questura. If you will go there at once, this agente di polizia will escort you."

John flushed. "I have given everyone a lot of trouble," he said. "I meant to tell you before going out to dinner, but you were not at the desk. The fact is that I have contacted my wife. She did make the flight to London after all, and I spoke to her on the telephone. It was all a great mistake."

The manager looked bewildered. "The signora is in London?" he repeated. He broke off, and exchanged a rapid conversation in Italian with the policeman. "It seems that the ladies maintain they did not go out for the day, except for a little shopping in the morning," he said, turning back to John. "Then who was it the signore saw on the vaporetto?"

John shook his head. "A very extraordinary mistake on my part which I still don't understand," he said. "Obviously, I did not see either my wife or the two ladies. I really am extremely sorry."

More rapid conversation in Italian. John noticed the clerk watching him with a curious expression in his eyes. The manager was obviously apologising on John's behalf to the policeman, who looked annoyed and gave tongue to this effect, his voice increasing in volume, to the manager's concern. The whole business had undoubtedly given enormous trouble to a great many people, not least the two unfortunate sisters.

"Look," said John, interrupting the flow, "will you tell the agente I will go with him to headquarters and apologise in person both to the police officer and to the ladies?"

The manager looked relieved. "If the signore would take the trouble," he said. "Naturally, the ladies were much distressed when a policeman interrogated them at their hotel, and they offered to accompany him to the Questura only because they were so distressed about the signora."

John felt more and more uncomfortable. Laura must never learn any of this. She would be outraged. He wondered if there were some penalty for giving the police misleading information involving a third party. His error began, in retrospect, to take on criminal proportions.

He crossed the Piazza San Marco, now thronged with after-dinner strollers and spectators at the cafés, all three orchestras going full blast in harmonious rivalry, while his companion kept a discreet two paces to his left and never uttered a word.

They arrived at the police station and mounted the stairs to the same inner room where he had been before. He saw immediately that it was not the officer he knew but another who sat behind the desk, a sallow-faced individual with a sour expression, while the two sisters, obviously upset—the active one in particular—were seated on chairs nearby, some underling in uniform standing behind them. John's escort went at once to the police officer, speaking in rapid Italian, while John himself, after a moment's hesitation, advanced towards the sisters.

"There has been a terrible mistake," he said. "I don't know how to apologise to you both. It's all my fault, mine entirely, the police are not to blame."

The active sister made as though to rise, her mouth twitching nervously, but he restrained her.

"We don't understand," she said, the Scots inflection strong. "We said good night to your wife last night at dinner, and we have not seen her since. The police came to our pension more than an hour ago and told us your wife was missing and you had filed a complaint against us. My sister is not very strong. She was considerably disturbed."

"A mistake. A frightful mistake," he repeated.

He turned towards the desk. The police officer was addressing him, his English very inferior to that of the previous interrogator. He had John's earlier statement on the desk in front of him, and tapped it with a pencil.

"So?" he queried. "This document all lies? You not speaka the truth?"

"I believed it to be true at the time," said John. "I could have sworn in a court of law that I saw my wife with these two ladies on a vaporetto in the Grand Canal this afternoon. Now I realise I was mistaken."

"We have not been near the Grand Canal all day," protested the sister, "not even on foot. We made a few purchases in the Merceria this morning, and remained indoors all afternoon. My sister was a little unwell. I have told the police officer this a dozen times, and the people at the pension would corroborate our story. He refused to listen."

"And the signora?" rapped the police officer angrily. "What happen to the signora?"

"The signora, my wife, is safe in England," explained John patiently. "I talked to her on the telephone just after seven. She did join the charter flight from the airport, and is now staying with friends."

"Then who you see on the vaporetto in the red coat?" asked the furious police officer. "And if not these signorine here, then what signorine?"

"My eyes deceived me," said John, aware that his English was likewise becoming strained. "I think I see my wife and these ladies but no, it was not so. My wife in aircraft, these ladies in pension all the time."

It was like talking stage Chinese. In a moment he would be bowing and putting his hands in his sleeves.

The police officer raised his eyes to heaven and thumped the table. "So all this work for nothing," he said. "Hotels and pensiones searched for the signorine and a missing signora inglese, when here we have plenty, plenty other things to do. You maka a mistake. You have perhaps too much vino at mezzo giorno and you see hundred signore in red coats in hundred vaporetti." He stood up, rumpling the papers on his desk. "And you, signorine," he said, "you wish to make complaint against this person?" He was addressing the active sister.

"Oh no," she said, "no, indeed. I quite see it was all a mistake. Our only wish is to return at once to our pension."

The police officer grunted. Then he pointed at John. "You very lucky man," he said. "These signorine could file complaint against you—very serious matter."

"I'm sure," began John, "I'll do anything in my power . . ."

"Please don't think of it," exclaimed the sister, horrified. "We would not hear of such a thing." It was her turn to apologise to the police officer. "I hope we need not take up any more of your valuable time," she said.

He waved a hand of dismissal and spoke in Italian to the underling. "This man walk with you to the pension," he said. "Buona sera, signorine," and, ignoring John, he sat down again at his desk.

"I'll come with you," said John, "I want to explain exactly what happened."

They trooped down the stairs and out of the building, the blind sister leaning on her twin's arm, and once outside she turned her sightless eyes to John.

"You saw us," she said, "and your wife too. But not today. You saw us in the future."

Her voice was softer than her sister's, slower, she seemed to have some slight impediment in her speech.

"I don't follow," replied John, bewildered.

He turned to the active sister and she shook her head at him, frowning, and put her finger on her lips.

"Come along, dear," she said to her twin. "You know you're very tired, and I want to get you home." Then sotto voce to John, "She's psychic. Your wife told you, I believe, but I don't want her to go into trance here in the street."

God forbid, thought John, and the little procession began to move slowly along the street, away from police headquarters, a canal to the left of them. Progress was slow, because of the blind sister, and there were two bridges. John was completely lost after the first turning, but it couldn't have mattered less. Their police escort was with them, and anyway, the sisters knew where they were going.

"I must explain," said John softly. "My wife would never forgive me if I didn't," and as they walked he went over the whole inexplicable story once again, beginning with the telegram received the night before and the conversation with Mrs. Hill, the decision to return to England the following day, Laura by air, and John himself by car and train. It no longer sounded as dramatic as it had done when he had made his statement to the police officer, when, possibly because of his conviction of something uncanny, the description of the two vaporettos passing one another in the middle of the Grand Canal had held a sinister quality, suggesting abduction on the part of the sisters, the pair of them holding a bewildered Laura captive. Now that neither of the women had any further menace for him he spoke more naturally, yet with great sincerity, feeling for the first time that they were somehow both in sympathy with him and would understand.

"You see," he explained, in a final endeavour to make amends for having gone to the police in the first place, "I truly believed I had seen you with Laura, and I thought . . ." he hesitated, because this had been the police officer's suggestion and not his, "I thought that perhaps Laura had some sudden loss of memory, had met you at the airport, and you had brought her back to Venice to wherever you were staying."

They had crossed a large square and were approaching a house at one end of it, with a sign, "Pensione," above the door. Their escort paused at the entrance.

"Is this it?" asked John.

"Yes," said the sister. "I know it is nothing much from the outside, but it is clean and comfortable, and was recommended by friends." She turned to the escort. "Grazie," she said to him, "grazie tanto."

The man nodded briefly, wished them "Buona notte," and disappeared across the campo.

"Will you come in?" asked the sister. "I am sure we can find you some coffee, or perhaps you prefer tea?"

"No, really," John thanked her, "I must get back to the hotel. I'm making an early start in the morning. I just want to make quite sure you do understand what happened, and that you forgive me."

"There is nothing to forgive," she replied. "It is one of the many examples of second sight that my sister and I have experienced time and time again, and I should very much like to record it for our files, if you will permit it."

"Well as to that, of course," he told her, "but I myself find it hard to understand. It has never happened to me before."

"Not consciously, perhaps," she said, "but so many things happen to us of which we are not aware. My sister felt you had psychic understanding. She told your wife. She also told your wife, last night in the restaurant, that you were to experience trouble, danger, that you should leave Venice. Well, don't you believe now that the telegram was proof of this? Your son was ill, possibly dangerously ill, and so it was necessary for you to return home immediately. Heaven be praised your wife flew home to be by his side."

"Yes, indeed," said John, "but why should I see her on the vaporetto with you and your sister when she was actually on her way to England?"

"Thought transference, perhaps," she answered. "Your wife may have been thinking about us. We gave her our address, should you wish to get in touch with us. We shall be here another ten days. And she knows that we would pass on any message that my sister might have from your little one in the spirit world."

"Yes," said John awkwardly, "yes, I see. It's very good of you." He had a sudden rather unkind picture of the two sisters putting on headphones in their bedroom, listening for a coded message from poor Christine. "Look, this is our address in London," he said. "I know Laura will be pleased to hear from you."

He scribbled their address on a sheet torn from his pocket diary, even, as a bonus thrown in, the telephone number, and handed it to her. He could imagine the outcome. Laura springing it on him one evening that the "old dears" were passing through London on their way to Scotland, and the last they could do was to offer them hospitality, even the spare room for the night. Then a séance in the living room, tambourines appearing out of thin air.

"Well, I must be off," he said. "Good night, and apologies, once again, for all that has happened this evening." He shook hands with the first sister, then turned to her blind twin. "I hope," he said, "that you are not too tired."

The sightless eyes were disconcerting. She held his hand fast and would not let it go. "The child," she said, speaking in an odd staccato voice, "the child . . . I can see the child . . ." and then, to his dismay, a bead of froth appeared at the corner of her mouth, her head jerked back, and she half-collapsed in her sister's arms.

"We must get her inside," said the sister hurriedly. "It's all right, she's not ill, it's beginning of a trance state."

Between them they helped the twin, who had gone rigid, into the house, and sat her down on the nearest chair, the sister supporting her. A woman came running from some inner room. There was a strong smell of spaghetti from the back regions. "Don't worry," said the sister, "the signorina and I can manage. I think you had better go. Sometimes she is sick after these turns."

"I'm most frightfully sorry . . ." John began, but the sister had already turned her back and, with the signorina, was bending over her twin, from whom peculiar choking sounds were proceeding. He was obviously in the way, and after a final gesture of courtesy, "Is there anything I can do?" which received no reply, he turned on his heel and began walking across the square. He looked back once, and saw they had closed the door.

What a finale to the evening! And all his fault. Poor old girls, first dragged to police headquarters and put through an interrogation, and then a psychic fit on top of it all. More likely epilepsy. Not much of a life for the other sister, but she seemed to take it in her stride. An additional hazard, though, if it happened in a restaurant or in the street. And not particularly welcome under his and Laura's roof should the sisters ever find themselves beneath it, which he prayed would never happen.

Meanwhile, where the devil was he? The square, with the inevitable church at one end, was quite deserted. He could not remember which way they had come from police headquarters, there had seemed to be so many turnings.

Wait a minute, the church itself had a familiar appearance. He drew nearer to it, looking for the name which was sometimes on notices at the entrance. San Giovanni in Bragora, that rang a bell. He and Laura had gone inside one morning to look at a painting by Cima da Conegliano. Surely it was only a stone's throw from the Riva degli Schiavoni and the open wide waters of the San Marco lagoon, with all the bright lights of civilisation and the strolling tourists? He remembered taking a small turning from the Schiavoni and they had arrived at the church. Wasn't that the alleyway ahead? He plunged along it, but halfway down he hesitated. It didn't seem right, although it was familiar for some unknown reason.

Then he realised that it was not the alley they had taken the morning they visited the church, but the one they had walked along the previous evening, only he was approaching it from the opposite direction. Yes, that was it, in which case it would be quicker to go on and cross the little bridge over the narrow canal, and he would find the Arsenal on his left and the street leading down to the Riva degli Schiavoni to his right. Simpler than retracing his steps and getting lost once more in the maze of back streets.

He had almost reached the end of the alley, and the bridge was in sight, when he saw the child. It was the same little girl with the pixie hood who had leapt between the tethered boats the preceding night and vanished up the cellar steps of one of the houses. This time she was running from the direction of the church the other side, making for the bridge. She was running as if her life depended on it, and in a moment he saw why. A man was in pursuit, who, when she glanced backwards for a moment, still running, flattened himself against a wall, believing himself unobserved. The child came on, scampering across the bridge, and John, fearful of alarming her further, backed into an open doorway that led into a small court.

He remembered the drunken yell of the night before which had come from one of the houses near where the man was hiding now. This is it, he thought, the fellow's after her again, and with a flash of intuition he connected the two events, the child's terror then and now, and the murders reported in the newspapers, supposedly the work of some madman. It could be coincidence, a child running from a drunken relative, and yet, and yet . . . His heart began thumping in his chest, instinct warning him to run himself, now, at once, back along the alley the way he had come —but what about the child? What was going to happen to the child?

Then he heard her running steps. She hurtled through the open doorway into the court in which he stood, not seeing him, making for the rear of the house that flanked it, where steps led presumably to a back entrance. She was sobbing as she ran, not the ordinary cry of a frightened child, but the panic-stricken intake of breath of a helpless being in despair. Were there parents in the house who would protect her, whom he could warn? He hesitated a moment, then followed her down the steps and through the door at the bottom, which had burst open at the touch of her hands as she hurled herself against it.

"It's all right," he called. "I won't let him hurt you, it's all right," cursing his lack of Italian, but possibly an English voice might reassure her. But it was no use—she ran sobbing up another flight of stairs, which were spiral, twisting, leading to the floor above, and already it was too late for him to retreat. He could hear sounds of the pursuer in the courtyard behind, someone shouting in Italian, a dog barking. This is it, he thought, we're in it together, the child and I. Unless we can bolt some inner door above he'll get us both.

He ran up the stairs after the child, who had darted into a room leading off a small landing, and followed her inside and slammed the door, and, merciful heaven, there was a bolt which he rammed into its socket. The child was crouching by the open window. If he shouted for help someone would surely hear, someone would surely come before the man in pursuit threw himself against the door and it gave, because there was no one but themselves, no parents, the room was bare except for a mattress on an old bed, and a heap of rags in one corner.

"It's all right," he panted, "it's all right," and held out his hand, trying to smile.

The child struggled to her feet and stood before him, the pixie hood falling from her head onto the floor. He stared at her, incredulity turning to horror, to fear. It was not a child at all but a little thick-set woman dwarf, about three feet high, with a great square adult head too big for her body, grey locks hanging shoulder-length, and she wasn't sobbing any more, she was grinning at him, nodding her head up and down.

Then he heard the footsteps on the landing outside and the hammering on the door, and a barking dog, and not one voice but several voices, shouting, "Open up! Police!" The creature fumbled in her sleeve, drawing a knife, and as she threw it at him with hideous strength, piercing his throat, he stumbled and fell, the sticky mess covering his protecting hands.

And he saw the vaporetto with Laura and the two sisters steaming down the Grand Canal, not today, not tomorrow, but the day after that, and he knew why they were together and for what purpose they had come. The creature was gibbering in its corner. The hammering and the voices and the barking dog grew fainter, and, "Oh, God," he thought, "what a bloody silly way to die . . ."

The Apple Tree

It was three months after she died that he first noticed the apple tree. He had known of its existence, of course, with the others, standing upon the lawn in front of the house, sloping upwards to the field beyond. Never before, though, had he been aware of this particular tree looking in any way different from its fellows, except that it was the third one on the left, a little apart from the rest and leaning more closely to the terrace.

It was a fine clear morning in early spring, and he was shaving by the open window. As he leant out to sniff the air, the lather on his face, the razor in his hand, his eye fell upon the apple tree. It was a trick of light, perhaps, something to do with sun coming up over the woods, that happened to catch the tree at this particular moment; but the likeness was unmistakable.

He put his razor down on the window ledge and stared. The tree was scraggy and of a depressing thinness, possessing none of the gnarled solidity of its companions. Its few branches, growing high up on the trunk like narrow shoulders on a tall body, spread themselves in martyred resignation, as though chilled by the fresh morning air. The roll of wire circling the tree, and reaching to about halfway up the trunk from the base, looked like a grey tweed skirt covering lean limbs; while the topmost branch, sticking up into the air above the ones below, yet sagging slightly, could have been a drooping head poked forward in an attitude of weariness.

How often he had seen Midge stand like this, dejected. No matter where it was, whether in the garden, or in the house, or even shopping in the town, she would take upon herself this same stooping posture, suggesting that life treated her hardly, that she had been singled out from her fellows to carry some impossible burden, but in spite of it would endure to the end without complaint. "Midge, you look worn out, for heaven's sake sit down and take a rest!" But the words would be received with the inevitable shrug of the shoulder, the inevitable sigh, "Someone has got to keep things going," and straightening herself she would embark upon the dreary routine of unnecessary tasks she forced herself to do, day in, day out, through the interminable changeless years.

He went on staring at the apple tree. That martyred bent position, the stooping top, the weary branches, the few withered leaves that had not blown away with the wind and rain of the past winter and now shivered in the spring breeze like wispy hair; all of it protested soundlessly to the owner of the garden looking upon it, "I am like this because of you, because of your neglect."

He turned away from the window and went on shaving. It would not do to let his imagination run away with him and start building fancies in his mind just when he was settling at long last to freedom. He bathed and dressed and went down to breakfast. Eggs and bacon were waiting for him on the hotplate, and he carried the dish to the single place laid for him at the dining table. *The Times,* folded smooth and new, was ready for him to read. When Midge was alive he had handed it to her first, from long custom, and when she gave it back to him after breakfast, to take with him to the study, the pages were always in the wrong order and folded crookedly, so that part of the pleasure of reading it was spoilt. The news, too, would be stale to him after she had read the worst of it aloud, which was a morning habit she used to take upon herself, always adding some derogatory remark of her own about what she read. The birth of a daughter to mutual friends would bring a click of the tongue, a little jerk of the head, "Poor things, another girl," or if a son, "A boy can't be much fun to educate these days." He used to think it psychological, because they themselves were childless, that she should so grudge the entry of new life into the world; but as time passed it became thus with all bright or joyous things, as though there was some fundamental blight upon good cheer.

"It says here that more people went on holiday this year than ever before. Let's hope they enjoyed themselves, that's all." But no hope lay in her words, only disparagement. Then, having finished breakfast, she would push back her chair and sigh and say, "Oh well . . . ," leaving the sentence unfinished; but the sigh, the shrug of the shoulders, the slope of her long, thin back as she stooped to clear the dishes from the serving table—thus sparing work for the daily maid—was all part of her long-term reproach, directed at him, that had marred their existence over a span of years.

Silent, punctilious, he would open the door for her to pass through to the kitchen quarters, and she would labour past him, stooping under the weight of the laden tray that there was no need for her to carry, and presently, through the half-open door, he would hear the swish of the running water from the pantry tap. He would return to his chair and sit down again, the crumpled *Times,* a smear of marmalade upon it, lying against the toast rack; and once again, with monotonous insistence, the question hammered at his mind, "What have I done?"

It was not as though she nagged. Nagging wives, like mothers-in-law, were chestnut jokes for music halls. He could not remember Midge ever losing her temper or quarrelling. It was just that the undercurrent of reproach, mingled with suffering nobly born, spoilt the atmosphere of his home and drove him to a sense of furtiveness and guilt.

Perhaps it would be raining and he, seeking sanctuary within his study, electric fire aglow, his after-breakfast pipe filling the small room with smoke, would settle down before his desk in a pretence of writing letters, but in reality to hide, to feel the snug security of four safe walls that were his alone. Then the door would open and Midge, struggling into a raincoat, her wide-brimmed felt hat pulled low over her brow, would pause and wrinkle her nose in distaste.

"Phew! What a fug."

He said nothing, but moved slightly in his chair, covering with his arm the novel he had chosen from a shelf in idleness.

"Aren't you going into the town?" she asked him.

"I had not thought of doing so."

"Oh! Oh, well, it doesn't matter." She turned away again towards the door.

"Why, is there anything you want done?"

"It's only the fish for lunch. They don't deliver on Wednesdays. Still, I can go myself if you are busy. I only thought . . ."

She was out of the room without finishing her sentence.

"It's all right, Midge," he called, "I'll get the car and go and fetch it presently. No sense in getting wet."

Thinking she had not heard, he went out into the hall. She was standing by the open front door, the mizzling rain driving in upon her. She had a long flat basket over her arm and was drawing on a pair of gardening gloves.

"I'm bound to get wet in any case," she said, "so it doesn't make much odds. Look at those flowers, they all need staking. I'll go for the fish when I've finished seeing to them."

Argument was useless. She had made up her mind. He shut the front door after her and sat down again in the study. Somehow the room no longer felt so snug, and a little later, raising his head to the window, he saw her hurry past, her raincoat not buttoned properly and flapping, little drips of water forming on the brim of her hat and the garden basket filled with limp Michaelmas daisies already dead. His conscience pricking him, he bent down and turned out one bar of the electric fire.

Or yet again it would be spring, it would be summer. Strolling out hatless into the garden, his hands in his pockets, with no other purpose in his mind but to feel the sun upon his back and stare out upon the woods and fields and the slow winding river, he would hear, from the bedrooms above, the high-pitched whine of the Hoover slow down suddenly, gasp and die. Midge called down to him as he stood there on the terrace.

"Were you going to do anything?" she said.

He was not. It was the smell of spring, of early summer, that had driven him out into the garden. It was the delicious knowledge that being retired now, no longer working in the City, time was a thing of no account, he could waste it as he pleased.

"No," he said, "not on such a lovely day. Why?"

"Oh, never mind," she answered, "it's only that the wretched drain under the kitchen window has gone wrong again. Completely plugged up and choked. No one ever sees to it, that's why. I'll have a go at it myself this afternoon."

Her face vanished from the window. Once more there was a gasp, a rising groan of sound, and the Hoover warmed to its task again. What foolishness that such an interruption could damp the brightness of the day. Not the demand, nor the task itself—clearing a drain was in its own way a schoolboy piece of folly, playing with mud—but that wan face of hers looking out upon the sunlit terrace, the hand that went up wearily to push back a strand of falling hair, and the inevitable sigh before she turned from the window, the unspoken "I wish I had the time to stand and do nothing in the sun. Oh, well . . ."

He had ventured to ask once why so much cleaning of the house was necessary. Why there must be the incessant turning out of rooms. Why chairs must be lifted to stand upon other chairs, rugs rolled up and ornaments huddled together on a sheet of newspaper. And why, in particular, the sides of the upstairs corridor, on which no one ever trod, must be polished laboriously by hand, Midge and the daily woman taking it in turns to crawl upon their knees the whole endless length of it, like slaves of bygone days.

Midge had stared at him, not understanding.

"You'd be the first to complain," she said, "if the house was like a pigsty. You like your comforts."

So they lived in different worlds, their minds not meeting. Had it been always so? He did not remember. They had been married nearly twenty-five years and were two people who, from force of habit, lived under the same roof.

When he had been in business, it seemed different. He had not noticed it so much. He came home to eat, to sleep, and to go up by train again in the morning. But when he retired he became aware of her forcibly, and day by day his sense of her resentment, of her disapproval, grew stronger.

Finally, in that last year before she died, he felt himself engulfed in it, so that he was led into every sort of petty deception to get away from her, making a pretence of going up to London to have his hair cut, to see the dentist, to lunch with an old business friend; and in reality he would be sitting by his club window, anonymous, at peace.

It was mercifully swift, the illness that took her from him. Influenza, followed by pneumonia, and she was dead within a week. He hardly knew how it happened, except that as usual she was overtired and caught a cold, and would not stay in bed. One evening, coming home by the late train from London, having sneaked into a cinema during the afternoon, finding release amongst the crowd of warm friendly people enjoying themselves —for it was a bitter December day—he found her bent over the furnace in the cellar, poking and thrusting at the lumps of coke.

She looked up at him, white with fatigue, her face drawn.

"Why, Midge, what on earth are you doing?" he said.

"It's the furnace," she said, "we've had trouble with it all day, it won't stay alight. We shall have to get the men to see it tomorrow. I really cannot manage this sort of thing myself."

There was a streak of coal dust on her cheek. She let the stubby poker fall on the cellar floor. She began to cough, and as she did so winced with pain.

"You ought to be in bed," he said, "I never heard of such nonsense. What the dickens does it matter about the furnace?"

"I thought you would be home early," she said, "and then you might have known how to deal with it. It's been bitter all day, I can't think what you found to do with yourself in London."

She climbed the cellar stairs slowly, her back bent, and when she reached the top she stood shivering and half-closed her eyes.

"If you don't mind terribly," she said, "I'll get your supper right away, to have it done with. I don't want anything myself."

"To hell with my supper," he said, "I can forage for myself. You go up to bed. I'll bring you a hot drink."

"I tell you, I don't want anything," she said. "I can fill my hot water bottle myself. I only ask one thing of you. And that is to remember to turn out the lights everywhere, before you come up." She turned into the hall, her shoulders sagging.

"Surely a glass of hot milk?" he began uncertainly, starting to take off his overcoat; and as he did so the torn half of the ten-and-sixpenny seat at the cinema fell from his pocket onto the floor. She saw it. She said nothing. She coughed again and began to drag herself upstairs.

The next morning her temperature was a hundred and three. The doctor came and said she had pneumonia. She asked if she might go to a private ward in the cottage hospital, because having a nurse in the house would make too much work. This was on the Tuesday morning. She went there right away, and they told him on the Friday evening that she was not likely to live through the night. He stood inside the room, after they told him, looking down at her in the high impersonal hospital bed, and his heart was wrung with pity, because surely they had given her too many pillows, she was propped too high, there could be no rest for her that way. He had brought some flowers, but there seemed no purpose now in giving them to the nurse to arrange, because Midge was too ill to look at them. In a sort of delicacy he put them on a table beside the screen, when the nurse was bending down to her.

"Is there anything she needs?" he said. "I mean, I can easily . . ." He did not finish the sentence, he left it in the air, hoping the nurse would understand his intention, that he was ready to go off in the car, drive somewhere, fetch what was required.

The nurse shook her head. "We will telephone you," she said, "if there is any change."

What possible change could there be, he wondered, as he found himself outside the hospital? The white pinched face upon the pillows would not alter now, it belonged to no one.

Midge died in the early hours of Saturday morning.

He was not a religious man, he had no profound belief in immortality, but when the funeral was over, and Midge was buried, it distressed him to think of her poor lonely body lying in that brand-new coffin with the brass handles: it seemed such a churlish thing to permit. Death should be different. It should be like bidding farewell to someone at a station before a long journey, but without the strain. There was something of indecency in this haste to bury underground the thing that but for ill chance would be a living breathing person. In his distress he fancied he could hear Midge saying with a sigh, "Oh, well . . ." as they lowered the coffin into the open grave.

He hoped with fervour that after all there might be a future in some unseen Paradise and that poor Midge, unaware of what they were doing to her mortal remains, walked somewhere in green fields. But who with, he wondered? Her parents had died in India many years ago; she would not have much in common with them now if they met her at the gates of Heaven. He had a sudden picture of her waiting her turn in a queue, rather far back, as was always her fate in queues, with that large shopping bag of woven straw which she took everywhere, and on her face that patient martyred look. As she passed through the turnstile into Paradise she looked at him, reproachfully.

These pictures, of the coffin and the queue, remained with him for about a week, fading a little day by day. Then he forgot her. Freedom was his, and the sunny empty house, the bright crisp winter. The routine he followed belonged to him alone. He never thought of Midge until the morning he looked out upon the apple tree.

Later that day he was taking a stroll round the garden, and he found himself drawn to the tree through curiosity. It had been stupid fancy after all. There was nothing singular about it. An apple tree like any other apple tree. He remembered then that it had always been a poorer tree than its fellows, was in fact more than half dead, and at one time there had been talk of chopping it

down, but the talk came to nothing. Well, it would be something
for him to do over the weekend. Axing a tree was healthy exercise, and apple wood smelt good. It would be a treat to have it
burning on the fire.

Unfortunately wet weather set in for nearly a week after that
day, and he was unable to accomplish the task he had set himself.
No sense in pottering out of doors this weather, and getting a chill
into the bargain. He still noticed the tree from his bedroom window. It began to irritate him, humped there, straggling and thin,
under the rain. The weather was not cold, and the rain that fell
upon the garden was soft and gentle. None of the other trees wore
this aspect of dejection. There was one young tree—only planted
a few years back, he recalled quite well—growing to the right of
the old one and standing straight and firm, the lithe young
branches lifted to the sky, positively looking as if it enjoyed the
rain. He peered through the window at it, and smiled. Now why
the devil should he suddenly remember that incident, years back,
during the war, with the girl who came to work on the land for a
few months at the neighbouring farm? He did not suppose he had
thought of her in months. Besides, there was nothing to it. At
weekends he had helped them at the farm himself—war work of a
sort—and she was always there, cheerful and pretty and smiling;
she had dark curling hair, crisp and boyish, and a skin like a very
young apple.

He looked forward to seeing her, Saturdays and Sundays; it was
an antidote to the inevitable news bulletins put on throughout the
day by Midge, and to ceaseless war talk. He liked looking at the
child—she was scarcely more than that, nineteen or so—in her
slim breeches and gay shirts; and when she smiled it was as
though she embraced the world.

He never knew how it happened, and it was such a little thing;
but one afternoon he was in the shed doing something to the tractor, bending over the engine, and she was beside him, close to his
shoulder, and they were laughing together; and he turned round,
to take a bit of waste to clean a plug, and suddenly she was in his
arms and he was kissing her. It was a happy thing, spontaneous
and free, and the girl so warm and jolly, with her fresh young
mouth. Then they went on with the work of the tractor, but united
now, in a kind of intimacy that brought gaiety to them both, and
peace as well. When it was time for the girl to go and feed the pigs

he followed her from the shed, his hand on her shoulder, a careless gesture that meant nothing really, a half caress; and as they came out into the yard he saw Midge standing there, staring at them.

"I've got to go in to a Red Cross meeting," she said. "I can't get the car to start. I called you. You didn't seem to hear."

Her face was frozen. She was looking at the girl. At once guilt covered him. The girl said good evening cheerfully to Midge, and crossed the yard to the pigs.

He went with Midge to the car and managed to start it with the handle. Midge thanked him, her voice without expression. He found himself unable to meet her eyes. This, then, was adultery. This was sin. This was the second page in a Sunday newspaper— "Husband Intimate with Land Girl in Shed. Wife Witnesses Act." His hands were shaking when he got back to the house and he had to pour himself a drink. Nothing was ever said. Midge never mentioned the matter. Some craven instinct kept him from the farm the next weekend, and then he heard that the girl's mother had been taken ill and she had been called back home.

He never saw her again. Why, he wondered, should he remember her suddenly, on such a day, watching the rain falling on the apple trees? He must certainly make a point of cutting down the old dead tree, if only for the sake of bringing more sunshine to the little sturdy one; it hadn't a fair chance, growing there so close to the other.

On Friday afternoon he went round to the vegetable garden to find Willis, the jobbing gardener, who came three days a week, to pay him his wages. He wanted, too, to look in the toolshed and see if the axe and saw were in good condition. Willis kept everything neat and tidy there—this was Midge's training—and the axe and saw were hanging in their accustomed place upon the wall.

He paid Willis his money, and was turning away when the man suddenly said to him, "Funny thing, sir, isn't it, about the old apple tree?"

The remark was so unexpected that it came as a shock. He felt himself change colour.

"Apple tree? What apple tree?" he said.

"Why, the one at the far end, near the terrace," answered Willis. "Been barren as long as I've worked here, and that's some years now. Never an apple from her, nor as much as a sprig of blossom. We were going to chop her up that cold winter, if you remember, and we never did. Well, she's taken on a new lease now. Haven't you noticed?" The gardener watched him smiling, a knowing look in his eye.

What did the fellow mean? It was not possible that he had been struck also by that fantastic freak resemblance—no, it was out of the question, indecent, blasphemous; besides, he had put it out of his own mind now, he had not thought of it again.

"I've noticed nothing," he said, on the defensive.

Willis laughed. "Come round to the terrace, sir," he said, "I'll show you."

They went together to the sloping lawn, and when they came to the apple tree Willis put his hand up and pulled down a branch within reach. It creaked a little as he did so, as though stiff and unyielding, and Willis brushed away some of the dry lichen and revealed the spiky twigs. "Look there, sir," he said. "She's growing buds. Look at them, feel them for yourself. There's life here yet, and plenty of it. Never known such a thing before. See this branch too." He released the first, and leant up to reach another.

Willis was right. There were buds in plenty, but so small and brown that it seemed to him they scarcely deserved the name, they were more like blemishes upon the twig, dusty, and dry. He put his hands in his pockets. He felt a queer distaste to touch them.

"I don't think they'll amount to much," he said.

"I don't know, sir," said Willis, "I've got hopes. She's stood the winter, and if we get no more bad frosts there's no knowing what we'll see. It would be some joke to watch the old tree blossom. She'll bear fruit yet." He patted the trunk with his open hand, in a gesture at once familiar and affectionate.

The owner of the apple tree turned away. For some reason he felt irritated with Willis. Anyone would think the damned tree lived. And now his plan to axe the tree, over the weekend, would come to nothing.

"It's taking the light from the young tree," he said. "Surely it would be more to the point if we did away with this one, and gave the little one more room?"

He moved across to the young tree and touched a limb. No lichen here. The branches smooth. Buds upon every twig, curling tight. He let go the branch and it sprang away from him, resilient.

"Do away with her, sir," said Willis, "while there's still life in her? Oh no, sir, I wouldn't do that. She's doing no harm to the young tree. I'd give the old tree one more chance. If she doesn't bear fruit, we'll have her down next winter."

"All right, Willis," he said, and walked swiftly away. Somehow he did not want to discuss the matter any more.

That night, when he went to bed, he opened the window wide as usual and drew back the curtains; he could not bear to wake up in the morning and find the room close. It was full moon, and the light shone down upon the terrace and the lawn above it, ghostly pale and still. No wind blew. A hush upon the place. He leant out, loving the silence. The moon shone full upon the little apple tree, the young one. There was a radiance about it in this light that gave it a fairy-tale quality. Small and lithe and slim, the young tree might have been a dancer, her arms upheld, poised ready on her toes for flight. Such a careless, happy grace about it. Brave young tree. Away to the left stood the other one, half of it in shadow still. Even the moonlight could not give it beauty. What in heaven's name was the matter with the thing that it had to stand there, humped and stooping, instead of looking upwards to the light? It marred the still quiet night, it spoilt the setting. He had been a fool to give way to Willis and agree to spare the tree. Those ridiculous buds would never blossom, and even if they did . . .

His thoughts wandered, and for the second time that week he found himself remembering the land girl and her joyous smile. He wondered what had happened to her. Married probably, with a young family. Made some chap happy, no doubt. Oh, well . . . He smiled. Was he going to make use of that expression now? Poor Midge! Then he caught his breath and stood quite still, his hand upon the curtain. The apple tree, the one on the left, was no longer in shadow. The moon shone upon the withered branches, and they looked like skeleton's arms raised in supplication. Frozen arms, stiff and numb with pain. There was no wind, and the other trees were motionless; but there, in those topmost branches, something shivered and stirred, a breeze that came from nowhere and died away again. Suddenly a branch fell from the apple tree to the ground below. It was the near branch, with the small dark buds upon it, which he would not touch. No rustle, no breath of movement came from the other trees. He went on staring at the branch as it lay there on the grass, under the moon. It stretched across the shadow of the young tree close to it, pointing as though in accusation.

For the first time in his life that he could remember he drew the curtains over the window to shut out the light of the moon.

Willis was supposed to keep to the vegetable garden. He had never shown his face much round the front when Midge was alive. That was because Midge attended to the flowers. She even used to mow the grass, pushing the wretched machine up and down the slope, her back bent low over the handles.

It had been one of the tasks she set herself, like keeping the bedrooms swept and polished. Now Midge was no longer there to attend to the front garden and to tell him where he should work, Willis was always coming through to the front. The gardener liked the change. It made him feel responsible.

"I can't understand how that branch came to fall, sir," he said on the Monday.

"What branch?"

"Why, the branch on the apple tree. The one we were looking at before I left."

"It was rotten, I suppose. I told you the tree was dead."

"Nothing rotten about it, sir. Why, look at it. Broke clean off."

Once again the owner was obliged to follow his man up the slope above the terrace. Willis picked up the branch. The lichen upon it was wet, bedraggled-looking, like matted hair.

"You didn't come again to test the branch, over the weekend, and loosen it in some fashion, did you, sir?" asked the gardener.

"I most certainly did not," replied the owner, irritated. "As a matter of fact I heard the branch fall, during the night. I was opening the bedroom window at the time."

"Funny. It was a still night, too."

"These things often happen to old trees. Why you bother about this one I can't imagine. Anyone would think . . ."

He broke off; he did not know how to finish the sentence.

"Anyone would think that the tree was valuable," he said.

The gardener shook his head. "It's not the value," he said. "I don't reckon for a moment that this tree is worth any money at all. It's just that after all this time, when we thought her dead, she's alive and kicking, as you might say. Freak of nature, I call it. We'll hope no other branches fall before she blossoms."

Later, when the owner set off for his afternoon walk, he saw the man cutting away the grass below the tree and placing new wire around the base of the trunk. It was quite ridiculous. He did not pay the fellow a fat wage to tinker about with a half-dead tree. He ought to be in the kitchen garden, growing vegetables. It was too much effort, though, to argue with him.

He returned home about half-past five. Tea was a discarded meal since Midge had died, and he was looking forward to his armchair by the fire, his pipe, his whisky-and-soda, and silence.

The fire had not long been lit and the chimney was smoking. There was a queer, rather sickly smell about the living room. He threw open the windows and went upstairs to change his heavy shoes. When he came down again the smoke still clung about the room and the smell was as strong as ever. Impossible to name it. Sweetish, strange. He called to the woman out in the kitchen.

"There's a funny smell in the house," he said. "What is it?"

The woman came out into the hall from the back.

"What sort of a smell, sir?" she said, on the defensive.

"It's in the living room," he said. "The room was full of smoke just now. Have you been burning something?"

Her face cleared. "It must be the logs," she said. "Willis cut them up specially, sir, he said you would like them."

"What logs are those?"

"He said it was apple wood, sir, from a branch he had sawed up. Apple wood burns well, I've always heard. Some people fancy it very much. I don't notice any smell myself, but I've got a slight cold."

Together they looked at the fire. Willis had cut the logs small. The woman, thinking to please him, had piled several on top of one another, to make a good fire to last. There was no great blaze. The smoke that came from them was thin and poor. Greenish in colour. Was it possible she did not notice that sickly rancid smell?

"The logs are wet," he said abruptly. "Willis should have known better. Look at them. Quite useless on my fire."

The woman's face took on a set, rather sulky expression. "I'm very sorry," she said. "I didn't notice anything wrong with them when I came to light the fire. They seemed to start well. I've always understood apple wood was very good for burning, and Willis said the same. He told me to be sure and see that you had these on the fire this evening, he had made a special job of cutting them for you. I thought you knew about it and had given orders."

"Oh, all right," he answered, abruptly. "I dare say they'll burn in time. It's not your fault."

He turned his back on her and poked at the fire, trying to separate the logs. While she remained in the house there was nothing he could do. To remove the damp smouldering logs and throw them somewhere round the back, and then light the fire afresh with dry sticks would arouse comment. He would have to go through the kitchen to the back passage where the kindling wood was kept, and she would stare at him, and come forward and say, "Let me do it, sir. Has the fire gone out then?" No, he must wait until after supper, when she had cleared away and washed up and gone off for the night. Meanwhile, he would endure the smell of the apple wood as best he could.

He poured out his drink, lit his pipe and stared at the fire. It gave out no heat at all, and with the central heating off in the house the living room struck chill. Now and again a thin wisp of the greenish smoke puffed from the logs, and with it seemed to come that sweet sickly smell, unlike any sort of wood smoke that he knew. That interfering fool of a gardener . . . Why saw up the logs? He must have known they were damp. Riddled with damp. He leant forward, staring more closely. Was it damp, though, that oozed there in a thin trickle from the pale logs? No, it was sap, unpleasant, slimy.

He seized the poker, and in a fit of irritation thrust it between the logs, trying to stir them to flame, to change that green smoke into a normal blaze. The effort was useless. The logs would not burn. And all the while the trickle of sap ran onto the grate and the sweet smell filled the room, turning his stomach. He took his glass and his book and went and turned on the electric fire in the study and sat in there instead.

It was idiotic. It reminded him of the old days, how he would make a pretence of writing letters, and go and sit in the study because of Midge in the living room. She had a habit of yawning in the evenings, when her day's work was done; a habit of which she was quite unconscious. She would settle herself on the sofa with her knitting, the click-click of the needles going fast and furious; and suddenly they would start, those shattering yawns, rising from the depths of her, a prolonged "Ah . . . Ah . . . Hi-oh!" followed by the inevitable sigh. Then there would be silence except for the knitting needles, but as he sat behind his book, waiting, he knew that within a few minutes another yawn would come, another sigh.

A hopeless sort of anger used to stir within him, a longing to throw down his book and say, "Look, if you are so tired, wouldn't it be better if you went to bed?"

Instead, he controlled himself, and after a little while, when he could bear it no longer, he would get up and leave the living room, and take refuge in the study. Now he was doing the same thing, all over again, because of the apple logs. Because of the damned sickly smell of the smouldering wood.

He went on sitting in his chair by the desk, waiting for supper. It was nearly nine o'clock before the daily woman had cleared up, turned down his bed and gone for the night.

He returned to the living room, which he had not entered since leaving it earlier in the evening. The fire was out. It had made some effort to burn, because the logs were thinner than they had been before, and had sunk low into the basket grate. The ash was meagre, yet the sickly smell clung to the dying embers. He went out into the kitchen and found an empty scuttle and brought it back into the living room. Then he lifted the logs into it, and the ashes too. There must have been some damp residue in the scuttle, or the logs were still not dry, because as they settled there they seemed to turn darker than before, with a kind of scum upon them. He carried the scuttle down to the cellar, opened the door of the central heating furnace, and threw the lot inside.

He remembered then, too late, that the central heating had been given up now for two or three weeks, owing to the spring weather, and that unless he relit it now the logs would remain there, untouched, until the following winter. He found paper, matches, and a can of paraffin, and setting the whole alight, closed the door of the furnace, and listened to the roar of flames. That would settle it. He waited a moment and then went up the steps, back to the kitchen passage, to lay and relight the fire in the living room. The business took time, he had to find kindling and coal, but with patience he got the new fire started, and finally settled himself down in his armchair before it.

He had been reading perhaps for twenty minutes before he became aware of the banging door. He put down his book and listened. Nothing at first. Then, yes, there it was again. A rattle, a slam of an unfastened door in the kitchen quarters. He got up and went along to shut it. It was the door at the top of the cellar stairs. He could have sworn he had fastened it. The catch must have worked loose in some way. He switched on the light at the head of the stairs, and bent to examine the catch. There seemed nothing wrong with it. He was about to close the door firmly when he noticed the smell again. The sweet sickly smell of smouldering apple wood. It was creeping up from the cellar, finding its way to the passage above.

Suddenly, for no reason, he was seized with a kind of fear, a feeling of panic almost. What if the smell filled the whole house through the night, came up from the kitchen quarters to the floor above, and while he slept found its way into his bedroom, choking him, stifling him, so that he could not breathe? The thought was ridiculous, insane—and yet . . .

Once more he forced himself to descend the steps into the cellar. No sound came from the furnace, no roar of flames. Wisps of smoke, thin and green, oozed their way from the fastened furnace door; it was this that he had noticed from the passage above.

He went to the furnace and threw open the door. The paper had all burnt away, and the few shavings with them. But the logs, the apple logs, had not burnt at all. They lay there as they had done when he threw them in, one charred limb above another, black and huddled, like the bones of someone darkened and dead by fire. Nausea rose in him. He thrust his handkerchief into his mouth, choking. Then, scarcely knowing what he did, he ran up the steps to find the empty scuttle, and with a shovel and tongs tried to pitch the logs back into it, scraping for them through the narrow door of the furnace. He was retching in his belly all the while. At last the scuttle was filled, and he carried it up the steps and through the kitchen to the back door.

He opened the door. Tonight there was no moon and it was raining. Turning up the collar of his coat he peered about him in the darkness, wondering where he should throw the logs. Too wet and dark to stagger all the way to the kitchen garden and chuck them on the rubbish heap, but in the field behind the garage the grass was thick and long and they might lie there hidden. He crunched his way over the gravel drive, and coming to the fence beside the field threw his burden onto the concealing grass. There they could rot and perish, grow sodden with rain, and in the end become part of the mouldy earth; he did not care. The responsibility was his no longer. They were out of his house, and it did not matter what became of them.

He returned to the house, and this time made sure the cellar door was fast. The air was clear again, the smell had gone.

He went back to the living room to warm himself before the fire, but his hands and feet, wet with the rain, and his stomach, still queasy from the pungent apple smoke, combined together to chill his whole person, and he sat there, shuddering.

He slept badly when he went to bed that night, and awoke in the morning feeling out of sorts. He had a headache, and an ill-tasting tongue. He stayed indoors. His liver was thoroughly upset. To relieve his feelings he spoke sharply to the daily woman.

"I've caught a bad chill," he said to her, "trying to get warm last night. So much for apple wood. The smell of it has affected my inside as well. You can tell Willis, when he comes tomorrow."

She looked at him in disbelief.

"I'm sure I'm very sorry," she said. "I told my sister about the wood last night, when I got home, and that you had not fancied it. She said it was most unusual. Apple wood is considered quite a luxury to burn, and burns well, what's more."

"This lot didn't, that's all I know," he said to her, "and I never want to see any more of it. As for the smell . . . I can taste it still, it's completely turned me up."

Her mouth tightened, "I'm sorry," she said. And then, as she left the dining room, her eye fell on the empty whisky bottle on the sideboard. She hesitated a moment, then put it on her tray.

"You've finished with this, sir?" she said.

Of course he had finished with it. It was obvious. The bottle was empty. He realised the implication, though. She wanted to suggest that the idea of apple-wood smoke upsetting him was all my eye, he had done himself too well. Damned impertinence.

"Yes," he said, "you can bring another in its place."

That would teach her to mind her own business.

He was quite sick for several days, queasy and giddy, and finally rang up the doctor to come and have a look at him. The story of the apple wood sounded nonsense, when he told it, and the doctor, after examining him, appeared unimpressed.

"Just a chill on the liver," he said, "damp feet, and possibly something you've eaten combined. I hardly think wood smoke has much to do with it. You ought to take more exercise, if you're inclinded to have a liver. Play golf. I don't know how I should keep fit without my weekend golf." He laughed, packing up his bag. "I'll make you up some medicine," he said, "and once this rain has cleared off I should get out and into the air. It's mild enough, and all we want now is a bit of sunshine to bring everything on. Your garden is farther ahead than mine. Your fruit trees are ready to blossom." And then, before leaving the room, he added, "You mustn't forget, you had a bad shock a few months ago. It takes time to get over these things. You're still missing your wife, you know. Best thing is to get out and about and see people. Well, take care of yourself."

His patient dressed and went downstairs. The fellow meant well, of course, but his visit had been a waste of time. "You're still missing your wife, you know." How little the doctor understood. Poor Midge . . . At least he himself had the honesty to admit that he did not miss her at all, that now she was gone he could breathe, he was free, and that apart from the upset liver he had not felt so well for years.

During the few days he had spent in bed the daily woman had taken the opportunity to spring-clean the living room. An unnecessary piece of work, but he supposed it was part of the legacy Midge had left behind her. The room looked scrubbed and straight and much too tidy. His own personal litter cleared, books and papers neatly stacked. It was an infernal nuisance, really, having anyone to do for him at all. It would not take much for him to sack her and fend for himself as best he could. Only the bother, the tie of cooking and washing up, prevented him. The ideal life, of course, was that led by a man out East, or in the South Seas, who took a native wife. No problem there. Silence, good service, perfect waiting, excellent cooking, no need for conversation; and then, if you wanted something more than that, there she was, young, warm, a companion for the dark hours. No criticism ever, the obedience of an animal to its master, and the lighthearted laughter of a child. Yes, they had wisdom all right, those fellows who broke away from convention. Good luck to them.

He strolled over to the window and looked out up the sloping lawn. The rain was stopping and tomorrow it would be fine; he would be able to get out, as the doctor had suggested. The man was right, too, about the fruit trees. The little one near the steps was in flower already, and a blackbird had perched himself on one of the branches, which swayed slightly under his weight.

The raindrops glistened and the opening buds were very curled and pink, but when the sun broke through tomorrow they would turn white and soft against the blue of the sky. He must find his old camera, and put a film in it, and photograph the little tree. The others would be in flower, too, during the week. As for the old one, there on the left, it looked as dead as ever; or else the so-called buds were so brown they did not show up from this distance. Perhaps the shedding of the branch had been its finish. And a good job, too.

He turned away from the window and set about rearranging the room to his taste, spreading his things about. He liked pottering, opening drawers, taking things out and putting them back again. There was a red pencil in one of the side tables that must have slipped down behind a pile of books and been found during the turnout. He sharpened it, gave it a sleek fine point. He found a new film in another drawer, and kept it out to put in his camera in the morning. There were a number of papers and old photographs in the drawer, heaped in a jumble, and snapshots too, dozens of them. Midge used to look after these things at one time and put them in albums; then during the war she must have lost interest, or had too many other things to do.

All this junk could really be cleared away. It would have made a fine fire the other night, and might have got even the apple logs to burn. There was little sense in keeping any of it. This appalling photo of Midge, for instance, taken heaven knows how many years ago, not long after their marriage, judging from the style of it. Did she really wear her hair that way? That fluffy mop, much too thick and bushy for her face, which was long and narrow even then. The low neck, pointing to a V, and the dangling earrings, and the smile, too eager, making her mouth seem larger than it was. In the left-hand corner she had written "To my own darling Buzz, from his loving Midge." He had completely forgotten his old nickname. It had been dropped years back, and he seemed to remember he had never cared for it: he had found it ridiculous and embarrassing and had chided her for using it in front of people.

He tore the photograph in half and threw it on the fire. He watched it curl up upon itself and burn, and the last to go was that vivid smile. My own darling Buzz . . . Suddenly he remembered the evening dress in the photograph. It was green, not her colour ever, turning her sallow; and she had bought it for some special occasion, some big dinner party with friends who were celebrating their wedding anniversary. The idea of the dinner had been to invite all those friends and neighbours who had been married roughly around the same time, which was the reason Midge and he had gone.

There was a lot of champagne, and one or two speeches, and much conviviality, laughter, and joking—some of the joking rather broad—and he remembered that when the evening was over, and they were climbing into the car to drive away, his host, with a gust of laughter, said, "Try paying your addresses in a top hat, old boy, they say it never fails!" He had been aware of Midge beside him, in that green evening frock, sitting very straight and still, and on her face that same smile which she had worn in the photograph just destroyed, eager yet uncertain, doubtful of the meaning of the words that her host, slightly intoxicated, had let fall upon the evening air, yet wishing to seem advanced, anxious to please, and more than either of these things desperately anxious to attract.

When he had put the car away in the garage and gone into the house he had found her waiting there, in the living room, for no reason at all. Her coat was thrown off to show the evening dress, and the smile, rather uncertain, was on her face.

He yawned, and settling himself down in a chair picked up a book. She waited a little while, then slowly took up her coat and went upstairs. It must have been shortly afterwards that she had that photograph taken. "My own darling Buzz, from his loving Midge." He threw a great handful of dry sticks onto the fire. They crackled and split and turned the photograph to ashes. No damp green logs tonight . . .

It was fine and warm the following day. The sun shone, and the birds sang. He had a sudden impulse to go to London. It was a day for sauntering along Bond Street, watching the passing crowds. A day for calling in at his tailors, for having a haircut, for eating a dozen oysters at his favourite bar. The chill had left him. The pleasant hours stretched before him. He might even look in at a matinee.

The day passed without incident, peaceful, untiring, just as he had planned, making a change from day-by-day country routine. He drove home about seven o'clock, looking forward to his drink and to his dinner. It was so warm he did not need his overcoat, not even now, with the sun gone down. He waved a hand to the farmer, who happened to be passing the gate as he turned into the drive.

"Lovely day," he shouted.

The man nodded, smiled. "Can do with plenty of these from now on," he shouted back. Decent fellow. They had always been very matey since those war days, when he had driven the tractor.

He put away the car and had a drink, and while waiting for supper took a stroll around the garden. What a difference those hours of sunshine had made to everything. Several daffodils were out, narcissi too, and the green hedgerows fresh and sprouting. As for the apple trees, the buds had burst, and they were all of them in flower. He went to his little favourite and touched the blossom. It felt soft to his hand and he gently shook a bough. It was firm, well-set, and would not fall. The scent was scarcely perceptible as yet, but in a day or two, with a little more sun, perhaps a shower or two, it would come from the open flower and softly fill the air, never pungent, never strong, a modest scent. A scent which you would have to find for yourself, as the bees did. Once found it stayed with you, it lingered always, alluring, comforting, and sweet. He patted the little tree, and went down the steps into the house.

Next morning, at breakfast, there came a knock on the dining-room door, and the daily woman said that Willis was outside and wanted to have a word with him. He asked Willis to step in.

The gardener looked aggrieved. Was it trouble, then?

"I'm sorry to bother you, sir," he said, "but I had a few words with Mr. Jackson this morning. He's been complaining."

Jackson was the farmer who owned the neighbouring fields.

"What's he complaining about?"

"Says I've been throwing wood over the fence into his field, and the young foal out there, with the mare, tripped over it and went lame. I've never thrown wood over the fence in my life, sir. Quite nasty he was, sir. Spoke of the value of the foal, and it might spoil his chances to sell it."

"I hope you told him, then, it wasn't true."

"I did, sir. But the point is someone has been throwing wood

over the fence. He showed me the very spot. Just behind the garage. I went with Mr. Jackson, and there they were. Logs had
been tipped there, sir. I thought it best to come to you about it before I spoke in the kitchen, otherwise you know how it is, there
would be unpleasantness."

He felt the gardener's eye upon him. No way out, of course.
And it was Willis's fault in the first place.

"No need to say anything in the kitchen, Willis," he said. "I
threw the logs there myself. You brought them into the house,
without my asking you to do so, with the result that they put out
my fire, filled the room with smoke, and ruined an evening. I
chucked them over the fence in a devil of a temper, and if they
have damaged Jackson's foal you can apologise for me, and tell
him I'll pay him compensation. All I ask is that you don't bring
any more logs like those into the house again."

"No, sir. I understand they had not been a success. I didn't
think, though, that you would go so far as to throw them out."

"Well, I did. And there's an end to it."

"Yes, sir." He made as if to go, but before he left the dining
room he paused and said, "I can't understand about the logs not
burning, all the same. I took a small piece back to the wife, and it
burnt lovely in our kitchen, bright as anything."

"It did not burn here."

"Anyway, the old tree is making up for one spoilt branch, sir.
Have you seen her this morning?"

"No."

"It's yesterday's sun that has done it, sir, and the warm night.
Quite a treat she is, with all the blossom. You should go out and
take a look at her directly."

Willis left the room, and he continued his breakfast.

Presently he went out onto the terrace. At first he did not go up
onto the lawn; he made a pretence of seeing to other things, of
getting the heavy garden seat out, now that the weather was set
fair. And then, fetching a pair of clippers, he did a bit of pruning
to the few roses, under the windows. Yet, finally, something drew
him to the tree.

It was just as Willis said. Whether it was the sun, the warmth,
the mild still night, he could not tell; but the small brown buds
had unfolded themselves, had ripened into flower, and now spread
themselves above his head into a fantastic cloud of white, moist

blossom. It grew thickest at the top of the tree, the flowers so clustered together that they looked like wad upon wad of soggy cotton wool, and all of it, from the topmost branches to those nearer to the ground had this same pallid colour of sickly white.

It did not resemble a tree at all; it might have been a flapping tent, left out in the rain by campers who had gone away, or else a mop, a giant mop, whose streaky surface had been caught somehow by the sun, and so turned bleached. The blossom was too thick, too great a burden for the long thin trunk, and the moisture clinging to it made it heavier still. Already, as if the effort had been too much, the lower flowers, those nearest the ground, were turning brown; yet there had been no rain.

Well, there it was. Willis had been proved right. The tree had blossomed. But instead of blossoming to life, to beauty, it had somehow, deep in nature, gone awry and turned a freak. A freak which did not know its texture or its shape, but thought to please. Almost as though it said, self-conscious, with a smirk, "Look. All this is for you."

Suddenly he heard a step behind him. It was Willis.

"Fine sight, sir, isn't it?"

"Sorry, I don't admire it. The blossom is far too thick."

The gardener stared at him and said nothing. It struck him that Willis must think him very difficult, very hard, and possibly eccentric. He would go and discuss him in the kitchen with the daily woman.

He forced himself to smile at Willis.

"Look here," he said, "I don't mean to damp you. But all this blossom doesn't interest me. I prefer it small and light and colourful, like the little tree. But you take some of it back home, to your wife. Cut as much of it as you like, I don't mind at all. I'd like you to have it."

He waved his arm, generously. He wanted Willis to go now, and fetch a ladder, and carry the stuff away.

The man shook his head. He looked quite shocked.

"No, thank you, sir, I wouldn't dream of it. It would spoil the tree. I want to wait for the fruit. That's what I'm banking on, the fruit."

There was no more to be said.

"All right, Willis. Don't bother, then."

He went back to the terrace. But when he sat down there in the sun, looking up the sloping lawn, he could not see the little tree at all, standing modest and demure above the steps, her soft flowers lifting to the sky. She was dwarfed and hidden by the freak, with its great cloud of sagging petals, already wilting, dingy white, onto the grass beneath. And whichever way he turned his chair, this way or that upon the terrace, it seemed to him that he could not escape the tree, that it stood there above him, reproachful, anxious, desirous of the admiration that he could not give.

That summer he took a longer holiday than he had done for many years—a bare ten days with his old mother in Norfolk, instead of the customary month that he had been used to spend with Midge, and the rest of August and the whole of September in Switzerland and Italy.

He took his car, and so was free to motor from place to place as the mood inclined. He cared little for sightseeing or excursions, and was not much of a climber. What he liked most was to come upon a little town in the cool of the evening, pick out a small but comfortable hotel, and then stay there, if it pleased him, for two or three days at a time, doing nothing, mooching.

He liked sitting about in the sun all morning, at some café or restaurant, with a glass of wine in front of him, watching the people; so many gay young creatures seemed to travel nowadays. He enjoyed the chatter of conversation around him, as long as he did not have to join in; and now and again a smile would come his way, a word or two of greeting from some guest in the same hotel, but nothing to commit him, merely a sense of being in the swim, of being a man of leisure on his own, abroad.

The difficulty in the old days, on holiday anywhere with Midge, would be her habit of striking up acquaintance with people, some other couple who struck her as looking "nice" or, as she put it, "our sort." It would start with conversation over coffee, and then pass on to mutual planning of shared days, car drives in four-somes—he could not bear it, the holiday would be ruined.

Now, thank heaven, there was no need for this. He did what he liked, in his own time. There was no Midge to say, "Well, shall we be moving?" when he was still sitting contentedly over his wine, no Midge to plan a visit to some old church that did not interest him.

He put on weight during his holiday, and he did not mind.

There was no one to suggest a good long walk to keep fit after the rich food, thus spoiling the pleasant somnolence that comes with coffee and dessert; no one to glance, surprised, at the sudden wearing of a jaunty shirt, a flamboyant tie.

Strolling through the little towns and villages, hatless, smoking a cigar, receiving smiles from the jolly young folk around him, he felt himself a dog. This was the life, no worries, no cares. No "We have to be back on the fifteenth because of that committee meeting at the hospital"; no "We can't possibly leave the house shut up for longer than a fortnight, something might happen." Instead, the bright lights of a little country fair, in a village whose name he did not even bother to find out; the tinkle of music, boys and girls laughing, and he himself, after a bottle of the local wine, bowing to a young thing with a gay handkerchief round her head and sweeping her off to dance under the hot tent. No matter if her steps did not harmonize with his—it was years since he had danced—this was the thing, this was it. He released her when the music stopped, and off she ran, giggling, back to her young friends, laughing at him no doubt. What of it? He had had his fun.

He left Italy when the weather turned, at the end of September, and was back home the first week in October. No problem to it. A telegram to the daily woman, with the probable date of arrival, and that was all. Even a brief holiday with Midge and the return meant complications. Written instructions about groceries, milk and bread; airing of beds, lighting of fires, reminders about the delivery of the morning papers. The whole business turned into a chore.

He turned into the drive on a mellow October evening and there was smoke coming from the chimneys, the front door open, and his pleasant home awaiting him. No rushing through to the back regions to learn of possible plumbing disasters, breakages, water shortages, food difficulties; the daily woman knew better than to bother him with these. Merely, "Good evening, sir. I hope you had a good holiday. Supper at the usual time?" And then silence. He could have his drink, light his pipe, and relax; the small pile of letters did not matter. No feverish tearing of them open, and then the start of the telephoning, the hearing of those endless one-sided conversations between women friends. "Well? How are things? Really? My dear . . . And what did you say to that . . . She did? . . . I can't possibly on Wednesday . . ."

He stretched himself contentedly, stiff after his drive, and gazed comfortably around the cheerful, empty living room. He was hungry, after his journey up from Dover, and the chop seemed rather meagre after foreign fare. But there it was, it wouldn't hurt him to return to plainer food. A sardine on toast followed the chop, and then he looked about him for dessert.

There was a plate of apples on the sideboard. He fetched them and put them down in front of him on the dining-room table. Poor-looking things. Small and wizened, dullish brown in colour. He bit into one, but as soon as the taste of it was on his tongue he spat it out. The thing was rotten. He tried another. It was just the same. He looked more closely at the pile of apples. The skins were leathery and rough and hard; you would expect the insides to be sour. On the contrary they were pulpy soft, and the cores were yellow. Filthy-tasting things. A stray piece stuck to his tooth and he pulled it out. Stringy, beastly . . .

He rang the bell, and the woman came through from the kitchen.

"Have we any other dessert?" he said.

"I am afraid not, sir. I remembered how fond you were of apples, and Willis brought in these from the garden. He said they were especially good, and just ripe for eating."

"Well, he's quite wrong. They're uneatable."

"I'm very sorry, sir. I wouldn't have put them through had I known. There's a lot more outside, too. Willis brought in a great basketful."

"All the same sort?"

"Yes, sir. The small brown ones. No other kind, at all."

"Never mind, it can't be helped. I'll look for myself in the morning."

He got up from the table and went through to the living room. He had a glass of port to take away the taste of the apples, but it seemed to make no difference, not even a biscuit with it. The pulpy rotten tang clung to his tongue and the roof of his mouth, and in the end he was obliged to go up to the bathroom and clean his teeth. The maddening thing was that he could have done with a good clean apple, after that rather indifferent supper: something with a smooth clear skin, the inside not too sweet, a little sharp in flavour. He knew the kind. Good biting texture. You have to pick them, of course, at just the right moment.

He dreamt that night he was back again in Italy, dancing under the tent in the little cobbled square. He woke with the tinkling music in his ear, but he could not recall the face of the peasant girl or remember the feel of her, tripping against his feet. He tried to recapture the memory, lying awake, over his morning tea, but it eluded him.

He got up out of bed and went over to the window, to glance at the weather. Fine enough, with a light nip in the air.

Then he saw the tree. The sight of it came as a shock, it was so unexpected. Now he realised at once where the apples had come from the night before. The tree was laden, bowed down, under her burden of fruit. They clustered, small and brown, on every branch, diminishing in size as they reached the top, so that those on the high boughs, not grown yet to full size, looked like nuts. They weighed heavy on the tree, and because of this it seemed bent and twisted out of shape, the lower branches nearly sweeping the ground; and on the grass, at the foot of the tree, were more and yet more apples, windfalls, the first-grown, pushed off by their clamouring brothers and sisters. The ground was covered with them, many split open and rotting where the wasps had been. Never in his life had he seen a tree so laden with fruit. It was a miracle that it had not fallen under the weight.

He went out before breakfast—curiosity was too great—and stood beside the tree, staring at it. There was no mistake about it, these were the same apples that had been put in the dining room last night. Hardly bigger than tangerines, and many of them smaller than that, they grew so close together on the branches that to pick one you would be forced to pick a dozen.

There was something monstrous in the sight, something distasteful; yet it was pitiful too that the months had brought this agony upon the tree, for agony it was, there could be no other word for it. The tree was tortured by fruit, groaning under the weight of it, and the frightful part about it was that not one of the fruit was eatable. Every apple was rotten through and through. He trod them underfoot, the windfalls on the grass, there was no escaping them; and in a moment they were mush and slime, clinging about his heels—he had to clean the mess off with wisps of grass.

It would have been far better if the tree had died, stark and bare, before this ever happened. What use was it to him or anyone, this load of rotting fruit, littering up the place, fouling the

ground? And the tree itself, humped, as it were, in pain, and yet
he could almost swear triumphant, gloating.

Just as in spring, when the mass of fluffy blossom, colourless
and sodden, dragged the reluctant eye away from the other trees,
so it did now. Impossible to avoid seeing the tree, with its burden
of fruit. Every window in the front part of the house looked out
upon it. And he knew how it would be. The fruit would cling there
until it was picked, staying upon the branches through October
and November, and it never would be picked, because nobody
could eat it. He could see himself being bothered with the tree
throughout the autumn. Whenever he came out onto the terrace
there it would be, sagging and loathsome.

It was extraordinary the dislike he had taken to the tree. It was
a perpetual reminder of the fact that he . . . well, he was blessed
if he knew what . . . a perpetual reminder of all the things he
most detested, and always had, he could not put a name to them.
He decided then and there that Willis should pick the fruit and
take it away, sell it, get rid of it, anything, as long as he did not
have to eat it, and as long as he was not forced to watch the tree
drooping there, day after day, throughout the autumn.

He turned his back upon it and was relieved to see that none of
the other trees had so degraded themselves to excess. They carried
a fair crop, nothing out of the way, and, as he might have known,
the young tree, to the right of the old one, made a brave little
show on its own, with a light load of medium-sized, rosy-looking
apples, not too dark in colour, but freshly reddened where the sun
had ripened them. He would pick one now, and take it in, to eat
with breakfast. He made his choice, and the apple fell at the first
touch into his hand. It looked so good that he bit into it with appetite. That was it, juicy, sweet-smelling, sharp, the dew upon it
still. He did not look back at the old tree. He went indoors, hungry, to breakfast.

It took the gardener nearly a week to strip the tree, and it was
plain he did it under protest.

"I don't care what you do with them," said his employer. "You
can sell them and keep the money, or you can take them home
and feed them to your pigs. I can't stand the sight of them, and
that's all there is to it. Find a long ladder, and start on the job
right away."

It seemed to him that Willis, from sheer obstinacy, spun out the time. He would watch the man from the windows act as though in slow motion. First the placing of the ladder. Then the laborious climb, and the descent to steady it again. After that the performance of plucking off the fruit, dropping them, one by one, into the basket. Day after day it was the same. Willis was always there on the sloping lawn with his ladder, under the tree, the branches creaking and groaning, and beneath him on the grass baskets, pails, basins, any receptacle that would hold the apples.

At last the job was finished. The ladder was removed, the baskets and pails also, and the tree was stripped bare. He looked out at it, the evening of that day, in satisfaction. No more rotting fruit to offend his eye. Every single apple gone.

Yet the tree, instead of seeming lighter from the loss of its burden, looked, if it were possible, more dejected than ever. The branches still sagged, and the leaves, withering now to the cold autumnal evening, folded upon themselves and shivered. "Is this my reward?" it seemed to say. "After all I've done for you?"

As the light faded, the shadow of the tree cast a blight upon the dank night. Winter would soon come. And the short, dull days.

He had never cared much for the fall of the year. In the old days, when he went up to London every day to the office, it had meant that early start by train, on a nippy morning. And then, before three o'clock in the afternoon, the clerks were turning on the lights, and as often as not there would be fog in the air, murky and dismal, and a slow chugging journey home, daily breaders like himself sitting five abreast in a carriage, some of them with colds in their heads. Then the long evening followed, with Midge opposite him before the living-room fire, and he listening, or feigning to listen, to the account of her days and the things that had gone wrong.

If she had not shouldered any actual household disaster, she would pick upon some current event to cast a gloom. "I see fares are going up again, what about your season ticket?" or "This business in South Africa looks nasty, quite a long bit about it on the six o'clock news," or yet again "Three more cases of polio over at the isolation hospital. I don't know, I'm sure, what the medical world thinks it's doing . . ."

Now, at least, he was spared the rôle of listener, but the memory of those long evenings was with him still, and when the lights were lit and the curtains were drawn he would be reminded of the click-click of the needles, the aimless chatter, and the "Hi-oh" of the yawns. He began to drop in, sometimes before supper, sometimes afterwards, at the Green Man, the old public house a quarter of a mile away on the main road. Nobody bothered him there. He would sit in a corner, having said good evening to genial Mrs. Hill, the proprietress, and then, with a cigarette and a whisky and soda, watch the local inhabitants stroll in to have a pint, to throw a dart, to gossip.

In a sense it made a continuation of his summer holiday. It bore resemblance, admittedly slight, to the carefree atmosphere of the cafés and the restaurants; and there was a kind of warmth about the bright smoke-filled bar, crowded with working men who did not bother him, which he found pleasant, comforting. These visits cut into the length of the dark winter evenings, making them more tolerable.

A cold in the head, caught in mid-December, put a stop to this for more than a week. He was obliged to keep to the house. And it was odd, he thought to himself, how much he missed the Green Man, and how sick to death he became of sitting about in the living room or the study, with nothing to do but read or listen to the wireless. The cold and the boredom made him morose and irritable, and the enforced inactivity turned his liver sluggish. He needed exercise. Whatever the weather, he decided towards the end of yet another cold grim day, he would go out tomorrow. The sky had been heavy from midafternoon and threatened snow, but no matter, he could not stand the house for a further twenty-four hours without a break.

The final edge to his irritation came with the fruit tart at supper. He was in that final stage of a bad cold when the taste is not yet fully returned, appetite is poor, but there is a certain emptiness within that needs ministration of a particular kind. A bird might have done it. Half a partridge, roasted to perfection, followed by a cheese soufflé. As well ask for the moon. The daily woman, not gifted with imagination, produced plaice, of all fish the most tasteless, the most dry. When she had borne the remains of this away —he had left most of it upon his plate—she returned with a tart, and because hunger was far from being satisfied he helped himself to it liberally.

One taste was enough. Choking, spluttering, he spat out the contents of his spoon upon the plate. He got up and rang the bell.

The woman appeared, a query on her face, at the unexpected summons.

"What the devil is this stuff?"

"Jam tart, sir."

"What sort of jam?"

"Apple jam, sir. Made from my own bottling."

He threw down his napkin on the table.

"I guessed as much. You've been using some of those apples that I complained to you about months ago. I told you and Willis quite distinctly that I would not have any of those apples in the house."

The woman's face became tight and drawn.

"You said, sir, not to cook the apples, or to bring them in for dessert. You said nothing about not making jam. I thought they would taste all right as jam. And I made some myself, to try. It was perfectly all right. So I made several bottles of jam from the apples Willis gave me. We always made jam here, madam and myself."

"Well, I'm sorry for your trouble, but I can't eat it. Those apples disagreed with me in the autumn, and whether they are made into jam or whatever you like they will do so again. Take the tart away, and don't let me see it, or the jam, again. I'll have some coffee in the living room."

He went out of the room, trembling. It was fantastic that such a small incident should make him feel so angry. God! What fools people were. She knew, Willis knew, that he disliked the apples, loathed the taste and the smell of them, but in their cheese-paring way they decided that it would save money if he was given home-made jam, jam made from the apples he particularly detested.

He swallowed down a stiff whisky and lit a cigarette.

In a moment or two she appeared with the coffee. She did not retire immediately on putting down the tray.

"Could I have a word with you, sir?"

"What is it?"

"I think it would be for the best if I gave in my notice."

Now this, on top of the other. What a day, what an evening.

"What reason? Because I can't eat apple tart?"

"It's not just that, sir. Somehow I feel things are very different from what they were. I have meant to speak several times."

"I don't give much trouble, do I?"

"No, sir. Only in the old days, when madam was alive, I felt my work was appreciated. Now it's as though it didn't matter one way or the other. Nothing's ever said, and although I try to do my best I can't be sure. I think I'd be happier if I went where there was a lady again who took notice of what I did."

"You are the best judge of that, of course. I'm sorry if you haven't liked it here lately."

"You were away so much too, sir, this summer. When madam was alive it was never for more than a fortnight. Everything seems so changed. I don't know where I am, or Willis either."

"So Willis is fed up too?"

"That's not for me to say, of course. I know he was upset about the apples, but that's some time ago. Perhaps he'll be speaking to you himself."

"Perhaps he will. I had no idea I was causing so much concern to you both. All right, that's quite enough. Good night."

She went out of the room. He stared moodily about him. Good riddance to them both, if that was how they felt. Things aren't the same. Everything so changed. Damned nonsense. As for Willis being upset about the apples, what infernal impudence. Hadn't he a right to do what he liked with his own tree? To hell with his cold and with the weather. He couldn't stand sitting about in front of the fire thinking about Willis and the cook. He would go down to the Green Man and forget the whole thing.

He put on his overcoat and muffler and his old cap and walked briskly down the road, and in twenty minutes he was sitting in his usual corner in the Green Man, with Mrs. Hill pouring out his whisky and expressing her delight to see him back. One or two of the habitués smiled at him, asked after his health.

"Had a cold, sir? Same everywhere. Everyone's got one."

"That's right."

"Well, it's the time of year, isn't it?"

"Got to expect it. It's when it's on the chest it's nasty."

"No worse than being stuffed up, like, in the head."

"That's right. One's as bad as the other. Nothing to it."

Likeable fellows. Friendly. Not harping at one, not bothering.

"Another whisky, please."

"There you are, sir. Do you good. Keep out the cold."

Mrs. Hill beamed behind the bar. Large comfortable old soul. Through a haze of smoke he heard the chatter, the deep laughter, the click of the darts, the jocular roar at a bull's-eye.

". . . and if it comes on to snow, I don't know how we shall manage," Mrs. Hill was saying, "them being so late delivering the coal. If we had a load of logs it would help us out, but what do you think they're asking? Two pounds a load. I mean to say . . ."

He leant forward and his voice sounded far away, even to himself.

"I'll let you have some logs," he said.

Mrs. Hill turned round. She had not been talking to him.

"Excuse me?" she said.

"I'll let you have some logs," he repeated. "Got an old tree, up at home, needed sawing down for months. Do it for you tomorrow."

He nodded, smiling.

"Oh no, sir. I couldn't think of putting you to the trouble. The coal will turn up, never fear."

"No trouble at all. A pleasure. Like to do it for you, the exercise, you know, do me good. Putting on weight. You count on me."

He got down from his seat and reached, rather carefully, for his coat.

"It's apple wood," he said. "Do you mind apple wood?"

"Why no," she answered, "any wood will do. But can you spare it, sir?"

He nodded, mysteriously. It was a bargain, it was a secret.

"I'll bring it down to you in my trailer tomorrow night," he said.

"Careful, sir," she said, "mind the step . . ."

He walked home, through the cold crisp night, smiling to himself. He did not remember undressing or getting into bed, but when he woke the next morning the first thought that came to his mind was the promise he had made about the tree.

It was not one of Willis's days, he realised with satisfaction. There would be no interfering with his plan. The sky was heavy and snow had fallen in the night. More to come. But as yet nothing to worry about, nothing to hamper him.

He went through to the kitchen garden, after breakfast, to the tool shed. He took down the saw, the wedges and the axe. He might need all of them. He ran his thumb along the edges. They would do. As he shouldered his tools and walked back to the front garden he laughed to himself, thinking that he must resemble an executioner of old days, setting forth to behead some wretched victim in the Tower.

He laid his tools down beneath the apple tree. It would be an act of mercy, really. Never had he seen anything so wretched, so utterly woebegone, as the apple tree. There couldn't be any life left in it. Not a leaf remained. Twisted, ugly, bent, it ruined the appearance of the lawn. Once it was out of the way the whole setting of the garden would change.

A snowflake fell onto his hand, then another. He glanced down past the terrace to the dining-room window. He could see the woman laying his lunch. He went down the steps and into the house. "Look," he said, "if you like to leave my lunch ready in the oven, I think I'll fend for myself today. I may be busy, and I don't want to be pinned down for time. Also it's going to snow. You had better go off early today and get home, in case it becomes really bad. I can manage perfectly well. And I prefer it."

Perhaps she thought his decision came through offence at her giving notice the night before. Whatever she thought, he did not mind. He wanted to be alone. He wanted no face peering from the window.

She went off at about twelve-thirty, and as soon as she had gone he went to the oven and got his lunch. He meant to get it over, so that he could give up the whole short afternoon to the felling of the tree.

No more snow had fallen, apart from a few flakes that did not lie. He took off his coat, rolled up his sleeves, and seized the saw. With his left hand he ripped away the wire at the base of the tree. Then he placed the saw about a foot from the bottom and began to work it, backwards, forwards.

For the first dozen strokes all went smoothly. The saw bit into the wood, the teeth took hold. Then after a few moments the saw began to bind. He had been afraid of that.

He tried to work it free, but the opening that he had made was not yet large enough, and the tree gripped upon the saw and held it fast. He drove in the first wedge, with no result. He drove in the second, and the opening gaped a little wider, but still not wide enough to release the saw.

He pulled and tugged at the saw, to no avail. He began to lose his temper. He took up his axe and started hacking at the tree, pieces of the trunk flying outwards, scattering on the grass.

That was more like it. That was the answer.

Up and down went the heavy axe, splitting and tearing at the tree. Off came the peeling bark, the great white strips of under-wood, raw and stringy. Hack at it, blast at it, gouge at the tough tissue, throw the axe away, claw at the rubbery flesh with the bare hand. Not far enough yet, go on, go on.

There goes the saw, and the wedge, released. Now up with the axe again. Down there, heavy, where the stringy threads cling so steadfast. Now she's groaning, now she's splitting, now she's rock-ing and swaying, hanging there upon one bleeding strip. Boot her, then. That's it, kick her, kick her again, one final blow, she's over, she's falling . . . she's down . . . damn her, blast her . . . she's down, splitting the air with sound, and all her branches spread about her on the ground.

He stood back, wiping the sweat from his forehead, from his chin. The wreckage surrounded him on either side, and below him, at his feet, gaped the torn, white jagged stump of the axed tree.

It began snowing.

His first task, after felling the apple tree, was to hack off the branches and the smaller boughs, and so to grade the wood in stacks, which made it easier to drag away.

The small stuff, bundled and roped, would do for kindling; Mrs. Hill would no doubt be glad of that as well. He brought the car, with the trailer attached, to the garden gate, hard by the ter-race. This chopping up of the branches was simple work; much of it could be done with a hook. The fatigue came with bending and tying the bundles, and then heaving them down past the terrace and through the gate up onto the trailer. The thicker branches he disposed of with the axe, then split them into three or four lengths, which he could also rope and drag, one by one, to the trailer.

He was fighting all the while against time. The light, what there was of it, would be gone by half-past four, and the snow went on falling. The ground was already covered, and when he paused for a moment in his work, and wiped the sweat away from his face, the thin frozen flakes fell upon his lips and made their way, insidious and soft, down his collar to his neck and body. If he lifted his eyes to the sky he was blinded at once. The flakes came thicker, faster, swirling about his head, and it was as though the heaven had turned itself into a canopy of snow, ever descending, coming nearer, closer, stifling the earth. The snow fell upon the torn boughs and the hacked branches, hampering his work. If he rested but an instant to draw breath and renew his strength, it seemed to throw a protective cover, soft and white, over the pile of wood.

He could not wear gloves. If he did so he had no grip upon his hook or his axe, nor could he tie the rope and drag the branches. His fingers were numb with cold, soon they would be too stiff to bend. He had a pain now, under the heart, from the strain of dragging the stuff onto the trailer; and the work never seemed to lessen. Whenever he returned to the fallen tree the pile of wood would appear as high as ever, long boughs, short boughs, a heap of kindling there, nearly covered with the snow, which he had forgotten: all must be roped and fastened and carried or pulled away.

It was after half-past four, and almost dark, when he had disposed of all the branches, and nothing now remained but to drag the trunk, already hacked into three lengths, over the terrace to the waiting trailer.

He was very nearly at the point of exhaustion. Only his will to be rid of the tree kept him to the task. His breath came slowly, painfully, and all the while the snow fell into his mouth and into his eyes and he could barely see.

He took his rope and slid it under the cold slippery trunk, knotting it fiercely. How hard and unyielding was the naked wood, and the bark was rough, hurting his numb hands.

"That's the end of you," he muttered, "that's your finish."

Staggering to his feet he bore the weight of the heavy trunk over his shoulder, and began to drag it slowly down over the slope to the terrace and to the garden gate. It followed him, bump . . . bump . . . down the steps of the terrace. Heavy and lifeless, the last bare limbs of the apple tree dragged in his wake through the wet snow.

It was over. His task was done. He stood panting, one hand upon the trailer. Now nothing more remained but to take the stuff down to the Green Man before the snow made the drive impossible. He had chains for the car, he had thought of that already.

He went into the house to change the clothes that were clinging to him and to have a drink. Never mind about his fire, never mind about drawing curtains, seeing what there might be for supper, all the chores the daily woman usually did—that would come later. He must have his drink and get the wood away.

His mind was numb and weary, like his hands and his whole body. For a moment he thought of leaving the job until the following day, flopping down into the armchair, and closing his eyes. No, it would not do. Tomorrow there would be more snow, tomorrow the drive would be two or three feet deep. He knew the signs. And there would be the trailer, stuck outside the garden gate, with the pile of wood inside it, frozen white. He must make the effort and do the job tonight.

He finished his drink, changed, and went out to start the car. It was still snowing, but now that darkness had fallen a colder, cleaner feeling had come into the air, and it was freezing. The dizzy, swirling flakes came more slowly now, with precision.

The engine started and he began to drive downhill, the trailer in tow. He drove slowly, and very carefully, because of the heavy load. And it was an added strain, after the hard work of the afternoon, peering through the falling snow, wiping the windscreen. Never had the lights of the Green Man shone more cheerfully as he pulled up into the little yard.

He blinked as he stood within the doorway, smiling to himself.

"Well, I've brought your wood," he said.

Mrs. Hill stared at him from behind the bar, one or two fellows turned and looked at him, and a hush fell upon the dart players.

"You never . . ." began Mrs. Hill, but he jerked his head at the door and laughed at her.

"Go and see," he said, "but don't ask me to unload it tonight."

He moved to his favourite corner, chuckling to himself, and there they all were, exclaiming and talking and laughing by the door, and he was quite a hero, the fellows crowding round with questions, and Mrs. Hill pouring out his whisky and thanking him and laughing and shaking her head. "You'll drink on the house tonight," she said.

"Not a bit of it," he said, "this is my party. Rounds one and two to me. Come on, you chaps."

It was festive, warm, jolly, and good luck to them all, he kept saying, good luck to Mrs. Hill, and to himself, and to the whole world. When was Christmas? Next week, the week after? Well, here's to it, and a merry Christmas. Never mind the snow, never mind the weather. For the first time he drank with them, he laughed with them, he even threw a dart with them, and there they all were in that warm stuffy smoke-filled bar, and he felt they liked him, he belonged, he was no longer "the gentleman" from the house up the road.

The hours passed, and some of them went home, and others took their place, and he was still sitting there, hazy, comfortable, the warmth and the smoke blending together. Nothing of what he heard or saw made very much sense but somehow it did not seem to matter, for there was jolly, fat, easygoing Mrs. Hill to minister to his needs, her face glowing at him over the bar.

Another face swung into his view, that of one of the labourers from the farm, with whom, in the old war days, he had shared the driving of the tractor. He leant forward, touching the fellow on the shoulder.

"What happened to the little girl?" he said.

The man lowered his tankard. "Beg pardon, sir?" he said.

"You remember. The little land girl. She used to milk the cows, feed the pigs, up at the farm. Pretty girl, dark curly hair, always smiling."

Mrs. Hill turned round from serving another customer.

"Does the gentleman mean May, I wonder?" she asked.

"Yes, that's it, that was the name, young May," he said.

"Why, didn't you hear about it, sir?" said Mrs. Hill, filling up his glass. "We were all very much shocked at the time, everyone was talking of it, weren't they, Fred?"

"That's right, Mrs. Hill."

The man wiped his mouth with the back of his hand.

"Killed," he said, "thrown from the back of some chap's motor-bike. Going to be married very shortly. About four years ago, now. Dreadful thing, eh? Nice kid, too."

"We all sent a wreath, from just around," said Mrs. Hill. "Her mother wrote back, very touched, and sent a cutting from the local paper, didn't she, Fred? Quite a big funeral they had, ever so many floral tributes. Poor May. We were all fond of May."

"That's right," said Fred.

"And fancy you never hearing about it, sir!" said Mrs. Hill.

"No," he said, "no, nobody ever told me. I'm sorry about it. Very sorry."

He stared in front of him at his half-filled glass.

The conversation went on around him but he was no longer part of the company. He was on his own again, silent, in his corner. Dead. That poor, pretty girl was dead. Thrown off a motorbike. Been dead for three or four years. Some careless, bloody fellow, taking a corner too fast, the girl behind him, clinging onto his belt, laughing probably in his ear, and then crash . . . finish. No more curling hair, blowing about her face, no more laughter.

May, that was the name; he remembered clearly now. He could see her smiling over her shoulder, when they called to her. "Coming," she sang out, and put a clattering pail down in the yard and went off, whistling, with big clumping boots. He had put his arm about her and kissed her for one brief, fleeting moment. May, the land girl, with the laughing eyes.

"Going, sir?" said Mrs. Hill.

"Yes. Yes, I think I'll be going now."

He stumbled to the entrance and opened the door. It had frozen hard during the past hour and it was no longer snowing. The heavy pall had gone from the sky and the stars shone.

"Want a hand with the car, sir?" said someone.

"No, thank you," he said, "I can manage."

He unhitched the trailer and let it fall. Some of the wood lurched forward heavily. That would do tomorrow. Tomorrow, if he felt like it, he would come down again and help to unload the wood. Not tonight. He had done enough. Now he was really tired; now he was spent.

It took him some time to start the car, and before he was half-way up the side road leading to his house he realised that he had made a mistake to bring it at all. The snow was heavy all about him, and the track he had made earlier in the evening was now covered. The car lurched and slithered, and suddenly the right wheel dipped and the whole body plunged sideways. He had got into a drift.

He climbed out and looked about him. The car was deep in the drift, impossible to move without two or three men to help him, and even then, if he went for assistance, what hope was there of trying to continue further, with the snow just as thick ahead? Better leave it. Try again in the morning, when he was fresh. No sense in hanging about now, spending half the night pushing and shoving at the car, all to no purpose. No harm would come to it, here on the side road; nobody else would be coming this way to-night.

He started walking up the road towards his own drive. It was bad luck that he had got the car into the drift. In the centre of the road the going was not bad and the snow did not come above his ankles. He thrust his hands deep in the pockets of his overcoat and ploughed on, up the hill, the countryside a great white waste on either side of him.

He remembered that he had sent the daily woman home at midday and that the house would strike cheerless and cold on his return. The fire would have gone out, and in all probability the furnace too. The windows, uncurtained, would stare bleakly down at him, letting in the night. Supper to get into the bargain. Well, it was his own fault. No one to blame but himself. This was the moment when there should be someone waiting, someone to come running through from the living room to the hall, opening the front door, flooding the hall with light. "Are you all right, darling? I was getting anxious."

He paused for breath at the top of the hill and saw his home shrouded by trees, at the end of the short drive. It looked dark and forbidding, without a light in any window. There was more friendliness in the open, under the bright stars, standing on the crisp white snow, than in the sombre house.

He had left the side gate open, and he went through that way to the terrace, shutting the gate behind him. What a hush had fallen upon the garden—there was no sound at all. It was as though some spirit had come and put a spell upon the place, leaving it white and still.

He walked softly over the snow towards the apple trees.

Now the young one stood alone, above the steps, dwarfed no longer; and with her branches spread, glistening white, she belonged to the spirit world, a world of fantasy and ghosts. He wanted to stand beside the little tree and touch the branches, to make certain she was still alive, that the snow had not harmed her, so that in the spring she would blossom once again.

She was almost within his reach when he stumbled and fell, his foot twisted underneath him, caught in some obstacle hidden by the snow. He tried to move his foot but it was jammed, and he knew suddenly, by the sharpness of the pain biting his ankle, that what had trapped him was the jagged split stump of the old apple tree he had felled that afternoon.

He leant forward on his elbows, in an attempt to drag himself along the ground, but such was his position, in falling, that his leg was bent backwards, away from his foot, and every effort that he made only succeeded in imprisoning the foot still more firmly in the grip of the trunk. He felt for the ground, under the snow, but wherever he felt his hands touched the small broken twigs from the apple tree that had scattered there, when the tree fell, and then were covered by the falling snow. He shouted for help, knowing in his heart no one could hear.

"Let me go," he shouted, "let me go," as though the thing that held him there in its mercy had the power to release him, and as he shouted tears of frustration and of fear ran down his face. He would have to lie there all night, held fast in the clutch of the old apple tree. There was no hope, no escape, until they came to find him in the morning, and supposing it was then too late, that when they came he was dead, lying stiffly in the frozen snow?

Once more he struggled to release his foot, swearing and sobbing as he did so. It was no use. He could not move. Exhausted, he laid his head upon his arms, and wept. He sank deeper, ever deeper into the snow, and when a stray piece of brushwood, cold and wet, touched his lips, it was like a hand, hesitant and timid, feeling its way towards him in the darkness.

The Pool

The children ran out onto the lawn. There was space all around them, and light, and air, with the trees indeterminate beyond. The gardener had cut the grass. The lawn was crisp and firm now, because of the hot sun through the day; but near the summerhouse where the tall grass stood there were dewdrops like frost clinging to the narrow stems.

The children said nothing. The first moment always took them by surprise. The fact that it waited, thought Deborah, all the time they were away; that day after day while they were at school, or in the Easter holidays with the aunts at Hunstanton being blown to bits, or in the Christmas holidays with their father in London riding on buses and going to theatres—the fact that the garden waited for them was a miracle known only to herself. A year was so long. How did the garden endure the snows clamping down upon it, or the chilly rain that fell in November? Surely sometimes it must mock the slow steps of Grandpapa pacing up and down the terrace in front of the windows, or Grandmama calling to Patch? The garden had to endure month after month of silence, while the children were gone. Even the spring and the days of May and June were wasted, all those mornings of butterflies and darting birds, with no one to watch but Patch gasping for breath on a cool stone slab. So wasted was the garden, so lost.

"You must never think we forget," said Deborah in the silent voice she used to her own possessions. "I remember, even at school, in the middle of French"—but the ache then was unbearable, that it should be the hard grain of a desk under her hands, and not the grass she bent to touch now. The children had had an argument once about whether there was more grass in the world or more sand, and Roger said that of course there must be more sand because of under the sea; in every ocean all over the world there would be sand, if you looked deep down. But there could be grass too, argued Deborah, a waving grass, a grass that nobody had ever seen, and the colour of that ocean grass would be darker than any grass on the surface of the world, in fields or prairies or people's gardens in America. It would be taller than trees and it would move like corn in a wind.

They had run in to ask somebody adult, "What is there most of in the world, grass or sand?" both children hot and passionate from the argument. But Grandpapa stood there in his old panama hat looking for clippers to trim the hedge—he was rummaging in the drawer full of screws—and he said, "What? What?" impatiently.

The boy turned red—perhaps it was a stupid question—but the girl thought, he doesn't know, they never know, and she made a face at her brother to show that she was on his side. Later they asked their grandmother, and she, being practical, said briskly, "I should think sand. Think of all the grains," and Roger turned in triumph. "I told you so!" The grains. Deborah had not considered the grains. The magic of millions and millions of grains clinging together in the world and under the oceans made her sick. Let Roger win, it did not matter. It was better to be in the minority of the waving grass.

Now, on this first evening of summer holiday, she knelt and then lay full-length on the lawn, and stretched her hands out on either side like Jesus on the Cross, only face downwards, and murmured over and over again the words she had memorised from Confirmation preparation. "A full, perfect and sufficient sacrifice . . . a full, perfect and sufficient sacrifice . . . satisfaction, and oblation, for the sins of the whole world." To offer herself to the earth, to the garden, the garden that had waited patiently all these months since last summer, surely this must be her first gesture.

"Come on," said Roger, rousing himself from his appreciation of how Willis the gardener had mown the lawn to just the right closeness for cricket, and without waiting for his sister's answer he ran to the summerhouse and made a dive at the long box in the corner where the stumps were kept. He smiled as he lifted the lid. The familiarity of the smell was satisfying. Old varnish and chipped paint, and surely that must be the same spider and the same cobweb? He drew out the stumps one by one, and the bails, and there was the ball—it had not been lost after all, as he had feared. It was worn, though, a greyish red—he smelt it and bit it, to taste the shabby leather. Then he gathered the things in his arms and went out to set up the stumps.

"Come and help me measure the pitch," he called to his sister, and looking at her, squatting in the grass with her face hidden, his heart sank, because it meant that she was in one of her absent moods and would not concentrate on the cricket.

"Deb?" he called anxiously. "You are going to play?"

Deborah heard his voice through the multitude of earth sounds, the heartbeat and the pulse. If she listened with her ear to the ground there was a humming much deeper than anything that bees did, or the sea at Hunstanton. The nearest to it was the wind, but the wind was reckless. The humming of the earth was patient. Deborah sat up, and her heart sank just as her brother's had done, for the same reason in reverse. The monotony of the game ahead would be like a great chunk torn out of privacy.

"How long shall we have to be?" she called.

The lack of enthusiasm dampened the boy. It was not going to be any fun at all if she made favour of it. He must be firm, though. Any concession on his part she snatched and turned to her advantage.

"Half an hour," he said, and then, for encouragement's sake, "You can bat first."

Deborah smelt her knees. They had not yet got the country smell, but if she rubbed them in the grass, and in the earth too, the white London look would go.

"All right," she said, "but no longer than half an hour."

He nodded quickly, and so as not to lose time measured out the pitch and then began ramming the stumps in the ground. Deborah went into the summerhouse to get the bats. The familiarity of the little wooden hut pleased her as it had her brother. It was a long time now, many years, since they had played in the summerhouse, making yet another house inside this one with the help of broken deck chairs; but, just as the garden waited for them a whole year, so did the summerhouse, the windows on either side, cobweb-wrapped and stained, gazing out like eyes. Deborah did her ritual of bowing twice. If she should forget this, on her first entrance, it spelt ill luck.

She picked out the two bats from the corner, where they were stacked with old croquet hoops, and she knew at once that Roger would choose the one with the rubber handle, even though they could not bat at the same time, and for the whole of the holidays she must make do with the smaller one, that had half the whipping off. There was a croquet clip lying on the floor. She picked it up and put it on her nose and stood a moment, wondering how it would be if forever more she had to live thus, nostrils pinched, making her voice like Punch. Would people pity her?

"Hurry," shouted Roger, and she threw the clip into the corner, then quickly returned when she was halfway to the pitch, because she knew the clip was lying apart from its fellows, and she might wake in the night and remember it. The clip would turn malevolent, and haunt her. She replaced him on the floor with two others, and now she was absolved and the summerhouse at peace.

"Don't get out too soon," warned Roger as she stood in the crease he had marked for her, and with a tremendous effort of concentration Deborah forced her eyes to his retreating figure and watched him roll up his sleeves and pace the required length for his run-up. Down came the ball and she lunged out, smacking it in the air in an easy catch. The impact of ball on bat stung her hands. Roger missed the catch on purpose. Neither of them said anything.

"Who shall I be?" called Deborah.

The game could only be endured, and concentration kept, if Roger gave her a part to play. Not an individual, but a country.

"You're India," he said, and Deborah felt herself grow dark and lean. Part of her was tiger, part of her was sacred cow, the long grass fringing the lawn was jungle, the roof of the summerhouse a minaret.

Even so, the half hour dragged, and, when her turn came to bowl, the ball she threw fell wider every time, so that Roger, flushed and self-conscious because their grandfather had come out onto the terrace and was watching them, called angrily, "Do try."

Once again the effort at concentration, the figure of their grandfather—a source of apprehension to the boy, for he might criticise them—acting as a spur to his sister. Grandpapa was an Indian god, and tribute must be paid to him, a golden apple. The apple must be flung to slay his enemies. Deborah muttered a prayer, and the ball she bowled came fast and true and hit Roger's off-stump. In the moment of delivery their grandfather had turned away and pottered back again through the french windows of the drawing room.

Roger looked round swiftly. His disgrace had not been seen. "Jolly good ball," he said. "It's your turn to bat again."

But his time was up. The stable clock chimed six. Solemnly Roger drew stumps.

"What shall we do now?" he asked.

Deborah wanted to be alone, but if she said so, on this first evening of the holiday, he would be offended.

"Go to the orchard and see how the apples are coming on," she suggested, "and then round by the kitchen garden in case the raspberries haven't all been picked. But you have to do it all without meeting anyone. If you see Willis or anyone, even the cat, you lose a mark."

It was these sudden inventions that saved her. She knew her brother would be stimulated at the thought of outwitting the gardener. The aimless wander round the orchard would turn into a stalking exercise.

"Will you come too?" he asked.

"No," she said, "you have to test your skill."

He seemed satisfied with this and ran off towards the orchard, stopping on the way to cut himself a switch from the bamboo.

As soon as he had disappeared Deborah made for the trees fringing the lawn, and once in the shrouded wood felt herself safe. She walked softly along the alleyway to the pool. The late sun sent shafts of light between the trees and onto the alleyway, and a myriad insects webbed their way in the beams, ascending and descending like angels on Jacob's ladder. But were they insects, wondered Deborah, or particles of dust, or even split fragments of light itself, beaten out and scattered by the sun?

It was very quiet. The woods were made for secrecy. They did not recognise her as the garden did. They did not care that for a whole year she could be at school, or at Hunstanton, or in London. The woods would never miss her: they had their own dark, passionate life.

Deborah came to the opening where the pool lay, with the five alleyways branching from it, and she stood a moment before advancing to the brink, because this was holy ground and required atonement. She crossed her hands on her breast and shut her eyes. Then she kicked off her shoes. "Mother of all things wild, do with me what you will," she said aloud. The sound of her own voice gave her a slight shock. Then she went down on her knees and touched the ground three times with her forehead.

The first part of her atonement was accomplished, but the pool demanded sacrifice, and Deborah had come prepared. There was a stub of pencil she had carried in her pocket throughout the school term which she called her luck. It had teeth marks on it, and a chewed piece of rubber at one end. This treasure must be given to the pool just as other treasures had been given in the past, a miniature jug, a crested button, a china pig. Deborah felt for the stub of pencil and kissed it. She had carried and caressed it for so many lonely months, and now the moment of parting had come. The pool must not be denied. She flung out of her right hand, her eyes still shut, and heard the faint plop as the stub of pencil struck the water. Then she opened her eyes, and saw in mid-pool a ripple. The pencil had gone, but the ripple moved, gently shaking the water lilies. The movement symbolised acceptance.

Deborah, still on her knees and crossing her hands once more, edged her way to the brink of the pool and then, crouching there beside it, looked down into the water. Her reflection wavered up at her, and it was not the face she knew, not even the looking-glass face which anyway was false, but a disturbed image, dark-skinned and ghostly. The crossed hands were like the petals of the water lilies themselves, and the colour was not waxen white but phantom green. The hair too was not the live clump she brushed every day and tied back with ribbon, but a canopy, a shroud. When the image smiled it became more distorted still. Uncrossing her hands, Deborah leant forward, took a twig, and drew a circle three times on the smooth surface. The water shook in ever widening ripples, and her reflection, broken into fragments, heaved and danced, a sort of monster, and the eyes were there no longer, nor the mouth.

Presently the water became still. Insects, long-legged flies and beetles with spread wings hummed upon it. A dragonfly had all the magnificence of a lily leaf to himself. He hovered there, rejoicing. But when Deborah took her eyes off him for a moment he was gone. At the far end of the pool, beyond the clustering lilies, green scum had formed, and beneath the scum were rooted, tangled weeds. They were so thick, and had lain in the pool so long, that if a man walked into them from the bank he would be held and choked. A fly, though, or a beetle, could sit upon the surface, and to him the pale green scum would not be treacherous at all, but a resting place, a haven. And if someone threw a stone, so that the ripples formed, eventually they came to the scum, and rocked it, and the whole of the mossy surface moved in rhythm, a dancing floor for those who played upon it.

There was a dead tree standing by the far end of the pool. He could have been fir or pine, or even larch, for time had stripped him of identity. He had no distinguishing mark upon his person, but with grotesque limbs straddled the sky. A cap of ivy crowned his naked head. Last winter a dangling branch had broken loose, and this now lay in the pool half-submerged, the green scum dripping from the withered twigs. The soggy branch made a vantage point for birds, and as Deborah watched a nestling suddenly flew from the undergrowth enveloping the dead tree, and perched for an instant on the mossy filigree. He was lost in terror. The parent bird cried warningly from some dark safety, and the nestling, pricking to the cry, took off from the branch that had offered him temporary salvation. He swerved across the pool, his flight mistimed, yet reached security. The chitter from the undergrowth told of his scolding. When he had gone, silence returned to the pool.

It was, so Deborah thought, the time for prayer. The water lilies were folding upon themselves. The ripples ceased. And that dark hollow in the centre of the pool, that black stillness where the water was deepest, was surely a funnel to the kingdom that lay below. Down that funnel had travelled the discarded treasures. The stub of pencil had lately plunged the depths. He had now been received as an equal among his fellows. This was the single law of the pool, for there were no other commandments. Once it was over, that first cold headlong flight, Deborah knew that the softness of the welcoming water took away all fear. It lapped the face and cleansed the eyes, and the plunge was not into darkness at all but into light. It did not become blacker as the pool was penetrated, but paler, more golden-green, and the mud that people told themselves was there was only a defence against strangers. Those who belonged, who knew, went to the source at once, and there were caverns and fountains and rainbow-coloured seas. There were shores of the whitest sand. There was soundless music.

Once again Deborah closed her eyes and bent lower to the pool. Her lips nearly touched the water. This was the great silence, when she had no thoughts, and was accepted by the pool. Waves of quiet ringed themselves about her, and slowly she lost all feeling, and had no knowledge of her legs, or of her kneeling body, or of her cold, clasped hands. There was nothing but the intensity of peace. It was a deeper acceptance than listening to the earth, because the earth was of the world, the earth was a throbbing pulse, but the acceptance of the pool meant another kind of hearing, a closing in of the waters, and just as the lilies folded so did the soul submerge.

"Deborah . . . ? Deborah . . . ?" Oh, no! Not now, don't let them call me back now! It was as though someone had hit her on the back, or jumped out at her from behind a corner, the sharp and sudden clamour of another life destroyed the silence, the secrecy. And then came the tinkle of the cowbells. It was the signal from their grandmother that the time had come to go in. Not imperious and ugly with authority, like the clanging bell at school summoning those at play to lessons or chapel, but a reminder, nevertheless, that Time was all-important, that life was ruled to order, that even here, in the holiday home the children loved, the adult reigned supreme.

"All right, all right," muttered Deborah, standing up and thrusting her numbed feet into her shoes. This time the rather raised tone of "Deborah?" and the more hurried clanging of the cowbells, brought long ago from Switzerland, suggested a more imperious Grandmama than the tolerant one who seldom questioned. It must mean their supper was already laid, soup perhaps getting cold, and the farce of washing hands, of tidying, of combing hair, must first be gone through.

"Come on, Deb," and now the shout was close, was right at hand, privacy lost forever, for her brother came running down the alleyway swishing his bamboo stick in the air.

"What *have* you been doing?" The question was an intrusion and a threat. She would never have asked him what he had been doing, had he wandered away wanting to be alone, but Roger, alas, did not claim privacy. He liked companionship, and his question now, asked half in irritation, half in resentment, came really from the fear that he might lose her.

"Nothing," said Deborah.

Roger eyed her suspiciously. She was in that mooning mood. And it meant, when they went to bed, that she would not talk. One of the best things, in the holidays, was having the two adjoining rooms and calling through to Deb, making her talk.

"Come on," he said, "they've rung," and the making of their grandmother into "they," turning a loved individual into something impersonal, showed Deborah that even if he did not understand he was on her side. He had been called from play, just as she had.

They ran from the woods to the lawn, and onto the terrace. Their grandmother had gone inside, but the cowbells hanging by the french windows were still jangling.

The custom was for the children to have their supper first, at seven, and it was laid for them in the dining room on a hotplate. They served themselves. At a quarter to eight their grandparents had dinner. It was called dinner, but this was a concession to their status. They ate the same as the children, though Grandpapa had a savoury which was not served to the children. If the children were late for supper then it put out Time, as well as Agnes, who cooked for both generations, and it might mean five minutes' delay before Grandpapa had his soup. This shook routine.

The children ran up to the bathroom to wash, then downstairs to the dining room. Their grandfather was standing in the hall. Deborah sometimes thought that he would have enjoyed sitting with them while they ate their supper, but he never suggested it. Grandmama had warned them, too, never to be a nuisance, or indeed to shout, if Grandpapa was near. This was not because he was nervous, but because he liked to shout himself.

"There's going to be a heat wave," he said. He had been listening to the news.

"That will mean lunch outside tomorrow," said Roger swiftly. Lunch was the meal they took in common with the grandparents, and it was the moment of the day he disliked. He was nervous that his grandfather would ask him how he was getting on at school.

"Not for me, thank you," said Grandpapa. "Too many wasps."

Roger was at once relieved. This meant that he and Deborah would have the little round garden table to themselves. But Deborah felt sorry for her grandfather as he went back into the drawing room. Lunch on the terrace could be gay, and would liven him up. When people grew old they had so few treats.

"What do you look forward to most in the day?" she once asked her grandmother.

"Going to bed," was the reply, "and filling my two hot-water bottles." Why work through being young, thought Deborah, to this?

Back in the dining room the children discussed what they should do during the heat wave. It would be too hot, Deborah said, for cricket. But they might make a house, suggested Roger, in the trees by the paddock. If he got a few old boards from Willis, and nailed them together like a platform, and borrowed the orchard ladder, then they could take fruit and bottles of orange squash and keep them up there, and it would be a camp from which they could spy on Willis afterwards.

Deborah's first instinct was to say she did not want to play, but she checked herself in time. Finding the boards and fixing them would take Roger a whole morning. It would keep him employed. "Yes, it's a good idea," she said, and to foster his spirit of adventure she looked at his notebook, as they were drinking their soup, and approved of items necessary for the camp while he jotted them down. It was all part of the daylong deceit she practised to express understanding of his way of life.

When they had finished supper they took their trays to the kitchen and watched Agnes, for a moment, as she prepared the second meal for the grandparents. The soup was the same, but garnished. Little croûtons of toasted bread were added to it. And the butter was made into pats, not cut in a slab. The savoury tonight was to be cheese straws. The children finished the ones that Agnes had burnt. Then they went through to the drawing room to say good night. The older people had both changed. Grandpapa was in a smoking jacket, and wore soft slippers. Grandmama had a dress that she had worn several years ago in London. She had a cardigan round her shoulders like a cape.

"Go carefully with the bath water," she said. "We'll be short if there's no rain."

They kissed her smooth, soft skin. It smelt of rose leaves. Grandpapa's chin was sharp and bony. He did not kiss Roger.

"Be quiet overhead," whispered their grandmother. The children nodded. The dining room was underneath their rooms, and any jumping about or laughter would make a disturbance.

Deborah felt a wave of affection for the two old people. Their lives must be empty and sad. "We *are* glad to be here," she said. Grandmama smiled. This was how she lived, thought Deborah, on little crumbs of comfort.

Once out of the room their spirits soared, and to show relief Roger chased Deborah upstairs, both laughing for no reason. Undressing, they forgot the instructions about the bath, and when they went into the bathroom—Deborah was to have first go—the water was gurgling into the overflow. They tore out the plug in a panic, and listened to the waste roaring down the pipe to the drain below. If Agnes did not have the wireless on she would hear it.

The children were too old now for boats or play, but the bathroom was a place for confidences, for a sharing of those few tastes they agreed upon, or, after quarrelling, for moody silence. The one who broke silence first would then lose face.

"Willis has a new bicycle," said Roger. "I saw it propped against the shed. I couldn't try it because he was there. But I shall tomorrow. It's a Raleigh."

He liked all practical things, and the trying of the gardener's bicycle would give an added interest to the morning of next day. Willis had a bag of tools in a leather pouch behind the saddle. These could all be felt and the spanners, smelling of oil, tested for shape and usefulness.

"If Willis died," said Deborah, "I wonder what age he would be."

It was the kind of remark that Roger resented always. What had death to do with bicycles? "He's sixty-five," he said, "so he'd be sixty-five."

"No," said Deborah, "what age when he got *there*."

Roger did not want to discuss it. "I bet I can ride it round the stables if I lower the seat," he said. "I bet I don't fall off."

But if Roger would not rise to death, Deborah would not rise to the wager. "Who cares?" she said.

The sudden streak of cruelty stung the brother. Who cared indeed . . . The horror of an empty world encompassed him, and to give himself confidence he seized the wet sponge and flung it out of the window. They heard it splosh on the terrace below.

"Grandpapa will step on it, and slip," said Deborah, aghast.

The image seized them, and choking back laughter they covered their faces. Hysteria doubled them up. Roger rolled over and over on the bathroom floor. Deborah, the first to recover, wondered why laughter was so near to pain, why Roger's face, twisted now in merriment, was yet the same crumpled thing when his heart was breaking.

"Hurry up," she said briefly, "let's dry the floor," and as they wiped the linoleum with their towels the action sobered them both.

Back in their bedrooms, the door open between them, they watched the light slowly fading. But the air was warm like day. Their grandfather and the people who said what the weather was going to be were right. The heat wave was on its way. Deborah, leaning out of the open window, fancied she could see it in the sky, a dull haze where the sun had been before; and the trees beyond the lawn, day-coloured when they were having their supper in the dining room, had turned into night birds with outstretched wings. The garden knew about the promised heat wave, and rejoiced: the lack of rain was of no consequence yet, for the warm air was a trap, lulling it into a drowsy contentment.

The dull murmur of their grandparents' voices came from the dining room below. What did they discuss, wondered Deborah. Did they make those sounds to reassure the children, or were their voices part of their unreal world? Presently the voices ceased, and then there was a scraping of chairs, and voices from a different quarter, the drawing room now, and a faint smell of their grandfather's cigarette.

Deborah called softly to her brother but he did not answer. She went through to his room, and he was asleep. He must have fallen asleep suddenly, in the midst of talking. She was relieved. Now she could be alone again, and not have to keep up the pretence of sharing conversation. Dusk was everywhere, the sky a deepening black. "When they've gone up to bed," thought Deborah, "then I'll be truly alone." She knew what she was going to do. She waited there, by the open window, and the deepening sky lost the veil that covered it, the haze disintegrated, and the stars broke through. Where there had been nothing was life, dusty and bright, and the waiting earth gave off a scent of knowledge. Dew rose from the pores. The lawn was white.

Patch, the old dog, who slept at the end of Grandpapa's bed on a plaid rug, came out onto the terrace and barked hoarsely. Deborah leant out and threw a piece of creeper onto him. He shook his back. Then he waddled slowly to the flower tub above the steps and cocked his leg. It was his nightly routine. He barked once more, staring blindly at the hostile trees, and went back into the drawing room. Soon afterwards, someone came to close the windows—Grandmama, thought Deborah, for the touch was light. "They are shutting out the best," said the child to herself, "all the meaning, and all the point." Patch, being an animal, should know better. He ought to be in a kennel where he could watch, but instead, grown fat and soft, he preferred the bumpiness of her grandfather's bed. He had forgotten the secrets. So had they, the old people.

Deborah heard her grandparents come upstairs. First her grandmother, the quicker of the two, and then her grandfather, more laboured, saying a word or two to Patch as the little dog wheezed his way up. There was a general clicking of lights and shutting of doors. Then silence. How remote, the world of the grandparents, undressing with curtains closed. A pattern of life unchanged for so many years. What went on without would never be known. "He that has ears to hear, let him hear," said Deborah, and she thought of the callousness of Jesus which no priest could explain. Let the dead bury their dead. All the people in the world, undressing now, or sleeping, not just in the village but in cities and capitals, they were shutting out the truth, they were burying their dead. They wasted silence.

The stable clock struck eleven. Deborah pulled on her clothes. Not the cotton frock of the day, but her old jeans that Grandmama disliked, rolled up above her knees. And a jersey. Sandshoes with a hole that did not matter. She was cunning enough to go down by the back stairs. Patch would bark if she tried the front stairs, close to the grandparents' rooms. The back stairs led past Agnes' room, which smelt of apples though she never ate fruit. Deborah could hear her snoring. She would not even wake on Judgement Day. And this led her to wonder on the truth of that fable too, for there might be so many millions by then who liked their graves—Grandpapa, for instance, fond of his routine, and irritated at the sudden riot of trumpets.

Deborah crept past the pantry and the servants' hall—it was only a tiny sitting room for Agnes, but long usage had given it the dignity of the name—and unlatched and unbolted the heavy back door. Then she stepped outside, onto the gravel, and took the long way round by the front of the house so as not to tread on the terrace, fronting the lawns and the garden.

The warm night claimed her. In a moment it was part of her. She walked on the grass, and her shoes were instantly soaked. She flung up her arms to the sky. Power ran to her fingertips. Excitement was communicated from the waiting trees, and the orchard, and the paddock; the intensity of their secret life caught at her and made her run. It was nothing like the excitement of ordinary looking forward, of birthday presents, of Christmas stockings, but the pull of a magnet—her grandfather had shown her once how it worked, little needles springing to the jaws—and now night and the sky above were a vast magnet, and the things that waited below were needles, caught up in the great demand.

Deborah went on to the summerhouse, and it was not sleeping like the house fronting the terrace but open to understanding, sharing complicity. Even the dusty windows caught the light, and the cobwebs shone. She rummaged for the old lilo and the motheaten car rug that Grandmama had thrown out two summers ago, and bearing them over her shoulder she made her way to the pool. The alleyway was ghostly, and Deborah knew, for all her mounting tension, that the test was hard. Part of her was still body-bound, and afraid of shadows. If anything stirred she would jump and know true terror. She must show defiance, though. The woods expected it. Like old wise lamas they expected courage.

She sensed approval as she ran the gauntlet, the tall trees watching. Any sign of turning back, of panic, and they would crowd upon her in a choking mass, smothering protest. Branches would become arms, gnarled and knotty, ready to strangle, and the leaves of the higher trees fold in and close like the sudden furling of giant umbrellas. The smaller undergrowth, obedient to the will, would become a briary of a million thorns where animals of no known world crouched snarling, their eyes on fire. To show fear was to show misunderstanding. The woods were merciless.

Deborah walked the alleyway to the pool, her left hand holding the lilo and the rug on her shoulder, her right hand raised in salutation. This was a gesture of respect. Then she paused before the pool and laid down her burden beside it. The lilo was to be her bed, the rug her cover. She took off her shoes, also in respect, and lay down upon the lilo. Then, drawing the rug to her chin, she lay flat, her eyes upon the sky. The gauntlet of the alleyway over, she had no more fear. The woods had accepted her, and the pool was the final resting place, the doorway, the key.

"I shan't sleep," thought Deborah. "I shall just lie awake here all the night and wait for morning, but it will be a kind of introduction to life, like being confirmed."

The stars were thicker now than they had been before. No space in the sky without a prick of light, each star a sun. Some, she thought, were newly born, white-hot, and others wise and colder, nearing completion. The law encompassed them, fixing the riotous path, but how they fell and tumbled depended upon themselves. Such peace, such stillness, such sudden quietude, excitement gone. The trees were no longer menacing but guardians, and the pool was primeval water, the first, the last.

Then Deborah stood at the wicket gate, the boundary, and there was a woman with outstretched hand, demanding tickets. "Pass through," she said when Deborah reached her. "We saw you coming." The wicket gate became a turnstile. Deborah pushed against it and there was no resistance, she was through.

"What is it?" she asked. "Am I really here at last? Is this the bottom of the pool?"

"It could be," smiled the woman. "There are so many ways. You just happened to choose this one."

Other people were pressing to come through. They had no faces, they were only shadows. Deborah stood aside to let them by, and in a moment they had gone, all phantoms.

"Why only now, tonight?" asked Deborah. "Why not in the afternoon, when I came to the pool?"

"It's a trick," said the woman. "You seize on the moment in time. We were here this afternoon. We're always here. Our life goes on around you, but nobody knows it. The trick's easier by night, that's all."

"Am I dreaming, then?" asked Deborah.

"No," said the woman, "this isn't a dream. And it isn't death, either. It's the secret world."

The secret world . . . It was something Deborah had always known, and now the pattern was complete. The memory of it, and the relief, were so tremendous that something seemed to burst inside her heart.

"Of course . . ." she said, "of course . . ." and everything that had ever been fell into place. There was no disharmony. The joy was indescribable, and the surge of feeling, like wings about her in the air, lifted her away from the turnstile and the woman, and she had all knowledge. That was it—the invasion of knowledge.

"I'm not myself, then, after all," she thought. "I knew I wasn't. It was only the task given," and, looking down, she saw a little child who was blind trying to find her way. Pity seized her. She bent down and put her hands on the child's eyes, and they opened, and the child was herself at two years old. The incident came back. It was when her mother died and Roger was born.

"It doesn't matter after all," she told the child. "You are not lost. You don't have to go on crying." Then the child that had been herself melted, and became absorbed in the water and the sky, and the joy of the invading flood intensified so that there was no body at all but only being. No words, only movements. And the beating of wings. This above all, the beating of wings.

"Don't let me go!" It was a pulse in her ear, and a cry, and she saw the woman at the turnstile put up her hands to hold her. Then there was such darkness, such dragging, terrible darkness, and the beginning of pain all over again, the leaden heart, the tears, the misunderstanding. The voice saying "No!" was her own harsh, worldly voice, and she was staring at the restless trees, black and ominous against the sky. One hand trailed in the water of the pool.

Deborah sat up, sobbing. The hand that had been in the pool was wet and cold. She dried it on the rug. And suddenly she was seized with such fear that her body took possession, and throwing aside the rug she began to run along the alleyway, the dark trees mocking and the welcome of the women at the turnstile turned to treachery. Safety lay in the house behind the closed curtains, security was with the grandparents sleeping in their beds, and like a leaf driven before a whirlwind Deborah was out of the woods and across the silver soaking lawn, up the steps beyond the terrace and through the garden gate to the back door.

The slumbering solid house received her. It was like an old staid person who, surviving many trials, had learnt experience. "Don't take any notice of them," it seemed to say, jerking its head —did a house have a head?—towards the woods beyond. "They've made no contribution to civilisation. I'm man-made, and different. This is where you belong, dear child. Now settle down."

Deborah went back again upstairs and into her bedroom. Nothing had changed. It was still the same. Going to the open window she saw that the woods and the lawn seemed unaltered from the moment, how long back she did not know, when she had stood there, deciding upon the visit to the pool. The only difference now was in herself. The excitement had gone, the tension too. Even the terror of those last moments, when her flying feet had brought her to the house, seemed unreal.

She drew the curtains, just as her grandmother might have done, and climbed into bed. Her mind was now preoccupied with practical difficulties, like explaining the presence of the lilo and the rug beside the pool. Willis might find them, and tell her grandfather. The feel of her own pillow, and of her own blankets, reassured her. Both were familiar. And being tired was familiar too, it was a solid bodily ache, like the tiredness after too much jumping or cricket. The thing was, though—and the last remaining conscious thread of thought decided to postpone conclusion until the morning—which was real? This safety of the house, or the secret world?

2

When Deborah woke next morning she knew at once that her mood was bad. It would last her for the day. Her eyes ached, and her neck was stiff, and there was a taste in her mouth like magnesia. Immediately Roger came running into her room, his face refreshed and smiling from some dreamless sleep, and jumped on her bed.

"It's come," he said, "the heat wave's come. It's going to be ninety in the shade."

Deborah considered how best she could damp his day. "It can go to a hundred for all I care," she said. "I'm going to read all morning."

His face fell. A look of bewilderment came into his eyes. "But the house?" he said. "We'd decided to have a house in the trees, don't you remember? I was going to get some planks from Willis."

Deborah turned over in bed and humped her knees. "You can, if you like," she said. "I think it's a silly game."

She shut her eyes, feigning sleep, and presently she heard his feet patter slowly back to his own room, and then the thud of a ball against the wall. If he goes on doing that, she thought maliciously, Grandpapa will ring his bell, and Agnes will come panting up the stairs. She hoped for destruction, for grumbling and snapping, and everyone falling out, not speaking. That was the way of the world.

The kitchen, where the children breakfasted, faced west, so it did not get the morning sun. Agnes had hung up flypapers to catch wasps. The cereal, puffed wheat, was soggy. Deborah complained, mashing the mess with her spoon.

"It's a new packet," said Agnes. "You're mighty particular all of a sudden."

"Deb's got out of bed the wrong side," said Roger.

The two remarks fused to make a challenge. Deborah seized the nearest weapon, a knife, and threw it at her brother. It narrowly missed his eye, but cut his cheek. Surprised, he put his hand to his face and felt the blood. Hurt, not by the knife but by his sister's action, his face turned red and his lower lip quivered. Deborah ran out of the kitchen and slammed the door. Her own violence distressed her, but the power of the mood was too strong. Going onto the terrace, she saw that the worst had happened. Willis had found the lilo and the rug, and had put them to dry in the sun. He was talking to her grandmother. Deborah tried to slip back into the house, but it was too late.

"Deborah, how very thoughtless of you," said Grandmama. "I tell you children every summer that I don't mind your taking the things from the hut into the garden if only you'll put them back."

Deborah knew she should apologise, but the mood forbade it. "That old rug is full of moth," she said contemptuously, "and the lilo has a rainproof back. It doesn't hurt them."

They both stared at her, and her grandmother flushed, just as Roger had done when she had thrown the knife at him. Then her grandmother turned her back and continued giving some instructions to the gardener.

Deborah stalked along the terrace, pretending that nothing had happened, and skirting the lawn she made her way towards the orchard and so to the fields beyond. She picked up a windfall, but as soon as her teeth bit into it the taste was green. She threw it away. She went and sat on a gate and stared in front of her, looking at nothing. Such deception everywhere. Such sour sadness. It was like Adam and Eve being locked out of paradise. The Garden of Eden was no more. Somewhere, very close, the woman at the turnstile waited to let her in, the secret world was all about her, but the key was gone. Why had she ever come back? What had brought her?

People were going about their business. The old man who came three days a week to help Willis was sharpening his scythe behind the toolshed. Beyond the field where the lane ran towards the main road she could see the top of the postman's head. He was pedalling his bicycle towards the village. She heard Roger calling, "Deb? Deb . . . ?" which meant that he had forgiven her, but still the mood held sway and she did not answer. Her own dullness made her own punishment. Presently a knocking sound told her that he had got the planks from Willis and had embarked on the building of his house. He was like his grandfather; he kept to the routine set for himself.

Deborah was consumed with pity. Not for the sullen self humped upon the gate, but for all of them going about their business in the world who did not hold the key. The key was hers, and she had lost it. Perhaps if she worked her way through the long day the magic would return with evening and she would find it once again. Or even now. Even now, by the pool, there might be a clue, a vision.

Deborah slid off the gate and went the long way round. By skirting the fields, parched under the sun, she could reach the other side of the wood and meet no one. The husky wheat was stiff. She had to keep close to the hedge to avoid brushing it, and the hedge was tangled. Foxgloves had grown too tall and were bending with empty sockets, their flowers gone. There were nettles everywhere. There was no gate into the wood, and she had to climb the pricking hedge with the barbed wire tearing her knickers. Once in the wood some measure of peace returned, but the alleyways this side had not been scythed, and the grass was long. She had to wade through it like a sea, brushing it aside with her hands.

She came upon the pool from behind the monster tree, the hybrid whose naked arms were like a dead man's stumps, projecting at all angles. This side, on the lip of the pool, the scum was carpet-thick, and all the lilies, coaxed by the risen sun, had opened wide. They basked as lizards bask on hot stone walls. But here, with stems in water, they swung in grace, cluster upon cluster, pink and waxen white, "They're asleep," thought Deborah. "So is the wood. The morning is not their time," and it seemed to her beyond possibility that the turnstile was at hand and the woman waiting, smiling. "She said they were always there, even in the day, but the truth is that being a child I'm blinded in the day. I don't know how to see."

She dipped her hands in the pool, and the water was tepid brown. She tasted her fingers, and the taste was rank. Brackish water, stagnant from long stillness. Yet beneath . . . beneath, she knew, by night the woman waited, and not only the woman but the whole secret world. Deborah began to pray. "Let it happen again," she whispered. "Let it happen again. Tonight. I won't be afraid."

The sluggish pool made no acknowledgement, but the very silence seemed a testimony of faith, of acceptance. Beside the pool, where the imprint of the lilo had marked the moss, Deborah found a kirby grip, fallen from her hair during the night. It was proof of the visitation. She threw it into the pool as part of the treasury. Then she walked back into the ordinary day and the heat wave, and her black mood was softened. She went to find Roger in the orchard. He was busy with the platform. Three of the boards were fixed, and the noisy hammering was something that had to be borne. He saw her coming, and as always, after trouble, sensed that her mood had changed and mention must never be made of it. Had he called, "Feeling better?" it would have revived the antagonism, and she might not play with him all the day. Instead, he took no notice. She must be the first to speak.

Deborah waited at the foot of the tree, then bent, and handed him up an apple. It was green, but the offering meant peace. He ate it manfully. "Thanks," he said. She climbed into the tree beside him and reached for the box of nails. Contact had been renewed. All was well between them.

3

The hot day spun itself out like a web. The heat haze stretched across the sky, dun-coloured and opaque. Crouching on the burning boards of the apple tree, the children drank ginger beer and fanned themselves with dock leaves. They grew hotter still. When the cowbells summoned them for lunch they found that their grandmother had drawn the curtains of all the rooms downstairs, and the drawing room was a vault and strangely cool. They flung themselves into chairs. No one was hungry. Patch lay under the piano, his soft mouth dripping saliva. Grandmama had changed into a sleeveless linen dress never before seen, and Grandpapa, in a dented panama, carried a fly whisk used years ago in Egypt.

"Ninety-one," he said grimly, "on the Air Ministry roof. It was on the one o'clock news."

Deborah thought of the men who must measure heat, toiling up and down on this Ministry roof with rods and tapes and odd-shaped instruments. Did anyone care but Grandpapa?

"Can we take our lunch outside?" asked Roger.

His grandmother nodded. Speech was too much effort, and she sank languidly into her chair at the foot of the dining-room table. The roses she had picked last night had wilted.

The children carried chicken drumsticks to the summerhouse. It was too hot to sit inside, but they sprawled in the shadow it cast, their heads on faded cushions shedding kapok. Somewhere, far above their heads, an aeroplane climbed like a small silver fish, and was lost in space.

"A Meteor," said Roger. "Grandpapa says they're obsolete."

Deborah thought of Icarus, soaring towards the sun. Did he know when his wings began to melt? How did he feel? She stretched out her arms and thought of them as wings. The finger-tips would be the first to curl, and then turn cloggy soft, and use-less. What terror in the sudden loss of height, the drooping power . . .

Roger, watching her, hoped it was some game. He threw his picked drumstick into a flower bed and jumped to his feet.

"Look," he said, "I'm a Javelin," and he too stretched his arms and ran in circles, banking. Jet noises came from his clenched teeth. Deborah dropped her arms and looked at the drumstick. What had been clean and white from Roger's teeth was now earth-brown. Was it offended to be chucked away? Years later, when everyone was dead, it would be found, moulded like a fossil. Nobody would care.

"Come on," said Roger.

"Where to?" she asked.

"To fetch the raspberries," he said.

"You go," she told him.

Roger did not like going into the dining room alone. He was self-conscious. Deborah made a shield from the adult eyes. In the end he consented to fetch the raspberries without her on condition that she played cricket after tea. After tea was a long way off.

She watched him return, walking very slowly, bearing the plates of raspberries and clotted cream. She was seized with sudden pity, that same pity which, earlier, she had felt for all people other than herself. How absorbed he was, how intent on the moment that held him. But tomorrow he would be some old man far away, the garden forgotten, and this day long past.

"Grandmama says it can't go on," he announced. "There'll have to be a storm."

But why? Why not forever? Why not breathe a spell so that all of them could stay locked and dreaming like the courtiers in *The Sleeping Beauty*, never knowing, never waking, cobwebs in their hair and on their hands, tendrils imprisoning the house itself?

"Race me," said Roger, and to please him she plunged her spoon into the mush of raspberries but finished last, to his delight.

No one moved during the long afternoon. Grandmama went upstairs to her room. The children saw her at her window in her petticoat drawing the curtains close. Grandpapa put his feet up in the drawing room, a handkerchief over his face. Patch did not stir from his place under the piano. Roger, undefeated, found employment still. He first helped Agnes to shell peas for supper, squatting on the back-door step while she relaxed on a lopsided basket chair dragged from the servants' hall. This task finished, he discovered a tin bath, put away in the cellar, in which Patch had been washed in younger days. He carried it to the lawn and filled it with water. Then he stripped to bathing trunks and sat in it solemnly, an umbrella over his head to keep off the sun.

Deborah lay on her back behind the summerhouse, wondering what would happen if Jesus and Buddha met. Would there be discussion, courtesy, an exchange of views like politicians at summit talks? Or were they after all the same person, born at separate times? The queer thing was that this topic, interesting now, meant nothing in the secret world. Last night, through the turnstile, all problems disappeared. They were nonexistent. There was only the knowledge and the joy.

She must have slept, because when she opened her eyes she saw to her dismay that Roger was no longer in the bath but was hammering the cricket stumps into the lawn. It was a quarter to five.

"Hurry up," he called, when he saw her move. "I've had tea."

She got up and dragged herself into the house, sleepy still, and giddy. The grandparents were in the drawing room, refreshed from the long repose of the afternoon. Grandpapa smelt of eau de cologne. Even Patch had come to and was lapping his saucer of cold tea.

"You look tired," said Grandmama critically. "Are you feeling all right?"

Deborah was not sure. Her head was heavy. It must have been sleeping in the afternoon, a thing she never did.

"I think so," she answered, "but if anyone gave me roast pork I know I'd be sick."

"No one suggested you should eat roast pork," said her grandmother, surprised. "Have a cucumber sandwich, they're cool enough."

Grandpapa was lying in wait for a wasp. He watched it hover over his tea, grim, expectant. Suddenly he slammed at the air with his whisk. "Got the brute," he said in triumph. He ground it into the carpet with his heel. It made Deborah think of Jehovah.

"Don't rush around in the heat," said Grandmama. "It isn't wise. Can't you and Roger play some nice, quiet game?"

"What sort of game?" asked Deborah.

But her grandmother was without invention. The croquet mallets were all broken. "We might pretend to be dwarfs and use the heads," said Deborah, and she toyed for a moment with the idea of squatting to croquet. Their knees would stiffen, though, it would be too difficult.

"I'll read aloud to you, if you like," said Grandmama.

Deborah seized upon the suggestion. It delayed cricket. She ran out onto the lawn and padded the idea to make it acceptable to Roger.

"I'll play afterwards," she said, "and that ice cream that Agnes has in the fridge, you can eat all of it. I'll talk tonight in bed."

Roger hesitated. Everything must be weighed. Three goods to balance evil.

"You know that stick of sealing wax Daddy gave you?" he said.

"Yes."

"Can I have it?"

The balance for Deborah too. The quiet of the moment in opposition to the loss of the long thick stick so brightly red.

"All right," she grudged.

Roger left the cricket stumps and they went into the drawing room. Grandpapa, at the first suggestion of reading aloud, had disappeared, taking Patch with him. Grandmama had cleared away the tea. She found her spectacles and the book. It was *Black Beauty*. Grandmama kept no modern children's books, and this made common ground for the three of them. She read the terrible chapter where the stable lad lets Beauty get overheated and gives him a cold drink and does not put on his blanket. The story was suited to the day. Even Roger listened entranced. And Deborah, watching her grandmother's calm face and hearing her careful voice reading the sentences, thought how strange it was that Grandmama could turn herself into Beauty with such ease. She *was* a horse, suffering there with pneumonia in the stable, being saved by the wise coachman.

After the reading, cricket was anticlimax, but Deborah must keep her bargain. She kept thinking of Black Beauty writing the book. It showed how good the story was, Grandmama said, because no child had ever yet questioned the practical side of it, or posed the picture of a horse with a pen in its hoof.

"A modern horse would have a typewriter," thought Deborah, and she began to bowl to Roger, smiling to herself as she did so because of the twentieth-century Beauty clacking with both hoofs at a machine.

This evening, because of the heat wave, the routine was changed. They had their baths first, before their supper, for they were hot and exhausted from the cricket. Then, putting on pyjamas and cardigans, they ate their supper on the terrace. For once Grandmama was indulgent. It was still so hot that they could not take chill, and the dew had not yet risen. It made a small excitement, being in pyjamas on the terrace. Like people abroad, said Roger. Or natives in the South Seas, said Deborah. Or beach-combers who had lost caste. Grandpapa, changed into a white tropical jacket, had not lost caste.

"He's a white trader," whispered Deborah. "He's made a fortune out of pearls."

Roger choked. Any joke about his grandfather, whom he feared, had all the sweet agony of danger.

"What's the thermometer say?" asked Deborah.

Her grandfather, pleased at her interest, went to inspect it.

"Still above eighty," he said with relish.

Deborah, when she cleaned her teeth later, thought how pale her face looked in the mirror above the washbasin. It was not brown, like Roger's, from the day in the sun, but wan and yellow. She tied back her hair with a ribbon, and the nose and chin were peaky sharp. She yawned largely, as Agnes did in the kitchen on Sunday afternoons.

"Don't forget you promised to talk," said Roger quickly.

Talk . . . That was the burden. She was so tired she longed for the white smoothness of her pillow, all blankets thrown aside, bearing only a single sheet. But Roger, wakeful on his bed, the door between them wide, would not relent. Laughter was the one solution, and to make him hysterical, and so exhaust him sooner, she fabricated a day in the life of Willis, from his first morning kipper to his final glass of beer at the village inn. The adventures in between would have tried Gulliver. Roger's delight drew protests from the adult world below. There was the sound of a bell, and then Agnes came up the stairs and put her head round the corner of Deborah's door.

"Your Granny says you're not to make so much noise," she said.

Deborah, spent with invention, lay back and closed her eyes. She could go no further. The children called good night to each other, both speaking at the same time, from agelong custom, beginning with their names and addresses and ending with the world, the universe, and space. Then the final main "Good night," after which neither must ever speak, on pain of unknown calamity.

"I must try and keep awake," thought Deborah, but the power was not in her. Sleep was too compelling, and it was hours later that she opened her eyes and saw her curtains blowing and the forked flash light the ceiling, and heard the trees tossing and sobbing against the sky. She was out of bed in an instant. Chaos had come. There were no stars, and the night was sulphurous. A great crack split the heavens and tore them in two. The garden groaned. If the rain would only fall there might be mercy, and the trees, imploring, bowed themselves this way and that, while the vivid lawn, bright in expectation, lay like a sheet of metal exposed to flame. Let the waters break. Bring down the rain.

Suddenly the lightning forked again, and standing there, alive yet immobile, was the woman by the turnstile. She stared up at the

windows of the house, and Deborah recognised her. The turnstile
was there, inviting entry, and already the phantom figures, passing
through it, crowded towards the trees beyond the lawn. The secret
world was waiting. Through the long day, while the storm was
brewing, it had hovered there unseen beyond her reach, but now
that night had come, and the thunder with it, the barriers were
down. Another crack, mighty in its summons, the turnstile
yawned, and the woman with her hand upon it smiled and
beckoned.

Deborah ran out of the room and down the stairs. Somewhere
somebody called—Roger, perhaps, it did not matter—and Patch
was barking; but caring nothing for concealment she went through
the dark drawing room and opened the french window onto the
terrace. The lightning searched the terrace and lit the paving, and
Deborah ran down the steps onto the lawn where the turnstile
gleamed.

Haste was imperative. If she did not run the turnstile might be
closed, the woman vanish, and all the wonder of the sacred world
be taken from her. She was in time. The woman was still waiting.
She held out her hand for tickets, but Deborah shook her head. "I
have none." The woman, laughing, brushed her through into the
secret world where there were no laws, no rules, and all the
faceless phantoms ran before her to the woods, blown by the rising wind. Then the rain came. The sky, deep brown as the lightning pierced it, opened, and the water hissed to the ground,
rebounding from the earth in bubbles. There was no order now in
the alleyway. The ferns had turned to trees, the trees to Titans.
All moved in ecstasy, with sweeping limbs, but the rhythm was
broken up, tumultuous, so that some of them were bent backwards, torn by the sky, and others dashed their heads to the undergrowth where they were caught and beaten.

In the world behind, laughed Deborah as she ran, this would be
punishment, but here in the secret world it was a tribute. The
phantoms who ran beside her were like waves. They were linked
one with another, and they were, each one of them, and Deborah
too, part of the night force that made the sobbing and the laughter. The lightning forked where they willed it, and the thunder
cracked as they looked upwards to the sky.

The pool had come alive. The water lilies had turned to hands,
with palms upraised, and in the far corner, usually so still under

the green scum, bubbles sucked at the surface, steaming and multiplying as the torrents fell. Everyone crowded to the pool. The phantoms bowed and crouched by the water's edge, and now the woman had set up her turnstile in the middle of the pool, beckoning them once more. Some remnant of a sense of social order rose in Deborah and protested.

"But we've already paid," she shouted, and remembered a second later that she had passed through free. Must there be duplication? Was the secret world a rainbow, always repeating itself, alighting on another hill when you believed yourself beneath it? No time to think. The phantoms had gone through. The lightning, streaky white, lit the old dead monster tree with his crown of ivy, and because he had no spring now in his joints he could not sway in tribute with the trees and ferns, but had to remain there, rigid, like a crucifix.

"And now . . . and now . . . and now . . ." called Deborah.

The triumph was that she was not afraid, was filled with such wild acceptance . . . She ran into the pool. Her living feet felt the mud and the broken sticks and all the tangle of old weeds, and the water was up to her armpits and her chin. The lilies held her. The rain blinded her. The woman and the turnstile were no more.

"Take me too," cried the child. "Don't leave me behind!" In her heart was a savage disenchantment. They had broken their promise, they had left her in the world. The pool that claimed her now was not the pool of secrecy, but dank, dark, brackish water choked with scum.

4

"Grandpapa says he's going to have it fenced round," said Roger. "It should have been done years ago. A proper fence, then nothing can ever happen. But barrow-loads of shingle tipped in it first. Then it won't be a pool, but just a dewpond. Dewponds aren't dangerous."

He was looking at her over the edge of her bed. He had risen in status, being the only one of them downstairs, the bearer of tidings good or ill, the go-between. Deborah had been ordered two days in bed.

"I should think by Wednesday," he went on, "you'd be able to play cricket. It's not as if you're hurt. People who walk in their sleep are just a bit potty."

"I did not walk in my sleep," said Deborah.

"Grandpapa said you must have done," said Roger. "It was a good thing that Patch woke him up and he saw you going across the lawn . . ." Then, to show his release from tension, he stood on his hands.

Deborah could see the sky from her bed. It was flat and dull. The day was a summer day that had worked through storm. Agnes came into the room with junket on a tray. She looked important.

"Now run off," she said to Roger. "Deborah doesn't want to talk to you. She's supposed to rest."

Surprisingly, Roger obeyed, and Agnes placed the junket on the table beside the bed. "You don't feel hungry, I expect," she said. "Never mind, you can eat this later, when you fancy it. Have you got a pain? It's usual, the first time."

"No," said Deborah.

What had happened to her was personal. They had prepared her for it at school, but nevertheless it was a shock, not to be discussed with Agnes. The woman hovered a moment, in case the child asked questions; but, seeing that none came, she turned and left the room.

Deborah, her cheek on her hand, stared at the empty sky. The heaviness of knowledge lay upon her, a strange, deep sorrow.

"It won't come back," she thought. "I've lost the key."

The hidden world, like ripples on the pool so soon to be filled in and fenced, was out of her reach forever.

The Blue Lenses

This was the day for the bandages to be removed and the blue lenses fitted. Marda West put her hand up to her eyes and felt the crêpe binder, and the layer upon layer of cotton wool beneath. Patience would be rewarded at last. The days had passed into weeks since her operation, and she had lain there suffering no physical discomfort, but only the anonymity of darkness, a negative feeling that the world and the life around was passing her by. During the first few days there had been pain, mercifully allayed by drugs, and then the sharpness of this wore down, dissolved, and she was left with a sense of great fatigue, which they assured her was reaction after shock. As for the operation itself, it had been successful. Here was definite promise. A hundred per cent successful.

"You will see," the surgeon told her, "more clearly than ever before."

"But how can you tell?" she urged, desiring her slender thread of faith to be reinforced.

"Because we examined your eyes when you were under the anaesthetic," he replied, "and again since, when we put you under for a second time. We would not lie to you, Mrs. West."

This reassurance came from them two or three times a day, and she had to steel herself to patience as the weeks wore by, so that she referred to the matter perhaps only once every twenty-four hours, and then by way of a trap, to catch them unawares. "Don't throw the roses out. I should like to see them," she would say, and the day nurse would be surprised into the admission, "They'll be over before you can do that." Which meant that she would not see this week.

Actual dates were never mentioned. Nobody said, "On the fourteenth of the month you will have your eyes." And the subterfuge continued, the pretence that she did not mind and was content to wait. Even Jim, her husband, was now classed in the category of "them," the staff of the hospital, and no longer treated as a confidant.

Once, long ago, every qualm and apprehension had been admitted and shared. This was before the operation. Then, fearful of pain and blindness, she had clung to him and said, "What if I never see again, what will happen to me?" picturing herself as helpless and maimed. And Jim, whose anxiety was no less harsh than hers, would answer, "Whatever comes, we'll go through it together."

Now, for no known reason except that darkness, perhaps, had made her more sensitive, she was shy to discuss her eyes with him. The touch of his hand was the same as it had ever been, and his kiss, and the warmth of his voice; but always, during these days of waiting, she had the seed of fear that he, like the staff at the hospital, was being too kind. The kindness of those who knew towards the one who must not be told. Therefore, when at last it happened, when at his evening visit the surgeon said, "Your lenses will be fitted tomorrow," surprise was greater than joy. She could not say anything, and he had left the room before she could thank him. It was really true. The long agony had ended. She permitted herself only a last feeler, before the day nurse went off duty— "They'll take some getting used to, and hurt a bit at first"—her statement of fact put as a careless question. But the voice of the woman who had tended her through so many weary days replied, "You won't know you've got them, Mrs. West."

Such a calm, comfortable voice, and the way she shifted the pillows and held the glass to the patient's lips, the hand smelling faintly of the Morny French Fern soap with which she washed her, these things gave confidence and implied that she could not lie.

"Tomorrow I shall see you," said Marda West, and the nurse, with the cheerful laugh that could be heard sometimes down the corridor outside, answered, "Yes, I'll give you your first shock."

It was a strange thought how memories of coming into the nursing home were now blunted. The staff who had received her were dim shadows, the room assigned to her, where she still lay, like a wooden box built only to entrap. Even the surgeon, brisk and efficient during those two rapid consultations when he had recommended an immediate operation, was a voice rather than a presence. He gave his orders and the orders were carried out, and it was difficult to reconcile this bird-of-passage with the person who, those several weeks ago, had asked her to surrender herself to him, who had in fact worked this miracle upon the membranes and the tissues which were her living eyes.

"Aren't you feeling excited?" This was the low, soft voice of her night nurse, who, more than the rest of them, understood what she had endured. Nurse Brand, by day, exuded a daytime brightness; she was a person of sunlight, of bearing the fresh flowers, of admitting visitors. The weather she described in the world outside appeared to be her own creation. "A real scorcher," she would say, flinging open windows, and her patient would sense the cool uniform, the starched cap, which somehow toned down the penetrating heat. Or else she might hear the steady fall of rain and feel the slight chill accompanying it. "This is going to please the gardeners, but it'll put paid to Matron's day on the river."

Meals, too, even the dullest of lunches, were made to appear delicacies through her method of introduction. "A morsel of brill *au beurre?*" she would suggest happily, whetting reluctant appetite, and the boiled fish that followed must be eaten for all its tastelessness, because otherwise it would seem to let down Nurse Brand, who had recommended it. "Apple fritters—you can manage two, I'm sure," and the tongue began to roll the imaginary fritter, crisp as a flake and sugared, which in reality had a languid, leathery substance. And so her cheerful optimism brooked no discontent—it would be offensive to complain, lacking in backbone to admit, "Let me just lie. I don't want anything."

The night brought consolation and Nurse Ansel. She did not expect courage. At first, during pain, it had been Nurse Ansel who had administered the drugs. It was she who had smoothed the pillows and held the glass to the parched lips. Then, with the passing weeks, there had been the gentle voice and the quiet encouragement. "It will soon pass. This waiting is the worst." At night the patient had only to touch the bell, and in a moment Nurse Ansel was by the bed. "Can't sleep? I know, it's wretched for you. I'll give you just two and a half grains, and the night won't seem so long."

How compassionate, that smooth and silken voice. The imagination, making fantasies through enforced rest and idleness, pictured some reality with Nurse Ansel that was not hospital—a holiday abroad, perhaps, for the three of them, and Jim playing golf with an unspecified male companion, leaving her, Marda, to wander with Nurse Ansel. All she did was faultless. She never annoyed. The small shared intimacies of nighttime brought a bond between nurse and patient that vanished with the day, and when she went off duty, at five minutes to eight in the morning, she would whisper, "Until this evening," the very whisper stimulating anticipation, as though eight o'clock that night would not be clocking-in but an assignation.

Nurse Ansel understood complaint. When Marda West said wearily, "It's been such a long day," her answering "Has it?" implied that for her too the day had dragged, that in some hostel she had tried to sleep and failed, that now only did she hope to come alive.

It was with a special secret sympathy that she would announce the evening visitor. "Here is someone you want to see, a little earlier than usual," the tone suggesting that Jim was not the husband of ten years but a troubadour, a lover, someone whose bouquet of flowers had been plucked in an enchanted garden and now brought to a balcony. "What gorgeous lilies!" the exclamation half a breath and half a sigh, so that Marda West imagined exotic dragon-petalled beauties growing to heaven, and Nurse Ansel, a litttle priestess, kneeling. Then, shyly, the voice would murmur, "Good evening, Mr. West. Mrs. West is waiting for you." She would hear the gentle closing of the door, the tiptoeing out with the lilies and the almost soundless return, the scent of flowers filling the room.

It must have been during the fifth week that Marda West had tentatively suggested, first to Nurse Ansel and then to her husband, that perhaps when she returned home the night nurse might go with them for the first week. It would chime with Nurse Ansel's own holiday. Just a week. Just so that Marda West could settle to home again.

"Would you like me to?" Reserve lay in the voice, yet promise too.

"I would. It's going to be so difficult at first." The patient, not knowing what she meant by difficult, saw herself as helpless still, in spite of the new lenses, and needing the protection and the reassurance that up to the present only Nurse Ansel had given her. "Jim, what about it?"

His comment was something between surprise and indulgence. Surprise that his wife considered a nurse a person in her own right, and indulgence because it was the whim of a sick woman. At least, that was how it seemed to Marda West, and later, when the evening visit was over and he had gone home, she said to the night nurse, "I can't make out whether my husband thought it a good idea or not."

The answer was quiet yet reassuring. "Don't worry. Mr. West is reconciled."

But reconciled to what? The change in routine? Three people round the table, conversation, the unusual status of a guest who, devoting herself to her hostess, must be paid? (Though the last would not be mentioned, but glossed over at the end of a week in an envelope.)

"Aren't you feeling excited?" Nurse Ansel, by the pillow, touched the bandages, and it was the warmth in the voice, the certainty that only a few hours now would bring revelation, which stifled at last all lingering doubt of success. The operation had not failed. Tomorrow she would see once more.

"In a way," said Marda West, "it's like being born again. I've forgotten how the world looks."

"Such a wonderful world," murmured Nurse Ansel, "and you've been patient for so long."

The sympathetic hand expressed condemnation of all those who had insisted upon bandages through the waiting weeks. Greater indulgence might have been granted had Nurse Ansel herself been in command and waved a wand.

"It's queer," said Marda West, "tomorrow you won't be a voice to me any more. You'll be a person."

"Aren't I a person now?"

A note of gentle teasing, of pretended reproach, which was all part of the communication between them, so soothing to the patient. This must surely, when sight came back, be forgone.

"Yes, of course, but it's bound to be different."

"I don't see why."

Even knowing she was dark and small—for so Nurse Ansel had described herself—Marda West must be prepared for surprise at the first encounter, the tilt of the head, the slant of the eyes, or perhaps some unexpected facial form like too large a mouth, too many teeth.

"Look, feel . . ." and not for the first time Nurse Ansel took her patient's hand and passed it over her own face, a little em-

barrassing, perhaps, because it implied surrender, the patient's
hand a captive. Marda West, withdrawing it, said with a laugh, "It
doesn't tell me a thing."

"Sleep then. Tomorrow will come too soon." There came the
familiar routine of the bell put within reach, the last-minute drink,
the pill, and then the soft, "Good night, Mrs. West. Ring if you
want me."

"Thank you. Good night."

There was always a slight sense of loss, of loneliness, as the
door closed and she went away, and a feeling of jealousy, too, because there were other patients who received these same mercies,
and who, in pain, would also ring their bells. When she awoke—
and this often happened in the small hours—Marda West would
no longer picture Jim at home, lonely on his pillow, but would
have an image of Nurse Ansel, seated perhaps by someone's bed,
bending to give comfort, and this alone would make her reach for
the bell, and press her thumb upon it, and say, when the door
opened, "Were you having a nap?"

"I never sleep on duty."

She would be seated, then, in the cubbyhole midway along the
passage, perhaps drinking tea or entering particulars of charts into
a ledger. Or standing beside a patient, as she now stood beside
Marda West.

"I can't find my handkerchief."

"Here it is. Under your pillow all the time."

A pat on the shoulder (and this in itself was a sort of delicacy),
a few moments of talk to prolong companionship, and then she
would be gone, to answer other bells and other requests.

"Well, we can't complain of the weather!" Now it was the day
itself, and Nurse Brand coming in like the first breeze of morning,
a hand on a barometer set fair. "All ready for the great event?"
she asked. "We must get a move on, and keep your prettiest
nightie to greet your husband."

It was her operation in reverse. This time in the same room,
though, and not a stretcher, but only the deft hands of the surgeon
with Nurse Brand to help him. First came the disappearance of
the crêpe, the lifting of the bandages and lint, the very slight prick
of an injection to dull feeling. Then he did something to her eye-

lids. There was no pain. Whatever he did was cold, like the slipping of ice where the bandages have been, yet soothing too.

"Now, don't be disappointed," he said. "You won't know any difference for about half an hour. Everything will seem shadowed. Then it will gradually clear. I want you to lie quietly during that time."

"I understand. I won't move."

The longed-for moment must not be too sudden. This made sense. The dark lenses, fitted inside her lids, were temporary for the first few days. Then they would be removed and others fitted.

"How much shall I see?" The question dared at last.

"Everything. But not immediately in colour. Just like wearing sunglasses on a bright day. Rather pleasant."

His cheerful laugh gave confidence, and when he and Nurse Brand had left the room she lay back again, waiting for the fog to clear and for that summer day to break in upon her vision, however subdued, however softened by the lenses.

Little by little the mist dissolved. The first object was angular, a wardrobe. Then a chair. Then, moving her head, the gradual forming of the window's shape, the vases on the sill, the flowers Jim had brought her. Sounds from the street outside merged with the shapes, and what had seemed sharp before was now in harmony. She thought to herself, "I wonder if I can cry? I wonder if the lenses will keep back tears," but, feeling the blessing of sight restored, she felt the tears as well, nothing to be ashamed of—one or two which were easily brushed away.

All was in focus now. Flowers, the washbasin, the glass with the thermometer in it, her dressing gown. Wonder and relief were so great that they excluded thought.

"They weren't lying to me," she thought. "It's happened. It's true."

The texture of the blanket covering her, so often felt, could now be seen as well. Colour was not important. The dim light caused by the blue lenses enhanced the charm, the softness of all she saw. It seemed to her, rejoicing in form and shape, that colour would never matter. There was time enough for colour. The blue symmetry of vision itself was all-important. To see, to feel, to blend the two together. It was indeed rebirth, the discovery of a world long lost to her.

There seemed to be no hurry now. Gazing about the small room and dwelling upon every aspect of it was richness, something to savour. Hours could be spent just looking at the room and feeling it, travelling through the window and to the windows of the houses opposite.

"Even a prisoner," she decided, "could find comfort in his cell if he had been blinded first, and had recovered his sight."

She heard Nurse Brand's voice outside, and turned her head to watch the opening door.

"Well . . . are we happy once more?"

Smiling, she saw the figure dressed in uniform come into the room, bearing a tray, her glass of milk upon it. Yet, incongruous, absurd, the head with the uniformed cap was not a woman's head at all. The thing bearing down upon her was a cow . . . a cow on a woman's body. The frilled cap was perched upon wide horns. The eyes were large and gentle, but cow's eyes, the nostrils broad and humid, and the way she stood there, breathing, was the way a cow stood placidly in pasture, taking the day as it came, content, unmoved.

"Feeling a bit strange?"

The laugh was a woman's laugh, a nurse's laugh, Nurse Brand's laugh, and she put the tray down on the cupboard beside the bed. The patient said nothing. She shut her eyes, then opened them again. The cow in the nurse's uniform was with her still.

"Confess now," said Nurse Brand, "you wouldn't know you had the lenses in, except for the colour."

It was important to gain time. The patient stretched out her hand carefully for the glass of milk. She sipped the milk slowly. The mask must be worn on purpose. Perhaps it was some kind of experiment connected with the fitting of the lenses—though how it was supposed to work she could not imagine. And it was surely taking rather a risk to spring such a surprise, and, to people weaker than herself who might have undergone the same operation, downright cruel?

"I see very plainly," she said at last. "At least, I think I do."

Nurse Brand stood watching her, with folded arms. The broad uniformed figure was much as Marda West had imagined it, but that cow's head tilted, the ridiculous frill of the cap perched on the horns . . . where did the head join the body, if mask it in fact was?

"You don't sound too sure of yourself," said Nurse Brand. "Don't say you're disappointed, after all we've done for you."

The laugh was cheerful, as usual, but she should be chewing grass, the slow jaws moving from side to side.

"I'm sure of myself," answered her patient, "but I'm not so sure of you. Is it a trick?"

"Is what a trick?"

"The way you look . . . your . . . face?"

Vision was not so dimmed by the blue lenses that she could not distinguish a change of expression. The cow's jaws distinctly dropped.

"Really, Mrs. West!" This time the laugh was not so cordial. Surprise was very evident. "I'm as the good God made me. I dare say he might have made a better job of it."

The nurse, the cow, moved from the bedside towards the window and drew the curtains more sharply back, so that the full light filled the room. There was no visible join to the mask: the head blended to the body. Marda West saw how the cow, if she stood at bay, would lower her horns.

"I didn't mean to offend you," she said, "but it *is* just a little strange. You see . . ."

She was spared explanation because the door opened and the surgeon came into the room. At least, the surgeon's voice was recognisable as he called, "Hullo! How goes it?" and his figure in the dark coat and the sponge-bag trousers was all that an eminent surgeon's should be, but . . . that terrier's head, ears pricked, the inquisitive, searching glance? In a moment surely he would yap, and a tail wag swiftly?

This time the patient laughed. The effect was ludicrous. It must be a joke. It was, it had to be; but why go to such expense and trouble, and what in the end was gained by the deception? She checked her laugh abruptly as she saw the terrier turn to the cow, the two communicate with each other soundlessly. Then the cow shrugged its too ample shoulders.

"Mrs. West thinks us a bit of a joke," she said. But the nurse's voice was not overpleased.

"I'm all for that," said the surgeon. "It would never do if she took a dislike to us, would it?"

Then he came and put his hand out to his patient, and bent close to observe her eyes. She lay very still. He wore no mask either. None, at least, that she could distinguish. The ears were pricked, the sharp nose questing. He was even marked, one ear black, the other white. She could picture him at the entrance to a fox's lair, sniffing, then quick on the scent scuffing down the tunnel, intent upon the job for which he was trained.

"Your name ought to be Jack Russell," she said aloud.

"I beg your pardon?"

He had straightened himself but still stood beside the bed, and the bright eye had a penetrating quality, one ear cocked.

"I mean," Marda West searched for words, "the name seems to suit you better than your own."

She felt confused. Mr. Edmund Greaves, with all the letters after him on the plate in Harley Street, what must he think of her?

"I know a James Russell," he said to her, "but he's an orthopaedic surgeon and breaks your bones. Do you feel I've done that to you?"

His voice was brisk, but he sounded a little surprised, as Nurse Brand had done. The gratitude which was owed to their skill was not forthcoming.

"No, no, indeed," said the patient hastily, "nothing is broken at all, I'm in no pain. I see clearly. Almost too clearly in fact."

"That's as it should be," he said, and the laugh that followed resembled a short sharp bark.

"Well, nurse," he went on, "the patient can do everything within reason except remove the lenses. You've warned her, I suppose?"

"I was about to, sir, when you came in."

Mr. Greaves turned his pointed terrier nose to Marda West.

"I'll be in on Thursday," he said, "to change the lenses. In the meantime, it's just a question of washing out the eyes with a solution three times a day. They'll do it for you. Don't touch them yourself. And above all don't fiddle with the lenses. A patient did that once and lost his sight. He never recovered it."

"If you tried that," the terrier seemed to say, "you would get what you deserved. Better not make the attempt. My teeth are sharp."

"I understand," said the patient slowly. But her chance had gone. She could not now demand an explanation. Instinct warned her that he would not understand. The terrier was saying something to the cow, giving instructions. Such a sharp staccato sen-

tence, and the foolish head nodded in answer. Surely on a hot day
the flies would bother her—or would the frilled cap keep insects
away?

As they moved to the door the patient made a last attempt.

"Will the permanent lenses," she asked, "be the same as these?"

"Exactly the same," yapped the surgeon, "except that they
won't be tinted. You'll see the natural colour. Until Thursday,
then."

He was gone, and the nurse with him. She could hear the murmur of voices outside the door. What happened now? If it was really some kind of test, did they remove their masks instantly? It
seemed to Marda West of immense importance that she should
find this out. The trick was not truly fair: it was a misuse of
confidence. She slipped out of bed and went to the door. She
could hear the surgeon say, "One and a half grains. She's a little
overwrought. It's the reaction, of course."

Bravely, she flung open the door. They were standing there in
the passage, wearing the masks still. They turned to look at her,
and the sharp bright eyes of the terrier, the deep eyes of the cow,
both held reproach, as though the patient, by confronting them,
had committed a breach of etiquette.

"Do you want anything, Mrs. West?" asked Nurse Brand.

Marda West stared beyond them down the corridor. The whole
floor was in the deception. A maid, carrying dustpan and brush,
coming from the room next door, had a weasel's head upon her
small body, and the nurse advancing from the other side was a little prancing kitten, her cap coquettish on her furry curls, the doctor beside her a proud lion. Even the porter, arriving at that moment in the lift opposite, carried a boar's head between his
shoulders. He lifted out luggage, uttering a boar's heavy grunt.

The first sharp prick of fear came to Marda West. How could
they have known she would open the door at that minute? How
could they have arranged to walk down the corridor wearing
masks, the other nurses and the other doctor, and the maid appear
out of the room next door, and the porter come up in the lift?
Something of her fear must have shown in her face, for Nurse
Brand, the cow, took hold of her and led her back into her room.

"Are you feeling all right, Mrs. West?" she asked anxiously.

Marda West climbed slowly into bed. If it was a conspiracy,
what was it all for? Were the other patients to be deceived as well?

"I'm rather tired," she said. "I'd like to sleep."

"That's right," said Nurse Brand, "you got a wee bit excited."

She was mixing something in the medicine glass, and this time, as Marda West took the glass, her hand trembled. Could a cow see clearly how to mix medicine? Supposing she made a mistake?

"What are you giving me?" she asked.

"A sedative," answered the cow.

Buttercups and daisies. Lush green grass. Imagination was strong enough to taste all three in the mixture. The patient shuddered. She lay down on her pillow and Nurse Brand drew the curtains close.

"Now just relax," she said, "and when you wake up you'll feel so much better." The heavy head stretched forward—in a moment it would surely open its jaws and moo.

The sedative acted swiftly. Already a drowsy sensation filled the patient's limbs.

Soon peaceful darkness came, but she awoke, not to the sanity she had hoped for, but to lunch brought in by the kitten. Nurse Brand was off duty.

"How long must it go on for?" asked Marda West. She had resigned herself to the trick. A dreamless sleep had restored energy and some measure of confidence. If it was somehow necessary to the recovery of her eyes, or even if they did it for some unfathomable reason of their own, it was their business.

"How do you mean, Mrs. West?" asked the kitten, smiling. Such a flighty little thing, with its pursed-up mouth, and even as it spoke it put a hand to its cap.

"This test on my eyes," said the patient, uncovering the boiled chicken on her plate. "I don't see the point of it. Making yourselves such guys. What is the object?"

The kitten, serious, if a kitten could be serious, continued to stare at her. "I'm sorry, Mrs. West," she said, "I don't follow you. Did you tell Nurse Brand you couldn't see properly yet?"

"It's not that I can't see," replied Marda West. "I see perfectly well. The chair is a chair. The table is a table. I'm about to eat boiled chicken. But why do you look like a kitten, and a tabby kitten at that?"

Perhaps she sounded ungracious. It was hard to keep her voice steady. The nurse—Marda West remembered the voice, it was

Nurse Sweeting, and the name suited her—drew back from the trolley table.

"I'm sorry," she said, "if I don't come up to scratch. I've never been called a cat before."

Scratch was good. The claws were out already. She might purr to the lion in the corridor, but she was not going to purr to Marda West.

"I'm not making it up," said the patient. "I see what I see. You are a cat, if you like, and Nurse Brand's a cow."

This time the insult must sound deliberate. Nurse Sweeting had fine whiskers to her mouth. The whiskers bristled.

"If you please, Mrs. West," she said, "will you eat your chicken, and ring the bell when you are ready for the next course?"

She stalked from the room. If she had a tail, thought Marda West, it would not be wagging, like Mr. Greaves's, but twitching angrily.

No, they could not be wearing masks. The kitten's surprise and resentment had been too genuine. And the staff of the hospital could not possibly put on such an act for one patient, for Marda West alone—the expense would be too great. The fault must lie in the lenses, then. The lenses, by their very nature, by some quality beyond the layman's understanding, must transform the person who was perceived through them.

A sudden thought struck her, and pushing the trolley table aside she climbed out of bed and went over to the dressing table. Her own face stared back at her from the looking glass. The dark lenses concealed the eyes, but the face was at least her own.

"Thank heaven for that," she said to herself, but it swung her back to thoughts of trickery. That her own face should seem unchanged through the lenses suggested a plot, and that her first idea of masks had been the right one. But why? What did they gain by it? Could there be a conspiracy amongst them to drive her mad? She dismissed the idea at once—it was too fanciful. This was a reputable London nursing home, and the staff was well known. The surgeon had operated on royalty. Besides, if they wanted to send her mad, or kill her even, it would be simple with drugs. Or with anaesthetics. They could have given her too much anaesthetic during the operation, and just let her die. No one would take the roundabout way of dressing up staff and doctors in animals' masks.

She would try one further proof. She stood by the window, the curtain concealing her, and watched for passers-by. For the moment there was no one in the street. It was the lunch hour, and traffic was slack. Then, at the other end of the street, a taxi crossed, too far away for her to see the driver's head. She waited. The porter came out from the nursing home and stood on the steps, looking up and down. His boar's head was clearly visible. He did not count though. He could be part of the plot. A van drew near, but she could not see the driver . . . yes, he slowed as he went by the nursing home and craned from his seat, and she saw the squat frog's head, the bulging eyes.

Sick at heart, she left the window and climbed back into bed. She had no further appetite and pushed away her plate, the rest of the chicken untasted. She did not ring her bell, and after a while the door opened. It was not the kitten. It was the little maid with the weasel's head.

"Will you have plum tart or ice cream, madam?" she asked.

Marda West, her eyes half-closed, shook her head. The weasel, shyly edging forward to take the tray, said, "Cheese, then, and coffee to follow?"

The head joined the neck without any fastening. It could not be a mask, unless some designer, some genius, had invented masks that merged with the body, blending fabric to skin.

"Coffee only," said Marda West.

The weasel vanished. Another knock on the door and the kitten was back again, her back arched, her fluff flying. She plonked the coffee down without a word, and Marda West, irritated—for surely, if anyone was to show annoyance, it should be herself?— said sharply, "Shall I pour you some milk in the saucer?"

The kitten turned. "A joke's a joke, Mrs. West," she said, "and I can take a laugh with anyone. But I can't stick rudeness."

"Miaow," said Marda West.

The kitten left the room. No one, not even the weasel, came to remove the coffee. The patient was in disgrace. She did not care. If the staff of the nursing home thought they could win this battle, they were mistaken. She went to the window again. An elderly cod, leaning on two sticks, was being helped into a waiting car by the boar-headed porter. It could not be a plot. They could not know she was watching them. Marda went to the telephone and asked the exchange to put her through to her husband's office. She remembered a moment afterwards that he would still be at lunch. Nevertheless, she got the number, and as luck had it he was there.

"Jim . . . Jim, darling."

"Yes?"

The relief to hear the loved familiar voice. She lay back on the bed, the receiver to her ear.

"Darling, when can you get here?"

"Not before this evening, I'm afraid. It's one hell of a day, one thing after another. Well, how did it go? Is everything O.K.?"

"Not exactly."

"What do you mean? Can't you see? Greaves hasn't bungled it has he?"

How was she to explain what had happened to her? It sounded so foolish over the telephone.

"Yes, I can see. I can see perfectly. It's just that . . . that all the nurses look like animals. And Greaves, too. He's a fox terrier. One of those little Jack Russells they put down the foxes' holes."

"What on earth are you talking about?"

He was saying something to his secretary at the same time, something about another appointment, and she knew from the tone of his voice that he was busy, very busy, and she had chosen the worst time to ring him up. "What do you mean about Jack Russell?" he repeated.

Marda West knew it was no use. She must wait till he came. Then she would try to explain everything, and he would be able to find out for himself what lay behind it.

"Oh, never mind," she said, "I'll tell you later."

"I'm sorry," he told her, "but I really am in a tearing hurry. If the lenses don't help you, tell somebody. Tell the nurses, the Matron."

"Yes," she said, "yes."

Then she rang off. She put down the telephone. She picked up a magazine, one left behind at some time or other by Jim himself, she supposed. She was glad to find that reading did not hurt her eyes. Nor did the blue lenses make any difference, for the photographs of men and women looked normal as they had always done. Wedding groups, social occasions, débutantes, all were as usual. It was only here, in the nursing home itself and in the street outside, that they were different.

It was much later in the afternoon that Matron called in to have a word with her. She knew it was Matron because of her clothes. But inevitably now, without surprise, she observed the sheep's head.

"I hope you're quite comfortable, Mrs. West?"

A note of gentle enquiry in the voice. A suspicion of a baa?

"Yes, thank you."

Marda West spoke guardedly. It would not do to ruffle the Matron. Even if the whole affair was some gigantic plot, it would be better not to aggravate her.

"The lenses fit well?"

"Very well."

"I'm so glad. It was a nasty operation, and you've stood the period of waiting so very well."

That's it, thought the patient. Butter me up. Part of the game, no doubt.

"Only a few days, Mr. Greaves said, and then you will have them altered and the permanent ones fitted."

"Yes, so he said."

"It's rather disappointing not to observe colour, isn't it?"

"As things are, it's a relief."

The retort slipped out before she could check herself. The Matron smoothed her dress. And if you only knew, thought the patient, what you look like, with that tape under your sheep's chin, you would understand what I mean.

"Mrs. West . . ." The Matron seemed uncomfortable, and turned her sheep's head away from the woman in the bed. "Mrs. West, I hope you won't mind what I'm going to say, but our nurses do a fine job here and we are all very proud of them. They work long hours, as you know, and it is not really very kind to mock them, although I am sure you intended it in fun."

Baa . . . Baa . . . Bleat away. Marda West tightened her lips.

"Is it because I called Nurse Sweeting a kitten?"

"I don't know what you called her, Mrs. West, but she was quite distressed. She came to me in the office nearly crying."

Spitting, you mean, spitting and scratching. Those capable little hands are really claws.

"It won't happen again."

She was determined not to say more. It was not her fault. She had not asked for lenses that deformed, for trickery, for make-believe.

"It must come very expensive," she added, "to run a nursing home like this."

"It is," said the Matron. Said the sheep. "It can only be done because of the excellence of the staff, and the co-operation of all our patients."

The remark was intended to strike home. Even a sheep can turn.

"Matron," said Marda West, "don't let's fence with each other. What is the object of it all?"

"The object of what, Mrs. West?"

"This tomfoolery, this dressing up." There, she had said it. To enforce her argument she pointed at the Matron's cap. "Why pick on that particular disguise? It's not even funny."

There was silence. The Matron, who had made as if to sit down to continue her chat, changed her mind. She moved slowly to the door.

"We, who were trained at St. Hilda's, are proud of our badge," she said. "I hope, when you leave us in a few days, Mrs. West, that you will look back on us with greater tolerance than you appear to have now."

She left the room. Marda West picked up the magazine she had thrown down, but the matter was dull. She closed her eyes. She opened them again. She closed them once more. If the chair had become a mushroom and the table a haystack, then the blame could have been put upon the lenses. Why was it only people who had changed. What was so wrong with people? She kept her eyes shut when her tea was brought her, and when the voice said pleasantly, "Some flowers for you, Mrs. West," she did not even open them, but waited for the owner of the voice to leave the room. The flowers were carnations. The card was Jim's. And the message on it said, "Cheer up. We're not as bad as we seem."

She smiled, and buried her face in the flowers. Nothing false about them. Nothing strange about the scent. Carnations were carnations, fragrant, graceful. Even the nurse on duty who came to put them in water could not irritate her with her pony's head. After all, it was trim little pony, with a white star on its forehead. It would do well in the ring. "Thank you," smiled Marda West.

The curious day dragged on, and she waited restlessly for eight o'clock. She washed and changed her nightgown, and did her hair. She drew her own curtains and switched on the bedside lamp. A strange feeling of nervousness had come upon her. She realised, so strange had been the day, that she had not once thought about Nurse Ansel. Dear, comforting, bewitching Nurse Ansel. Nurse Ansel, who was due to come on duty at eight. Was she also in the conspiracy? If she was, then Marda West would have a show-down. Nurse Ansel would never lie. She would go up to her, and put her hands on her shoulders, and take the mask in her two hands, and say to her, "There, now take it off. You won't deceive me." But if it was the lenses, if all the time it was the lenses that were at fault, how was she to explain it?

She was sitting at the dressing table, putting some cream on her face, and the door must have opened without her being aware; but she heard the well-known voice, the soft beguiling voice, and it said to her, "I nearly came before. I didn't dare. You would have thought me foolish." It slid slowly into view, the long snake's head, the twisting neck, the pointed barbed tongue swiftly thrusting and swiftly withdrawn, it came into view over her shoulders, through the looking glass.

Marda West did not move. Only her hand, mechanically, continued to cream her cheek. The snake was not motionless: it turned and twisted all the time, as though examining the pots of cream, the scent, the powder.

"How does it feel to see yourself again?"

Nurse Ansel's voice emerging from the head seemed all the more grotesque and horrible, and the very fact that as she spoke the darting tongue spoke too paralysed action. Marda West felt sickness rise in her stomach, choking her, and suddenly physical reaction proved too strong. She turned away, but as she did so the steady hands of the nurse gripped her, she suffered herself to be led to her bed, she was lying down, eyes closed, the nausea passing.

"Poor dear, what have they been giving you? Was it the sedative? I saw it on your chart," and the gentle voice, so soothing and so calm, could only belong to one who understood. The patient did not open her eyes. She did not dare. She lay there on the bed, waiting.

"It's been too much for you," said the voice. "They should have kept you quiet, the first day. Did you have visitors?"

"No."

"Nevertheless, you should have rested. You look really pale. We can't have Mr. West seeing you like this. I've half a mind to telephone him to stay away."

"No . . . please, I want to see him. I must see him."

Fear made her open her eyes, but directly she did so the sickness gripped her again, for the snake's head, longer than before, was twisting out of its nurse's collar, and for the first time she saw the hooded eye, a pin's head, hidden. She put her hand over her mouth to stifle her cry.

A sound came from Nurse Ansel, expressing disquiet.

"Something has turned you very sick," she said. "It can't be the sedative. You've often had it before. What was the dinner this evening?"

"Steamed fish. I wasn't hungry."

"I wonder if it was fresh. I'll see if anyone has complained. Meanwhile, lie still, dear, and don't upset yourself."

The door quietly opened and closed again, and Marda West, disobeying instructions, slipped from her bed and seized the first weapon that came to hand, her nail scissors. Then she returned to her bed again, her heart beating fast, the scissors concealed beneath the sheet. Revulsion had been too great. She must defend herself, should the snake approach her. Now she was certain that what was happening was real, was true. Some evil force encompassed the nursing home and its inhabitants, the Matron, the nurses, the visiting doctors, her surgeon—they were all caught up in it, they were all partners in some gigantic crime, the purpose of which could not be understood. Here, in Upper Watling Street, the malevolent plot was in process of being hatched, and she, Marda West, was one of the pawns; in some way they were to use her as an instrument.

One thing was very certain. She must not let them know that she suspected them. She must try and behave with Nurse Ansel as she had done hitherto. One slip, and she was lost. She must pretend to be better. If she let sickness overcome her, Nurse Ansel might bend over her with that snake's head, that darting tongue.

The door opened and she was back. Marda West clenched her hands under the sheet. Then she forced a smile.

"What a nuisance I am," she said. "I felt giddy, but I'm better now."

The gliding snake held a bottle in her hand. She came over to the washbasin and, taking the medicine glass, poured out three drops.

"This should settle it, Mrs. West," she said, and fear gripped the patient once again, for surely the words themselves constituted a threat. "This should settle it"—settle what? Settle her finish? The liquid had no colour, but that meant nothing. She took the medicine glass handed to her, and invented a subterfuge.

"Could you find me a clean handkerchief, in the drawer there?"

"Of course."

The snake turned its head, and as it did so Marda West poured the contents of the glass onto the floor. Then fascinated, repelled, she watched the twisting head peer into the contents of the dressing-table drawer, search for a handkerchief, and bring it back again. Marda West held her breath as it drew near the bed, and this time she noticed that the neck was not the smooth glowworm neck that it had seemed on first encounter, but had scales upon it, zigzagged. Oddly, the nurse's cap was not ill-fitting. It did not perch incongruously as had the caps of kitten, sheep and cow. She took the handkerchief.

"You embarrass me," said the voice, "staring at me so hard. Are you trying to read my thoughts?"

Marda West did not answer. The question might be a trap.

"Tell me," the voice continued, "are you disappointed? Do I look as you expected me to look?"

Still a trap. She must be careful. "I think you do," she said slowly, "but it's difficult to tell with the cap. I can't see your hair."

Nurse Ansel laughed, the low, soft laugh that had been so alluring during the long weeks of blindness. She put up her hands, and in a moment the whole snake's head was revealed, the flat, broad top, the tell-tale adder's V. "Do you approve?" she asked.

Marda West shrank back against her pillow. Yet once again she forced herself to smile.

"Very pretty," she said, "very pretty indeed."

The cap was replaced, the long neck wriggled, and then, deceived, it took the medicine glass from the patient's hand and put it back upon the washbasin. It did not know everything.

"When I go home with you," said Nurse Ansel, "I needn't wear uniform—that is, if you don't want me to. You see, you'll be a private patient then, and I your personal nurse for the week I'm with you."

Marda West felt suddenly cold. In the turmoil of the day she had forgotten the plans. Nurse Ansel was to be with them for a week. It was all arranged. The vital thing was not to show fear. Nothing must seem changed. And then, when Jim arrived, she would tell him everything. If he could not see the snake's head as she did—and indeed, it was possible that he would not, if her hypervision was caused by the lenses—he must just understand that for reasons too deep to explain she no longer trusted Nurse Ansel, could not, in fact, bear her to come home. The plan must be altered. She wanted no one to look after her. She only wanted to be home again, with him.

The telephone rang on the bedside table and Marda West seized it, as she might seize salvation. It was her husband.

"Sorry to be late," he said. "I'll jump into a taxi and be with you right away. The lawyer kept me."

"Lawyer?" she asked.

"Yes, Forbes & Millwall, you remember, about the trust fund."

She had forgotten. There had been so many financial discussions before the operation. Conflicting advice, as usual. And finally Jim had put the whole business into the hands of the Forbes & Millwall people.

"Oh, yes. Was it satisfactory?"

"I think so. Tell you directly."

He rang off, and looking up she saw the snake's head watching her. No doubt, thought Marda West, no doubt you would like to know what we were saying to one another.

"You must promise not to get too excited when Mr. West comes." Nurse Ansel stood with her hand upon the door.

"I'm not excited. I just long to see him, that's all."

"You're looking very flushed."

"It's warm in here."

The twisting neck craned upward, then turned to the window. For the first time Marda West had the impression that the snake was not entirely at its ease. It sensed tension. It knew, it could not help but know, that the atmosphere had changed between nurse and patient.

"I'll open the window just a trifle at the top."

If you were all snake, thought the patient, I could push you through. Or would you coil yourself round my neck and strangle me?

The window was opened, and pausing a moment, hoping perhaps for a word of thanks, the snake hovered at the end of the bed. Then the neck settled in the collar, the tongue darted rapidly in and out, and with a gliding motion Nurse Ansel left the room.

Marda West waited for the sound of the taxi in the street outside. She wondered if she could persuade Jim to stay the night in the nursing home. If she explained her fear, her terror, surely he would understand. She would know in an instant if he had sensed anything wrong himself. She would ring the bell, make a pretext of asking Nurse Ansel some question, and then, by the expression on his face, by the tone of his voice, she would discover whether he saw what she saw herself.

The taxi came at last. She heard it slow down, and then the door slammed and, blessedly, Jim's voice rang out in the street below. The taxi went away. He would be coming up in the lift. Her heart began to beat fast, and she watched the door. She heard his footstep outside, and then his voice again—he must be saying something to the snake. She would know at once if he had seen the head. He would come into the room either startled, not believing his eyes, or laughing, declaring it a joke, a pantomime. Why did he not hurry? Why must they linger there, talking, their voices hushed?

The door opened, the familiar umbrella and bowler hat the first objects to appear around the corner, then the comforting burly figure, but—God . . . no . . . please God, not Jim too, not Jim, forced into a mask, forced into an organisation of devils, of liars . . . Jim had a vulture's head. She could not mistake it. The brooding eye, the blood-tipped beak, the flabby folds of flesh. As she lay in sick and speechless horror, he stood the umbrella in a corner and put down the bowler hat and the folded overcoat.

"I gather you're not too well," he said, turning his vulture's head and staring at her, "feeling a bit sick and out of sorts. I won't stay long. A good night's rest will put you right."

She was too numb to answer. She lay quite still as he approached the bed and bent to kiss her. The vulture's beak was sharp.

"It's reaction, Nurse Ansel says," he went on, "the sudden

shock of being able to see again. It works differently with different people. She says it will be much better when we get you home."

We . . . Nurse Ansel and Jim. The plan still held, then.

"I don't know," she said faintly, "that I want Nurse Ansel to come home."

"Not want Nurse Ansel?" He sounded startled. "But it was you who suggested it. You can't suddenly chop and change."

There was no time to reply. She had not rung the bell, but Nurse Ansel herself came into the room. "Cup of coffee, Mr. West?" she said. It was the evening routine. Yet tonight it sounded strange, as though it had been arranged outside the door.

"Thanks, Nurse, I'd love some. What's this nonsense about not coming home with us?" The vulture turned to the snake, the snake's head wriggled, and Marda West knew, as she watched them, the snake with darting tongue, the vulture with his head hunched between his man's shoulders, that the plan for Nurse Ansel to come home had not been her own after all; she remembered now that the first suggestion had come from Nurse Ansel herself. It had been Nurse Ansel who had said that Marda West needed care during convalescence. The suggestion had come after Jim had spent the evening laughing and joking and his wife had listened, her eyes bandaged, happy to hear him. Now, watching the smooth snake whose adder's V was hidden beneath the nurse's cap, she knew too why Nurse Ansel wanted to return with her, and she knew too why Jim had not opposed it, why in fact he had accepted the plan at once, had declared it a good one.

The vulture opened its bloodstained beak. "Don't say you two have fallen out?"

"Impossible." The snake twisted its neck, looked sideways at the vulture, and added, "Mrs. West is just a little bit tired tonight. She's had a trying day, haven't you, dear?"

How best to answer? Neither must know. Neither the vulture, nor the snake, nor any of the hooded beasts surrounding her and closing in, must ever guess, must ever know.

"I'm all right," she said. "A bit mixed-up. As Nurse Ansel says, I'll be better in the morning."

The two communicated in silence, sympathy between them. That, she realised now, was the most frightening thing of all. Animals, birds and reptiles had no need to speak. They moved, they looked, they knew what they were about. They would not destroy her, though. She had, for all her bewildered terror, the will to live.

"I won't bother you," said the vulture, "with these documents tonight. There's no violent hurry anyway. You can sign that at home."

"What documents?"

If she kept her eyes averted she need not see the vulture's head. The voice was Jim's, steady and reassuring.

"The trust fund papers Forbes & Millwall gave me. They suggest I should become a co-director of the fund."

The words struck a chord, a thread of memory belonging to the weeks before her operation. Something to do with her eyes. If the operation was not successful she would have difficulty in signing her name.

"What for?" she asked, her voice unsteady. "After all, it is my money."

He laughed. And, turning to the sound, she saw the beak open. It gaped like a trap, and then closed again.

"Of course it is," he said. "That's not the point. The point is that I should be able to sign for you, if you should be ill or away."

Marda West looked at the snake, and the snake, aware, shrank into its collar and slid towards the door. "Don't stay too long, Mr. West," murmured Nurse Ansel. "Our patient must have a real rest tonight."

She glided from the room and Marda West was left alone with her husband. With the vulture.

"I don't propose to go away," she said, "or be ill."

"Probably not. That's neither here nor there. These fellows always want safeguards. Anyway, I won't bore you with it now."

Could it be that the voice was overcasual? That the hand, stuffing the document into the pocket of the greatcoat, was a claw? This was a possibility, a horror, perhaps, to come. The bodies changing too, hands and feet becoming wings, claws, hoofs, paws, with no touch of humanity left to the people about her. The last thing to go would be the human voice. When the human voice went, there would be no hope. The jungle would take over, multitudinous sounds and screams coming from a hundred throats.

"Did you really mean that," Jim asked, "about Nurse Ansel?"

Calmly she watched the vulture pare his nails. He carried a file in his pocket. She had never thought about it before—it was part of Jim like his fountain pen and his pipe. Yet now there was reasoning behind it: a vulture needed sharp claws for tearing its victim.

"I don't know," she said. "It seemed to me rather silly to go home with a nurse, now that I can see again."

He did not answer at once. The head sank deeper between the shoulders. His dark city suit was like the humped feathers of a large brooding bird. "I think she's a treasure," he said. "And you're bound to feel groggy at first. I vote we stick to the plan. After all, if it doesn't work we can always send her away."

"Perhaps," said his wife.

She was trying to think if there was anyone left whom she could trust. Her family was scattered. A married brother in South Africa, friends in London, no one with whom she was intimate. Not to this extent. No one to whom she could say that her nurse had turned into a snake, her husband into a vulture. The utter hopelessness of her position was like damnation itself. This was her hell. She was quite alone, coldly conscious of the hatred and cruelty about her.

"What will you do this evening?" she asked quietly.

"Have dinner at the club, I suppose," he answered. "It's becoming rather monotonous. Only two more days of it, thank goodness. Then you'll be home again."

Yes, but once at home, once back there, with a vulture and a snake, would she not be more completely at their mercy than she was here?

"Did Greaves say Thursday for certain?" she asked.

"He told me so this morning, when he telephoned. You'll have the other lenses then, the ones that show colour."

The ones that would show the bodies too. That was the explanation. The blue lenses only showed the heads. They were the first test. Greaves, the surgeon, was in this too, very naturally. He had a high place in the conspiracy—perhaps he had been bribed. Who was it, she tried to remember, who had suggested the operation in the first place? Was it the family doctor, after a chat with Jim? Didn't they both come to her together and say that this was the only chance to save her eyes? The plot must lie deep in the past, extend right back through the months, perhaps the years. But, in heaven's name, for what purpose? She sought wildly in her memory to try to recall a look, or sign, or word which would give her some insight into this dreadful plot, this conspiracy against her person or her sanity.

"You look pretty peaky," he said suddenly. "Shall I call Nurse Ansel?"

"No . . ." It broke from her, almost a cry.

"I think I'd better go. She said not to stay long."

He got up from the chair, a heavy, hooded figure, and she closed her eyes as he came to kiss her good night. "Sleep well, my poor pet, and take it easy."

In spite of her fear she felt herself clutch at his hand.

"What is it?" he asked.

The well-remembered kiss would have restored her, but not the stab of the vulture's beak, the thrusting bloodstained beak. When he had gone she began to moan, turning her head upon the pillow.

"What am I to do?" she said. "What am I to do?"

The door opened again and she put her hand to her mouth. They must not hear her cry. They must not see her cry. She pulled herself together with a tremendous effort.

"How are you feeling, Mrs. West?"

The snake stood at the bottom of the bed, and by her side the house physician. She had always liked him, a young pleasant man, and although like the others he had an animal's head it did not frighten her. It was a dog's head, an Aberdeen's, and the brown eyes seemed to quiz her. Long ago, as a child, she had owned an Aberdeen.

"Could I speak to you alone?" she asked.

"Of course. Do you mind, nurse?" He jerked his head at the door, and she had gone. Marda West sat up in bed and clasped her hands.

"You'll think me very foolish," she began, "but it's the lenses. I can't get used to them."

He came over, the trustworthy Aberdeen, head cocked in sympathy.

"I'm sorry about that," he said. "They don't hurt you, do they?"

"No," she said, "no, I can't feel them. It's just that they make everyone look strange."

"They're bound to do that, you know. They don't show colour." His voice was cheerful, friendly. "It comes as a bit of a shock when you've worn bandages so long," he said, "and you mustn't forget you were pulled about quite a bit. The nerves behind the eyes are still very tender."

"Yes," she said. His voice, even his head, gave her confidence. "Have you known people who've had this operation before?"

"Yes, scores of them. In a couple of days you'll be as right as rain." He patted her on the shoulder. Such a kindly dog. Such a sporting, cheerful dog, like the long-dead Angus. "I'll tell you another thing," he continued. "Your sight may be better after this than it's ever been before. You'll actually see more clearly in every way. One patient told me that it was as though she had been wearing spectacles all her life, and then, because of the operation, she realised she saw all her friends and her family as they really were."

"As they really were?" She repeated his words after him.

"Exactly. Her sight had always been poor, you see. She had thought her husband's hair was brown, but in reality it was red, bright red. A bit of a shock at first. But she was delighted."

The Aberdeen moved from the bed, patted the stethoscope on his jacket, and nodded his head. "Mr. Greaves did a wonderful job on you. I can promise you that," he said. "He was able to strengthen a nerve he thought had perished. You've never had the use of it before—it wasn't functioning. So who knows, Mrs. West, you may have made medical history. Anyway, sleep well and the best of luck. See you in the morning. Good night." He trotted from the room. She heard him call good night to Nurse Ansel as he went down the corridor.

The comforting words had turned to gall. In one sense they were a relief, because his explanation seemed to suggest there was no plot against her. Instead, like the woman patient before her with the deepened sense of colour, she had been given vision. She used the words he had used himself. Marda West could see people as they really were. And those whom she had loved and trusted most were in truth a vulture and a snake . . .

The door opened and Nurse Ansel, with the sedative, entered the room.

"Ready to settle down, Mrs. West?" she asked.

"Yes, thank you."

There might be no conspiracy, but even so all trust, all faith, were over.

"Leave it with a glass of water. I'll take it later."

She watched the snake put the glass on the bedside table. She watched her tuck in the sheet. Then the twisting neck peered closer and the hooded eyes saw the nail scissors half-hidden beneath the pillow.

"What have you got there?"

The tongue darted and withdrew. The hand stretched out for the scissors. "You might have cut yourself. I'll put them away, shall I, for safety's sake?"

Her one weapon was pocketed, not replaced on the dressing table. The very way Nurse Ansel slipped the scissors into her pocket suggested that she knew of Marda West's suspicions. She wanted to leave her defenceless.

"Now, remember to ring your bell if you want anything."

"I'll remember."

The voice that had once seemed tender was oversmooth and false. How deceptive are ears, thought Marda West, what traitors to truth. And for the first time she became aware of her own new latent power, the power to tell truth from falsehood, good from evil.

"Good night, Mrs. West."

"Good night."

Lying awake, her bedside clock ticking, the accustomed traffic sounds coming from the street outside, Marda West decided upon her plan. She waited until eleven o'clock, an hour past the time when she knew that all the patients were settled and asleep. Then she switched out her light. This would deceive the snake, should she come to peep at her through the window slide in the door. The snake would believe that she slept. Marda West crept out of bed. She took her clothes from the wardrobe and began to dress. She put on her coat and shoes and tied a scarf over her head. When she was ready she went to the door and softly turned the handle. All was quiet in the corridor. She stood there motionless. Then she took one step across the threshold and looked to the left, where the nurse on duty sat. The snake was there. The snake was sitting crouched over a book. The light from the ceiling shone upon her head, and there could be no mistake. There were the trim uniform, the white starched front, the stiff collar, but rising from the collar the twisting neck of the snake, the long, flat, evil head.

Marda West waited. She was prepared to wait for hours. Presently the sound she hoped for came, the bell from a patient. The snake lifted its head from the book and checked the red light on the wall. Then, slipping on her cuffs, she glided down the corridor to the patient's room. She knocked and entered. Directly she had disappeared Marda West left her own room and went to the head of the staircase. There was no sound. She listened carefully, and then crept downstairs. There were four flights, four floors, but the stairway itself was not visible from the cubbyhole where the night nurses sat on duty. Luck was with her.

Down in the main hall the lights were not so bright. She waited at the bottom of the stairway until she was certain of not being observed. She could see the night porter's back—his head was not visible, for he was bent over his desk—but when it straightened she noticed the broad fish face. She shrugged her shoulders. She had not dared all this way to be frightened by a fish. Boldly she walked through the hall. The fish was staring at her.

"Do you want anything, madam?" he said.

He was as stupid as she expected. She shook her head.

"I'm going out. Good night," she said, and she walked straight past him, out of the swing door, and down the steps into the street. She turned swiftly to the left, and, seeing a taxi at the further end, called and raised her hand. The taxi slowed and waited. When she came to the door she saw that the driver had the squat black face of an ape. The ape grinned. Some instinct warned her not to take the taxi.

"I'm sorry," she said. "I made a mistake."

The grin vanished from the face of the ape. "Make up your mind, lady," he shouted, and let in his clutch and swerved away.

Marda West continued walking down the street. She turned right, and left, and right again, and in the distance she saw the lights of Oxford Street. She began to hurry. The friendly traffic drew her like a magnet, the distant lights, the distant men and women. When she came to Oxford Street she paused, wondering of a sudden where she should go, whom she could ask for refuge. And it came to her once again that there was no one, no one at all; because the couple passing her now, a toad's head on a short black body clutching a panther's arm, could give her no protection, and the policeman standing at the corner was a baboon, the woman talking to him a little prinked-up pig. No one was human, no one was safe, the man a pace or two behind her was like Jim, another vulture. There were vultures on the pavement opposite. Coming towards her, laughing, was a jackal.

She turned and ran. She ran, bumping into them, jackals, hyenas, vultures, dogs. The world was theirs, there was no human left. Seeing her run they turned and looked at her, they pointed, they screamed and yapped, they gave chase, their footsteps followed her. Down Oxford Street she ran, pursued by them, the night all darkness and shadow, the light no longer with her, alone in an animal world.

"Lie quite still, Mrs. West, just a small prick, I'm not going to hurt you."

She recognised the voice of Mr. Greaves, the surgeon, and dimly she told herself that they had got hold of her again. She was back at the nursing home, and it did not matter now—she might as well be there as anywhere else. At least in the nursing home the animal heads were known.

They had replaced the bandages over her eyes, and for this she was thankful. Such blessed darkness, the evil of the night hidden.

"Now, Mrs. West, I think your troubles are over. No pain and no confusion with these lenses. The world's in colour again."

The bandages were being lightened after all. Layer after layer removed. And suddenly everything was clear, was day, and the face of Mr. Greaves smiled down at her. At his side was a rounded, cheerful nurse.

"Where are your masks?" asked the patient.

"We didn't need masks for this little job," said the surgeon. "We were only taking out the temporary lenses. That's better, isn't it?"

She let her eyes drift round the room. She was back again all right. This was the shape, there was the wardrobe, the dressing table, the vases of flowers. All in natural colour, no longer veiled. But they could not fob her off with stories of a dream. The scarf she had put round her head before slipping away in the night lay on the chair.

"Something happened to me, didn't it?" she said. "I tried to get away."

The nurse glanced at the surgeon. He nodded his head.

"Yes," he said, "you did. And, frankly, I don't blame you. I blame myself. Those lenses I inserted yesterday were pressing upon a tiny nerve, and the pressure threw out your balance. That's all over now."

His smile was reassuring. And the large warm eyes of Nurse Brand—it must surely be Nurse Brand—gazed down at her in sympathy.

"It was very terrible," said the patient. "I can never explain how terrible."

"Don't try," said Mr. Greaves. "I can promise you it won't happen again."

The door opened and the young physician entered. He too was smiling. "Patient fully restored?" he asked.

"I think so," said the surgeon. "What about it, Mrs. West?"

Marda West stared gravely at the three of them, Mr. Greaves, the house physician and Nurse Brand, and she wondered what palpitating wounded tissue could so transform three individuals into prototypes of an animal kingdom, what cell linking muscle to imagination.

"I thought you were dogs," she said. "I thought you were a hunt terrier, Mr. Greaves, and that you were an Aberdeen."

The house physician touched his stethoscope and laughed.

"But I am," he said, "it's my native town. Your judgement was not wholly out, Mrs. West. I congratulate you."

Marda West did not join in the laugh.

"That's all right for you," she said. "Other people were not so pleasant." She turned to Nurse Brand. "I thought you were a cow," she said, "a kind cow. But you had sharp horns."

This time it was Mr. Greaves who took up the laugh. "There you are, nurse," he said, "just what I've often told you. Time they put you out to grass and to eat the daisies."

Nurse Brand took it in good part. She straightened the patient's pillows and her smile was benign. "We get called some funny things from time to time," she said. "That's all part of the job."

The doctors were moving towards the door, still laughing, and Marda West, sensing the normal atmosphere, the absence of all strain, said, "Who found me, then? What happened? Who brought me back?"

Mr. Greaves glanced back at her from the door. "You didn't get very far, Mrs. West, and a damn good job for you, or you mightn't be here now. The porter followed you."

"It's all finished with now," said the house physician, "and the episode lasted five minutes. You were safely in your bed before any harm was done, and I was here. So that was that. The person who really had the full shock was poor Nurse Ansel when she found you weren't in your bed."

Nurse Ansel . . . The revulsion of the night before was not so easily forgotten. "Don't say our little starlet was an animal too?" smiled the house doctor. Marda West felt herself colour. Lies would have to begin. "No," she said quickly, "no, of course not."

"Nurse Ansel is here now," said Nurse Brand. "She was so upset when she went off duty that she wouldn't go back to the hostel to sleep. Would you care to have a word with her?"

Apprehension seized the patient. What had she said to Nurse Ansel in the panic and fever of the night? Before she could answer the house doctor opened the door and called down the passage.

"Mrs. West wants to say good morning to you," he said. He was smiling all over his face. Mr. Greaves waved his hand and was gone, Nurse Brand went after him, and the house doctor, saluting with his stethoscope and making a mock bow, stepped back against the wall to admit Nurse Ansel. Marda West stared, then tremulously began to smile, and held out her hand.

"I'm sorry," she said, "you must forgive me."

How could she have seen Nurse Ansel as a snake! The hazel eyes, the clear olive skin, the dark hair trim under the frilled cap. And that smile, that slow, understanding smile.

"Forgive you, Mrs. West?" said Nurse Ansel. "What have I to forgive you for? You've been through a terrible ordeal."

Patient and nurse held hands. They smiled at one another. And, oh heaven, thought Marda West, the relief, the thankfulness, the load of doubt and despair that was swept away with the new-found sight and knowledge.

"I still don't understand what happened," she said, clinging to the nurse. "Mr. Greaves tried to explain. Something about a nerve."

Nurse Ansel made a face towards the door. "He doesn't know himself," she whispered, "and he's not going to say either, or he'll find himself in trouble. He fixed those lenses too deep, that's all. Too near a nerve. I wonder it didn't kill you."

She looked down at her patient. She smiled with her eyes. She was so pretty, so gentle. "Don't think about it," she said. "You're going to be happy from now on. Promise me?"

"I promise," said Marda West.

The telephone rang, and Nurse Ansel let go her patient's hand and reached for the receiver. "You know who this is going to be," she said. "Your poor husband." She gave the receiver to Marda West.

"Jim . . . Jim, is that you?"

The loved voice sounding so anxious at the other end. "Are you all right?" he said. "I've been through to Matron twice, she said she would let me know. What the devil has been happening?"

Marda West smiled and handed the receiver to the nurse.

"You tell him," she said.

Nurse Ansel held the receiver to her ear. The skin of her hand was olive smooth, the nails gleaming with soft pink polish.

"Is that you, Mr. West?" she said. "Our patient gave us a fright, didn't she?" She smiled and nodded at the woman in the bed. "Well, you don't have to worry any more. Mr. Greaves changed the lenses. They were pressing on a nerve, and everything is now all right. She can see perfectly. Yes, Mr. Greaves said we could come home tomorrow."

The endearing voice blended to the soft colouring, the hazel eyes. Marda West reached once more for the receiver.

"Jim, I had a hideous night," she said. "I'm only just beginning to understand it now. A nerve in the brain . . ."

"So I gather," he said. "How damnable. Thank God they traced it. That fellow Greaves can't have known his job."

"It can't happen again," she said. "Now the proper lenses are in, it can't happen again."

"It had better not," he said, "or I'll sue him. How are you feeling in yourself?"

"Wonderful," she said, "bewildered, but wonderful."

"Good girl," he said. "Don't excite yourself. I'll be along later."

His voice went. Marda West gave the receiver to Nurse Ansel, who replaced it on the stand.

"Did Mr. Greaves really say I could go home tomorrow?" she asked.

"Yes, if you're good." Nurse Ansel smiled and patted her patient's hand. "Are you sure you still want me to come with you?" she asked.

"Why, yes," said Marda West. "Why, it's all arranged."

She sat up in bed and the sun came streaming through the window, throwing light on the roses, the lilies, the tall-stemmed iris. The hum of traffic outside was close and friendly. She thought of her garden waiting for her at home, and her own bedroom, her own possessions, the day-by-day routine of home to be taken up again with sight restored, the anxiety and fear of the past months put away forever.

"The most precious thing in the world," she said to Nurse Ansel, "is sight. I know now. I know what I might have lost."

Nurse Ansel, hands clasped in front of her, nodded her head in sympathy. "You've got your sight back," she said, "that's the miracle. You won't ever lose it now."

She moved to the door. "I'll slip back to the hostel and get some rest," she said. "Now I know everything is well with you I'll be able to sleep. Is there anything you want before I go?"

"Give me my face cream and my powder," said the patient, "and my lipstick and the brush and comb."

Nurse Ansel fetched the things from the dressing table and put them within reach upon the bed. She brought the hand mirror too, and the bottle of scent, and with a little smile of intimacy sniffed at the stopper. "Gorgeous," she murmured. "This is what Mr. West gave you, isn't it?"

Already, thought Marda West, Nurse Ansel fitted in. She saw herself putting flowers in the small guest room, choosing the right books, fitting a portable wireless in case Nurse Ansel should be bored in the evenings.

"I'll be with you at eight o'clock."

The familiar words, said every morning now for so many days and weeks, sounded in her ear like a melody, loved through repetition. At last they were joined to the individual, the person who smiled, the one whose eyes promised friendship and loyalty.

"See you this evening."

The door closed. Nurse Ansel had gone. The routine of the nursing home, broken by the fever of the night before, resumed its usual pattern. Instead of darkness, light. Instead of negation, life.

Marda West took the stopper from the scent bottle and put it behind her ears. The fragrance filtered, becoming part of the warm, bright day. She lifted the hand mirror and looked into it. Nothing changed in the room, the street noises penetrated from outside, and presently the little maid who had seemed a weasel yesterday came in to dust the room. She said, "Good morning," but the patient did not answer. Perhaps she was tired. The maid dusted, and went her way.

Then Marda West took up the mirror and looked into it once more. No, she had not been mistaken. The eyes that stared back at her were doe's eyes, wary before sacrifice, and the timid deer's head was meek, already bowed.

Kiss Me Again, Stranger

I looked around for a bit, after leaving the army and before settling down, and then I found myself a job up Hampstead way, in a garage it was, at the bottom of Haverstock Hill near Chalk Farm, and it suited me fine. I'd always been one for tinkering with engines, and in R.E.M.E. that was my work and I was trained to it —it had always come easy to me, anything mechanical.

My idea of having a good time was to lie on my back in my greasy overalls under a car's belly, or a lorry's, with a spanner in my hand, working on some old bolt or screw, with the smell of oil about me, and someone starting up an engine, and the other chaps around clattering their tools and whistling. I never minded the smell or the dirt. As my old Mum used to say when I'd be that way as a kid, mucking about with a grease can, "It won't hurt him, it's clean dirt," and so it is, with engines.

The boss at the garage was a good fellow, easygoing, cheerful, and he saw I was keen on my work. He wasn't much of a mechanic himself, so he gave me the repair jobs, which was what I liked.

I didn't live with my old Mum—she was too far off, over Shepperton way, and I saw no point in spending half the day getting to and from my work. I like to be handy, have it on the spot, as it were. So I had a bedroom with a couple called Thompson, only about ten minutes' walk away from the garage. Nice people, they were. He was in the shoe business, cobbler I suppose he'd be called, and Mrs. Thompson cooked the meals and kept the house for him over the shop. I used to eat with them, breakfast and supper—we always had a cooked supper—and being the only lodger I was treated as family.

I'm one for routine. I like to get on with my job, and then when the day's work's over settle down to a paper and a smoke and a bit of music on the wireless, variety or something of the sort, and then turn in early. I never had much use for girls, not even when I was doing my time in the army. I was out in the Middle East, too, Port Said and that.

No, I was happy enough living with the Thompsons, carrying on much the same day after day, until that one night, when it happened. Nothing's been the same since. Nor ever will be. I don't know . . .

The Thompsons had gone to see their married daughter up at Highgate. They asked me if I'd like to go along, but somehow I didn't fancy barging in, so instead of staying home alone after leaving the garage I went down to the picture palace, and taking a look at the poster saw it was cowboy and Indian stuff—there was a picture of a cowboy sticking a knife into the Indian's guts. I like that—proper baby I am for westerns—so I paid my one and twopence and went inside. I handed my slip of paper to the usherette and said, "Back row, please," because I like sitting far back and leaning my head against the board.

Well, then I saw her. They dress the girls up no end in some of these places, velvet tams and all, making them proper guys. They hadn't made a guy out of this one, though. She had copper hair, page-boy style I think they call it, and blue eyes, the kind that look shortsighted but see further than you think, and go dark by night, nearly black, and her mouth was sulky-looking, as if she was fed up, and it would take someone giving her the world to make her smile. She hadn't freckles, nor a milky skin, but warmer than that, more like a peach, and natural too. She was small and slim, and her velvet coat—blue it was—fitted her close, and the cap on the back of her head showed up her copper hair.

I bought a programme—not that I wanted one, but to delay going in through the curtain—and I said to her, "What's the picture like?"

She didn't look at me. She just went on staring into nothing, at the opposite wall. "The knifing's amateur," she said, "but you can always sleep."

I couldn't help laughing. I could see she was serious though. She wasn't trying to have me on or anything.

"That's no advertisement," I said. "What if the manager heard you?"

Then she looked at me. She turned those blue eyes in my direction, still fed-up they were, not interested, but there was something in them I'd not seen before, and I've never seen it since, a kind of laziness like someone waking from a long dream and glad to find you there. Cat's eyes have that gleam sometimes, when you stroke them, and they purr and curl themselves into a ball and let you do anything you want. She looked at me this way a moment, and there was a smile lurking somewhere behind her mouth if you gave it a chance, and tearing my slip of paper in half she said, "I'm not paid to advertise. I'm paid to look like this and lure you inside."

She drew aside the curtains and flashed her torch in the darkness. I couldn't see a thing. It was pitch black, like it always is at first until you get used to it and begin to make out the shapes of the other people sitting there, but there were two great heads on the screen and some chap saying to the other, "If you don't come clean I'll put a bullet through you," and somebody broke a pane of glass and a woman screamed.

"Looks all right to me," I said, and began groping for somewhere to sit.

She said, "This isn't the picture, it's the trailer for next week," and she flicked on her torch and showed me a seat in the back row, one away from the gangway.

I sat through the advertisements and the newsreel, and then some chap came and played the organ, and the colours of the curtains over the screen went purple and gold and green—funny, I suppose they think they have to give you your money's worth—and looking around I saw the house was half-empty—and I guessed the girl had been right, the big picture wasn't going to be much, and that's why nobody much was there.

Just before the hall went dark again she came sauntering down the aisle. She had a tray of ice creams, but she didn't even bother to call them out and sell them. She could have been walking in her sleep, so when she went up the other aisle I beckoned to her.

"Got a sixpenny one?" I said.

She looked across at me. I might have been something dead under her feet, and then she must have recognised me, because that half smile came back again, and the lazy look in the eye, and she walked round the back of the seats to me.

"Wafer or cornet?" she said.

I didn't want either, to tell the truth. I just wanted to buy something from her and keep her talking.

"Which do you recommend?" I asked.

She shrugged her shoulders. "Cornets last longer," she said, and put one in my hand before I had time to give her my choice.

"How about one for you too?" I said.

"No, thanks," she said, "I saw them made."

And she walked off, and the place went dark, and there I was sitting with a great sixpenny cornet in my hand looking a fool. The damn thing slopped all over the edge of the holder, spilling onto my shirt, and I had to ram the frozen stuff into my mouth as quick as I could for fear it would all go on my knees, and I turned sideways, because someone came and sat in the empty seat beside the gangway.

I finished it at last, and cleaned myself up with my pocket handkerchief, and then concentrated on the story flashing across the screen. It was a western all right, carts lumbering over prairies, and a train full of bullion being held to ransom, and the heroine in breeches one moment and full evening dress the next. That's the way picture should be, not a bit like real life at all; but as I watched the story I began to notice the whiff of scent in the air, and I didn't know what it was or where it came from, but it was there just the same. There was a man to the right of me, and on my left were two empty seats, and it certainly wasn't the people in front, and I couldn't keep turning round and sniffing.

I'm not a great one for liking scent. It's too often cheap and nasty, but this was different. There was nothing stale about it, or stuffy, or strong; it was like the flowers they sell up in the West End in the big flower shops before you get them on the barrows— three bob a bloom sort of touch, rich chaps buy them for actresses and such—and it was so darn good, the smell of it there, in that murky old picture palace full of cigarette smoke, that it nearly drove me mad.

At last I turned right round in my seat, and I spotted where it came from. It came from the girl, the usherette; she was leaning on the backboard behind me, her arms folded across it.

"Don't fidget," she said. "You're wasting one and twopence. Watch the screen."

But not out loud, so that anyone could hear. In a whisper, for me alone. I couldn't help laughing to myself. The cheek of it! I knew where the scent came from now, and somehow it made me enjoy the picture more. It was as though she was beside me in one of the empty seats and we were looking at the story together.

When it was over, and the lights went on, I saw I'd sat through the last showing and it was nearly ten. Everyone was clearing off for the night. So I waited a bit, and then she came down with her torch and started squinting under the seats to see if anybody had dropped a glove or a purse, the way they do and only remember about afterwards when they got home, and she took no more notice of me than if I'd been a rag which no one would bother to pick up.

I stood up in the back row, alone—the house was clear now—and when she came to me she said, "Move over, you're blocking the gangway," and flashed about with her torch, but there was nothing there, only a empty packet of Player's which the cleaners would throw away in the morning. Then she straightened herself and looked me up and down, and taking off the ridiculous cap from the back of her head that suited her so well she fanned herself with it and said, "Sleeping here tonight?" and then went off, whistling under her breath, and disappeared through the curtains.

It was proper maddening. I'd never been taken so much with a girl in my life. I went into the vestibule after her, but she had gone through a door to the back, behind the box-office place, and the commissionaire chap was already getting the doors to and fixing them for the night. I went out and stood in the street and waited. I felt a bit of a fool, because the odds were that she would come out with a bunch of others, the way girls do. There was the one who had sold me my ticket, and I dare say there were other usherettes up in the balcony, and perhaps a cloakroom attendant too, and they'd all be giggling together, and I wouldn't have the nerve to go up to her.

In a few minutes, though, she came swinging out of the place alone. She had a mac on, belted, and her hands in her pockets, and she had no hat. She walked straight up the street, and she didn't look to right or left of her. I followed, scared that she would turn round and see me off, but she went on walking, fast and direct, staring straight in front of her, and as she moved her copper page-boy hair swung with her shoulders.

Presently she hesitated, then crossed over and stood waiting for a bus. There was a queue of four or five people, so she didn't see me join the queue, and when the bus came she climbed onto it, ahead of the others, and I climbed too, without the slightest notion where it was going, and I couldn't have cared less. Up the stairs she went with me after her, and settled herself in the back seat, yawning, and closed her eyes.

I sat myself down beside her, nervous as a kitten, the point
being that I never did that sort of thing as a rule and expected a
rocket, and when the conductor stumped up and asked for fares I
said, "Two sixpennies, please," because I reckoned she would
never be going the whole distance and this would be bound to
cover her fare and mine too.

He raised his eyebrows—they like to think themselves smart,
some of these fellows—and he said, "Look out for the bumps
when the driver changes gear. He's only just passed his test." And
he went down the stairs chuckling, telling himself he was no end
of a wag, no doubt.

The sound of his voice woke the girl, and she looked at me out
of her sleepy eyes, and looked too at the tickets in my hand—she
must have seen by the colour they were sixpennies—and she
smiled, the first real smile I had got out of her that evening, and
said without any sort of surprise, "Hullo, stranger."

I took out a cigarette, to put myself at ease, and offered her
one, but she wouldn't take it. She just closed her eyes again, to
settle herself to sleep. Then, seeing there was no one else to notice
up on the top deck, only an Air Force chap in the front slopped
over a newspaper, I put out my hand and pulled her head down
on my shoulder, and got my arm round her, snug and comfortable, thinking of course she'd throw it off and blast me to hell. She
didn't, though. She gave a sort of laugh to herself, and settled
down like as if she might have been in an armchair, and she said,
"It's not every night I get a free ride and a free pillow. Wake me
at the bottom of the hill, before we get to the cemetery."

I didn't know what hill she meant, or what cemetery, but I
wasn't going to wake her, not me. I had paid for two sixpennies,
and I was darn well going to get value for my money.

So we sat there together, jogging along in the bus, very close
and very pleasant, and I thought to myself that it was a lot more
fun than sitting at home in the bed-sit reading the football news,
or spending an evening up Highgate at Mr. and Mrs. Thompson's
daughter's place.

Presently I got more daring, and let my head lean against her,
and tightened up my arm a bit, not too obvious-like, but nicely.
Anyone coming up the stairs to the top deck would have taken us
for a courting couple.

Then, after we had had about fourpenny-worth, I got anxious.

The old bus wouldn't be turning round and going back again, when we reached the sixpenny limit; it would pack up for the night, we'd have come to the terminus. And there we'd be, the girl and I, stuck out somewhere at the back of beyond, with no return bus, and I'd got about six bob in my pocket and no more. Six bob would never pay for a taxi, not with a tip and all. Besides, there probably wouldn't be any taxis going.

What a fool I'd been not to come out with more money. It was silly, perhaps, to let it worry me, but I'd acted on impulse right from the start, and if only I'd known how the evening was going to turn out I'd have had my wallet filled. It wasn't often I went out with a girl, and I hate a fellow who can't do the thing in style. Proper slap-up at a Corner House—they're good these days with that help-yourself service—and if she had a fancy for something stronger than coffee or orangeade, well, of course as late as this it wasn't much use, but nearer home I knew where to go. There was a pub where my boss went, and you paid for your gin and kept it there, and could go in and have a drink from your bottle when you felt like it. They have the same sort of racket at the posh night clubs up West, I'm told, but they make you pay through the nose for it.

Anyway, here I was riding a bus to the Lord knows where, with my girl beside me—I called her "my girl" just as if she really was and we were courting—and bless me if I had the money to take her home. I began to fidget about, from sheer nerves, and I fumbled in one pocket after another, in case by a piece of luck I should come across a half crown, or even a ten-bob note I had forgotten all about, and I suppose I disturbed her with all this, because she suddenly pulled my ear and said, "Stop rocking the boat."

Well, I mean to say . . . It just got me. I can't explain why. She held my ear a moment before she pulled it, like as though she were feeling the skin and liked it, and then she just gave it a lazy tug. It's the kind of thing anyone would do to a child, and the way she said it, as if she had known me for years and we were out picnicking together, "Stop rocking the boat." Chummy, matey, yet better than either.

"Look here," I said, "I'm awfully sorry, I've been and done a darn silly thing. I took tickets to the terminus because I wanted to sit beside you, and when we get there we'll be turned out of the bus, and it will be miles from anywhere, and I've only got six bob in my pocket."

"You've got legs, haven't you?" she said.

"What d'you mean, I've got legs?"

"They're meant to walk on. Mine were," she answered.

Then I knew it didn't matter, and she wasn't angry either, and the evening was going to be all right. I cheered up in a second, and gave her a squeeze, just to show I appreciated her being such a sport—most girls would have torn me to shreds—and I said, "We haven't passed a cemetery, as far as I know. Does it matter very much?"

"Oh, there'll be others," she said. "I'm not particular."

I didn't know what to make of that. I thought she wanted to get out at the cemetery stopping point because it was her nearest stop for home, like the way you say, "Put me down at Woolworth's" if you live handy. I puzzled over it for a bit, and then I said, "How do you mean, there'll be others? It's not a thing you see often along a bus route."

"I was speaking in general terms," she answered. "Don't bother to talk, I like you silent best."

It wasn't a slap on the face, the way she said it. Fact was, I knew what she meant. Talking's all very pleasant with people like Mr. and Mrs. Thompson, over supper, and you say how the day has gone, and one of you reads a bit out of the paper, and the other says, "Fancy, there now," and so it goes on, in bits and pieces until one of you yawns, and somebody says, "Who's for bed?" Or it's nice enough with a chap like the boss, having a cuppa midmorning, or about three when there's nothing doing, "I tell you what I think, those blokes in the government are making a mess of things, no better than the last lot," and then we'll be interrupted with someone coming to fill up with petrol. And I like talking to my old Mum when I go and see her, which I don't do often enough, and she tells me how she spanked my bottom when I was a kid, and I sit on the kitchen table like I did then, and she bakes rock cakes and gives me peel, saying, "You always were one for peel." That's talk, that's conversation.

But I didn't want to talk to my girl. I just wanted to keep my arm round her the way I was doing, and rest my chin against her head, and that's what she meant when she said she liked me silent. I liked it too.

One thing bothered me a bit, and that was whether I could kiss her before the bus stopped and we were turned out at the terminus. I mean, putting an arm round a girl is one thing, and kissing her is another. It takes a little time as a rule to warm up. You start off with a long evening ahead of you, and by the time you've been to a picture or a concert, and then had something to eat and to drink, well, you've got yourselves acquainted, and it's the usual thing to end up with a bit of kissing and a cuddle, the girls expect it. Truth to tell, I was never much of a one for kissing. There was a girl I walked out with back home, before I went into the army, and she was quite a good sort, I liked her. But her teeth were a bit prominent, and even if you shut your eyes and tried to forget who it was you were kissing, well, you knew it was her, and there was nothing to it. Good old Doris from next door. But the opposite kind are even worse, the ones that grab you and nearly eat you. You come across plenty of them, when you're in uniform. They're much too eager, and they muss you about, and you get the feeling they can't wait for a chap to get busy about them. I don't mind saying it used to make me sick. Put me dead off, and that's a fact. I suppose I was born fussy. I don't know.

But now, this evening in the bus, it was all quite different. I don't know what it was about the girl—the sleepy eyes, and the copper hair, and somehow not seeming to care if I was there yet liking me at the same time; I hadn't found anything like this before. So I said to myself, "Now, shall I risk it, or shall I wait?" and I knew, from the way the driver was going and the conductor was whistling below and saying "good night" to the people getting off, that the final stop couldn't be far away; and my heart began to thump under my coat, and my neck grow hot below the collar—darn silly, only a kiss, you know, she couldn't kill me—and then . . . It was like diving off a springboard. I thought, "Here goes," and I bent down, and turned her face to me, and lifted her chin with my hand, and kissed her good and proper.

Well, if I was poetical, I'd say what happened then was a revelation. But I'm not poetical, and I can only say that she kissed me back, and it lasted a long time, and it wasn't a bit like Doris.

Then the bus stopped with a jerk, and the conductor called out in a singsong voice, "All out, please." Frankly, I could have wrung his neck.

She gave me a kick on the ankle. "Come on, move," she said,

and I stumbled from my seat and racketted down the stairs, she following behind, and there we were, standing in a street. It was beginning to rain too, not badly but just enough to make you notice and want to turn up the collar of your coat, and we were right at the end of a great wide street, with deserted unlighted shops on either side, the end of the world it looked to me, and sure enough there was a hill over to the left, and at the bottom of the hill a cemetery. I could see the railings and the white tombstones behind, and it stretched a long way, nearly halfway up the hill. There were acres of it.

"God darn it," I said, "is this the place you meant?"

"Could be," she said, looking over her shoulder vaguely, and then she took my arm. "What about a cup of coffee first?" she said.

First . . . ? I wondered if she meant before the long trudge home, or was this home? It didn't really matter. It wasn't much after eleven. And I could do with a cup of coffee, and a sandwich too. There was a stall across the road, and they hadn't shut up shop.

We walked over to it, and the driver was there too, and the conductor, and the Air Force fellow who had been up in front on the top deck. They were ordering cups of tea and sandwiches, and we had the same, only coffee. They cut them tasty at the stalls, the sandwiches, I've noticed it before, nothing stingy about it, good slices of ham between thick white bread, and the coffee is piping hot, full cups too, good value, and I thought to myself, "Six bob will see this lot all right."

I noticed my girl looking at the Air Force chap, sort of thoughtful-like, as though she might have seen him before, and he looked at her too. I couldn't blame him for that. I didn't mind either; when you're out with a girl it gives you a kind of pride if other chaps notice her. And you couldn't miss this one. Not my girl.

Then she turned her back on him, deliberate, and leant with her elbows on the stall, sipping her hot coffee, and I stood beside her doing the same. We weren't stuck up or anything, we were pleasant and polite enough, saying good evening all round, but anyone could tell that we were together, the girl and I, we were on our own. I liked that. Funny, it did something to me inside, gave me a protective feeling. For all they knew we might have been a married couple on our way home.

They were chaffing a bit, the other three and the chap serving the sandwiches and tea, but we didn't join in.

"You want to watch out, in that uniform," said the conductor to the Air Force fellow, "or you'll end up like those others. It's late too, to be out on your own."

They all started laughing. I didn't quite see the point, but I supposed it was a joke.

"I've been awake a long time," said the Air Force fellow. "I know a bad lot when I see one."

"That's what the others said, I shouldn't wonder," remarked the driver, "and we know what happened to them. Makes you shudder. But why pick on the Air Force, that's what I want to know?"

"It's the colour of our uniform," said the fellow. "You can spot it in the dark."

They went on laughing in that way. I lighted up a cigarette, but my girl wouldn't have one.

"I blame the war for all that's gone wrong with the women," said the coffee-stall bloke, wiping a cup and hanging it up behind. "Turned a lot of them balmy, in my opinion. They don't know the difference between right or wrong."

" 'Tisn't that, it's sport that's the trouble," said the conductor. "Develops their muscles and that, what weren't never meant to be developed. Take my two youngsters, f'r instance. The girl can knock the boy down any time, she's a proper little bully. Makes you think."

"That's right," agreed the driver, "equality of the sexes, they call it, don't they? It's the vote that did it. We ought never to have given them the vote."

"Garn," said the Air Force chap, "giving them the vote didn't turn the women balmy. They've always been the same, under the skin. The people out East know how to treat 'em. They keep 'em shut up, out there. That's the answer. Then you don't get any trouble."

"I don't know what my old woman would say if I tried to shut her up," said the driver. And they all started laughing again.

My girl plucked at my sleeve and I saw she had finished her coffee. She motioned with her head towards the street.

"Want to go home?" I said.

Silly. I somehow wanted the others to believe we were going

home. She didn't answer. She just went striding off, her hands in
the pockets of her mac. I said good night and followed her, but
not before I noticed the Air Force fellow staring after her over his
cup of tea.

She walked off along the street, and it was still raining, dreary
somehow, made you want to be sitting over a fire somewhere
snug, and when she had crossed the street, and had come to the
railings outside the cemetery she stopped, and looked up at me,
and smiled.

"What now?" I said.

"Tombstones are flat," she said, "sometimes."

"What if they are?" I asked, bewildered-like.

"You can lie down on them," she said.

She turned and strolled along, looking at the railings, and then
she came to one that was bent wide, and the next beside it broken,
and she glanced up at me and smiled again.

"It's always the same," she said. "You're bound to find a gap if
you look long enough."

She was through that gap in the railings as quick as a knife
through butter. You could have knocked me flat.

"Here, hold on," I said, "I'm not as small as you."

But she was off and away, wandering among the graves. I got
through the gap, puffing and blowing a bit, and then I looked
around, and bless me if she wasn't lying on a long flat gravestone,
with her arms under her head and her eyes closed.

Well, I wasn't expecting anything. I mean, it had been in my
mind to see her home and that. Date her up for the next evening.
Of course, seeing as it was late, we could have stopped a bit when
we came to the doorway of her place. She needn't have gone in
right away. But lying there on the gravestone wasn't hardly natural.

I sat down, and took her hand.

"You'll get wet lying there," I said. Feeble, but I didn't know
what else to say.

"I'm used to that," she said.

She opened her eyes and looked at me. There was a street light
not far away, outside the railings, so it wasn't all that dark, and
anyway in spite of the rain that night wasn't pitch-black, more
murky somehow. I wish I knew how to tell about her eyes, but I'm
not one for fancy talk. You know how a luminous watch shines in

the dark. I've got one myself. When you wake up in the night, there it is on your wrist, like a friend. Somehow my girl's eyes shone like that, but they were lovely too. And they weren't lazy cat's eyes any more. They were loving and gentle, and they were sad, too, all at the same time.

"Used to lying in the rain?" I said.

"Brought up to it," she answered. "They gave us a name in the shelters. The dead-end kids, they used to call us, in the war days."

"Weren't you never evacuated?" I asked.

"Not me," she said. "I never could stop any place. I always came back."

"Parents living?"

"No. Both of them killed by the bomb that smashed my home." She didn't speak tragic-like. Just ordinary.

"Bad luck," I said.

She didn't answer that one. And I sat there, holding her hand, wanting to take her home.

"You been on your job some time, at the picture house?" I asked.

"About three weeks," she said. "I don't stop anywhere long. I'll be moving on again soon."

"Why's that?"

"Restless," she said.

She put up her hands suddenly and took my face and held it. It was gentle the way she did it, not as you'd think.

"You've got a good kind face. I like it," she said to me.

It was queer. The way she said it made me feel daft and soft, not sort of excited like I had been in the bus, and I thought to myself, well, maybe this is it, I've found a girl at last I really want. But not for an evening, casual. For going steady.

"Got a bloke?" I asked.

"No," she said.

"I mean, regular."

"No, never."

It was a funny line of talk to be having in a cemetery, and she lying there like some figure carved on the old tombstone.

"I haven't got a girl either," I said. "Never think about it, the way other chaps do. Faddy, I guess. And then I'm keen on my job. Work in a garage, mechanic you know, repairs, anything that's going. Good pay. I've saved a bit, besides what I send my old Mum. I live in digs. Nice people, Mr. and Mrs. Thompson, and my boss at the garage is a nice chap too. I've never been lonely, and I'm not lonely now. But since I've seen you, it's made me think. You know, it's not going to be the same any more."

She never interrupted once, and somehow it was like speaking my thoughts aloud.

"Going home to the Thompsons is all very pleasant and nice," I said, "and you couldn't wish for kinder people. Good grub too, and we chat a bit after supper, and listen to the wireless. But d'you know, what I want now is different. I want to come along and fetch you from the cinema, when the programme's over, and you'd be standing there by the curtains, seeing the people out, and you'd give me a bit of a wink to show me you'd be going through to change your clothes and I could wait for you. And then you'd come out into the street, like you did tonight, but you wouldn't go off on your own, you'd take my arm, and if you didn't want to wear your coat I'd carry it for you, or a parcel maybe, or whatever you had. Then we'd go off to the Corner House or some place for supper, handy. We'd have a table reserved—they'd know us, the waitresses and them; they'd keep back something special, just for us."

I could picture it too, clear as anything. The table with the ticket on "Reserved." The waitress nodding at us, "Got curried eggs tonight." And we going through to get our trays, and my girl acting like she didn't know me, and me laughing to myself.

"D'you see what I mean?" I said to her. "It's not just being friends, it's more than that."

I don't know if she heard. She lay there looking up at me, touching my ear and my chin in that funny, gentle way. You'd say she was sorry for me.

"I'd like to buy you things," I said, "flowers sometimes. It's nice to see a girl with a flower tucked in her dress, it looks clean and fresh. And for special occasions, birthdays, Christmas, and that, something you'd seen in a shop window, and wanted, but hadn't liked to go in and ask the price. A brooch, perhaps, or a bracelet, something pretty. And I'd go in and get it when you weren't with me, and it'd cost much more than my week's pay, but I wouldn't mind."

I could see the expression on her face, opening the parcel. And she'd put it on, what I'd bought, and we'd go out together, and she'd be dressed up a bit for the purpose, nothing glaring I don't mean, but something that took the eye. You know, saucy.

"It's not fair to talk about getting married," I said, "not in these days, when everything's uncertain. A fellow doesn't mind the uncertainty, but it's hard on a girl. Cooped up in a couple of rooms maybe, and queueing and rations and all. They like their freedom, and being in a job, and not being tied down, the same as us. But it's nonsense the way they were talking back in the coffee stall just now. About girls not being the same as in old days, and the war to blame. As for the way they treat them out East—I've seen some of it. I suppose that fellow meant to be funny, they're all smart alecks in the Air Force, but it was a silly line of talk, I thought."

She dropped her hands to her side and closed her eyes. It was getting quite wet there on the tombstone. I was worried for her, though she had her mac of course, but her legs and feet were damp in her thin stockings and shoes.

"You weren't ever in the Air Force, were you?" she said.

Queer. Her voice had gone quite hard. Sharp, and different. Like as if she was anxious about something, scared even.

"Not me," I said, "I served my time with R.E.M.E. Proper lot they were. No swank, no nonsense. You know where you are with them."

"I'm glad," she said. "You're good and kind. I'm glad."

I wondered if she'd known some fellow in the R.A.F. who had let her down. They're a wild crowd, the ones I've come across. And I remembered the way she'd looked at the boy drinking his tea at the stall. Reflective, somehow. As if she was thinking back. I couldn't expect her not to have been around a bit, with her looks, and then brought up to play about the shelters, without parents, like she said. But I didn't want to think of her being hurt by anyone.

"Why, what's wrong with them?" I said. "What's the R.A.F. done to you?"

"They smashed my home," she said.

"That was the Germans, not our fellows."

"It's all the same, they're killers, aren't they?" she said.

I looked down at her, lying on the tombstone, and her voice wasn't hard any more, like when she'd asked me if I'd been in the Air Force, but it was tired, and sad, and oddly lonely, and it did something queer to my stomach, right in the pit of it, so that I wanted to do the darnedest silliest thing and take her home with me, back to where I lived with Mr. and Mrs. Thompson, and say to Mrs. Thompson—she was a kind old soul, she wouldn't mind—"Look, this is my girl. Look after her." Then I'd know she'd be safe, she'd be all right, nobody could do anything to hurt her. That was the thing I was afraid of suddenly, that someone would come along and hurt my girl.

I bent down and put my arms round her and lifted her up close.

"Listen," I said, "it's raining hard. I'm going to take you home. You'll catch your death, lying here on the wet stone."

"No," she said, her hands on my shoulders, "nobody ever sees me home. You're going back where you belong, alone."

"I won't leave you here," I said.

"Yes, that's what I want you to do. If you refuse I shall be angry. You wouldn't want that, would you?"

I stared at her, puzzled. And her face was queer in the murky old light there, whiter than before, but it was beautiful, Jesus Christ, it was beautiful. That's blasphemy. But I can't say it no other way.

"What do you want me to do?" I asked.

"I want you to go and leave me here, and not look back," she said, "like someone dreaming, sleepwalking, they call it. Go back walking through the rain. It will take you hours. It doesn't matter, you're young and strong and you've got long legs. Go back to your room, wherever it is, and get into bed, and go to sleep, and wake and have your breakfast in the morning, and go off to work, the same as you always do."

"What about you?"

"Never mind about me. Just go."

"Can I call for you at the cinema tomorrow night? Can it be like what I was telling you, you know . . . going steady?"

She didn't answer. She only smiled. She sat quite still, looking in my face, and then she closed her eyes and threw back her head and said, "Kiss me again, stranger."

I left her, like she said. I didn't look back. I climbed through the railings of the cemetery, out onto the road. No one seemed to be about, and the coffee stall by the bus stop had closed down, the boards were up.

I started walking the way the bus had brought us. The road was

straight, going on forever. A High Street it must have been. There
were shops on either side, and it was right away northeast of London, nowhere I'd ever been before. I was proper lost, but it didn't
seem to matter. I felt like a sleepwalker, just as she said.

I kept thinking of her all the time. There was nothing else, only
her face in front of me as I walked. They had a word for it in the
Army, when a girl gets a fellow that way, so he can't see straight
or hear right or know what he's doing; and I thought it a lot of
cock, or it only happened to drunks, and now I knew it was true
and it had happened to me. I wasn't going to worry any more
about how she'd get home; she'd told me not to, and she must
have lived handy, she'd never have ridden out so far else, though
it was funny living such a way from her work. But maybe in time
she'd tell me more, bit by bit. I wouldn't drag it from her. I had
one thing fixed in my mind, and that was to pick her up the next
evening from the picture palace. It was firm and set, and nothing
would budge me from that. The hours in between would just be a
blank for me until 10 P.M. came round.

I went on walking in the rain, and presently a lorry came along
and I thumbed a lift, and the driver took me a good part of the
way before he had to turn left in the other direction, and so I got
down and walked again, and it must have been close on three
when I got home.

I would have felt bad, in an ordinary way, knocking up Mr.
Thompson to let me in, and it had never happened before either,
but I was all lit up inside from loving my girl, and I didn't seem to
mind. He came down at last and opened the door. I had to ring
several times before he heard, and there he was, grey with sleep,
poor old chap, his pyjamas all crumpled from the bed.

"Whatever happened to you?" he said. "We've been worried,
the wife and me. We thought you'd been knocked down, run over.
We came back here and found the house empty and your supper
not touched."

"I went to the pictures," I said.

"The pictures?" He stared up at me, in the passageway. "The
pictures stop at ten o'clock."

"I know," I said, "I went walking after that. Sorry. Good night."

And I climbed up the stairs to my room, leaving the old chap
muttering to himself and bolting the door, and I heard Mrs.

Thompson calling from her bedroom, "What is it? Is it him? Is he come home?"

I'd put them to trouble and to worry, and I ought to have gone in there and then and apologised, but I couldn't somehow, it wouldn't have come right; so I shut my door and threw off my clothes and got into bed, and it was like as if she was with me still, my girl, in the darkness.

They were a bit quiet at breakfast the next morning, Mr. and Mrs. Thompson. They didn't look at me. Mrs. Thompson gave me my kipper without a word, and he went on looking at his news-paper.

I ate my breakfast, and then I said, "I hope you had a nice evening up at Highgate?" and Mrs. Thompson, with her mouth a bit tight, she said, "Very pleasant, thank you, we were home by ten," and she gave a little sniff and poured Mr. Thompson out another cup of tea.

We went on being quiet, no one saying a word, and then Mrs. Thompson said, "Will you be in to supper this evening?" and I said, "No, I don't think so. I'm meeting a friend," and then I saw the old chap look at me over his spectacles.

"If you're going to be late," he said, "we'd best put out the key for you."

Then he went on reading his paper. You could tell they were proper hurt that I didn't tell them anything, or say where I was going.

I went off to work, and we were busy at the garage that day, one job after the other came along, and any other time I wouldn't have minded. I liked a full day and often worked overtime, but today I wanted to get away before the shops closed; I hadn't thought about anything else since the idea came into my head.

It was getting on for half past four, and the boss came to me and said, "I promised the doctor he'd have his Austin this evening, I said you'd be through with it by seven-thirty. That's O.K., isn't it?"

My heart sank. I'd counted on getting off early, because of what I wanted to do. Then I thought quickly that if the boss let me off now, and I went out to the shop before it closed, and came back again to do the job on the Austin, it would be all right, so I said, "I don't mind working a bit of overtime, but I'd like to slip out now, for half an hour, if you're going to be here. There's something I want to buy before the shops shut."

He told me that suited him, so I took off my overalls and washed and got my coat and I went off to the line of shops down at the bottom of Haverstock Hill. I knew the one I wanted. It was a jeweller's, where Mr. Thompson used to take his clock to be repaired, and it wasn't a place where they sold trash at all, but good stuff, solid silver frames and that, and cutlery.

There were rings, of course, and a few fancy bangles, but I didn't like the look of them. All the girls in the N.A.A.F.I. used to wear bangles with charms on them, quite common it was, and I went on staring in at the window and then I spotted it, right at the back.

It was a brooch. Quite small, not much bigger than your thumbnail, but with a nice blue stone on it and a pin at the back, and it was shaped like a heart. That was what got me, the shape. I stared at it a bit, and there wasn't a ticket to it, which meant it would cost a bit, but I went in and asked to have a look at it. The jeweller got it out of the window for me, and he gave it a bit of a polish and turned it this way and that, and I saw it pinned on my girl, showing up nice on her frock or her jumper, and I knew this was it.

"I'll take it," I said, and then asked him the price.

I swallowed a bit when he told me, but I took out my wallet and counted the notes, and he put the heart in a box wrapped up careful with cotton wool, and made a neat package of it tied with fancy string. I knew I'd have to get an advance from the boss before I went off work that evening, but he was a good chap and I was certain he'd give it to me.

I stood outside the jeweller's, with the packet for my girl safe in my breast pocket, and I heard the church clock strike a quarter to five. There was time to slip down to the cinema and make sure she understood about the date for the evening, and then I'd beat it fast up the road and get back to the garage, and I'd have the Austin done by the time the doctor wanted it.

When I got to the cinema my heart was beating like a sledgehammer and I could hardly swallow. I kept picturing to myself how she'd look, standing there by the curtains going in, with that velvet jacket and the cap on the back of her head.

There was a bit of a queue outside, and I saw they'd changed the programme. The poster of the western had gone, with the cowboy throwing a knife in the Indian's guts, and they had instead a lot of girls dancing, and some chap prancing in front of them with a walking stick. It was a musical.

I went in, and didn't go near the box office but looked straight to the curtains, where she'd be. There was an usherette there all right, but it wasn't her. This was a great tall girl, who looked silly in the clothes, and she was trying to do two things at once—tear off the slips of tickets as the people went past, and hang on to her torch at the same time.

I waited a moment. Perhaps they'd switched over positions and my girl had gone up to the circle. When the last lot had got in through the curtains and there was a pause and she was free, I went up to her and I said, "Excuse me, do you know where I could have a word with the other young lady?"

She looked at me. "What other young lady?"

"The one who was here last night, with copper hair," I said.

She looked at me closer then, suspicious-like.

"She hasn't shown up today," she said. "I'm taking her place."

"Not shown up?"

"No. And it's funny you should ask. You're not the only one. The police was here not long ago. They had a word with the manager, and the commissionaire too, and no one's said anything to me yet, but I think there's been trouble."

My heart beat different then. Not excited, bad. Like when someone's ill, took to hospital, sudden.

"The police?" I said. "What were they here for?"

"I told you, I don't know," she answered, "but it was something to do with her, and the manager went with them to the police station, and he hasn't come back yet. This way, please, circle on the left, stalls to the right."

I just stood there, not knowing what to do. It was like as if the floor had been knocked away from under me.

The tall girl tore another slip off a ticket and then she said to me, over her shoulder, "Was she a friend of yours?"

"Sort of," I said. I didn't know what to say.

"Well, if you ask me, she was queer in the head, and it wouldn't surprise me if she'd done away with herself and they'd found her dead. No, ice creams served in the interval, after the newsreel."

I went out and stood in the street. The queue was growing for the cheaper seats, and there were children too, talking, excited. I brushed past them and started walking up the street, and I felt sick inside, queer. Something had happened to my girl. I knew it now. That was why she had wanted to get rid of me last night, and for me not to see her home. She was going to do herself in, there in the cemetery. That's why she talked funny and looked so white, and now they'd found her, lying there on the gravestone by the railings.

If I hadn't gone away and left her she'd have been all right. If I'd stayed with her just five minutes longer, coaxing her, I'd have got her round to my way of thinking and seen her home, standing no nonsense, and she'd be at the picture palace now, showing the people to their seats.

It might be it wasn't as bad as what I feared. It might be she was found wandering, lost her memory and got picked up by the police and taken off, and then they found out where she worked and that, and now the police wanted to check up with the manager at the cinema to see if it was so. If I went down to the police station and asked them there, maybe they'd tell me what had happened, and I could say she was my girl, we were walking out, and it wouldn't matter if she didn't recognise me even, I'd stick to the story. I couldn't let down my boss, I had to get that job done on the Austin, but afterwards, when I'd finished, I could go down to the police station.

All the heart had gone out of me, and I went back to the garage hardly knowing what I was doing, and for the first time ever the smell of the place turned my stomach, the oil and the grease, and there was a chap roaring up his engine, before backing out his car, and a great cloud of smoke coming from his exhaust, filling the workshop with stink.

I went and got my overalls, and put them on, and fetched the tools, and started on the Austin, and all the time I was wondering what it was that had happened to my girl, if she was down at the police station, lost and lonely, or if she was lying somewhere . . . dead. I kept seeing her face all the time like it was last night.

It took me an hour and a half, not more, to get the Austin ready for the road, filled up with petrol and all, and I had her facing outwards to the street for the owner to drive out, but I was all in by then, dead tired, and the sweat pouring down my face. I had a bit of a wash and put on my coat, and I felt the package in the breast pocket. I took it out and looked at it, done so neat with the fancy ribbon, and I put it back again, and I hadn't noticed the boss come in—I was standing with my back to the door.

"Did you get what you want?" he said, cheerful-like and smiling.

He was a good chap, never out of temper, and we got along well.

"Yes," I said.

But I didn't want to talk about it. I told him the job was done and the Austin was ready to drive away. I went to the office with him so that he could note down the work done, and the overtime, and he offered me a fag from the packet lying on his desk beside the evening paper.

"I see Lady Luck won the three-thirty," he said. "I'm a couple of quid up this week."

He was entering my work in his ledger, to keep the payroll right.

"Good for you," I said.

"Only backed it for a place, like a clot," he said. "She was twenty-five to one. Still, it's all in the game."

I didn't answer. I'm not one for drinking, but I needed one bad, just then. I mopped my forehead with my handkerchief. I wished he'd get on with the figures, and say good night, and let me go.

"Another poor devil's had it," he said. "That's the third now in three weeks, ripped right up the guts, same as the others. He died in hospital this morning. Looks like there's a hoodoo on the R.A.F."

"What was it, flying jets?" I asked.

"Jets?" he said. "No, damn it, murder. Sliced up the belly, poor sod. Don't you ever read the papers? It's the third one in three weeks, done identical, all Air Force fellows, and each time they've found 'em near a graveyard or a cemetery. I was saying just now, to that chap who came in for petrol, it's not only men who go off their rockers and turn sex maniacs, but women too. They'll get this one all right though, you see. It says in the paper they've a line on her, and expect an arrest shortly. About time too, before another poor blighter cops it."

He shut up his ledger and stuck his pencil behind his ear.

"Like a drink?" he said. "I've got a bottle of gin in the cupboard."

"No," I said, "no, thanks very much. I've . . . I've got a date."

"That's right," he said smiling, "enjoy yourself."

I walked down the street and bought an evening paper. It was like what he said about the murder. They had it on the front page. They said it must have happened about 2 A.M. Young fellow in the Air Force, in northeast London. He had managed to stagger to a call box and get through to the police, and they found him there on the floor of the box when they arrived.

He made a statement in the ambulance before he died. He said a girl called to him, and he followed her, and he thought it was just a bit of love-making—he'd seen her with another fellow drinking coffee at a stall a little while before—and he thought she'd thrown this other fellow over and had taken a fancy to him, and then she got him, he said, right in the guts.

It said in the paper that he had given the police a full description of her, and it said also that the police would be glad if the man who had been seen with the girl earlier in the evening would come forward to help in identification.

I didn't want the paper any more. I threw it away. I walked about the streets till I was tired, and when I guessed Mr. and Mrs. Thompson had gone to bed I went home, and groped for the key they'd left on a piece of string hanging inside the letterbox, and I let myself in and went upstairs to my room.

Mrs. Thompson had turned down the bed and put a Thermos of tea for me, thoughtful-like, and the evening paper, the late edition.

They'd got her. About three o'clock in the afternoon. I didn't read the writing nor the name nor anything. I sat down on my bed, and took up the paper, and there was my girl staring up at me from the front page.

Then I took the package from my coat and undid it, and threw away the wrapper and the fancy string, and sat there looking down at the little heart I held in my hand.

The Chamois

We were told there were chamois in the Pindus. The report came to us in a roundabout way. A member of the British school of archaeology in Athens, writing to Stephen about the season's "dig," reported that he had dined with a friend, John Evans, who had been staying in one of the monasteries at Meteora. During his three-day visit, a man from Kalabaka with supplies for the monastery told one of the monks that a bus driver, bringing passengers over the pass from Malakasi, had stopped for his usual five minutes at the store, and picked up a rumour from the storekeeper that woodcutters had seen a doe and a kid flit past the young beech growth about five hundred yards away. The story was as vague as that. Yet it was enough to make Stephen cancel our Austrian plans, and book seats on the Athens plane for the following week.

This is what it means to be a fanatic—but a fanatic, that is to say, in a very special sense. It has little in common with the obsession of the politician or the artist, for instance, for both of these understand in a greater or lesser degree the impulse which drives them. But the sportsman-fanatic—that is another matter entirely. His thoughts fixed solely on a vision of that mounted trophy against the wall, the eyes now dead that were once living, the tremulous nostrils stilled, the sensitive pricked ears closed to sound at the instant when the rifle shot echoed from the naked rocks, this man hunts his quarry through some instinct unknown even to himself.

Stephen was a sportsman of this kind. It was not the skill needed that drove him, nor the delight and excitement of the stalk itself, but a desire, so I told myself, to destroy something beautiful and rare. Hence his obsession with chamois.

Chamois, as all sportsmen know, have become scarce through the years. They are hardly seen today in Switzerland and Austria. Stephen tried to explain the reasons once. The breakup of the big estates, two world wars, promiscuous shooting by peasants which would have been forbidden in the old days, and the growing popularity of the Alps, and indeed of every region of mountains amongst climbers and tourists—all this has led to a general trampling and desecration of land once sacred to the chamois.

He is the shyest of all creatures. He shuns human beings, and does not mix with other deer. Always on the alert for anything that may threaten his safety, his note of warning is a curious shrill whistle; and the first hint of danger will send him headlong to the highest and most inaccessible crags. The buck lives alone at all times of the year, except in the late fall, in the brief rutting season, when the chemical change in his blood drives him to the doe. This, according to Stephen, is the moment to catch him; this is when he falls a prey. Watchfulness, intuition of danger, that sixth sense which normally keeps him safe, all these lie in abeyance because of the urge for a mate. He deserts the narrow ledges and the steep cliff faces, and follows the little herd of does and yearlings, the secretive shy mothers who have no need of him until now; and then blood answers blood, the chase begins, the wild scamper over rock and precipice, the little kids surprised at the sudden fever of their mothers, so quickly stirred and put to flight by the black stranger. For he is black in winter, the adult chamois buck: the reddish-yellow summer coat has gone, and the thick protecting fur covers him, the wave of long hair rising on his back like a crest.

When Stephen talked about stalking chamois his whole expression changed. The features became more aquiline, the nose sharpened, the chin narrowed, and his eyes—steel blue—somehow took on the cold brilliance of a northern sky. I am being very frank about my husband. He attracted me at those times, and he repelled me too. This man, I told myself when I first met him, is a perfectionist. And he has no compassion. Gratified like all women who find themselves sought after and desired—a mutual love for Sibelius had been our common ground at our first encounter—after a few weeks in his company I shut my eyes to further judgment, because being with him gave me pleasure. It flattered my self-esteem. The perfectionist, admired by other women, now sought me. Marriage was in every sense a *coup*. It was only afterwards that I knew myself deceived.

Some men are born adult, without the redeeming and endearing faults of childhood; Stephen was one of them. Born and bred in the hard home of a Scots father and an Italian mother—none of your beautiful opera singers, but the daughter of a Milan industrialist—he shook off all family ties at fifteen, and began earning his living in a shipping office in Glasgow. Those early days would make a book, and it may get written one day, but not now. Now I want to tell how we sought the chamois.

Stephen handed me the letter across the breakfast table, and said briefly, "I shall telegraph Bruno right away and say we have changed our plans." Bruno was the Austrian friend who, at great trouble to himself and with much forethought and care, had arranged the shoot in his own Alpine district, solely to please Stephen. Chamois had been the bait. Deer in plenty would not have tempted him: it must be chamois.

"What's the difference," I asked, "between chamois in Austria and chamois in northern Greece?"

The sport meant nothing to me. I went for adventure, for mountain air. Stephen was welcome to go off by himself all day, either alone or with other friends armed with rifles. My holiday worked in, a breathing space, stock-taking for a woman who had not borne children.

"The difference," said Stephen, his blue eyes colder than ever, "lies in the rarity of the prey. I have never heard of anyone who has shot chamois in the Pindus, or anywhere else in Greece."

"Then probably the story is not true," I suggested. "The woodcutters saw a wild goat, and mistook it for a chamois."

"Probably," said Stephen, but he got up from the breakfast table, and a few minutes afterwards I heard him give out the telegram on the phone to his friend in Austria.

I watched his back, and the powerful shoulders. He looked taller than his six feet two inches because of his build, and his voice became impatient as he spelt out the Austrian address, which the telephone operator did not immediately understand. It held the same impatience with a mentality less quick and incisive than his own that had been apparent to me ten years previously, when we had become engaged. He had taken me to see that austere house of his near Portland Place—a far cry from the shipping office in Glasgow, for he was head of the London office by then—and the trophies on the wall. I wondered straightaway how he could sit at peace there, of an evening, with the row of heads staring down at him. There were no pictures, no flowers: only the heads of chamois. The concession to melody was the radiogram and the stack of records of classical music.

Foolishly, I had asked, "Why only chamois?"

He answered at once, "They fear Man."

This might have led to an argument about animals in general, domestic, wild, and those which adapt themselves to the whims and vagaries of the human race; but instead he changed the subject abruptly, put on a Sibelius record, and presently made love to me, intently but without emotion. I was surprised but pleased. I thought, "We are suited to one another. There will be no demands. Each of us will be self-contained and not beholden to the other."

All this came true, but something was amiss. There was a flaw —not only the nonappearance of children, but a division of the spirit. The communion of flesh which brought us together was in reality a chasm, and I despised the bridge we made. Perhaps he did as well. I had been endeavouring for ten years to build for myself a ledge of safety.

"So we are going to Greece?" I said to Stephen that evening, when he came home rather later than usual, and threw down the air tickets and a brochure and a map. "You've definitely made up your mind, although you haven't confirmed the rumour about the chamois seen near a mountain pass?"

"I have confirmed the rumour," said Stephen. "I traced the fellow Evans to a bank in Athens, and put through a call to him. He says the story is true. The monk at Meteora had spoken since to the bus driver himself. The driver is a brother-in-law of the man who owns the store and saw the woodcutters. There are no wild goats in the area. It was chamois all right."

A smile should be a means of communication. It is not always, though, and it was not with Stephen when he spoke of chamois. The smile was secretive, an answer to a question which he put to himself, but without pleasure. Then he left the living room and went to the music room—we called it that because of the radiogram, and the television, and my piano, an odd juxtaposition of objects that bore a relation to one another—and I knew he was standing there, looking up at the chamois trophies on the wall. There were twenty altogether, including three does and two kids shot in error. They were all exquisitely cured and mounted, a silver plate beneath each head giving the date and place of the kill. As I said before, chamois are scarce these days. They retreat more and more to the inaccessible crags. There are no longer the big chamois drives in Switzerland, and for stalking you must know your territory, and your host too, for these matters are not easily arranged.

When Stephen returned from the music room he was wiping his hands on a rag, and I knew from his same smile that he had been cleaning his rifle. It was not the comforted smile of one pottering with a favourite hobby—the photographic expert, the Sunday painter, the carpenter—or even the country well-being of the sportsman before an annual partridge drive (I had brothers once who shot). This was a killer's smile, obeying an impulse deep within himself.

"Snap out of it," I said suddenly.

He looked across at me, startled, as I was myself, by the curious note of urgency in my voice.

"Snap out of what?" he asked.

"This obsession with chamois," I said. "It isn't balanced."

I thought for a moment that he would hit me. The look of terror—and it was terror, swiftly and indecently unmasked—came and went at the speed of thought, to be replaced by anger, the cold anger of a man caught off guard.

"You don't have to come with me," he said. "Make your own plans. I'm going. Do as you please."

He did not reply to my attack, though. The answer was evasion.

"Oh, I'll come, right enough," I said. "I may be in search of something myself, for all you know."

I did the irritating, wifely thing of tidying, snapping off the dead head of a flower, straightening a cushion, but I felt his eyes on my back. It was not a comfortable sensation. However, the tension passed, and at dinner we were on our usual easy footing of mutual tolerance, and this continued through the days that followed before our departure.

A certain date in mid-October found us on the plane for Athens. The letter of regret and disappointment from our friend in Austria had been thrown, almost unskimmed, into the wastepaper basket. Instead, new contacts, arranged through Stephen's own shipping firm, had fixed our itinerary in Greece. Use people, whenever you can, as a means to an end. This was one of Stephen's maxims. Drop them when they no longer serve your purpose.

I do not give the year of this particular October in case there should be any recognition of individuals. It is enough to say that it

was in the early fifties, there was as yet no Cyprus question, the
summer had been hot, and there had been two earthquakes.

It might have been midsummer still when we landed to drop
and pick up passengers in Rome. As we stood on the hot tarmac
the sun was merciless, and the ugly high buildings fringing the airport, alternating with wasteland, gave off a yellow glare. How
different was Athens. A cool serenity seemed to come to us even
in the aircraft, as we stared down on Corinth bathed in the afterglow of sunset; and the airport—at the time I speak of—was like
a casual provincial station, with attendants in shirt sleeves smiling,
handling passports and baggage checks as though all time were
theirs and would endure forever.

A rattling bus took us into Athens. I liked my husband's company when travelling. He never fussed, tickets were not mislaid,
and he left me to sort impressions for myself. There was no elbow
jerking, no sudden exclamations at new things perceived. But
later, over a drink or at dinner, we would find we had usually noticed the same points of beauty or interest. This thread of appreciation was one of our few links.

That evening we were met at the airport terminus by a Greek
from the shipping firm contacted by Stephen—his name was inevitably George—and taken to our hotel. Once bathed and changed,
we were joined by Stephen's archaeologist friend, whom I will call
Burns, and the John Evans who had stayed at Meteora and first
passed on the rumour of the chamois. They had come to take us
out to dinner. These arrangements were all part of Stephen's
clocklike mind, his talent for seizing upon the essential.

There was to be no ambling in Athens for us, no strolling on
the Acropolis. Later, when we returned from the Pindus, if we
had the time, said Stephen, but meanwhile one certainty alone lay
ahead of us, the knowledge that tickets had already been taken on
the train leaving Athens for the north the following morning. I
can remember still the look of bewilderment on the face of young
John Evans, an expert on Byzantine churches; and even Burns,
who knew something of Stephen's vagaries, was shocked at what
must have seemed excess of passion.

"You surely could afford one day," he said, "or even half a day.
I could call for you early, with my car . . ." but Stephen brushed
him aside.

"How's the weather in the north?" he asked. "You've checked that the road over the pass is open?"

I left them to it, the pointing of fingers on maps, the tracing of mountain villages, the tracks and contours on maps of larger scale, and basked for the one evening allowed to me in the casual, happy atmosphere of the taverna where we dined. I enjoyed poking my finger in a pan and choosing my own piece of lamb. I liked the chatter and the laughter from neighbouring tables. The gay intensity of talk—none of which I could understand, naturally—reminded me of left-bank Paris. A man from one table would suddenly rise to his feet and stroll over to another, discussion would follow, argument at heat perhaps swiftly dissolving into laughter. This, I thought to myself, has been happening through the centuries under this same sky, in the warm air with a bite to it, the sap drink pungent as the sap running through the veins of these Greeks, witty and cynical as Aristophanes himself, in the shadow, unmoved, inviolate, of Athene's Parthenon.

"The cabin store will be open then?" pursued Stephen. "They don't shut down when the weather breaks? And the bus runs from Kalabaka until the pass is closed by snow?"

I felt it time to intervene. Our hosts were drained, and had no more to give.

"Listen, Stephen" I said, "if the pass is closed, and the store is burnt to the ground, I'm still willing to take a groundsheet and sleep in the open, so long as you find your chamois. Let's give it a miss until tomorrow. I want to see the Parthenon by moonlight."

I had my way. They floodlight it now, to great advantage I am told, but it was not so then, and since it was late in the year there were few tourists. My companions were all intelligent men, including my own husband, and they had the sense to stay mute. I suppose, being a woman, I confuse beauty with sentiment, but, as I looked on the Parthenon for the first time in my life, I found myself crying. It had never happened to me before. Your sunset weepers I despise. It was not full moon, or anywhere near it. The half circle put me in mind of the labrys, the Cretan double axe, and the pillars were the most ghostly in consequence. What a shock for the modern aesthete, I thought when my crying was done, if he could see the ruddy glow of colour, the painted eyes, the garish lips, the orange-reds and blues that were there once, and Athene herself a giantess on her pedestal touched by the rising sun. Even in those distant times the exigencies of a state religion had brought their own traffic, the buying and selling of doves, of trinkets: to find himself, a man had to go to the woods, to the hills.

"Come on," said Stephen. "It's beautiful and stark, if you like, but so is St. Pancras station at 4 A.M. It depends on your association of ideas."

We crammed into Burns's small car, and went back to our hotel.

We left Athens early the next morning, seen off at the station by our still-bewildered friends. Stephen, of course, had no regrets. As to myself, it was like being dragged from Paris at seventeen, having glimpsed the Champs-Élysées overnight. Athens had that same surge of life, that same bright air, the crowded morning streets at once urgent and indolent.

We rattled our way north. Stephen at his maps again, myself at the window. The plains of Thessaly to me spelt armies of the past, to my husband the narrowing of distance between us and the chamois.

We changed trains at one point. Where it was I cannot remember. There were signs of a recent earthquake, houses in half, buildings in rubble, unmoving to our eyes who had seen all this in war. The bright light faded. It began to rain. The earth turned yellow-brown, and dispirited women, their faces veiled from the hidden sun like Moslems, scratched at the lean ground. As we passed through empty stations donkeys brayed. A rising wind drove the rain slantways. In the far distance I saw mountains, and touching Stephen on the knees I pointed to them. Once again he consulted his map. Somewhere, amongst that misty range, snowcapped and hidden from us, would be Olympus, stronghold of the gods. Not for us, alas, that ultimate discovery. Our trek was westward, to the chamois.

Kalabaka, crouching muddied and wet at the foot of rockbound Meteora, offered no temptation as a refuge. Nevertheless, it was our station of descent. Rapid enquiries—and Stephen's smattering of Greek seemed to me well laced with Italian—soon showed that we had, in the full sense of the phrase, missed our bus. There was only one a day, at this time of the year, which climbed the winding road to the pass: and it left in the early morning. Stephen was not to be deterred. Means of transport other than bus must be found, and we sat down in the ticket collector's office—ourselves, the ticket collector, a bearded patriarch, a young boy, the ticket collector's brother-in-law, who happened to be passing by—all gesturing, arguing in high excitement the possibility of our reaching the top of the pass before nightfall.

The ticket collector's brother-in-law brought light out of darkness. His nephew had a car. A good car. A car that not only held the road and the twists in the road, but whose lights worked. The three of us went to a café to celebrate, and while we pledged each other in coffee dregs and ouzo the nephew's car was driven to a nearby garage to be filled with petrol. The nephew had a walleye. I could not help wondering if the walleye would affect his driving. As we started off, taking the road out of Kalabaka like a speedway, it occurred to me that the walleye gave him confidence, making him unconscious of danger. It was his left eye, and as we started to climb it was this side of his face that was turned to the precipices.

Climbing a mountain road by car is always a doubtful pleasure. As a test of skill for experts it is endurable. In northern Greece, however, after autumn rains, when the road is heavy with loose stones and falls of earth, and it is late afternoon, and the car's chassis shakes in protest, and its engine groans as it approaches each fresh bend, and the walleyed chauffeur suddenly seizes the crucifix hanging on the dashboard and kisses it with fervour, in these circumstances climbing a mountain road brings destruction of thought. Stephen, on the right side of the car, had only bank to daunt him, but I, glancing leftwards through the window to the tumbling gorge below, was less happily placed. The grunts of the chauffeur, harmonising with each change of gear as we came to the bends in the road, were not conducive to a sense of security, nor, as I peered ahead through the rain, was the long sight of the distant bridge spanning a ravine over which we must in some five minutes cross. The bridge looked broken. Planks from it appeared tossed amongst the boulders far below. I was not altogether surprised that our walleyed driver kissed his crucifix, but his action did not increase my confidence.

The dusk crept upon us. Our chauffeur switched on his lights. This, more than the kissing of the crucifix, seemed a measure of defeat, for they hardly broke the growing dark. The road wound its way ever upward, and at no place was there a possibility of turning and going back to Kalabaka. Like Roland in *Childe Harold,* we must go on, naught else remained to do. I shut my eyes. And it was only then, after a moment or two, that I heard Stephen say beside me, "What's the matter? Feeling sick?" I could only conclude that, as always, my husband lacked perception.

The final roar of the engine and a furious grinding of gears warned me that death was imminent, and, not to miss the experience, I opened my eyes. We had come to our journey's end.

I do not know what buildings stand at Malakasi today. For all I know there may be a motel. In the year of which I speak there was a log cabin at the top of the pass, standing a little apart from the road, with room enough for a bus or lorry to park beside it. Forests of beech surrounded the cabin. The rain had ceased. The crisp cold air had all the stark invigoration that comes with a height of some seven thousand feet. A single light shone from the window of the cabin. Our driver sounded his horn, and as he did so the door of the cabin opened and a man stood on the threshold.

"Come on," said Stephen, "help me unload. We'll leave them to the explanations."

My trepidation had vanished the moment the car stopped. One sniff of that mountain air was like a whiff of alcohol to an addict. I got out and stamped and stretched my legs, and if Stephen had said to me that we were to start climbing now, on foot, striking off through the trees in darkness in search of chamois, I would have followed him. Instead, we carried our traps through to the log cabin.

While Stephen interposed his odd mixture of Greek and Italian in the torrent of discussion taking place between the walleyed driver and the tenant of the cabin, I had time to look around me. The room was half café, half store, shaped like a short L, the floor earth-covered, a ladder rising from it to the lofts above, and a small kitchen at one end. I could smell food, something cooking in a pan. There were rows of goods, cigarettes, chocolate, coils of rope, toothpaste, cloths—all the things you find in a well-stocked village shop—and the owner, a cheerful-looking man of middle age, received us without surprise, shaking our hands in true Greek courtesy. Indeed, it might have been every day that a fanatical

Englishman in search of the mythical chamois arrived at his store after dark demanding supper and a bed.

I made gestures of smoking, and pointed to his store of cartons behind the counter, but he brushed the idea aside, and with a bow offered me one from his own packet. Then, bowing still, he led me up the ladder to the communicating rooms above, and I saw that we must all of us, proprietor, walleyed driver, Stephen and myself, share the pile of blankets for the night, heaped carelessly upon the wooden floor—unless I removed myself, in modesty, to a cupboard. I smiled and nodded, hoping to express appreciation, and followed my host down the ladder to the store below.

The first person I saw was Stephen. He had taken his rifle from its cover, and was showing it to a small, rat-faced man who had appeared in shirt sleeves from the kitchen. The rat-faced man was nodding in great excitement, and then, in fine pantomime, made a pretence of crouching, animal fashion, after which he leapt in the air, to the applause of our walleyed driver.

"It's all right," called Stephen at sight of me, "there's no mistake. These are the chaps who know the woodcutters who saw the chamois."

His voice was triumphant. Foolishly, I was reminded of the House that Jack built. This was the bull, that worried the dog, that killed the cat, that ate the malt . . . Had we come all this way to the top of the Pindus mountains only to destroy?

"Fine," I said, shrugging my shoulders, and making a concession to femininity I took out my lipstick. There was a little cracked mirror hanging behind the counter. The men watched in admiration. My status was established. I knew that, without a word from me, those blankets in the room above would be redistributed before the night was older, and the best folded for me in the cupboard apart. The Greeks paid tribute to Gaia before the birth of Zeus.

"That small chap understands Italian," said Stephen, as we sat down to eggs fried in oil and a tinned sardine. "He was in some prison camp during the war. He says the woodcutters have gone down for the winter, but there's some fellow still grazing goats a couple of hundred feet higher up, above the tree line, who knows all about chamois. He sometimes calls in here during the evening. He may look in tonight."

I glanced across at our three companions. The rat-faced cook had returned to his pots and pans, and our walleyed driver was being shaved by the proprietor of the store. He leant back at ease, a towel round his shoulders, his face in lather, the walleye staring up in confidence at the broad-shouldered, smiling proprietor, who leant over him, razor in hand. Somewhere a cracked loudspeaker gave forth a South American song. We were at the top of a Pindus pass. Nothing was really out of place.

I finished spooning sheep's cream from a saucer—our dessert— and Stephen began drawing a chamois head on the bare boards of our table. The proprietor of the store came to watch, and with him our walleyed driver, newly shaved. Somewhere outside, I thought I heard a dog barking, but no one paid any attention, the men too intent upon the chamois head. I got up and went to the door. Observation before supper had warned me that, if I desired to wash, a stream ran beside the road and lost itself in the gorge below. I went out into the night and crunched across the gravel clearing to the stream. Last evening the quarter moon upon the Parthenon, and now the nearby naked Pindus beeches seven thousand feet closer to the stars. No wind to stir the leaves that yet remained. The sky looked wider than it did at home.

I washed in the gully by the road, and once more heard the barking of a dog. I raised my head, and looked beyond the log cabin to a narrow plateau stretching to the very lip of the gorge. Something moved there in the darkness. I dried my hands on my woollen jersey, and crossed back over the road, past the clearing by the cabin, towards the plateau. Someone whistled. The sound was uncanny, heard there on the mountain pass, remote from town and village. It was the hissing whistle blown between tooth and lip heard on the sidewalk of a garish city, and the woman who hears it quickens her step instinctively. I paused. Then I saw the herd of goats, crowded together, bedded for the night, the narrow plateau their pillow. Two dogs stood guardian, one at either end. And motionless, in the midst of his herd, hooded, leaning on his crook, stood their master, staring not at me but at the hills above. It must have been he who whistled.

I watched them a moment, the man, and the bedded goats, and the sentinel dogs, and they seemed to me remote from the little world of the log cabin and the men within. To look upon them was intrusion. They belonged elsewhere. Their very stillness put them apart and gave me a strange feeling of disquiet. Yet why the whistle? Why the lewd, low hiss of warning? I turned away, went back to the cabin, and opened the door.

The store with its earth floor, its canned food, its coils of rope, and the chattering voices of the men—all three of them now bending over Stephen, absorbed in his drawing—was somehow welcoming. Even the cracked loudspeaker and the confused babble of Radio Athens seemed at that moment reassuring, part of a life that was familiar. I went and sat down at the table beside Stephen, and helped myself to another of the proprietor's cigarettes.

"They're here," said Stephen, not bothering to look at me, and sketching in a stunted bush beside his chamois head.

"Who's here?" I asked.

"Chamois," he answered. "They were seen again two days ago."

I don't know why—perhaps I was tired, for our journey had been long that day: we had left Athens in the early morning, and the drive up to the pass had told on nerve and muscle—but a wave of depression came upon me with his words. I wanted to say, "Oh, be damned to chamois. Can't we forget them until to-morrow?" but to do so would have brought tension between us, happily stilled since leaving London. So I said nothing and watched him draw, the smoke from the cigarette making my eyes smart, and presently, yawning, I let my head rest on the wall behind me and dozed, like a nodding passenger in a railway carriage.

The change of music woke me. Radio Athens had become an accordion. I opened my eyes, and the rat-faced cook had turned into entertainer, and was now sitting cross-legged on his chair, instrument in hand, applauded by the proprietor and the walleyed driver, and by Stephen too. His song was melancholy, wild, Slav, bred in heaven knows what bald Macedonian vale by a long-forgotten forebear, but there was rhythm somewhere, and ferocity as well, and his thin voice like a reed was also the pipe of Pan.

It was only when he had finished, and laid his accordion down, that I noticed we were no longer five, but six. The goatherd from the night had come to join us. He sat on a bench apart, still wrapped in his hooded burnous, leaning upon his crook, but the swinging lamp from the beam shone upon his face and into his eyes. They were the strangest eyes I had ever looked upon. Golden brown in colour, large and widely set, they stared from his narrow face as though suddenly startled into life. I thought, at first glance, that the abrupt cessation of the music had surprised him; but when the expression did not change, but remained constant, with all the alert watchfulness of one poised for flight or for attack, I knew myself mistaken, that he was perhaps blind, that his wide stare was in reality the sightless gaze of a man without vision. Then he shifted his posture and said something to the proprietor of the store; and from the way he moved, catching a packet of cigarettes thrown to him, I saw that he was not blind, but on the contrary had a sight keener than most men—for the cigarettes were poorly thrown and the catch was quick—and the eyes, shifting now to the rest of us round the table, and finally resting upon Stephen, were now larger, if possible, than before, and the searching stare impossible to hold.

I said to Stephen in a low voice, "Do you think he's mad?"

"No," said my husband. "He lives a lot alone. He's the fellow they've been talking about. We're going with him in the morning."

My spirits ebbed. The doze against the wall had rested me, and I was no longer tired. But apprehension filled me.

"Going with him where?" I asked. The man was watching us.

"He has a hut in the forest," said Stephen impatiently. "It's all settled. An hour's climb from here. He'll put us up."

From the way Stephen spoke, he might have been arranging a weekend with some obliging golfing friend. I looked at the goatherd again. The honey-coloured eyes never moved from Stephen's face, and his whole body was taut, as though he waited for us to spring, and must seize advantage first.

"I don't think he likes us," I said.

"Rubbish," said Stephen, and rising to his feet he picked up his rifle.

The goatherd moved. It was strange, he was by the door. I had not seen him shift from chair to door, so swift had been his passage. Yet he was standing there, his hand on the latch, and the door was open. No one noticed anything unusual in the quickness of the flight—if flight it was. Stephen's back was turned. The rat-faced cook was strumming his accordion. The proprietor and the walleyed driver were sitting down to dominoes.

"Come to bed," said Stephen. "You're dead on your feet."

The door closed. The goatherd had gone. I had shifted my eyes for the passing of a second, and I had not seen him go. I followed Stephen up the ladder to the lofts above.

"You're for the cupboard," said my husband. "I'll turn in with the chaps." Already he was choosing his particular heap of blankets.

"What about the man?" I asked.

"What man?"

"The goatherd. The one we're to go with in the morning."

"Oh, he'll wrap himself in his hood out there with the goats."

Stephen took off his coat, and I groped my way to the cupboard. Below, the rat-faced cook had started once more upon the accordion, and the reedy voice floated up through the floorboards. A crack in the planking of my cupboard gave me a view upon a narrow strand of plateau beyond the cabin. I could see a single beech tree, and a star. Beneath the tree stood the hooded figure leaning upon a crook. I lay down on my blankets. The cold air from the crack in the planking blew upon my face. Presently the sound of the accordion stopped. The voices too. I heard the men come up the ladder to the loft, and go into the room with Stephen. Later their varying snores told me of their sleep, and of Stephen's too. I listened, every sense alert, for a sound I somehow knew must come. I heard it, finally, more distant than before. Not a bird's cry, nor a shepherd's call to his dogs, but more penetrating, more intense; the low whistle of one who sees a woman on a street.

2

Something in me grudges sleep to others when my own night has been poor. The sight of Stephen, tackling fried eggs again at seven, and drinking the muddied grains of coffee, fresh-shaved too from water boiled by the cook, was unbearably irritating as I climbed down the ladder to the store below.

He hailed me cheerfully. "Slept like a top," he said. "How was the cupboard?"

"The Little Ease," I told him, remembering Harrison Ainsworth's *Tower of London* and the torture chamber, and I glanced with a queasy stomach at the egg yolk on his oily plate.

"Better get something inside you," he said. "We've a steep

climb ahead of us. If you don't want to face it, you can always drive back to Kalabaka with our walleyed friend."

I felt myself a drag upon his day. The bread, brought yesterday, I supposed, in the bus from north or west, was moderately fresh, and I spread it with honey. I would have given much for French coffee instead of the Greek-Turkish brew that never satisfied a void.

"What exactly do you mean to do?" I asked.

Stephen had the inevitable large-scale map on the table in front of him. "We're here," he said, pointing to the cross he had marked on the map, "and we have to walk to this." A speck in the nick of a fold showed our destination. "That is where the goatherd —his name is Jesus, by the way, but he answers to Zus—has his lair. It's primitive, I gather, but clean. We'll carry stores with us from here. That extra rucksack will prove a godsend."

It was all very well for Stephen. He had slept. The smell of brewing eggs was nauseous. I hastily swallowed my coffee dregs and went outside. The bright clear day helped to pull me together. There was no sign of the goatherd with his unlikely name, nor of his goats. Our driver from Kalabaka was washing his car. He greeted me with enthusiasm, and then made great play of gesturing to the woods above us, bending himself as if under a rucksack, and shaking his head. Laughing, he pointed downwards where the road twisted like a snake to the depths beneath, and from the road to his car. His meaning was plain. I would do better to return with him. The thought of the descent was worse than the climb to the unknown. And somehow, now that morning had come, now that I could breathe the sharp air and glimpse the great sky, cloudless and blue above the yet golden beech trees, the unknown did not seem to hold much danger.

I washed in the stream—the saucepanned water in the kitchen amongst the oil did not tempt me—and while Stephen and I were packing our rucksacks the first bus of the day arrived, travelling from the west. It halted for five minutes, while the driver and the few passengers stretched their legs. Inevitably our walleyed chauffeur had a cousin among the passengers, inevitably the purpose of our journey became known, and we were surrounded at once by eager questioners, poking our rucksacks, peeping at Stephen's rifle, overwhelming the pair of us with advice we could not understand. The cousin had a sister in America. The supposed bond between us made him spokesman of the group.

"No good," he said, pointing to the trees, "too late, no good." And then, feigning the posture of one holding a gun, he said, "Bang . . . bang . . . bang . . ." rapidly. A chorus of approval came from his fellow passengers.

Stephen continued to strap his rucksack. The proprietor of the store came out carrying more goods for us to pack away. Perched on the top, incongruous, was a great packet of soapflakes and a bottle of bull's-eyes. Everybody suddenly started shaking hands.

When the bus pulled away down the road to Kalabaka, followed by our walleyed driver and his cousin in the car, it was as though our last link with sanity had snapped. I looked up, and saw the goatherd emerging from the trees. I stood my ground and waited. He was smaller than I had thought, barely my own height, and the hooded burnous dwarfed him further. He came and took my rucksack without a word, seizing at the same time the extra pack with the stores. He had the two slung over his shoulder in an instant.

"He can't very well take both," I murmured to Stephen.

"Rot," said my husband. "He won't notice them, any more than one of his own goats."

The proprietor and the cook stood waving at the door of the store. It seemed suddenly a home, a long-known refuge, in the full sunlight. I forgot the cupboard where I had spent the night, and the oily eggs. The little store was friendly and the red earth comforting, the smiling proprietor and the rat-faced cook with his accordion men of good will. Then I turned my back on them, and followed Stephen and Jesus the goatherd through the trees.

We must have made a queer procession, no one speaking, the three of us in single file. The goats and the dogs had vanished. Perhaps this was the goatherd's second journey of the day. Our way lay through forest at first, mostly beech but pine as well, then clearings of tufty grass and box and shrub. As we climbed the trees thinned, the air became purer, sweeter, the range of mountains opened up on either side and above and beyond us, some of them already capped with snow. Now and again Stephen halted, not for breath—I believe he could have climbed without pause all day—but to swing his field glasses on the nearer ridge above the tree line, to the left of us. I knew better than to talk. So did our

guide. He was always just ahead, and when Stephen lifted the binoculars the goatherd followed their direction, his face impassive,
but those honey-coloured eyes staring wild and startled from beneath the gaping hood. It could be some disease, I told myself,
like goitre; yet the eyes were not full, they did not protrude. It was
the expression that was so unusual, so compelling, yet not compelling in an hypnotic, penetrating sense—these eyes did not only
see, but appeared to listen as well. And not to us. That was the
curious thing. Stephen and I were of no account. The goatherd,
although our beast of burden, did not listen or watch for us.

Now it was all sun, all sky, and the trees were beneath us, except for one lone blasted pine, lording it over a crisp sheet of recent snow, and above our heads, dark and formidable, circled our
first eagle. A dog came bounding over the ridge towards us, and
as we topped the rise I saw the goats, spread out and snuffing at
the ground. Hard against an overhanging rock was a cabin, a
quarter the size of our store below on the pass. Shelter from the
elements it might have been—I was no judge of that—but a hermit saint or an aesthete could not have picked upon a spot more
apt for contemplation or for beauty.

"H'm," said Stephen, "it looks central enough, if that's our
shakedown." Central. He might have been talking about the Underground at Piccadilly. "Hi, Zus!" he called, and jerked his head
towards the hut. "Is this the spot? Do we unload?" He was still
talking in Italian, believing, by some process of thought peculiar
to him, that the language meant more to the goatherd than English could.

The man replied in Greek. It was the first time I had heard him
speak. Once again, it was disconcerting. The voice was not harsh,
as I had expected, but oddly soft, and pitched a little high, like the
voice of a child. Had I, in fact, not guessed his age as forty or
thereabouts, I would have said that a child was speaking to us.

"Don't know what that was about," said Stephen to me, "but
I'm sure it's the place all right. Let's have a look at it."

The dogs, for the second one had now appeared, watched us
gravely. Their master led us to his refuge. Blinking, because of the
strong sunlight without, we lowered our heads from the beam and
stepped inside. It was just a plain wood shelter, with a partition
down the centre. There was no furniture, except for a bench at
one end on which stood a small Primus stove. The earth floor had

more sand on it than the floor of our overnight cabin store. It must have been built to serve as a shelter only in the case of sudden storm.

"Nothing wrong with this," said Stephen, looking about him. "We can spread out groundsheets on the floor and the sleeping bags on top."

The goatherd, our host, had stood aside as we explored his premises. Even the space behind the partition was unfurnished like the rest. There was not even a blanket. Now, silently, he unloaded our things for us, and left us to arrange them as we pleased.

"Funny sort of bloke," said Stephen. "Hardly the type to make us crack our ribs with laughter."

"It's his eyes," I said. "Have you noticed his eyes?"

"Yes," said Stephen, "they look a bit frozen. So would you be, if you lived up here for long."

Frozen, though, was a new thought. Frozen, petrified. A petrified forest was surely the life sap of a substance turned to stone. Were the goatherd's emotions petrified? Had he no blood in his veins, no warmth, no sap? Perhaps he was blasted, like the lone pine outside his hut. I helped my husband to unpack, and soon we had some semblance of comfort within the four blank walls.

It was only ten o'clock, but I was hungry. The proprietor of the store had put a tin opener amongst our rations, and I was soon eating ham, canned in the United States, and dates thrown in for good measure. I sat cross-legged in the sun outside the hut, and the eagle still soared above me in the sky.

"I'm off," said Stephen.

Glancing up, I saw that he had his cartridge bag at his belt, his field glasses round his neck, and his rifle slung over his shoulder. The easy camaraderie had gone, his manner was terse, abrupt. I scrambled to my feet. "You'll never keep up," he said. "You'll only hold us back."

"Us?" I asked.

"Friend Jesus has to set me on the way," replied my husband.

The goatherd, silent as ever, waited by a cairn of stones. He was unarmed, save for his shepherd's crook.

"Can you understand a word he says?" I spoke in doubt.

"Sign language is enough," said Stephen. "Enjoy yourself."

The goatherd had already turned, and Stephen followed. In a

moment they were lost in scrub. I had never felt more alone. I went into the hut to fetch my camera—the panorama was too good to miss, though it would be dull enough, no doubt, when it was printed—and the sight of the groundsheets, the rucksacks, the stores and my thicker jersey restored confidence. The height, the solitude, the bright sun and the scent of the air, these were things I loved; why, then, my seed of melancholy? The sense, hard to describe, of mutability?

I went outside and found a hollow, with a piece of rock at my back, and made myself a resting place near the browsing goats. The forest was below, and somewhere—in the depths—our lodging of last night. Away to the northeast, hidden from me by a range of mountains, were the plains of the civilized world. I smoked my first cigarette of the day, and watched the eagle. The hot sun made me drowsy, and I was short of sleep.

When I opened my eyes the sun had shifted, and it was half-past one by my watch. I had slept for over three hours. I got up and stretched, and as I did so the dog, watching me a few hundred yards away, growled. So did his companion. I called to them and moved towards the hut, and at this the pair of them advanced, snarling. I remained where I was. They crouched once more, and as long as I did not move they remained silent. One step, however, brought an instant snarl, and a stealthy lowering of the head, a forward padding movement as if to spring. I did not fancy being torn to pieces. I sat down again and waited, but, knowing my husband, I was aware that it might be nightfall before he returned. Meanwhile I must remain, marked by the dogs, the full force of the sun already spent. I could not even get to the hut for another jersey.

Somewhere, from what direction I could not tell, I heard a shot, and the sound echoed from the gorges far below. The dogs heard it too. They cocked their heads and stared. The goats rustled in the scrub, surprised, and one old patriarch, bearded to his breast, bleated his disapproval like some professor roused from sleep.

I waited for a second shot, but none came. I wondered if Stephen had found his mark, or missed. At any rate, he had sighted chamois. He would not have wasted his bullet on other game. If he had hit and killed, it would not be long before he returned, bearing his prey upon his shoulder. If he had hit and wounded only—but that would be unlike Stephen—he would go after the poor beast and shoot again.

I went on sitting above my hollow, close to the blasted pine. Then one of the dogs whined. I saw nothing. But the next moment the goatherd was behind me.

"Any luck?" I asked. I spoke in English, having no Greek, but the tone of my voice should tell him what I meant. His strange eyes stared down at me. Slowly he shook his head. He raised his hand, pointing over his shoulder. He continued to shake his head gently from side to side, and suddenly—fool that I was—I remembered that the Greek "yes," the affirmation, is always given with this same shake of the head, suggesting its opposite, denial. The child's voice coming from the impassive face said, "Nei," and this was repeated, the head still moving slowly.

"He has found them, then?" I said. "There are chamois?" and he reaffirmed his nei, which looked so much like contradiction, and went on staring at me with his great honey-coloured eyes, the frozen petrified eyes, until I was seized with a kind of horror, for they did not go with the gentle childish voice. I moved away through the scrub to put some distance between us, calling over my shoulder uselessly—for he could not understand me—"I'll go and find out what's happened." This time the dogs did not snarl, but stayed where they were, watching their master, and he remained motionless, leaning on his crook and staring after me.

I crawled through the scrub and up a track which I judged to be the one taken by Stephen and the goatherd earlier. Soon the scrub gave place to rock, a track of a sort beneath the overhanging face, and as I went I shouted, "Stephen!" for the sound of my voice must carry even as the sound of the rifle shot had done. I had no answer.

The world in which I found myself was sparse and bare, and I could see no footprints in the snow in front of me. Had Stephen come this way there must be footprints. Now from my vantage point it was as though the whole of Greece was spread beneath me, infinitely far, belonging to another age, another time, and I was indeed at the summit of my world and quite alone. I could see the forests and the foothills and the plains, and a river like a little silken thread, but my husband was not with me, nor anyone at all, not even the eagle that had soared above at midday.

"Stephen!" I shouted, my voice flat and feeble against the rock.

I stood and listened. It might be that I should hear a rifle shot again. Any sound would be welcome in such barren solitude. Yet when one came I was shocked out of immobility, for it was no rifle shot, but a whistle. That same lewd whistle to attract attention, coming from fifty feet above my head, from the jutting ledge, the overhanging rock. I saw his horns, his questing eyes, his satyr's face staring down at me, suspicious, curious, and he whistled again, a hiss, a mockery, and stamped his hoofs, releasing a crumbling stone. Then he was gone—the chamois was gone, my first live chamois—he was away and lost, but crouching below me, on a narrow lip over a precipice, clinging to the rock face, his rifle vanished, was a white-faced man who could not speak from fear, my husband, Stephen.

He could not move. I could not reach him. That was the horror. I could not reach him. He must have edged his way onto the lip of rock and found that he could go no further. In some extremity he had dropped his rifle. The thing that appalled me most was the terror on his face. Stephen, who rode roughshod over the feelings of his friends, Stephen the cold, the calculating. I threw myself down full-length on the ground and stretched out my hands. There was a gap between us of a few feet, no more.

"Keep your eyes turned to the rock," I said softly—instinct warned me not to speak too loudly—"edge your way inch by inch. If you got yourself there you must be able to return."

He did not answer. He moistened his lips with his tongue. He was deadly pale.

"Stephen," I said, "you've got to try."

He tried to speak, but nothing came, and as though to mock us both the lewd warning whistle of the chamois sounded once again. It was more distant now, and the chamois itself was out of sight on some unattainable fastness of his own, secure from human penetration.

It seemed to me that if Stephen had had his rifle with him he would not have been afraid. The loss of the rifle had unmanned him. All power, all confidence had gone, and with it, in some sickening way, his personality. The man clinging to the rock face was a puppet. Then I saw the goatherd, staring down at us from a rock above our heads.

"Please come," I called gently, "my husband's in danger."

He disappeared. A loose stone crumbled and fell past Stephen's head. I saw my husband's knuckles turn white under the strain. A moment's horror suggested that the crumbling of the stone had been intentional, that the goatherd had vanished on purpose, leaving Stephen to his fate. A movement behind me told me I had misjudged him. He was by my side.

I crawled away to let him have my place. He did not look at me, only at Stephen. He threw off his burnous, and I was aware of something lithe and compact, with a shock of black hair. He leapt onto the narrow lip beside Stephen and seized hold of him as an adult would seize a child, and all the six feet two of my husband's body was thrown like a sack across the goatherd's shoulder. I put my hand over my mouth to stifle the cry that must surely come. He was going to throw Stephen into the depths below. I shrank away, my legs turned to jelly, and the next moment the goatherd was back on the track beside me, and Stephen too; Stephen was sitting hunched on the ground, his face in his hands, rocking from side to side. When I looked back from him I saw that the goatherd was dressed in his burnous again, and was standing some little distance away from us, his head averted.

I was quietly sick into a hole I scooped out of the snow. Then I shut my eyes and waited. It seemed a very long time before I heard Stephen rise to his feet. I opened my eyes and looked up at him. The colour had returned to his face. The goatherd had gone.

"Now do you understand?" asked Stephen.

"Understand what?" I asked weakly.

"Why I must shoot chamois."

He stood there, defenceless without his rifle; and although he was no longer pale he was somehow shrunken in stature. One of his bootlaces was undone. I found myself staring at that rather than at his face.

"It's fear, isn't it?" I said. "Have you always had it?"

"Always," he answered, "from the very first. It's something I have to conquer. The chamois gives the greatest chance because he climbs the highest. The more I kill, the more I destroy fear." Then absently, as if thinking of something else, he pointed downward. "I dropped my rifle," he said. "I fired when I saw the brute, but it whistled at me instead of taking to its heels, and then the giddiness came, the giddiness that's part of fear."

I was still much shaken, but I got up and took his arm.

"Let's go back," I said. "I want a drink. Thank God for the brandy flasks."

His confidence was returning; nevertheless, he allowed me to lead him like a child. We made short work of the descent. When we came to the hut the two dogs were waiting on guard by the entrance, and the goatherd was gathering chips of wood to make kindling for a fire. He took no notice of us, and the dogs ignored us too. We went into the hut and took a good swig at our flasks. Then we lighted cigarettes and smoked for a while in silence, watching the goatherd with his armfuls of wood and scattered cones.

"You'll never tell anyone, will you?" Stephen said suddenly.

I looked at him, startled by the harsh note in his voice, betraying the strain he would not otherwise show. "You mean about the fear?"

"Yes," he replied. "I don't mind you knowing—you were bound to find out one day. And that fellow there—well, he's not the kind to talk. But I won't have anyone else knowing."

"Of course I won't say anything," I replied quickly, to reassure him, and after a moment I turned away and began wrestling with the Primus stove. First things first. We should both of us feel more normal if we had hot food inside us.

Baked beans have never tasted more delicious. And the retsina wine on top of brandy helped to dull speculation. The short day faded quickly. We had scarcely eaten and put on warmer jerseys when the temperature fell at least twenty degrees, the sky deepened, and the sun had gone. The fire at the threshold of the hut threw leaping flames into the air.

"Tomorrow," said Stephen, "I'll go and find my rifle."

I looked at him across the flames. His face was set, the face of the man I knew, the old Stephen.

"You'll never find it," I said. "It might be anywhere."

"I know the place," he replied impatiently, "amongst a heap of boulders and some dwarf pines. I marked it down."

I wondered how he proposed to get himself down there, knowing his limitations as I did now. He must have read my thoughts, for he added, "I can get round to it from here. There shouldn't be any difficulty."

I threw my cigarette into the heart of the fire. It was a mistake to smoke it. Somehow I had not much stomach for cigarettes to-night.

"If you do find it," I said, "what then?"

"A last crack at the chamois," he said.

His fanaticism, instead of cooling, had intensified. He was staring intently into the darkness over my shoulder. I turned and saw Jesus, the goatherd and his saviour, come towards us to drop more chips into the fire.

"Kalinykta," said Stephen.

It was the Greek for good night. And a sign of dismissal. The goatherd paused, and with a little gesture bowed to each of us in turn. *"Kalinykta,"* he said.

The voice was as shrouded as he himself in his burnous, the childish timbre of it muted in some strange fashion because of darkness. The hood was thrown further back than it had been, so that the sharp outline of his face was more revealed, and the firelight turned his skin ruddy, the staring eyes bright like live coals.

He withdrew and left us together. Presently the sharp air, for all the leaping flames, drove us to our sleeping bags inside the hut. We lit candles and read our Penguins for a time. Then Stephen fell asleep, and I blew out the candles and did likewise, worn with the emotion I'd been unable to express. What shocked me were my dreams. The goatherd had stripped off his burnous, and it was not Stephen that he carried in his arms but myself. I put out my hands to feel the shock of hair. It rose from his head like a black crest.

I woke, and lit the candle. Stephen was sleeping still. I went to the door of the hut, and saw that the fire had died; not even the ashes glowed. The moon, past its quarter mark and swelling, was hanging like a half cheese in the sky. The dogs, the goats, the goatherd had all gone. Silhouetted on the sky line beyond the blasted pine stood a chamois buck, his sharp horns curving backward, his listening head uptilted to the moon, and grazing beneath him, silently, delicately, were the does and the yearling kids.

3

It was a curious thing, I considered, as I brewed our breakfast tea on the Primus and spread cheese over slices of ham, but danger shared had brought Stephen and myself together. Or else I had turned compassionate. He was human after all, weak like the rest of us. He must have sensed my sympathy, because he talked at breakfast, telling me of adventures in the past, of near escapes.

"I remember once," he said, "falling some fifteen feet, but I only sprained an ankle."

He laughed in high good humour, and I thought that if he could joke at fear his battle was half-won.

"I'll come with you today," I told him, "when you look for your rifle."

"Will you?" he said. "Splendid. It's going to be fine, after that sharp frost. No mist about, the bugbear of all stalkers."

The zest, the keenness had returned. And what was more, I shared it. I wanted to stalk with him. This was a new emotion, something I could not explain. We ate our breakfast and straightened our sleeping bags, and going out into the sunlight I kicked at the ashes of last night's fire. There was no sign of the goatherd or his dogs, or of his flock either. He must have taken them to graze elsewhere. I hardly thought of him: I was anxious to be off. Stephen led the way down the forested mountainside, for he knew by instinct where he wished to go, and we scrambled over scrub and slag, and stunted bushes, part box, part thorn, away from the overhanging crags above.

High in the blue sky soared the eagle of yesterday, or perhaps his fellow, and as the sun rose and warmed us, so that we took off our jerseys and tied them round our waists, life seemed suddenly very good, very full. There was none of the strain that had been with us yesterday. I put it down to sleeping well, to the new bond shared, and to the absence of the goatherd Jesus.

When we had scrambled thus for half an hour or more Stephen said, "There it is—look, the sun's caught the barrel."

He smiled and ran ahead, and indeed I could see the shining metal, caught sideways between a thorn and a lump of rock. He seized his gun, and waved it above his head in triumph.

"I could never have gone home if I'd lost this," he said.

He handled the rifle with care, still smiling—it was almost a caress the way he stroked it. I watched him, indulgent for the first time in my life. He took a cloth from his pouch and began to polish it. I let my eyes roam above him to the rugged heights, to the lips and ledges where we had climbed yesterday. It was sparse and naked, bare of vegetation. A black speck like a humped rock caught my eye that I had not remembered the previous day. The black speck moved. I touched Stephen's elbow. "There . . ." I murmured, and put my pocket spyglass into his hand. Cautiously he lifted it to his eye.

"He's there," he whispered, "he's there, my buck of yesterday."

I had not thought Stephen could move so stealthily or so fast. He was away from me in a moment, crawling upward through the scrub, and seized with a curious enchantment I crawled after him. He motioned me back, and I lay still and looked through my glass again. Now the picture was indistinct: one second it looked like the chamois, and the next like our goatherd, yes, our goatherd. I called to Stephen.

"It isn't chamois," I said, "it's your saviour, Zus."

He glanced back at me over his shoulder, impatient, angry.

"What the hell are you shouting for?" he said. "He'll get away from us."

Once again I thrust my glass into his hand, crawling close to him to do so. "Look there," I said, "it isn't chamois."

He seized the glass, and after adjusting it to his eye gave it back with an exclamation of disgust.

"Are you mad?" he said. "Of course it's chamois. I can see the horns."

Then, shrill, unmistakable, came the whistle of warning, the mocking chamois call.

"Do you still think it isn't chamois?" said Stephen, and he put his rifle to his shoulder and fired. The explosion was like an echo to the whistle. It ricocheted away from the rocks above us, and carried to the depths below. The black speck leapt and vanished. Loose stones fell upon our heads.

"You've missed him," I said.

"No," said Stephen, "I'm going after him."

There was a gully immediately above us. He climbed to the left of it, I to the right, and as we made towards the jutting ledge where we had seen the black speck leap, neck and neck on opposite sides of the gully, I knew, with sudden certainty, that we were after different quarry. Stephen was after chamois. I was after Man. Both were symbolic of something abhorrent to our natures, and so held fascination and great fear. We wanted to destroy the thing that shamed us most.

My heart was singing as I climbed, and pounding too. It was worth having been born, having lived my span of years for this alone. There had been no other experience. Nothing else compared with the stalk, and I had my goatherd on the run. It was he who fled from me, not I from him.

I could see him now, jumping from rock to rock. How Stephen could mistake him for a chamois, God alone could tell. He had thrown off his burnous, and his shaggy head was like a wave crest, thick and black. It was glorious. I had no fear of the jutting rocks, and climbed them steadily and surely, with never a slip and never a moment's pause. Silence no longer mattered, for he knew I was after him.

"I'll get you," I called, "you can't escape. You know very well I've hunted you all my life."

Such savagery and power—I, who hated violence; intoxication, too, and wild delight. Once more the hiss, the whistle. Fear and warning and mockery in one. The rattle of stones, the scampering of hoofs.

"Lie down," shouted Stephen, "lie down. I'm going to shoot."

I remember laughing as the shot rang out. This time Stephen did not miss. The black form crumpled to its knees and fell. As I hauled myself to the ledge I saw the honey-coloured eyes glaze in death. They would never stare at me again. My husband had destroyed the thing that frightened me.

4

"He's smaller than I thought," said Stephen, turning the dead buck over with his feet, "and younger, too. Not more than five years old."

He lit a cigarette. I took it from him. Sweat was pouring from both of us. The eagle was still soaring against the sun.

"I shan't carry him back," said my husband. "I don't even want his head. That's my last chamois. Don't ask me why—I just know it, that's all. We'll leave him out here in grandeur, where he belongs. Nature has her own way of disposing of the dead." He glanced up at the eagle.

We left the chamois on the ledge of rock under the sky and climbed down again, through the scrub and stones, back to the hut and our belongings. The rucksacks and the sleeping bags seemed part of another life.

"No sign of our host," said Stephen, "and we've finished all the rations. Let's pack and spend tonight down at the store. We can catch the morning bus in the other direction. Go to Metsovon, and Ioannina, and down the west coast to Missolonghi and across to Delphi. You'd like that, wouldn't you?"

I did not answer, but I put out my hand to him for no reason. It was very peaceful, very still, on the quiet mountain. Suddenly Stephen kissed me. Then he put his hand in his pocket, and, bending down, placed two small metal objects in the white ash of the fire.

"We'll leave the empty cartridges for Jesus," Stephen said.

Not After Midnight

I am a schoolmaster by profession. Or was. I handed in my resignation to the Head before the end of the summer term in order to forestall inevitable dismissal. The reason I gave was true enough —ill health, caused by a wretched bug picked up on holiday in Crete, which might necessitate a stay in hospital of several weeks, various injections, etc. I did not specify the nature of the bug. He knew, though, and so did the rest of the staff. And the boys. My complaint is universal, and has been so through the ages, an excuse for jest and hilarious laughter from earliest times, until one of us oversteps the mark and becomes a menace to society. Then we are given the boot. The passer-by averts his gaze, and we are left to crawl out of the ditch alone, or stay there and die.

If I am bitter, it is because the bug I caught was picked up in all innocence. Fellow sufferers of my complaint can plead predisposition, poor heredity, family trouble, excess of the good life, and, throwing themselves on a psychoanalyst's couch, spill out the rotten beans within and so effect a cure. I can do none of this. The doctor to whom I endeavoured to explain what had happened listened with a superior smile, and then murmured something about emotionally destructive identification coupled with repressed guilt, and put me on a course of pills. They might have helped me if I had taken them. Instead I threw them down the drain and became more deeply imbued with the poison that seeped through me, made worse of course by the fatal recognition of my condition by the youngsters I had believed to be my friends, who nudged one another when I came into class, or, with stifled laughter, bent their loathsome little heads over their desks—until the moment arrived when I knew I could not continue, and took the decision to knock on the headmaster's door.

Well, that's over, done with, finished. Before I take myself to hospital or, alternatively, blot out memory, which is a second possibility, I want to establish what happened in the first place. So that, whatever becomes of me, this paper will be found, and the reader can make up his mind whether, as the doctor suggested, some want of inner balance made me an easy victim of super-stitious fear, or whether, as I myself believe, my downfall was caused by an age-old magic, insidious, evil, its origins lost in the dawn of history. Suffice to say that he who first made the magic deemed himself immortal, and with unholy joy infected others, sowing in his heirs, throughout the world and down the centuries, the seeds of self-destruction.

To return to the present. The time was April, the Easter holi-days. I had been to Greece twice before, but never Crete. I taught classics to the boys at the preparatory school, but my reason for visiting Crete was not to explore the sites of Knossos of Phaestus but to indulge a personal hobby. I have a minor talent for painting in oils, and this I find all-absorbing, whether on free days or in the school holidays. My work has been praised by one or two friends in the art world, and my ambition was to collect enough paintings to give a small exhibition. Even if none of them sold, the holding of a private show would be a happy achievement.

Here, briefly, a word about my personal life. I am a bachelor. Age forty-nine. Parents dead. Educated at Sherborne and Brasen-ose, Oxford. Profession, as you already know, schoolmaster. I play cricket and golf, badminton, and rather poor bridge. Inter-ests, apart from teaching, art, as I have already said, and occa-sional travel, when I can afford it. Vices, up to the present, liter-ally none. Which is not being self-complacent, but the truth is that my life has been uneventful by any standard. Nor has this bothered me. I am probably a dull man. Emotionally I have had no complications. I was engaged to a pretty girl, a neighbour, when I was twenty-five, but she married somebody else. It hurt at the time, but the wound healed in less than a year. One fault, if fault it is, I have always had, which perhaps accounts for my hitherto monotonous life. This is an aversion to becoming in-volved with people. Friends I possess, but at a distance. Once in-volved, trouble occurs, and too often disaster follows.

I set out for Crete in the Easter holidays with no encumbrance but a fair-sized suitcase and my painting gear. A travel agent had recommended a hotel overlooking the Gulf of Mirabello on the eastern coast, after I had told him I was not interested in archae-ological sights but wanted to paint. I was shown a brochure which seemed to meet my requirements. A pleasantly situated hotel close to the sea, and chalets by the water's edge where one slept and breakfasted. Clientèle well-to-do, and although I count myself no snob I cannot abide paper bags and orange peel. A couple of pictures painted the previous winter—a view of St. Paul's Cathedral under snow, and another one of Hampstead Heath, both sold to an obliging female cousin—would pay for my journey, and I permitted myself an added indulgence, though it was really a necessity—the hiring of a small Volkswagen on arrival at the airport of Kerakleion.

The flight, with an overnight stop in Athens, was pleasant and uneventful, the forty-odd miles' drive to my destination somewhat tedious, for being a cautious driver I took it slowly, and the twisting road, once I reached the hills, was decidedly hazardous. Cars passed me, or swerved towards me, hooting loudly. Also, it was very hot, and I was hungry. The sight of the blue Gulf of Mirabello and the splendid mountains to the east acted as a spur to sagging spirits, and once I arrived at the hotel, set delightfully in its own grounds, with lunch served to me on the terrace despite the fact that it was after two in the afternoon—how different from England!—I was ready to relax and inspect my quarters. Disappointment followed. The young porter led me down a garden path flagged on either side by brilliant geraniums to a small chalet bunched in by neighbours on either side, and overlooking, not the sea, but a part of the garden laid out for mini-golf. My next-door neighbours, an obviously English mother and her brood, smiled in welcome from their balcony, which was strewn with bathing suits drying under the sun. Two middle-aged men were engaged in mini-golf. I might have been in Maidenhead.

"This won't do," I said, turning to my escort. "I have come here to paint. I must have a view of the sea."

He shrugged his shoulders, murmuring something about the chalets beside the sea being fully booked. It was not his fault, of course. I made him trek back to the hotel with me, and addressed myself to the clerk at the reception desk.

"There has been some mistake," I said. "I asked for a chalet overlooking the sea, and privacy above all."

The clerk smiled, apologised, began ruffling papers, and the inevitable excuses followed. My travel agent had not specifically booked a chalet overlooking the sea. These were in great demand, and were fully booked. Perhaps in a few days there might be some cancellations, one never could tell, in the meantime he was sure I should be very comfortable in the chalet that had been allotted to me. All the furnishings were the same, my breakfast would be served me, etc., etc.

I was adamant. I would not be fobbed off with the English family and the mini-golf. Not having flown all those miles at considerable expense. I was bored by the whole affair, tired, and considerably annoyed.

"I am a professor of art," I told the clerk. "I have been commissioned to execute several paintings while I am here, and it is essential that I should have a view of the sea, and neighbours who will not disturb me."

(My passport states my occupation as professor. It sounds better than schoolmaster or teacher, and usually arouses respect in the attitude of reception clerks.)

The clerk seemed genuinely concerned, and repeated his apologies. He turned again to the sheaf of papers before him. Exasperated, I strode across the spacious hall and looked out of the door onto the terrace down to the sea.

"I cannot believe," I said, "that every chalet is taken. It's too early in the season. In summer, perhaps, but not now." I waved my hand towards the western side of the bay. "That group over there," I said, "down by the water's edge. Do you mean to say every single one of them is booked?"

He shook his head and smiled. "We do not usually open those until midseason. Also, they are more expensive. They have a bath as well as a shower."

"How much more expensive?" I hedged.

He told me. I made a quick calculation. I could afford it if I cut down on all other expenses. Had my evening meal in the hotel, and went without lunch. No extras in the bar, not even mineral water.

"Then there is no problem," I said grandly. "I will willingly pay more for privacy. And, if you have no objection, I should like to choose the chalet which would suit me best. I'll walk down to the sea now and then come back for the key, and your porter can bring my things."

I gave him no time to reply, but turned on my heel and went out onto the terrace. It paid to be firm. One moment's hesitation, and he would have fobbed me off with the stuffy chalet overlooking the mini-golf. I could imagine the consequences. The chattering children on the balcony next door, the possibly effusive mother, and the middle-aged golfers urging me to have a game. I could not have borne it.

I walked down through the garden to the sea, and as I did so my spirits rose. For this, of course, was what had been so highly coloured on the agent's brochure, and why I had flown so many miles. No exaggeration, either. Little whitewashed dwellings, discreetly set apart from one another, the sea washing the rocks below. There was a beach, from which doubtless people swam in high season, but no one was on it now, and, even if they should intrude, the chalets themselves were well to the left, inviolate, private. I peered at each in turn, mounting the steps, standing on the balconies. The clerk must have been telling the truth about none of them being let before full season, for all had their windows shuttered. All except one. And directly I mounted the steps and stood on the balcony I knew that it must be mine. This was the view I had imagined. The sea beneath me, lapping the rocks, the bay widening into the gulf itself, and beyond the mountains. It was perfect. The chalets to the east of the hotel, which was out of sight anyway, could be ignored. One, close to a neck of land, stood on its own like a solitary outpost with a landing stage below, but this would only enhance my picture when I came to paint it. The rest were mercifully hidden by rising ground. I turned, and looked through the open windows to the bedroom within. Plain whitewashed walls, a stone floor, a comfortable divan bed with rugs upon it. A bedside table with a lamp and telephone. But for these last it had all the simplicity of a monk's cell, and I wished for nothing more.

I wonder why this chalet, and none of its neighbours, was unshuttered, and stepping inside I heard from the bathroom beyond the sound of running water. Not further disappointment, and the place booked after all? I put my head round the open door, and saw that it was a little Greek maid swabbing the bathroom floor. She seemed startled at the sight of me. I gestured, pointed, said, "Is this taken?" She did not understand, but answered me in Greek. Then she seized her cloth and pail and, plainly terrified, brushed past me to the entrance, leaving her work unfinished.

I went back into the bedroom and picked up the telephone, and in a moment the smooth voice of the reception clerk answered.

"This is Mr. Grey," I told him, "Mr. Timothy Grey. I was speaking to you just now about changing my chalet."

"Yes, Mr. Grey," he replied. He sounded puzzled. "Where are you speaking from?"

"Hold on a minute," I said. I put down the receiver and crossed the room to the balcony. The number was above the open door. It was 62. I went back to the telephone. "I'm speaking from the chalet I have chosen," I said. "It happened to be open—one of the maids was cleaning the bathroom, and I'm afraid I scared her away. This chalet is ideal for my purpose. It is No. 62."

He did not answer immediately, and when he did he sounded doubtful. "No. 62?" he repeated. And then, after a moment's hesitation, "I am not sure if it is available."

"Oh, for heaven's sake . . ." I began, exasperated, and I heard him talking in Greek to someone beside him at the desk. The conversation went back and forth between them; there was obviously some difficulty, which made me all the more determined.

"Are you there?" I said. "What's the trouble?"

More hurried whispers, and then he spoke to me again. "No trouble, Mr. Grey. It is just that we feel you might be more comfortable in No. 57, which is a little nearer to the hotel."

"Nonsense," I said, "I prefer the view from here. What's wrong with No. 62? Doesn't the plumbing work?"

"Certainly the plumbing works," he assured me, while the whispering started again. "There is nothing wrong with the chalet. If you have made up your mind I will send down the porter with your luggage and the key."

He rang off, possibly to finish his discussion with the whisperer at his side. Perhaps they were going to step up the price. If they did, I would have further argument. The chalet was no different from its empty neighbours, but the position, dead centre to sea and mountains, was all I had dreamed and more. I stood on the balcony, looking out across the sea and smiling. What a prospect, what a place! I would unpack and have a swim, then put up my easel and do a preliminary sketch before starting serious work in the morning.

I heard voices, and saw the little maid staring at me from half-way up the garden path, cloth and pail still in hand. Then, as the young porter advanced downhill bearing my suitcase and painting gear, she must have realised that I was to be the occupant of No.

62, for she stopped him midway, and another whispered conversation began. I had evidently caused a break in the smooth routine of the hotel. A few moments later they climbed the steps to the chalet together, the porter to set down my luggage, the maid doubtless to finish her swabbing of the bathroom floor. I had no desire to be on awkward terms with either of them, and, smiling cheerfully, placed coins in both their hands.

"Lovely view," I said loudly, pointing to the sea. "Must go for a swim," and made breast-stroke gestures to show my intent, hoping for the ready smile of the native Greek, usually so responsive to good will.

The porter evaded my eyes and bowed gravely, accepting my tip nevertheless. As for the little maid, distress was evident in her face, and forgetting about the bathroom floor she hurried after him. I could hear them talking as they walked up the garden path together to the hotel.

Well, it was not my problem. Staff and management must sort out their troubles between them. I had got what I wanted, and that was all that concerned me. I unpacked and made myself at home. Then, slipping on bathing trunks, I stepped down to the ledge of rock beneath the balcony, and ventured a toe into the water. It was surprisingly chill, despite the hot sun that had been upon it all day. Never mind. I must prove my mettle, if only to myself. I took the plunge and gasped, and being a cautious swimmer at the best of times, especially in strange waters, swam round and round in circles rather like a sea-lion pup in a zoological pool.

Refreshing, undoubtedly, but a few minutes were enough, and as I climbed out again onto the rocks I saw that the porter and the little maid had been watching me all the time from behind a flowering bush up the garden path. I hoped I had not lost face. And anyway, why the interest? People must be swimming every day from the other chalets. The bathing suits on the various balconies proved it. I dried myself on the balcony, observing how the sun, now in the western sky behind my chalet, made dappled patterns on the water. Fishing boats were returning to the little harbour port a few miles distant, the chug-chug engines making a pleasing sound.

I dressed, taking the precaution of having a hot bath, for the first swim of the year is always numbing, and then set up my easel and instantly became absorbed. This was why I was here, and nothing else mattered. I worked for a couple of hours, and as the light failed, and the colour of the sea deepened and the mountains turned a softer purple blue, I rejoiced to think that tomorrow I should be able to seize this afterglow in paint instead of charcoal, and the picture would begin to come alive.

It was time to stop. I stacked away my gear, and before changing for dinner and drawing the shutters—doubtless there were mosquitoes, and I had no wish to be bitten—watched a motorboat with gently purring engine draw in softly to the eastward point with the landing stage away to my right. Three people aboard, fishing enthusiasts no doubt, a woman amongst them. One man, a local, probably, made the boat fast, and stepped on the landing stage to help the woman ashore. Then all three stared in my direction, and the second man, who had been standing in the stern, put up a pair of binoculars and fixed them on me. He held them steady for several minutes, focusing, no doubt, on every detail of my personal appearance, which is unremarkable enough, heaven knows, and would have continued had I not suddenly become annoyed and withdrawn into the bedroom, slamming the shutters to. How rude can you get, I asked myself? Then I remembered that these western chalets were all unoccupied, and mine was the first to open for the season. Possibly this was the reason for the intense interest I appeared to cause, beginning with members of the hotel staff and now embracing guests as well. Interest would soon fade. I was neither pop star nor millionaire. And my painting efforts, however pleasing to myself, were hardly likely to draw a fascinated crowd.

Punctually at eight o'clock I walked up the garden path to the hotel and presented myself in the dining room for dinner. It was moderately full and I was allotted a table in the corner, suitable to my single status, close to the screen dividing the service entrance from the kitchens. Never mind. I preferred this position to the centre of the room, where I could tell immediately that the hotel clientèle were on what my mother used to describe as an "all fellows to football" basis.

I enjoyed my dinner, treated myself—despite my de luxe chalet —to half a bottle of domestica wine, and was peeling an orange when an almighty crash from the far end of the room disturbed us all. Waiters hurried to the scene. Heads turned, mine amongst them. A hoarse American voice, hailing from the Deep South, called loudly, "For God's sake, clear up this goddarn mess!" It came from a square-shouldered man of middle age, whose face was so swollen and blistered by exposure to the sun that he looked as if he had been stung by a million bees. His eyes were sunk into his head, which was bald on top, with a grizzled thatch on either side, and the pink crown had the appearance of being tightly stretched, like the skin of a sausage about to burst. A pair of enormous ears the size of clams gave further distortion to his appearance, while a drooping wisp of moustache did nothing to hide the protruding underlip, thick as blubber and about as moist. I have seldom set eyes on a more unattractive individual. A woman, I suppose his wife, sat beside him, stiff and bolt upright, apparently unmoved by the debris on the floor, which appeared to consist chiefly of bottles. She was likewise middle-aged, with a mop of tow-coloured hair turning white, and a face as sunburnt as her husband's, but mahogany brown instead of red.

"Let's get the hell out of here and go to the bar!" The hoarse strains echoed across the room. The guests at the other tables turned discreetly back to their own dinner, and I must have been the only one to watch the unsteady exit of the bee-stung spouse and his wife—I could see the deaf-aid in her ear, hence possibly her husband's rasping tones—as he literally rolled past me to the bar, a lurching vessel in the wake of his steady partner. I silently commended the efficiency of the hotel staff, who made short work of clearing the wreckage.

The dining room emptied. "Coffee in the bar, sir," murmured my waiter. Fearing a crush and loud chatter I hesitated before entering, for the camaraderie of hotel bars has always bored me, but I hate going without my after-dinner coffee. I need not have worried. The bar was empty, apart from the white-coated server behind the bar, and the American sitting at a table with his wife. Neither of them was speaking. There were three empty beer bottles already on the table before him. Greek music played softly from some lair behind the bar. I sat myself on a stool and ordered coffee.

The bartender, who spoke excellent English, asked if I had spent a pleasant day. I told him yes, I had had a good flight, found the road from Herakleion hazardous, and my first swim rather cold. He explained that it was still early in the year. "In any case," I told him, "I have come to paint, and swimming will take second place. I have a chalet right on the waterfront, No. 62, and the view from the balcony is perfect."

Rather odd. He was polishing a glass, and his expression changed. He seemed about to say something, then evidently thought better of it, and continued with his work.

"Turn that goddamn record off!"

The hoarse, imperious summons filled the empty room. The barman made at once for the gramophone in the corner and adjusted the switch. A moment later the summons rang forth again.

"Bring me another bottle of beer!"

Now, had I been the bartender I should have turned to the man and, like a parent to a child, insisted that he say please. Instead, the brute was promptly served, and I was just downing my coffee when the voice from the table echoed through the room once more.

"Hi, you there, chalet No. 62. You're not superstitious?"

I turned on my stool. He was staring at me, glass in hand. His wife looked straight in front of her. Perhaps she had removed her deaf-aid. Remembering the maxim that one must humour madmen and drunks, I replied courteously enough.

"No," I said, "I'm not superstitious. Should I be?"

He began to laugh, his scarlet face creasing into a hundred lines.

"Well, goddarn it, I would be," he answered. "The fellow from that chalet was drowned only two weeks ago. Missing for two days, and then his body brought up in a net by a local fisherman, half-eaten by octopuses."

He began to shake with laughter, slapping his hand on his knee. I turned away in disgust, and raised my eyebrows in enquiry to the bartender.

"An unfortunate accident," he murmured. "Mr. Gordon such a nice gentleman. Interested in archaeology. It was very warm the night he disappeared, and he must have gone swimming after dinner. Of course the police were called. We were all most distressed here at the hotel. You understand, sir, we don't talk about it much. It would be bad for business. But I do assure you that bathing is perfectly safe. This is the first accident we have ever had."

"Oh, quite," I said.

Nevertheless . . . It was rather off-putting, the fact that the poor chap had been the last to use my chalet. However, it was not as though he had died in the bed. And I was not superstitious. I understood now why the staff had been reluctant to let the chalet again so soon, and why the little maid had been upset.

"I tell you one thing," boomed the revolting voice. "Don't go swimming after midnight, or the octopuses will get you too." This statement was followed by another outburst of laughter. Then he said, "Come on, Maud. We're for bed," and he noisily shoved the table aside.

I breathed more easily when the room was clear and we were alone.

"What an impossible man," I said. "Can't the management get rid of him?"

The bartender shrugged. "Business is business. What can they do? The Stolls have plenty of money. This is their second season here, and they arrived when we opened in March. They seem to be crazy about the place. It's only this year, though, that Mr. Stoll has become such a heavy drinker. He'll kill himself if he goes on at this rate. It's always like this, night after night. Yet his day must be healthy enough. Out at sea fishing from early morning until sundown."

"I dare say more bottles go over the side than he catches fish," I observed.

"Could be," the bartender agreed. "He never brings his fish to the hotel. The boatman takes them home, I dare say."

"I feel sorry for the wife."

The bartender shrugged. "She's the one with the money," he replied sotto voce, for a couple of guests had just entered the bar, "and I don't think Mr. Stoll has it all his own way. Being deaf may be convenient to her at times. But she never leaves his side, I'll grant her that. Goes fishing with him every day. Yes, gentlemen, what can I get for you?"

He turned to his new customers, and I made my escape. The cliché that it takes all sorts to make a world passed through my head. Thank heaven it was not my world, and Mr. Stoll and his deaf wife could burn themselves black under the sun all day at sea as far as I was concerned, and break beer bottles every evening into the bargain. In any event, they were not neighbours. No. 62 may have had the unfortunate victim of a drowning accident for

its last occupant, but at least this had insured privacy for its present tenant.

I walked down the garden path to my abode. It was a clear
starlit night. The air was balmy, and sweet with the scent of the
flowering shrubs planted thickly in the red earth. Standing on my
balcony I looked out across the sea towards the distant shrouded
mountains and the harbour lights from the little fishing port. To
my right winked the lights of the other chalets, giving a pleasing,
almost fairy impression, like a clever backcloth on a stage. Truly a
wonderful spot, and I blessed the travel agent who had recommended it.

I let myself in through my shuttered doorway and turned on the
bedside lamp. The room looked welcoming and snug; I could not
have been better housed. I undressed, and before getting into bed
remembered I had left a book I wanted to glance at on the balcony. I opened the shutters and picked it up from the deckchair
where I had thrown it, and once more, before turning in, glanced
out at the open sea. Most of the fairy lights had been extinguished, but the chalet that stood on its own on the extreme point
still had its light burning on the balcony. The boat, tied to the
landing stage, bore a riding light. Seconds later I saw something
moving close to my rocks. It was the snorkel of an underwater
swimmer. I could see the narrow pipe, like a minute periscope,
move steadily across the still, dark surface of the sea. Then it
disappeared to the far left out of sight. I drew my shutters and
went inside.

I don't know why it was, but the sight of that moving object was
somehow disconcerting. It made me think of the unfortunate man
who had been drowned during a midnight swim. My predecessor.
He too, perhaps, had sallied forth one balmy evening such as this,
intent on underwater exploration, and by so doing lost his life.
One would imagine the unhappy accident would scare off other
hotel visitors from swimming alone at night. I made a firm decision never to bathe except in broad daylight, and—chicken-
hearted, maybe—well within my depth.

I read a few pages of my book, then, feeling ready for sleep,
turned to switch out my light. In doing so I clumsily bumped the
telephone, which fell to the floor. I bent over, picked it up, luckily
no damage done, and saw that the small drawer that was part of
the fixture had fallen open. It contained a scrap of paper, or

rather card, with the name Charles Gordon upon it, and an address in Bloomsbury. Surely Gordon had been the name of my predecessor? The little maid, when she cleaned the room, had not thought to open the drawer. I turned the card over. There was something scrawled on the other side, the words "Not after midnight." And then, maybe as an afterthought, the figure 38. I replaced the card in the drawer and switched off the light. Perhaps I was overtired after the journey, but it was well past two before I finally got off to sleep. I lay awake for no rhyme or reason, listening to the water lapping against the rocks beneath my balcony.

I painted solidly for three days, never quitting my chalet except for the morning swim and my evening meal at the hotel. Nobody bothered me. An obliging waiter brought my breakfast, from which I saved rolls for midday lunch, the little maid made my bed and did her chores without disturbing me, and when I had finished my impressionistic scene on the afternoon of the third day I felt quite certain it was one of the best things I had ever done. It would take pride of place in the planned exhibition of my work. Well satisfied, I could now relax, and I determined to explore along the coast the following day, and discover another view to whip up inspiration. The weather was glorious. Warm as a good English June. And the best thing about the whole site was the total absence of neighbours. The other guests kept to their side of the domain, and, apart from bows and nods from adjoining tables as one entered the dining room for dinner, no one attempted to strike up acquaintance. I took good care to drink my coffee in the bar before the obnoxious Mr. Stoll had left his table.

I realised now that it was his boat which lay anchored off the point. They were away too early in the morning for me to watch their departure, but I used to spot them returning in the late afternoon; his square, hunched form was easily recognisable, and the occasional hoarse shout to the man in charge of the boat as they came to the landing stage. Theirs, too, was the isolated chalet on the point, and I wondered if he had picked it purposely in order to soak himself into oblivion out of sight and earshot of his nearest neighbours. Well, good luck to him, as long as he did not obtrude his offensive presence upon me.

Feeling the need of gentle exercise, I decided to spend the rest of the afternoon taking a stroll to the eastern side of the hotel grounds. Once again I congratulated myself on having escaped the cluster of chalets in this populated quarter. Mini-golf and tennis were in full swing, and the little beach was crowded with sprawling bodies on every available patch of sand. But soon the murmur of the world was behind me, and screened and safe behind the flowering shrubs I found myself on the point to the landing stage. The boat was not yet at its mooring, nor even in sight out in the gulf.

A sudden temptation to peep at the unpleasant Mr. Stoll's chalet swept upon me. I crept up the little path, feeling as furtive as a burglar on the prowl, and stared up at the shuttered windows. It was no different from its fellows, or mine for that matter, except for a telltale heap of bottles lying in a corner of the balcony. Brute . . . Then something else caught my eye. A pair of frog-feet, and a snorkel. Surely, with all that liquor inside him, he did not venture his carcass under water? Perhaps he sent the local Greek whom he employed as crew to seek for crabs. I remembered the snorkel on my first evening, close to the rocks, and the riding light in the boat.

I moved away, for I thought I could hear someone coming down the path and did not want to be caught prying, but before doing so I glanced up at the number of the chalet. It was 38. The figure had no particular significance for me then, but later on, changing for dinner, I picked up the tie-pin I had placed on my bedside table, and on sudden impulse opened the drawer beneath the telephone to look at my predecessor's card again. Yes, I thought so. The scrawled figure *was* 38. Pure coincidence, of course, and yet . . . "Not after midnight." The words suddenly had meaning. Stoll had warned me about swimming late on my first evening. Had he warned Gordon too? And Gordon had jotted down the warning on his card with Stoll's chalet number underneath? It made sense, but obviously poor Gordon had disregarded the advice. And so, apparently, did one of the occupants of Chalet 38.

I finished changing, and instead of replacing the card in the telephone drawer put it in my wallet. I had an uneasy feeling that it was my duty to hand it in to the reception desk in case it threw any light on my unfortunate predecessor's demise. I toyed with the thought through dinner but came to no decision. The point was, I might become involved, questioned by the police. And as far as I knew the case was closed. There was little point in my suddenly coming forward with a calling card lying forgotten in a drawer that probably had no significance at all.

It so happened that the people seated to the right of me in the dining room appeared to have gone, and the Stolls' table in the corner now came into view without my being obliged to turn my head. I could watch them without making it too obvious, and I was struck by the fact that he never once addressed a word to her. They made an odd contrast. She stiff as a ramrod, prim-looking, austere, forking her food to her mouth like a Sunday school teacher on an outing, and he, more scarlet than ever, like a great swollen sausage, pushing aside most of what the waiter placed before him after the first mouthful, and reaching out a pudgy, hairy hand to an ever-emptying glass.

I finished my dinner and went through to the bar to drink my coffee. I was early, and had the place to myself. The bartender and I exchanged the usual pleasantries and then, after an allusion to the weather, I jerked my head in the direction of the dining room.

"I noticed our friend Mr. Stoll and his lady spent the whole day at sea as usual," I said.

The bartender shrugged. "Day after day, it never varies," he replied, "and mostly in the same direction, westward out of the bay into the gulf. It can be squally, too, at times, but they don't seem to care."

"I don't know how she puts up with him," I said. "I watched them at dinner—he didn't speak to her at all. I wonder what the other guests make of him."

"They keep well clear, sir. You saw how it was for yourself. If he ever does open his mouth it's only to be rude. And the same goes for the staff. The girls dare not go in to clean the chalet until he's out of the way. And the smell!" He grimaced, and leant forward confidentially. "The girls say he brews his own beer. He lights the fire in the chimney, and has a pot standing, filled with rotting grain, like some sort of pig swill! Oh, yes, he drinks it right enough. Imagine the state of his liver, after what he consumed at dinner and afterwards here in the bar!"

"I suppose," I said, "that's why he keeps his balcony light on so late at night. Drinking pig swill until the small hours. Tell me, which of the hotel visitors is it who goes underwater swimming?"

The bartender looked surprised. "No one, to my knowledge. Not since the accident, anyway. Poor Mr. Gordon liked a night swim, at least so we supposed. He was one of the few visitors who ever talked to Mr. Stoll, now I think of it. They had quite a conversation here one evening in the bar."

"Indeed?"

"Not about swimming, though, or fishing either. They were discussing antiquities. There's a fine little museum here in the village, you know, but it's closed at present for repairs. Mr. Gordon had some connection with the British Museum in London."

"I wouldn't have thought," I said, "that would interest friend Stoll."

"Ah," said the bartender, "you'd be surprised. Mr. Stoll is no fool. Last year he and Mrs. Stoll used to take the car and visit all the famous sites, Knossos, Mallia, and other places not so well known. This year it's quite different. It's the boat and fishing every day."

"And Mr. Gordon," I pursued, "did he ever go fishing with them?"

"No, sir. Not to my knowledge. He hired a car, like you, and explored the district. He was writing a book, he told me, on archaeological finds in eastern Crete, and their connection with Greek mythology."

"Mythology?"

"Yes, I understood him to tell Mr. Stoll it was mythology, but it was all above my head, you can imagine, nor did I hear much of the conversation—we were busy that evening in the bar. Mr. Gordon was a quiet sort of gentleman, rather after your own style, if you'll excuse me, sir, seeming very interested in what they were discussing, all to do with the old gods. They were at it for over an hour."

H'm . . . I thought of the card in my wallet. Should I, or should I not, hand it over to the reception clerk at the desk? I said good night to the bartender and went back through the dining room to the hall. The Stolls had just left their table and were walking ahead of me. I hung back until the way was clear, surprised that they had turned their backs upon the bar and were making for the hall. I stood by the rack of postcards, to give myself an excuse for loitering, but out of their range of vision, and watched Mrs. Stoll take her coat from a hook in the lobby near the entrance, while her unpleasant husband visited the cloakroom, and then the pair of them walked out of the front door which led direct to the car park. They must be going for a drive. With Stoll at the wheel in his condition?

I hesitated. The reception clerk was on the telephone. It wasn't the moment to hand over the card. Some impulse, like that of a small boy playing detective, made me walk to my own car, and when Stoll's taillight was out of sight—he was driving a Mercedes —I followed in his wake. There was only the one road, and he was heading east towards the village and the harbour lights. I lost him, inevitably, on reaching the little port, for, instinctively making for the quayside opposite what appeared to be a main café, I thought he must have done the same. I parked the Volkswagen, and looked around me. No sign of the Mercedes. Just a sprinkling of other tourists like myself, and local inhabitants, strolling, or drinking in front of the café.

Oh well, forget it, I'd sit and enjoy the scene, have a lemonade. I must have sat there for over half an hour, savouring what is known as "local colour," amused by the passing crowd, Greek families taking the air, pretty, self-conscious girls eyeing the youths, who appeared to stick together, practising a form of segregation, a bearded Orthodox priest who smoked incessantly at the table next to me, playing some game of dice with a couple of very old men and of course the familiar bunch of hippies from my own country, considerably longer-haired than anybody else, dirtier, and making far more noise. When they switched on a transistor and squatted on the cobbled stones behind me, I felt it was time to move.

I paid for my lemonade, and strolled to the end of the quay and back—the line upon line of fishing boats would be colourful by day, and possibly the scene worth painting—and then I crossed the street, my eye caught by a glint of water inland, where a side road appeared to end in a cul-de-sac. This must be the feature mentioned in the guidebook as the Bottomless Pool, much frequented and photographed by tourists in the high season. It was larger than I had expected, quite a sizeable lake, the water full of scum and floating debris, and I did not envy those who had the temerity to use the diving board at the further end of it by day.

Then I saw the Mercedes. It was drawn up opposite a dimly lit café, and there was no mistaking the hunched figure at the table, beer bottles before him, the upright lady at his side, but to my surprise, and I may add disgust, he was not imbibing alone but appeared to be sharing his after-dinner carousal with a crowd of raucous fishermen at the adjoining table.

Clamour and laughter filled the air. They were evidently mocking him, Greek courtesy forgotten in their cups, while strains of song burst forth from some younger member of the clan, and suddenly he put out his hand and swept the empty bottles from his table onto the pavement, with the inevitable crash of broken glass and the accompanying cheers of his companions. I expected the local police to appear at any moment and break up the party, but there was no sign of authority. I did not care what happened to Stoll—a night in gaol might sober him up—but it was a wretched business for his wife. However, it wasn't my affair, and I was turning to go back to the quay when he staggered to his feet, applauded by the fishermen, and, lifting the remaining bottle from his table, swung it over his head. Then, with amazing dexterity for one in his condition, he pitched it like a discus thrower into the lake. It must have missed me by a couple of feet, and he saw me duck. This was too much. I advanced towards him, livid with rage.

"What the hell are you playing at?" I shouted.

He stood before me, swaying on his feet. The laughter from the café ceased as his cronies watched with interest. I expected a flood of abuse, but Stoll's swollen face creased into a grin, and he lurched forward and patted me on the arm.

"Know something?" he said. "If you hadn't been in the way I could have lobbed it into the centre of the goddamn pool. Which is more than any of those fellows could. Not a pure-blooded Cretan among them. They're all of them goddamn Turks."

I tried to shake him off, but he clung to me with the effusive affection of the habitual drunkard who has suddenly found, or imagines he has found, a lifelong friend.

"You're from the hotel, aren't you?" he hiccoughed. "Don't deny it, buddy boy, I've got a good eye for faces. You're the fellow who paints all day on his goddamn porch. Well, I admire you for it. Know a bit about art myself. I might even buy your picture."

His bonhomie was offensive, his attempt at patronage intolerable.

"I'm sorry," I said stiffly, "the picture is not for sale."

"Oh, come off it," he retorted. "You artists are all the same. Play hard to get until someone offers 'em a darn good price. Take Charlie Gordon now . . ." He broke off, peering slyly into my face. "Hang on, you didn't meet Charlie Gordon, did you?"

"No," I said shortly, "he was before my time."

"That's right, that's right," he agreed, "poor fellow's dead. Drowned in the bay there right under your rocks. At least, that's where they found him."

His slit eyes were practically closed in his swollen face, but I knew he was watching for my reaction.

"Yes," I said, "so I understand. He wasn't an artist."

"An artist?" Stoll repeated the word after me, then burst into a guffaw of laughter. "No, he was a connoisseur, and I guess that means the same goddamn thing to a chap like me. Charlie Gordon, connoisseur. Well, it didn't do him much good in the end, did it?"

"No," I said, "obviously not."

He was making an effort to pull himself together, and still rocking on his feet he fumbled for a packet of cigarettes and a lighter. He lit one for himself, then offered me the packet. I shook my head, telling him I did not smoke. Then, greatly daring, I observed, "I don't drink either."

"Good for you," he answered astonishingly, "neither do I. The beer they sell you here is all piss anyway, and the wine is poison." He looked over his shoulder to the group at the café and with a conspiratorial wink dragged me to the wall beside the pool.

"I told you all those bastards are Turks, and so they are," he said, "wine-drinking, coffee-drinking Turks. They haven't brewed the right stuff here for over five thousand years. They knew how to do it then."

I remembered what the bartender had told me about the pigswill in his chalet. "Is that so?" I enquired.

He winked again, and then his slit eyes widened, and I noticed that they were naturally bulbous and protuberant, a discoloured muddy brown with the whites red-flecked. "Know something?" he whispered hoarsely. "The scholars have got it all wrong. It was beer the Cretans drank here in the mountains, brewed from spruce and ivy long before wine. Wine was discovered centuries later by the goddamn Greeks."

He steadied himself, one hand on the wall, the other on my arm. Then he leant forward and was sick into the pool. I was very nearly sick myself.

"That's better," he said, "gets rid of the poison. Doesn't do to have poison in the system. Tell you what, we'll go back to the hotel and you shall come along and have a nightcap at our chalet. I've taken a fancy to you, Mr. What's-your-Name. You've got the right ideas. Don't drink, don't smoke, and you paint pictures. What's your job?"

It was impossible to shake myself clear, and I was forced to let him tow me across the road. Luckily the group at the café had now dispersed, disappointed, no doubt, because we had not come to blows, and Mrs. Stoll had climbed into the Mercedes and was sitting in the passenger seat in front.

"Don't take any notice of her," he said. "She's stone-deaf unless you bawl at her. Plenty of room at the back."

"Thank you," I said, "I've got my own car on the quay."

"Suit yourself," he answered. "Well, come on, tell me, Mr. Artist, what's your job? An academician?"

I could have left it at that, but some pompous strain in me made me tell the truth, in the foolish hope that he would then consider me too dull to cultivate.

"I'm a teacher," I said, "in a boys' preparatory school."

He stopped in his tracks, his wet mouth open wide in a delighted grin. "Oh, my God," he shouted, "that's rich, that's really rich. A goddamn tutor, a nurse to babes and sucklings. You're one of us, my buddy, you're one of us. And you've the nerve to tell me you've never brewed spruce and ivy!"

He was raving mad, of course, but at least this sudden burst of hilarity had made him free my arm, and he went on ahead of me to his car, shaking his head from side to side, his legs bearing his cumbersome body in a curious jog trot, one-two . . . one-two . . . like a clumsy horse.

I watched him climb into the car beside his wife, and then I moved swiftly away to make for the safety of the quayside, but he had turned his car with surprising agility, and had caught up with me before I reached the corner of the street. He thrust his head out of the window, smiling still.

"Come and call on us, Mr. Tutor, any time you like. You'll always find a welcome. Tell him so, Maud. Can't you see the fellow's shy?"

His bawling word of command echoed through the street. Strolling passers-by looked in our direction. The stiff, impassive face of Mrs. Stoll peered over her husband's shoulder. She seemed quite unperturbed, as if nothing was wrong, as if driving in a foreign village beside a drunken husband was the most usual pastime in the world.

"Good evening," she said in a voice without any expression. "Pleased to meet you, Mr. Tutor. Do call on us. Not after midnight. Chalet 38 . . ."

Stoll waved his hand, and the car went roaring up the street to cover the few kilometres to the hotel, while I followed behind, telling myself that this was one invitation I should never accept if my life depended on it.

It would not be true to say the encounter cast a blight on my holiday and put me off the place. A half truth, perhaps. I was angry and disgusted, but only with the Stolls. I awoke refreshed after a good night's sleep to another brilliant day, and nothing seems so bad in the morning. I had only the one problem, which was to avoid Stoll and his equally half-witted wife. They were out in their boat all day, so this was easy. By dining early I could escape them in the dining room. They never walked about the grounds, and meeting them face to face in the garden was not likely. If I happened to be on my balcony when they returned from fishing in the evening, and he turned his field glasses in my direction, I would promptly disappear inside my chalet. In any event, with luck, he might have forgotten my existence, or, if that was too much to hope for, the memory of our evening's conversation might have passed from his mind. The episode had been unpleasant, even, in a curious sense, alarming, but I was not going to let it spoil the days that remained to me.

The boat had left its landing stage by the time I came onto my balcony to have breakfast, and I intended to carry out my plan of exploring the coast with my painting gear, and, once absorbed in my hobby, could forget all about them. And I would not pass on to the management poor Gordon's scribbled card. I guessed now what had happened. The poor devil, without realising where his

conversation in the bar would lead him, had been intrigued by
Stoll's smattering of mythology and nonsense about ancient Crete,
and, as an archaeologist, had thought further conversation might
prove fruitful. He had accepted an invitation to visit Chalet 38
—the uncanny similarity of the words on the card and those
spoken by Mrs. Stoll still haunted me—though why he had
chosen to swim across the bay instead of walking the slightly
longer way by the rock path was a mystery. A touch of bravado,
perhaps? Who knows? Once in Stoll's chalet he had been induced,
poor victim, to drink some of the hell-brew offered by his host,
which must have knocked all sense and judgement out of him, and
when he took to the water once again, the carousal over, what followed was bound to happen. I only hoped he had been too far
gone to panic, and sank instantly. Stoll had never come forward
to give the facts, and that was that. Indeed, my theory of what had
happened was based on intuition alone, coincidental scraps that
appeared to fit, and prejudice. It was time to dismiss the whole
thing from my mind and concentrate on the day ahead.

Or rather, days. My exploration along the coast westward, in
the opposite direction from the harbour, proved even more successful than I had anticipated. I followed the winding road to the
left of the hotel, and having climbed for several kilometres descended again from the hills to sea level, where the land on my
right suddenly flattened out to what seemed to be a great stretch
of dried marsh, sun-baked, putty-coloured, the dazzling blue sea
affording a splendid contrast as it lapped the stretch of land on either side. Driving closer I saw that it was not marsh at all but salt
flats, with narrow causeways running between them, the flats
themselves contained by walls intersected by dykes to allow the
sea water to drain, leaving the salt behind. Here and there were
the ruins of abandoned windmills, their rounded walls like castle
keeps, and in a rough patch of ground a few hundred yards distant, and close to the sea, was a small church—I could see the
minute cross on the roof shining in the sun. Then the salt flats
ended abruptly, and the land rose once more to form the long,
narrow isthmus of Spinalongha beyond.

I bumped the Volkswagen down to the track leading to the flats.
The place was quite deserted. This, I decided, after viewing the
scene from every angle, would be my pitch for the next few days.
The ruined church in the foreground, the abandoned windmills

beyond, the salt flats on the left, and blue water rippling to the shore of the isthmus on my right.

I set up my easel, planted my battered felt hat on my head, and forgot everything but the scene before me. Those three days on the salt flats—for I repeated the expedition on successive days—were the high spot of my holiday. Solitude and peace were absolute. I never saw a single soul. The occasional car wound its way along the coast road in the distance and then vanished. I broke off for sandwiches and lemonade, which I'd brought with me, and then, when the sun was hottest, rested by the ruined windmill. I returned to the hotel in the cool of the evening, had an early dinner, and then retired to my chalet to read until bedtime. A hermit at his prayers could not have wished for greater seclusion.

The fourth day, having completed two separate paintings from different angles, yet loath to leave my chosen territory, which had now become a personal stamping ground, I stacked my gear in the car and struck off on foot to the rising terrain of the isthmus, with the idea of choosing a new site for the following day. Height might give an added advantage. I toiled up the hill, fanning myself with my hat, for it was extremely hot, and was surprised when I reached the summit to find how narrow was the isthmus, no more than a long neck of land with the sea immediately below me. Not the calm water that washed the salt flats I had left behind, but the curling crests of the outer gulf itself, whipped by a northerly wind that nearly blew my hat out of my hand. A genius might have caught those varying shades on canvas—turquoise blending into Aegean blue with wine-deep shadows beneath—but not an amateur like myself. Besides, I could hardly stand upright. Canvas and easel would have instantly blown away.

I climbed downwards towards a clump of broom affording shelter, where I could rest for a few minutes and watch that curling sea, and it was then that I saw the boat. It was moored close to a small inlet where the land curved and the water was comparatively smooth. There was no mistaking the craft: it was theirs all right. The Greek they employed as crew was seated in the bows, with a fishing line over the side, but from his lounging attitude the fishing did not seem to be serious, and I judged he was taking his siesta. He was the only occupant of the boat. I glanced directly beneath me to the spit of sand along the shore, and saw there was a rough stone building, more or less ruined, built against the cliff face, possibly used at one time as a shelter for sheep or goats. There was a haversack and a picnic basket lying by the entrance, and a coat. The Stolls must have landed earlier from the boat, although nosing the bows of the craft onto the shore must have been hazardous in the running sea, and were now taking their ease out of the wind. Perhaps Stoll was even brewing his peculiar mixture of spruce and ivy, with some goat dung added for good measure, and this lonely spot on the isthmus of Spinalongha was his "still."

Suddenly the fellow in the boat sat up, and winding in his line he moved to the stern and stood there, watching the water. I saw something move, a form beneath the surface, and then the form itself emerged, headpiece, goggles, rubber suiting, aqualung and all. Then it was hidden from me by the Greek bending to assist the swimmer to remove his top gear, and my attention was diverted to the ruined shelter on the shore. Something was standing in the entrance. I say "something" because doubtless owing to a trick of light, it had at first the shaggy appearance of a colt standing on its hind legs. Legs and even rump were covered with hair, and then I realised that it was Stoll himself, naked, his arms and chest as hairy as the rest of him. Only his swollen scarlet face proclaimed him for the man he was, with the enormous ears like saucers standing out from either side of his bald head. I had never in all my life seen a more revolting sight. He came out into the sunlight and looked towards the boat, and then, as if well pleased with himself and his world, strutted forward, pacing up and down the spit of sand before the ruined shelter with that curious movement I had noticed earlier in the village, not the rolling gait of a drunken man but a stumping jog trot, arms akimbo, his chest thrust forward, his backside prominent behind him.

The swimmer, having discarded goggles and aqualung, was now coming into the beach with long leisurely strokes, still wearing flippers—I could see them thrash the surface like a giant fish. Then, flippers cast aside on the sand, the swimmer stood up, and despite the disguise of the rubber suiting I saw, with astonishment, that it was Mrs. Stoll. She was carrying some sort of bag around her neck, and advancing up the sand to meet her strutting husband she lifted it over her head and gave it to him. I did not hear them exchange a word, and they went together to the hut and disappeared inside. As for the Greek, he had gone once more to the bows of the boat to resume his idle fishing.

I lay down under cover of the broom and waited. I would give them twenty minutes, half an hour, perhaps, then make my way back to the salt flats and my car. As it happened, I did not have to wait so long. It was barely ten minutes before I heard a shout below me on the beach, and peering through the broom I saw that they were both standing on the spit of sand, haversack, picnic basket and flippers in hand. The Greek was already starting the engine, and immediately afterwards he began to pull up the anchor. Then he steered the boat slowly inshore, touching it beside a ledge of rock where the Stolls had installed themselves. They climbed aboard, and in another moment the Greek had turned the boat, and it was heading out to sea away from the sheltered inlet and into the gulf. Then it rounded the point and was out of my sight.

Curiosity was too much for me. I scrambled down the cliff onto the sand and made straight for the ruined shelter. As I thought, it had been a haven for goats; the muddied floor reeked, and their droppings were everywhere. In a corner, though, a clearing had been made, and there were planks of wood, forming a sort of shelf. The inevitable beer bottles were stacked beneath this, but whether they had contained the local brew or Stoll's own poison I could not tell. The shelf itself held odds and ends of pottery, as though someone had been digging in a rubbish dump and had turned up broken pieces of discarded household junk. There was no earth upon them, though; they were scaled with barnacles, and some of them were damp, and it suddenly occurred to me that these were what archaeologists call "sherds," and came from the sea bed. Mrs. Stoll had been exploring, and exploring underwater, whether for shells or for something of greater interest I did not know, and these pieces scattered here were throwouts, of no use, and so neither she nor her husband had bothered to remove them. I am no judge of these things, and after looking around me, and finding nothing of further interest, I left the ruin.

The move was a fatal one. As I turned to climb the cliff I heard the throb of an engine, and the boat had returned once more, to cruise along the shore, so I judged from its position. All three heads were turned in my direction, and inevitably the squat figure in the stern had field glasses poised. He would have no difficulty, I feared, in distinguishing who it was that had just left the ruined shelter and was struggling up the cliff to the hill above.

I did not look back but went on climbing, my hat pulled down

well over my brows in the vain hope that it might afford some sort
of concealment. After all, I might have been any tourist who had
happened to be at that particular spot at that particular time. Nevertheless, I feared recognition was inevitable. I tramped back to
the car on the salt flats, tired, breathless and thoroughly irritated.
I wished I had never decided to explore the further side of the
peninsula. The Stolls would think I had been spying upon them,
which indeed was true. My pleasure in the day was spoilt. I decided to pack it in and go back to the hotel. Luck was against me,
though, for I had hardly turned onto the track leading from the
marsh to the road when I noticed that one of my tyres was flat. By
the time I had put on the spare wheel—for I am ham-fisted at all
mechanical jobs—forty minutes had gone by.

My disgruntled mood did not improve, when at last I reached
the hotel, to see that the Stolls had beaten me to it. Their boat was
already at its moorings beside the landing stage, and Stoll himself
was sitting on his balcony with field glasses trained upon my chalet. I stumped up the steps feeling as self-conscious as someone
under a television camera and went into my quarters, closing the
shutters behind me. I was taking a bath when the telephone rang.

"Yes?" Towel round the middle, dripping hands, it could not
have rung at a more inconvenient moment.

"That you, Mr. Tutor-boy?"

The rasping, wheezing voice was unmistakable. He did not
sound drunk, though.

"This is Timothy Grey," I replied stiffly.

"Grey or Black, it's all the same to me," he said. His tone was
unpleasant, hostile. "You were out on Spinalongha this afternoon.
Correct?"

"I was walking on the peninsula," I told him. "I don't know
why you should be interested."

"Oh, stuff it up," he answered, "you can't fool me. You're just
like the other fellow. You're nothing but a goddamn spy. Well, let
me tell you this. The wreck was clean-picked centuries ago."

"I don't know what you're talking about," I said. "What
wreck?"

There was a moment's pause. He muttered something under his
breath, whether to himself or to his wife I could not tell, but when
he resumed speaking his tone had moderated, something of
pseudo-bonhomie had returned.

"O.K. . . . O.K., Tutor-boy," he said. "We won't argue the point. Let us say you and I share an interest. Schoolmasters, university professors, college lecturers, we're all alike under the skin, and above it too sometimes." His low chuckle was offensive. "Don't panic, I won't give you away," he continued. "I've taken a fancy to you, as I told you the other night. You want something for your goddarn school museum, correct? Something you can show the pretty lads and your colleagues, too? Fine. Agreed. I've got just the thing. You call round here later this evening, and I'll make you a present of it. I don't want your goddamn money . . ." He broke off, chuckling again, and Mrs. Stoll must have made some remark, for he added, "That's right, that's right. We'll have a cosy little party, just the three of us. My wife's taken quite a fancy to you, too."

The towel round my middle slipped to the floor, leaving me naked. I felt vulnerable for no reason at all. And the patronising, insinuating voice infuriated me.

"Mr. Stoll," I said, "I'm not a collector for schools, colleges or museums. I'm not interested in antiquities. I am here on holiday to paint, for my own pleasure, and quite frankly I have no intention of calling upon you or any other visitor at the hotel. Good evening."

I slammed down the receiver and went back to the bathroom. Infernal impudence. Loathsome man. The question was, would he now leave me alone, or would he keep his glasses trained on my balcony until he saw me go up to the hotel for dinner, and then follow me, wife in tow, to the dining room? Surely he would not dare to resume the conversation in front of waiters and guests? If I guessed his intentions aright, he wanted to buy my silence by fobbing me off with some gift. Those daylong fishing expeditions of his were a mask for underwater exploration—hence his allusion to a wreck—during which he hoped to find, possibly had found already, objects of value that he intended to smuggle out of Crete. Doubtless he had succeeded in doing this the preceding year, and the Greek boatman would be well paid for holding his tongue.

This season, however, it had not worked to plan. My unfortunate predecessor at Chalet 62, Charles Gordon, himself an expert in antiquities, had grown suspicious. Stoll's allusion, "You're like the other fellow. Nothing but a goddamn spy," made this plain. What if Gordon had received an invitation to Chalet 38, not to drink the spurious beer but to inspect Stoll's collection and be offered a bribe for keeping silent? Had he refused, threatening to expose Stoll? Did he really drown accidentally, or had Stoll's wife followed him down into the water in her rubber suit and mask and flippers, and then, once beneath the surface . . . ?

My imagination was running away with me. I had no proof of anything. All I knew was that nothing in the world would get me to Stoll's chalet, and indeed, if he attempted to pester me again, I should have to tell the whole story to the management.

I changed for dinner, then opened my shutters a fraction and stood behind them, looking out towards his chalet. The light shone on his balcony, for it was already dusk, but he himself had disappeared. I stepped outside, locking the shutters behind me, and walked up the garden to the hotel.

I was just about to go through to the reception hall from the terrace when I saw Stoll and his wife sitting on a couple of chairs inside, guarding, as it were, the passageway to lounge and dining room. If I wanted to eat I had to pass them. Right, I thought. You can sit there all evening waiting. I went back along the terrace, and circling the hotel by the kitchens went round to the car park and got into the Volkswagen. I would have dinner down in the village, and damn the extra expense. I drove off in a fury, found an obscure taverna well away from the harbour itself, and instead of the three-course hotel meal I had been looking forward to on my en pension terms—for I was hungry after my day in the open and meagre sandwiches on the salt flats—I was obliged to content myself with an omelette, an orange and a cup of coffee.

It was after ten when I arrived back in the hotel. I parked the car, and skirting the kitchen quarters once again made my way furtively down the garden path to my chalet, letting myself in through the shutters like a thief. The light was still shining on Stoll's balcony, and by this time he was doubtless deep in his cups. If there was any trouble with him the next day I would definitely go to the management.

I undressed and lay reading in bed until after midnight, then, feeling sleepy, switched out my light and went across the room to open the shutters, for the air felt stuffy and close. I stood for a moment looking out across the bay. The chalet lights were all extinguished except for one. Stoll's, of course. His balcony light cast a yellow streak on the water beside his landing stage. The water rippled, yet there was no wind. Then I saw it. I mean, the snorkel. The little pipe was caught an instant in the yellow gleam, but before I lost it I knew that it was heading in a direct course for the rocks beneath my chalet. I waited. Nothing happened, there was no sound, no further ripple on the water. Perhaps she did this every evening. Perhaps it was routine, and while I was lying on my bed reading, oblivious of the world outside, she had been treading water close to the rocks The thought was discomforting, to say the least of it, that regularly after midnight she left her besotted husband asleep over his hell-brew of spruce and ivy and came herself, his underwater partner, in her black-seal rubber suit, her mask, her flippers, to spy upon Chalet 62. And on this night in particular, after the telephone conversation and my refusal to visit them, coupled with my new theory as to the fate of my predecessor, her presence in my immediate vicinity was more than ominous, it was threatening.

Suddenly, out of the dark stillness to my right, the snorkel pipe was caught in a finger-thread of light from my own balcony. Now it was almost immediately below me. I panicked, turned, and fled inside my room, closing the shutters fast. I switched off the balcony light and stood against the wall between my bedroom and bathroom, listening. The soft air filtered through the shutters beside me. It seemed an eternity before the sound I expected, dreaded, came to my ears. A kind of swishing movement from the balcony, a fumbling of hands, and heavy breathing. I could see nothing from where I stood against the wall, but the sounds came through the chinks in the shutters, and I knew she was there. I knew she was holding on to the hasp, and the water was dripping from the skintight rubber suit, and that even if I shouted, "What do you want?" she would not hear. No deaf-aids underwater, no mechanical device for soundless ears. Whatever she did by night must be done by sight, by touch.

She began to rattle on the shutters. I took no notice. She rattled again. Then she found the bell, and the shrill summons pierced the air above my head with all the intensity of a dentist's drill upon a nerve. She rang three times. Then silence. No more rattling of the shutters. No more breathing. She might yet be crouching on the balcony, the water dripping from the black rubber suit, waiting for me to lose patience, to emerge.

I crept away from the wall and sat down on the bed. There was

not a sound from the balcony. Boldly I switched on my bedside
light, half-expecting the rattling of the shutters to begin again, or
the sharp ping of the bell. Nothing happened, though. I looked at
my watch. It was half-past twelve. I sat there hunched on my bed,
my mind that had been so heavy with sleep now horribly awake,
full of foreboding, my dread of that sleek black figure increasing
minute by minute so that all sense and reason seemed to desert
me, and my dread was the more intense and irrational because the
figure in the rubber suit was female. What did she want?

I sat there for an hour or more until reason took possession
once again. She must have gone. I got up from the bed and went
to the shutters and listened. There wasn't a sound. Only the lapping of water beneath the rocks. Gently, very gently, I opened the
hasp and peered through the shutters. Nobody was there. I opened
them wider and stepped onto the balcony. I looked out across the
bay, and there was no longer any light shining from the balcony of
No. 38. The little pool of water beneath my shutters was evidence
enough of the figure that had stood there an hour ago, and the wet
footmarks leading down the steps towards the rocks suggested she
had gone the way she came. I breathed a sigh of relief. Now I
could sleep in peace.

It was only then that I saw the object at my feet, lying close to
the shutter's base. I bent and picked it up. It was a small package,
wrapped in some sort of waterproof cloth. I took it inside and examined it, sitting on the bed. Foolish suspicions of plastic bombs
came to my mind, but surely a journey underwater would neutral-
ise the lethal effect? The package was sewn about with twine,
crisscrossed. It felt quite light. I remembered the old classical prov-
erb, "Beware of the Greeks when they bear gifts." But the Stolls
were not Greeks, and, whatever lost Atlantis they might have
plundered, explosives did not form part of the treasure trove of
that vanished continent.

I cut the twine with a pair of nail scissors, then unthreaded it
piece by piece and unfolded the waterproof wrapping. A layer of
finely meshed net concealed the object within, and, this unra-
velled, the final token itself lay in my open hand. It was a small
jug, reddish in colour, with a handle on either side for safe holding. I had seen this sort of object before—the correct name, I believe, is rhyton—displayed behind glass cases in museums. The
body of the jug had been shaped cunningly and brilliantly into a

man's face, with upstanding ears like scallop shells, while protruding eyes and bulbous nose stood out above the leering, open mouth, the moustache drooping to the rounded beard that formed the base. At the top, between the handles, were the upright figures of three strutting men, their faces similar to that upon the jug, but here human resemblance ended, for they had neither hands nor feet but hooves, and from each of their hairy rumps extended a horse's tail.

I turned the object over. The same face leered at me from the other side. The same three figures strutted at the top. There was no crack, no blemish that I could see, except a faint mark on the lip. I looked inside the jug and saw a note lying on the bottom. The opening was too small for my hand, so I shook it out. The note was a plain white card, with words typed upon it. It read: "Silenus, earthborn satyr, half horse, half man, who, unable to distinguish truth from falsehood, reared Dionysus, god of intoxication, as a girl in a Cretan cave, then became his drunken tutor and companion."

That was all. Nothing more. I put the note back inside the jug, and the jug on the table at the far end of the room. Even then the lewd mocking face leered back at me, and the three strutting figures of the horsemen stood out in bold relief across the top. I was too weary to wrap it up again. I covered it with my jacket and climbed back into bed. In the morning I would cope with the laborious task of packing it up and getting my waiter to take it across to Chalet 38. Stoll could keep his rhyton—heaven knew what the value might be—and good luck to him. I wanted no part of it.

Exhausted, I fell asleep, but, oh God, to no oblivion. The dreams which came, and from which I struggled to awaken, but in vain, belonged to some other unknown world horribly intermingled with my own. Term had started, but the school in which I taught was on a mountaintop hemmed in by forest, though the school buildings were the same and the classroom was my own. My boys, all of them familiar faces, lads I knew, wore vine leaves in their hair, and had a strange, unearthly beauty both endearing and corrupt. They ran towards me, smiling, and I put my arms about them, and the pleasure they gave me was insidious and sweet, never before experienced, never before imagined, the man who pranced in their midst and played with them was not myself, not the self I knew, but a demon shadow emerging from a jug, strutting in his conceit as Stoll had done upon the spit of sand at Spinalongha.

I awoke after what seemed like centuries of time and indeed broad daylight seeped through the shutters, and it was a quarter to ten. My head was throbbing. I felt sick, exhausted. I rang for coffee, and looked out across the bay. The boat was at its moorings. The Stolls had not gone fishing. Usually they were away by nine. I took the jug from under my coat, and with fumbling hands began to wrap it up in the net and waterproof packing. I had made a botched job of it when the waiter came onto the balcony with my breakfast tray. He wished me good morning with his usual smile.

"I wonder," I said, "if you would do me a favour."

"You are welcome, sir," he replied.

"It concerns Mr. Stoll," I went on. "I believe he has Chalet 38 across the bay. He usually goes fishing every day, but I see his boat is still at the landing stage."

"That is not surprising," the waiter smiled. "Mr. and Mrs. Stoll left this morning by car."

"I see. Do you know when they will be back?"

"They will not be back, sir. They have left for good. They are driving to the airport en route for Athens. The boat is probably vacant now if you wish to hire it."

He went down the steps into the garden, and the jar in its waterproof packing was still lying beside the breakfast tray.

The sun was already fierce upon my balcony. It was going to be a scorching day, too hot to paint. And anyway, I wasn't in the mood. The events of the night before had left me tired, jaded, with a curious sapped feeling due not so much to the intruder beyond my shutters as to those interminable dreams. I might be free of the Stolls themselves, but not of their legacy.

I unwrapped it once again and turned it over in my hands. The leering, mocking face repelled me; its resemblance to the human Stoll was not pure fancy but compelling, sinister, doubtless his very reason for palming it off on me—I remembered the chuckle down the telephone—and if he possessed treasures of equal value to this rhyton, or even greater, then one object the less would not bother him. He would have a problem getting them through Customs, especially in Athens. The penalties were enormous for this sort of thing. Doubtless he had his contacts, knew what to do.

I stared at the dancing figures near the top of the jar, and once more I was struck by their likeness to the strutting Stoll on the shore of Spinalongha, his naked, hairy form, his protruding rump. Part man, part horse, a satyr . . . "Silenus, drunken tutor to the god Dionysus."

The jar was horrible, evil. Small wonder that my dreams had been distorted, utterly foreign to my nature. But not perhaps to Stoll's? Could it be that he too had realised its bestiality, but not until too late? The bartender had told me that it was only this year he had gone to pieces, taken to drink. There must be some link between his alcoholism and the finding of the jar. One thing was very evident, I must get rid of it—but how? If I took it to the management questions would be asked. They might not believe my story about its being dumped on my balcony the night before; they might suspect that I had taken it from some archaeological site, and then had second thoughts about trying to smuggle it out of the country or dispose of it somewhere on the island. So what? Drive along the coast and chuck it away, a rhyton centuries old and possibly priceless?

I wrapped it carefully in my jacket pocket and walked up the garden to the hotel. The bar was empty, the bartender behind his counter polishing glasses. I sat down on a stool in front of him and ordered a mineral water.

"No expedition today, sir?" he enquired.

"Not yet," I said. "I may go out later."

"A cool dip in the sea and a siesta on the balcony," he suggested, "and by the way, sir, I have something for you."

He bent down and brought out a small screw-topped bottle filled with what appeared to be bitter lemon.

"Left here last evening with Mr. Stoll's compliments," he said. "He waited for you in the bar until nearly midnight, but you never came. So I promised to hand it over when you did."

I looked at it suspiciously. "What is it?" I asked.

The bartender smiled. "Some of his chalet home-brew," he said. "It's quite harmless, he gave me a bottle for myself and my wife. She says it's nothing but lemonade. The real smelling stuff must have been thrown away. Try it." He had poured some into my mineral water before I could stop him.

Hesitant, wary, I dipped my finger into the glass and tasted it. It was like the barley water my mother used to make when I was a child. And equally tasteless. And yet . . . it left a sort of aftermath on the palate and the tongue. Not as sweet as honey nor as sharp as grapes, but pleasant, like the smell of raisins under the sun, curiously blended with the ears of ripening corn.

"Oh well," I said, "here's to the improved health of Mr. Stoll," and I drank my medicine like a man.

"I know one thing," said the bartender, "I've lost my best customer. They were away early this morning."

"Yes," I said, "so my waiter informed me."

"The best thing Mrs. Stoll could do would be to get him into hospital," the bartender continued. "Her husband's a sick man, and it's not just the drink."

"What do you mean?"

He tapped his forehead. "Something wrong up here," he said. "You could see for yourself how he acted. Something on his mind. Some sort of obsession. I rather doubt we shall see them again next year."

I sipped my mineral water, which was undoubtedly improved by the barley taste.

"What was his profession?" I asked.

"Mr. Stoll? Well, he told me he had been professor of classics in some American university, but you never could tell if he was speaking the truth or not. Mrs. Stoll paid the bills here, hired the boatman, arranged everything. Though he swore at her in public he seemed to depend on her. I sometimes wondered, though . . ."

He broke off.

"Wondered what?" I enquired.

"Well . . . She had a lot to put up with. I've seen her look at him sometimes, and it wasn't with love. Women of her age must seek some sort of satisfaction out of life. Perhaps she found it on the side while he indulged his passion for liquor and antiques. He had picked up quite a few items in Greece, and around the islands and here in Crete. It's not too difficult if you know the ropes."

He winked. I nodded, and ordered another mineral water. The warm atmosphere in the bar had given me a thirst.

"Are there any lesser known sites along the coast?" I asked. "I mean, places they might have gone ashore to from the boat?"

It may have been my fancy, but I thought he avoided my eye.

"I hardly know, sir," he said. "I dare say there are, but they would have custodians of some sort. I doubt if there are any places the authorities don't know about."

"What about wrecks?" I pursued. "Vessels that might have been sunk centuries ago, and are now lying on the sea bottom?"

He shrugged his shoulders. "There are always local rumours," he said casually, "stories that get handed down through generations. But it's mostly superstition. I've never believed in them myself, and I don't know anybody with education who does."

He was silent for a moment, polishing a glass. I wondered if I had said too much. "We all know small objects are discovered from time to time," he murmured, "and they can be of great value. They get smuggled out of the country, or if too much risk is involved they can be disposed of locally to experts and a good price paid. I have a cousin in the village connected with the local museum. He owns the café opposite the Bottomless Pool. Mr. Stoll used to patronise him. Papitos is the name. As a matter of fact, the boat hired by Mr. Stoll belongs to my cousin; he lets it out on hire to the visitors here at the hotel."

"I see."

"But there . . . you are not a collector, sir, and you're not interested in antiques."

"No," I said, "I am not a collector."

I got up from the stool and bade him good morning. I wondered if the small package in my pocket made a bulge.

I went out of the bar and strolled onto the terrace. Nagging curiosity made me wander down to the landing stage below the Stolls' chalet. The chalet itself had evidently been swept and tidied, the balcony cleared, the shutters closed. No trace remained of the last occupants. Before the day was over, in all probability, it would be opened for some English family who would strew the place with bathing suits.

The boat was at its moorings, and the Greek hand was swabbing down the sides. I looked out across the bay to my own chalet on the opposite side and saw it, for the first time, from Stoll's viewpoint. As he stood there, peering through his field glasses, it seemed clearer to me than ever before that he must have taken me for an interloper, a spy—possibly, even someone sent out from England to enquire into the true circumstances of Charles Gordon's death. Was the gift of the jar, the night before departure, a gesture of defiance? A bribe? Or a curse?

Then the Greek fellow on the boat stood up and faced towards me. It was not the regular boatman, but another one. I had not realised this before when his back was turned. The man who used to accompany the Stolls had been younger, dark, and this was an older chap altogether. I remembered what the bartender had told me about the boat belonging to his cousin, Papitos, who owned the café in the village by the Bottomless Pool.

"Excuse me," I called, "are you the owner of the boat?"

The man climbed onto the landing stage and stood before me.

"Nicolai Papitos is my brother," he said. "You want to go for trip round the bay? Plenty good fish outside. No wind today. Sea very calm."

"I don't want to fish," I told him. "I wouldn't mind an outing for an hour or so. How much does it cost?"

He gave me the sum in drachmae, and I did a quick reckoning and made it out to be not more than two pounds for the hour, though it would doubtless be double that sum to round the point and go along the coast as far as that spit of sand on the isthmus of Spinalongha. I took out my wallet to see if I had the necessary notes or whether I should have to return to the reception desk and cash a traveller's cheque.

"You charge to hotel," he said quickly, evidently reading my thoughts. "The cost go on your bill."

This decided me. Damn it all, my extras had been moderate to date.

"Very well," I said, "I'll hire the boat for a couple of hours."

It was a curious sensation to be chug-chugging across the bay as the Stolls had done so many times, the line of chalets in my wake, the harbour astern on my right and the blue waters of the open gulf ahead. I had no clear plan in mind. It was just that, for some inexplicable reason, I felt myself drawn towards that inlet near the shore where the boat had been anchored on the previous day. "The wreck was picked clean centuries ago . . ." Those had been Stoll's words. Was he lying? Or could it be that day after day, through the past weeks, that particular spot had been his hunting ground, and his wife, diving, had brought the dripping treasure from its sea bed to his grasping hands? We rounded the point, and inevitably, away from the sheltering arm that had hitherto encompassed us, the breeze appeared to freshen, the boat became more lively as the bows struck the short curling seas.

The long isthmus of Spinalongha lay ahead of us to the left, and I had some difficulty in explaining to my helmsman that I did not want him to steer into the comparative tranquillity of the waters bordering the salt flats, but to continue along the more exposed outward shores of the isthmus bordering the open sea.

"You want to fish?" he shouted above the roar of the engine. "You find very good fish in there," pointing to my flats of yesterday.

"No, no," I shouted back, "further on along the coast."

He shrugged. He couldn't believe I had no desire to fish, and I wondered, when we reached our destination, what possible excuse I could make for heading the boat inshore and anchoring, unless —and this seemed plausible enough—I pleaded that the motion of the boat was proving too much for me.

The hills I had climbed yesterday swung into sight above the bows, and then, rounding a neck of land, the inlet itself, the ruined shepherd's hut close to the shore.

"In there," I pointed. "Anchor close to the shore."

He stared at me, puzzled, and shook his head. "No good," he shouted, "too many rocks."

"Nonsense," I yelled. "I saw some people from the hotel anchored here yesterday."

Suddenly he slowed the engine, so that my voice rang out foolishly on the air. The boat danced up and down in the troughs of the short seas.

"Not a good place to anchor," he repeated doggedly. "Wreck there, fouling the ground."

So there was a wreck . . . I felt a mounting excitement, and I was not to be put off.

"I don't know anything about that," I replied, with equal determination, "but this boat did anchor here, just by the inlet. I saw it myself."

He muttered something to himself, and made the sign of the cross.

"And if I lose the anchor?" he said. "What do I say to my brother Nicolai?"

He was nosing the boat gently, very gently, towards the inlet, and then, cursing under his breath, he went forward to the bows and threw the anchor overboard. He waited until it held, then returned and switched off the engine.

"If you want to go in close, you must take the dinghy," he said sulkily. "I blow it up for you, yes?"

He went forward once again, and dragged out one of those inflatable rubber affairs they use on air-sea rescue craft.

"Very well," I said, "I'll take the dinghy."

In point of fact, it suited my purpose better. I could paddle close inshore, and would not have him breathing over my shoulder. At the same time, I couldn't forbear a slight prick to his pride.

"The man in charge of the boat yesterday anchored further in without mishap," I told him.

My helmsman paused in the act of inflating the dinghy.

"If he like to risk my brother's boat that is his affair," he said shortly. "I have charge of it today. Other fellow not turn up for work this morning, so he lose his job. I do not want to lose mine."

I made no reply. If the other fellow had lost his job it was probably because he had pocketed too many tips from Stoll.

The dinghy inflated and in the water, I climbed into it gingerly and began to paddle myself towards the shore. Luckily there was no run upon the spit of sand, and I was able to land successfully and pull the dinghy after me. I noticed that my helmsman was watching me with some interest from his safe anchorage, then, once he perceived that the dinghy was unlikely to come to harm, he turned his back and squatted in the bows of the boat, shoulders humped in protest, meditating, no doubt, upon the folly of English visitors.

My reason for landing was that I wanted to judge, from the shore, the exact spot where the boat had anchored yesterday. It was as I thought. Perhaps a hundred yards to the left of where we had anchored today, and closer inshore. The sea was smooth enough, I could navigate it perfectly in the rubber dinghy. I glanced towards the shepherd's hut, and saw my footprints of the day before. There were other footprints too. Fresh ones. The sand in front of the hut had been disturbed. It was as though something had lain there, and then been dragged to the water's edge where I stood now. The goatherd himself, perhaps, had visited the place with his flock earlier that morning.

I crossed over to the hut and looked inside. Curious . . . The little pile of rubble, odds and ends of pottery, had gone. The empty bottles still stood in the far corner, and three more had been added to their number, one of them half full. It was warm inside the hut, and I was sweating. The sun had been beating down on my bare head for nearly an hour—like a fool I had left my hat back in the chalet, not having prepared myself for this expedition —and I was seized with an intolerable thirst. I had acted on impulse, and was paying for it now. It was, in retrospect, an idiotic thing to have done. I might become completely dehydrated, pass out with heat stroke. The half bottle of beer would be better than nothing.

I did not fancy drinking from it after the goatherd, if it was indeed he who had brought it here; these fellows were none too clean. Then I remembered the jar in my pocket. Well, it would at least serve a purpose. I pulled the package out of its wrappings and poured the beer into it. It was only after I had swallowed the first draught that I realised it wasn't beer at all. It was barley water. It was the same home-brewed stuff that Stoll had left for me in the bar. Did the locals, then, drink it too? It was innocuous enough, I knew that; the bartender had tasted it himself, and so had his wife.

When I had finished the bottle I examined the jar once again. I don't know how it was, but somehow the leering face no longer seemed so lewd. It had a certain dignity that had escaped me before. The beard, for instance. The beard was shaped to perfection around the base—whoever had fashioned it was a master of his craft. I wondered whether Socrates had looked thus when he strolled in the Athenian agora with his pupils and discoursed on life. He could have done. And his pupils may not necessarily have been the young men whom Plato said they were, but of a tenderer age, like my lads at school, like those youngsters of eleven and twelve who had smiled upon me in my dreams last night.

I felt the scalloped ears, the rounded nose, the full soft lips of the tutor Silenus upon the jar, the eyes no longer protruding but questioning, appealing, and even the naked horsemen on the top had grown in grace. It seemed to me now they were not strutting in conceit but dancing with linked hands, filled with a gay abandon, a pleasing, wanton joy. It must have been my fear of the midnight intruder that had made me look upon the jar with such distaste.

I put it back in my pocket, and walked out of the hut and down the spit of beach to the rubber dinghy. Supposing I went to the fellow Papitos who had connections with the local museum, and asked him to value the jar? Supposing it was worth hundreds, thousands, and he could dispose of it for me, or tell me of a contact in London? Stoll must be doing this all the time, and getting away with it. Or so the bartender had hinted . . . I climbed into the dinghy and began to paddle away from the shore, thinking of the difference between a man like Stoll, with all his wealth, and myself. There he was, a brute with a skin so thick you couldn't pierce it with a spear, and his shelves back at home in the States loaded with loot. Whereas I . . . Teaching small boys on an inadequate salary, and all for what? Moralists said that money made no difference to happiness, but they were wrong. If I had a quarter of the Stolls' wealth I could retire, live abroad, on a Greek island, perhaps, and winter in some studio in Athens or Rome. A whole new way of life would open up, and just at the right moment, too, before I touched middle age.

I pulled out from the shore and made for the spot where I judged the boat to have anchored the day before. Then I let the dinghy rest, pulled in my paddles and stared down into the water. The colour was pale green, translucent, yet surely fathoms deep, for, as I looked down to the golden sands beneath, the sea bed had all the tranquillity of another world, remote from the one I knew. A shoal of fish, silver-bright and gleaming, wriggled their way towards a tress of coral hair that might have graced Aphrodite, but was seaweed moving gently in whatever currents lapped the shore. Pebbles that on land would have been no more than rounded stones were brilliant here as jewels. The breeze that rippled the gulf beyond the anchored boat would never touch these depths, but only the surface of the water, and as the dinghy floated on, circling slowly without pull of wind or tide, I wondered whether it was the motion in itself that had drawn the unhearing Mrs. Stoll to underwater swimming. Treasure was the excuse, to satisfy her husband's greed, but down there, in the depths, she would escape from a way of life that must have been unbearable.

Then I looked up at the hills above the retreating spit of sand, and I saw something flash. It was a ray of sunlight upon glass, and the glass moved. Someone was watching me through field glasses. I rested upon my paddles and stared. Two figures moved stealthily away over the brow of the hill, but I recognised them instantly. One was Mrs. Stoll, the other the Greek fellow who had acted as their crew. I glanced over my shoulder to the anchored boat. My helmsman was still staring out to sea. He had seen nothing.

The footsteps outside the hut were now explained. Mrs. Stoll, the boatman in tow, had paid a final visit to the hut to clear the rubble, and now, their mission accomplished, they would drive on to the airport to catch the afternoon plane to Athens, their journey made several miles longer by the detour along the coast road. And Stoll himself? Asleep, no doubt, at the back of the car upon the salt flats, awaiting their return.

The sight of that woman once again gave me a profound distaste for my expedition. I wished I had not come. And my helmsman had spoken the truth; the dinghy was now floating above rock. A ridge must run out here from the shore in a single reef. The sand had darkened, changed in texture, become grey. I peered closer into the water, cupping my eyes with my hands, and suddenly I saw the vast encrusted anchor, the shells and barnacles of centuries upon its spikes, and as the dinghy drifted on, the bones of the long-buried craft itself appeared, broken, sparless, her decks, if decks there had been, long since dismembered or destroyed.

Stoll had been right: her bones had been picked clean. Nothing of any value could now remain upon that skeleton. No pitchers, no jars, no gleaming coins. A momentary breeze rippled the water, and when it became clear again and all was still I saw the second anchor by the skeleton bows, and a body, arms outstretched, legs imprisoned in the anchor's jaws. The motion of the water gave the body life, as though, in some desperate fashion, it still struggled for release, but, trapped as it was, escape would never come. The days and nights would follow, months and years, and slowly the flesh would dissolve, leaving the frame impaled upon the spikes.

The body was Stoll's head, trunk, limbs grotesque, inhuman, as they swayed backwards and forwards at the bidding of the current.

I looked up once more to the crest of the hill, but the two figures had long since vanished, and in an appalling flash of intuition a picture of what had happened became vivid: Stoll strutting on the spit of sand, the half bottle raised to his lips, and then they struck him down and dragged him to the water's edge, and it was his wife who towed him, drowning, to his final resting place beneath the surface, there below me, impaled on the crusted anchor. I was sole witness to his fate, and no matter what lies she told to account for his disappearance I would remain silent; it was not my responsibility; guilt might increasingly haunt me, but I must never become involved.

I heard the sound of something choking beside me—I realise now it was myself, in horror and in fear—and I struck at the water with my paddles and started pulling away from the wreck back to the boat. As I did so my arm brushed against the jar in my pocket, and in sudden panic I dragged it forth and flung it overboard. Even as I did so, I knew the gesture was in vain. It did not sink immediately but remained bobbing on the surface, then slowly filled with that green translucent sea, pale as the barley liquid laced with spruce and ivy. Not innocuous but evil, stifling conscience, dulling intellect, the hell-brew of the smiling god Dionysus, which turned his followers into drunken sots, would claim another victim before long. The eyes in the swollen face stared up at me, and they were not only those of Silenus the satyr tutor, and of the drowned Stoll, but my own as well, as I should see them soon reflected in a mirror. They seemed to hold all knowledge in their depths, and all despair.

The Old Man

Did I hear you asking about the Old Man? I thought so. You're a newcomer to the district, here on holiday. We get plenty these days, during the summer months. Somehow they always find their way eventually over the cliffs down to this beach, and then they pause and look from the sea back to the lake. Just as you did.

It's a lovely spot, isn't it? Quiet and remote. You can't wonder at the old man choosing to live here.

I don't remember when he first came. Nobody can. Many years ago, it must have been. He was here when I arrived, long before the war. Perhaps he came to escape from civilisation, much as I did myself. Or maybe, where he lived before, the folks around made things too hot for him. It's hard to say. I had the feeling, from the very first, that he had done something, or something had been done to him, that gave him a grudge against the world. I remember the first time I set eyes on him I said to myself, "I bet that old fellow is one hell of a character."

Yes, he was living here beside the lake, along of his missus. Funny sort of lash-up they had, exposed to all the weather, but they didn't seem to mind.

I had been warned about him by one of the fellows from the farm, who advised me, with a grin, to give the old man who lived down by the lake a wide berth—he didn't care for strangers. So I went warily, and I didn't stay to pass the time of day. Nor would it have been any use if I had, not knowing a word of his lingo. The first time I saw him he was standing by the edge of the lake, looking out to sea, and from tact I avoided the piece of planking over the stream, which meant passing close to him, and crossed to the other side of the lake by the beach instead. Then, with an awkward feeling that I was trespassing and had no business to be there, I bobbed down behind a clump of gorse, took out my spyglass, and had a peep at him.

He was a big fellow, broad and strong—he's aged, of course, lately; I'm speaking of several years back—but even now you can see what he must have been once. Such power and drive behind him, and that fine head, which he carried like a king. There's an idea in that, too. No, I'm not joking. Who knows what royal blood he carries inside him, harking back to some remote ancestor? And now and again, surging in him—not through his own fault—it gets the better of him and drives him fighting mad. I didn't think about that at the time. I just looked at him, and ducked behind the gorse when I saw him turn, and I wondered to myself what went on in his mind, whether he knew I was there, watching him.

If he should decide to come up the lake after me I should look pretty foolish. He must have thought better of it, though, or perhaps he did not care. He went on staring out to sea, watching the gulls and the incoming tide, and presently he ambled off his side of the lake, heading for the missus and home and maybe supper.

I didn't catch a glimpse of her that first day. She just wasn't around. Living as they do, close in by the left bank of the lake, with no proper track to the place, I hardly had the nerve to venture close and come upon her face to face. When I did see her, though, I was disappointed. She wasn't much to look at after all. What I mean is, she hadn't got anything like his character. A placid, mild-tempered creature, I judged her.

They had both come back from fishing when I saw them, and were making their way up from the beach to the lake. He was in front, of course. She tagged along behind. Neither of them took the slightest notice of me, and I was glad, because the old man might have paused, and waited, and told her to get on back home, and then come down towards the rocks where I was sitting. You ask what I would have said, had he done so? I'm damned if I know. Maybe I would have got up, whistling and seeming unconcerned, and then, with a nod and a smile—useless, really, but instinctive, if you know what I mean—said good day and pottered off. I don't think he would have done anything. He'd just have stared after me, with those strange narrow eyes of his, and let me go.

After that, winter and summer, I was always down on the beach or the rocks, and they went on living their curious, remote existence, sometimes fishing in the lake, sometimes at sea. Occasionally I'd come across them in the harbour on the estuary, taking a look at the yachts anchored there, and the shipping. I used to wonder which of them made the suggestion. Perhaps suddenly he would be lured by the thought of the bustle and life of the harbour, and all the things he had either wantonly given up or never known, and he would say to her, "Today we are going into town." And she, happy to do whatever pleased him best, followed along.

You see, one thing that stood out—and you couldn't help noticing it—was that the pair of them were devoted to one another. I've seen her greet him when he came back from a day's fishing and had left her back home, and towards evening she'd come down the lake and onto the beach and down to the sea to wait for him. She'd see him coming from a long way off, and I would see him too, rounding the corner of the bay. He'd come straight in to the beach, and she would go to meet him, and they would embrace each other, not caring a damn who saw them. It was touching, if you know what I mean. You felt there was something lovable about the old man, if that's how things were between them. He might be a devil to outsiders, but he was all the world to her. It gave me a warm feeling for him, when I saw them together like that.

You asked if they had any family. I was coming to that. It's about the family I really wanted to tell you. Because there was a tragedy, you see. And nobody knows anything about it except me. I suppose I could have told someone, but if I had, I don't know . . . They might have taken the old man away, and she'd have broken her heart without him, and anyway, when all's said and done, it wasn't my business. I know the evidence against the old man was strong, but I hadn't positive proof, it might have been some sort of accident, and anyway, nobody made any enquiries at the time the boy disappeared, so who was I to turn busybody and informer?

I'll try and explain what happened. But you must understand that all this took place over quite a time, and sometimes I was away from home or busy, and didn't go near the lake. Nobody seemed to take any interest in the couple living there but myself, so that it was only what I observed with my own eyes that makes this story, nothing that I heard from anybody else, no scraps of gossip, or tales told about them behind their backs.

Yes, they weren't always alone, as they are now. They had four kids. Three girls and a boy. They brought up the four of them in that ramshackle old place by the lake, and it was always a wonder to me how they did it. God, I've known days when the rain lashed the lake into little waves that burst and broke on the muddy shore

near by their place, and turned the marsh into a swamp, and the
wind driving straight in. You'd have thought anyone with a grain of
sense would have taken his missus and his kids out of it and gone
off somewhere where they could get some creature comforts at
least. Not the old man. If he could stick it, I guess he decided she
could too, and the kids as well. Maybe he wanted to bring them
up the hard way.

Mark you, they were attractive youngsters. Especially the
youngest girl. I never knew her name, but I called her Tiny. She
had so much go to her. Chip off the old block, in spite of her size.

I can see her now, as a little thing, the first to venture paddling
in the lake, on a fine morning, way ahead of her sisters and the
brother.

The brother I nicknamed Boy. He was the eldest, and between
you and me a bit of a fool. He hadn't the looks of his sisters and
was a clumsy sort of fellow. The girls would play around on their
own, and go fishing, and he'd hang about in the background, not
knowing what to do with himself. If he possibly could he'd stay
around home, near his mother. Proper mother's boy. That's why I
gave him the name. Not that she seemed to fuss over him any
more than she did the others. She treated the four alike, as far as I
could tell. Her thoughts were always for the old man rather than
for them. But Boy was just a great baby, and I have an idea he
was simple.

Like their parents, the youngsters kept themselves to themselves. Been dinned into them, I dare say, by the old man. They
never came down to the beach on their own and played; and it
must have been a temptation, I thought, in full summer, when
people came walking over the cliffs down to the beach to bathe
and picnic. I suppose, for those strange reasons best known to
himself, the old man had warned them to have no truck with
strangers.

They were used to me pottering, day in, day out, fetching driftwood and that. And often I would pause and watch the kids playing by the lake. I didn't talk to them, though. They might have
gone back and told the old man. They used to look up when I
passed by, then glance away again, sort of shy. All but Tiny. Tiny
would toss her head and do a somersault, just to show off.

I sometimes watched them go off, the six of them—the old man,
the missus, Boy, and the three girls, for a day's fishing out to sea.

The old man, of course, in charge; Tiny eager to help, close to her dad; the missus looking about her to see if the weather was going to keep fine; the two other girls alongside; and Boy, poor simple Boy, always the last to leave home. I never knew what sport they had. They used to stay out late and I'd have left the beach by the time they came back again. But I guess they did well. They must have lived almost entirely on what they caught. Well, fish is said to be full of vitamins, isn't it? Perhaps the old man was a food faddist in his way.

Time passed, and the youngsters began to grow up. Tiny lost something of her individuality then, it seemed to me. She grew more like her sisters. They were a nice-looking trio, all the same. Quiet, you know, well-behaved.

As for Boy, he was enormous. Almost as big as the old man, but with what a difference! He had none of his father's looks, or strength, or personality; he was nothing but a great clumsy lout. And the trouble was, I believe the old man was ashamed of him. He didn't pull his weight in the home, I'm certain of that. And out fishing he was perfectly useless. The girls would work away like beetles, with Boy, always in the background, making a mess of things. If his mother was there he just stayed by her side.

I could see it rattled the old man to have such an oaf of a son. Irritated him, too, because Boy was so big. It probably didn't make sense to his intolerant mind. Strength and stupidity didn't go together. In any normal family, of course, Boy would have left home by now and gone out to work. I used to wonder if they argued about it back in the evenings, the missus and the old man, or if it was something never admitted between them but tacitly understood—Boy was no good.

Well, they did leave home at last. At least, the girls did.

I'll tell you how it happened.

It was a day in late autumn, and I happened to be over doing some shopping in the little town overlooking the harbour, three miles from this place, and suddenly I saw the old man, the missus, the three girls and Boy all making their way up to Pont—that's at the head of a creek going eastward from the harbour. There are a few cottages at Pont, and a farm and a church up behind. The family looked washed and spruced up, and so did the old man and the missus, and I wondered if they were going visiting. If they were, it was an unusual thing for them to do. But it's possible they had friends or acquaintances up there, of whom I knew nothing. Anyway, that was the last I saw of them, on the fine Saturday afternoon, making for Pont.

It blew hard over the weekend, a proper easterly gale. I kept indoors and didn't go out at all. I knew the seas would be breaking good and hard on the beach. I wondered if the old man and the family had been able to get back. They would have been wise to stay with their friends up Pont, if they had friends there.

It was Tuesday before the wind dropped and I went down to the beach again. Seaweed, driftwood, tar and oil all over the place. It's always the same after an easterly blow. I looked up the lake, towards the old man's shack, and I saw him there, with the missus, just by the edge of the lake. But there was no sign of the youngsters.

I thought it a bit funny, and waited around in case they should appear. They never did. I walked right round the lake, and from the opposite bank I had a good view of their place, and even took out my old spyglass to have a closer look. They just weren't there. The old man was pottering about as he often did when he wasn't fishing, and the missus had settled herself down to bask in the sun. There was only one explanation. They had left the family with friends in Pont. They had sent the family for a holiday.

I can't help admitting I was relieved, because for one frightful moment I thought maybe they had started off back home on the Saturday night and got struck by the gale; and, well—that the old man and his missus had got back safely, but not the kids. It couldn't be that, though. I should have heard. Someone would have said something. The old man wouldn't be pottering there in his usual unconcerned fashion and the missus basking in the sun. No, that must have been it. They had left the family with friends. Or maybe the girls and Boy had gone up country, gone to find themselves jobs at last.

Somehow it left a gap. I felt sad. So long now I had been used to seeing them all around, Tiny and the others. I had a strange sort of feeling that they had gone for good. Silly, wasn't it? To mind, I mean. There was the old man, and his missus, and the four youngsters, and I'd more or less watched them grow up, and now for no reason they had gone.

I wished then I knew even a word or two of his language, so

that I could have called out to him, neighbour-like, and said, "I see you and the missus are on your own. Nothing wrong, I hope?"

But there, it wasn't any use. He'd have looked at me with his strange eyes and told me to go to hell.

I never saw the girls again. No, never. They just didn't come back. Once I thought I saw Tiny, somewhere up the estuary, with a group of friends, but I couldn't be sure. If it was, she'd grown, she looked different. I tell you what I think. I think the old man and the missus took them with a definite end in view, that last weekend, and either settled them with friends they knew or told them to shift for themselves.

I know it sounds hard, not what you'd do for your own son and daughters, but you have to remember the old man was a tough customer, a law unto himself. No doubt he thought it would be for the best, and so it probably was, and if only I could know for certain what happened to the girls, especially Tiny, I wouldn't worry.

But I do worry sometimes, because of what happened to Boy.

You see, Boy was fool enough to come back. He came back about three weeks after that final weekend. I had walked down through the woods—not my usual way, but down to the lake by the stream that feeds it from a higher level. I rounded the lake by the marshes to the north, some distance from the old man's place, and the first thing I saw was Boy.

He wasn't doing anything. He was just standing by the marsh. He looked dazed. He was too far off for me to hail him; besides, I didn't have the nerve. But I watched him, as he stood there in his clumsy loutish way, and I saw him staring at the far end of the lake. He was staring in the direction of the old man.

The old man, and the missus with him, took not the slightest notice of Boy. They were close to the beach, by the plank bridge, and were either just going out to fish or coming back. And here was Boy, with his dazed stupid face, but not only stupid—frightened.

I wanted to say, "Is anything the matter?" but I didn't know how to say it. I stood there, like Boy, staring at the old man.

Then what we both must have feared would happen, happened.

The old man lifted his head and saw Boy.

He must have said a word to his missus, because she didn't move, she stayed where she was, by the bridge, but the old man turned like a flash of lightning and came down the other side of the lake towards the marshes, towards Boy. He looked terrible. I shall never forget his appearance. That magnificent head I had always admired now angry, evil; and he was cursing Boy as he came. I tell you, I heard him.

Boy, bewildered, scared, looked hopelessly about him for cover. There was none. Only the thin reeds that grew beside the marsh. But the poor fellow was so dumb he went in there, and crouched, and believed himself safe—it was a horrible sight.

I was just getting my own courage up to interfere when the old man stopped suddenly in his tracks, pulled up short as it were, and then, still cursing, muttering, turned back again and returned to the bridge. Boy watched him, from his cover of reeds, then, poor clot that he was, came out onto the marsh again, with some idea, I suppose, of striking for home.

I looked about me. There was no one to call. No one to give any help. And if I went and tried to get someone from the farm they would tell me not to interfere, that the old man was best left alone when he got in one of his rages, and anyway that Boy was old enough to take care of himself. He was as big as the old man. He could give as good as he got. I knew different. Boy was no fighter. He didn't know how.

I waited quite a time beside the lake but nothing happened. It began to grow dark. It was no use my waiting there. The old man and the missus left the bridge and went on home. Boy was still standing there on the marsh, by the lake's edge.

I called to him, softly. "It's no use. He won't let you in. Go back to Pont, or wherever it is you've been. Go to some place, anywhere, but get out of here."

He looked up, that same queer dazed expression on his face, and I could tell he hadn't understood a word I said.

I felt powerless to do any more. I went home myself. But I thought about Boy all evening, and in the morning I went down to the lake again, and I took a great stick with me to give me courage. Not that it would have been much good. Not against the old man.

Well . . . I suppose they had come to some sort of agreement, during the night. There was Boy, by his mother's side, and the old man was pottering on his own.

I must say, it was a great relief. Because, after all, what could I have said or done? If the old man didn't want Boy home, it was really his affair. And if Boy was too stupid to go, that was Boy's affair.

But I blamed the mother a good deal. After all, it was up to her to tell Boy he was in the way, and the old man was in one of his moods, and Boy had best get out while the going was good. But I never did think she had great intelligence. She did not seem to show much spirit at any time.

However, what arrangement they had come to worked for a time. Boy stuck close to his mother—I suppose he helped her at home, I don't know—and the old man left them alone and was more and more by himself.

He took to sitting down by the bridge, humped, staring out to sea, with a queer brooding look on him. He seemed strange, and lonely. I didn't like it. I don't know what his thoughts were, but I'm sure they were evil. It suddenly seemed a very long time since he and the missus and the whole family had gone fishing, a happy, contented party. Now everything had changed for him. He was thrust out in the cold, and the missus and Boy stayed together.

I felt sorry for him, but I felt frightened, too. Because I felt it could not go on like this indefinitely; something would happen.

One day I went down to the beach for driftwood—it had been blowing in the night—and when I glanced towards the lake I saw that Boy wasn't with his mother. He was back where I had seen him that first day, on the edge of the marsh. He was as big as his father. If he'd known how to use his strength he'd have been a match for him any day, but he hadn't the brains. There he was, back on the marsh, a great big frightened foolish fellow, and there was the old man, outside his home, staring down towards his son with murder in his eyes.

I said to myself, "He's going to kill him." But I didn't know how or when or where, whether by night, when they were sleeping, or by day, when they were fishing. The mother was useless, she would not prevent it. It was no use appealing to the mother. If only Boy would use one little grain of sense, and go . . .

I watched and waited until nightfall. Nothing happened.

It rained in the night. It was grey, and cold, and dim. December was everywhere, trees all bare and bleak. I couldn't get down to the lake until late afternoon, and then the skies had cleared and the sun was shining in that watery way it does in winter, a burst of it, just before setting below the sea.

I saw the old man, and the missus too. They were close together, by the old shack, and they saw me coming for they looked towards me. Boy wasn't there. He wasn't on the marsh, either. Nor by the side of the lake.

I crossed the bridge and went along the right bank of the lake, and I had my spyglass with me, but I couldn't see Boy. Yet all the time I was aware of the old man watching me.

Then I saw him. I scrambled down the bank, and crossed the marsh, and went to the thing I saw lying there, behind the reeds.

He was dead. There was a great gash on his body. Dried blood on his back. But he had lain there all night. His body was sodden with the rain.

Maybe you'll think I'm a fool, but I began to cry, like an idiot, and I shouted across to the old man, "You murderer, you bloody goddamned murderer." He did not answer. He did not move. He stood there, outside his shack with the missus, watching me.

You'll want to know what I did. I went back and got a spade, and I dug a grave for Boy, in the reeds behind the marsh, and I said one of my own prayers for him, being uncertain of his religion. When I had finished I looked across the lake to the old man.

And do you know what I saw?

I saw him lower his great head, and bend towards her and embrace her. And she lifted her head to him and embraced him too. It was both a requiem and a benediction. An atonement, and a giving of praise. In their strange way they knew they had done evil, but now it was over, because I had buried Boy and he was gone. They were free to be together again, and there was no longer a third to divide them.

They came out into the middle of the lake, and suddenly I saw the old man stretch his neck and beat his wings, and he took off from the water, full of power, and she followed him. I watched the two swans fly out to sea right into the face of the setting sun, and I tell you it was one of the most beautiful sights I ever saw in my life: the two swans flying there, alone, in winter.

The Birds

On December the third the wind changed overnight and it was winter. Until then the autumn had been mellow, soft. The leaves had lingered on the trees, golden red, and the hedgerows were still green. The earth was rich where the plough had turned it.

Nat Hocken, because of a wartime disability, had a pension and did not work full-time at the farm. He worked three days a week, and they gave him the lighter jobs: hedging, thatching, repairs to the farm buildings.

Although he was married, with children, his was a solitary disposition; he liked best to work alone. It pleased him when he was given a bank to build up, or a gate to mend at the far end of the peninsula, where the sea surrounded the farm land on either side. Then, at midday, he would pause and eat the pasty that his wife had baked for him, and sitting on the cliff's edge would watch the birds. Autumn was best for this, better than spring. In spring the birds flew inland, purposeful, intent; they knew where they were bound, the rhythm and ritual of their life brooked no delay. In autumn those that had not migrated overseas but remained to pass the winter were caught up in the same driving urge, but because migration was denied them followed a pattern of their own. Great flocks of them came to the peninsula, restless, uneasy, spending themselves in motion; now wheeling, circling in the sky, now settling to feed on the rich new-turned soil, but even when they fed it was as though they did so without hunger, without desire. Restlessness drove them to the skies again.

Black and white, jackdaw and gull, mingled in strange partnership, seeking some sort of liberation, never satisfied, never still. Flocks of starlings, rustling like silk, flew to fresh pasture, driven by the same necessity of movement, and the smaller birds, the finches and the larks, scattered from tree to hedge as if compelled.

Nat watched them, and he watched the sea birds too. Down in the bay they waited for the tide. They had more patience. Oyster-catchers, redshank, sanderling and curlew watched by the water's edge; as the slow sea sucked at the shore and then withdrew, leav-

ing the strip of seaweed bare and the shingle churned, the sea
birds raced and ran upon the beaches. Then that same impulse to
flight seized upon them too. Crying, whistling, calling, they
skimmed the placid sea and left the shore. Make haste, make
speed, hurry and begone; yet where, and to what purpose? The
restless urge of autumn, unsatisfying, sad, had put a spell upon
them and they must flock, and wheel, and cry; they must spill
themselves of motion before winter came.

Perhaps, thought Nat, munching his pasty by the cliff's edge, a
message comes to the birds in autumn, like a warning. Winter is
coming. Many of them perish. And like people who, apprehensive
of death before their time, drive themselves to work or folly, the
birds do likewise.

The birds had been more restless than ever this fall of the year,
the agitation more marked because the days were still. As the
tractor traced its path up and down the western hills, the figure of
the farmer silhouetted on the driving seat, the whole machine and
the man upon it would be lost momentarily in the great cloud of
wheeling, crying birds. There were many more than usual, Nat
was sure of this. Always, in autumn, they followed the plough, but
not in great flocks like these, nor with such clamour.

Nat remarked upon it, when hedging was finished for the day.
"Yes," said the farmer, "there are more birds about than usual;
I've noticed it too. And daring, some of them, taking no notice of
the tractor. One or two gulls came so close to my head this afternoon I thought they'd knock my cap off! As it was, I could
scarcely see what I was doing, when they were overhead and I had
the sun in my eyes. I have a notion the weather will change. It will
be a hard winter. That's why the birds are restless."

Nat, tramping home across the fields and down the lane to his
cottage, saw the birds still flocking over the western hills, in the
last glow of the sun. No wind, and the grey sea calm and full. Cam-
pion in bloom yet in the hedges, and the air mild. The farmer was
right, though, and it was that night the weather turned. Nat's bedroom faced east. He woke just after two and heard the wind in the
chimney. Not the storm and bluster of a sou'westerly gale, bringing the rain, but east wind, cold and dry. It sounded hollow in the
chimney, and a loose slate rattled on the roof. Nat listened, and he
could hear the sea roaring in the bay. Even the air in the small
bedroom had turned chill: a draught came under the skirting of

the door, blowing upon the bed. Nat drew the blanket round him, leant closer to the back of his sleeping wife, and stayed wakeful, watchful, aware of misgiving without cause.

Then he heard the tapping on the window. There was no creeper on the cottage walls to break loose and scratch upon the pane. He listened, and the tapping continued until, irritated by the sound, Nat got out of bed and went to the window. He opened it, and as he did so something brushed his hand, jabbing at his knuckles, grazing the skin. Then he saw the flutter of the wings and it was gone, over the roof, behind the cottage.

It was a bird, what kind of bird he could not tell. The wind must have driven it to shelter on the sill.

He shut the window and went back to bed, but feeling his knuckles wet put his mouth to the scratch. The bird had drawn blood. Frightened, he supposed, and bewildered, the bird, seeking shelter, had stabbed at him in the darkness. Once more he settled himself to sleep.

Presently the tapping came again, this time more forceful, more insistent, and now his wife woke at the sound, and turning in the bed said to him, "See to the window, Nat, it's rattling."

"I've already seen to it," he told her, "there's some bird there, trying to get in. Can't you hear the wind? It's blowing from the east, driving the birds to shelter."

"Send them away," she said. "I can't sleep with that noise."

He went to the window for the second time, and now when he opened it there was not one bird upon the sill but half a dozen; they flew straight into his face, attacking him.

He shouted, striking out at them with his arms, scattering them; like the first one, they flew over the roof and disappeared. Quickly he let the window fall and latched it.

"Did you hear that?" he said. "They went for me. Tried to peck my eyes." He stood by the window, peering into the darkness, and could see nothing. His wife, heavy with sleep, murmured from the bed.

"I'm not making it up," he said, angry at her suggestion. "I tell you the birds were on the sill, trying to get into the room."

Suddenly a frightened cry came from the room across the passage where the children slept.

"It's Jill," said his wife, roused at the sound, sitting up in bed. "Go to her, see what's the matter."

Nat lit the candle, but when he opened the bedroom door to cross the passage the draught blew out the flame.

There came a second cry of terror, this time from both children, and stumbling into their room he felt the beating of wings about him in the darkness. The window was wide open. Through it came the birds, hitting first the ceiling and the walls, then swerving in midflight, turning to the children in their beds.

"It's all right, I'm here," shouted Nat, and the children flung themselves, screaming, upon him, while in the darkness the birds rose and dived and came for him again.

"What is it, Nat, what's happened?" his wife called from the further bedroom, and swiftly he pushed the children through the door to the passage and shut it upon them, so that he was alone now, in their bedroom, with the birds.

He seized a blanket from the nearest bed, and using it as a weapon flung it to right and left about him in the air. He felt the thud of bodies, heard the fluttering of wings, but they were not yet defeated, for again and again they returned to the assault, jabbing his hands, his head, the little stabbing beaks sharp as a pointed fork. The blanket became a weapon of defence; he wound it about his head, and then in greater darkness beat at the birds with his bare hands. He dared not stumble to the door and open it, lest in doing so the birds should follow him.

How long he fought with them in the darkness he could not tell, but at last the beating of the wings about him lessened and then withdrew, and through the density of the blanket he was aware of light. He waited, listened; there was no sound except the fretful crying of one of the children from the bedroom beyond. The fluttering, the whirring of the wings had ceased.

He took the blanket from his head and stared about him. The cold grey morning light exposed the room. Dawn, and the open window, had called the living birds; the dead lay on the floor. Nat gazed at the little corpses, shocked and horrified. They were all small birds, none of any size; there must have been fifty of them lying there upon the floor. There were robins, finches, sparrows, blue tits, larks and bramblings, birds that by nature's law kept to their own flock and their own territory, and now, joining one with another in their urge for battle, had destroyed themselves against the bedroom walls, or in the strife had been destroyed by him.

Some had lost feathers in the fight, others had blood, his blood, upon their beaks.

Sickened, Nat went to the window and stared out across his patch of garden to the fields.

It was bitter cold, and the ground had all the hard black look of frost. Not white frost, to shine in the morning sun, but the black frost that the east wind brings. The sea, fiercer now with the turning tide, whitecapped and steep, broke harshly in the bay. Of the birds there was no sign. Not a sparrow chattered in the hedge beyond the garden gate, no early missel-thrush or blackbird pecked on the grass for worms. There was no sound at all but the east wind and the sea.

Nat shut the window and the door of the small bedroom, and went back across the passage to his own. His wife sat up in bed, one child asleep beside her, the smaller in her arms, his face bandaged. The curtains were tightly drawn across the window, the candles lit. Her face looked garish in the yellow light. She shook her head for silence.

"He's sleeping now," she whispered, "but only just. Something must have cut him, there was blood at the corner of his eyes. Jill said it was the birds. She said she woke up, and the birds were in the room."

His wife looked up at Nat, searching his face for confirmation. She looked terrified, bewildered, and he did not want her to know that he was also shaken, dazed almost, by the events of the past few hours.

"There are birds in there," he said, "dead birds, nearly fifty of them. Robins, wrens, all the little birds from hereabouts. It's as though madness seized them, with the east wind." He sat down on the bed beside his wife, and held her hand. "It's the weather," he said, "it must be that, it's the hard weather. They aren't the birds, maybe, from here around. They've been driven down, from up country."

"But Nat," whispered his wife, "it's only this night that the weather turned. There's been no snow to drive them. And they can't be hungry yet. There's food for them, out there, in the fields."

"It's the weather," repeated Nat. "I tell you, it's the weather."

His face too was drawn and tired, like hers. They stared at one another for a while without speaking.

"I'll go downstairs and make a cup of tea," he said.

The sight of the kitchen reassured him. The cups and saucers, neatly stacked upon the dresser, the table and chairs, his wife's roll of knitting on her basket chair, the children's toys in a corner cupboard.

He knelt down, raked out the old embers and relit the fire. The glowing sticks brought normality, the steaming kettle and the brown teapot comfort and security. He drank his tea, carried a cup to his wife. Then he washed in the scullery, and, putting on his boots, opened the back door.

The sky was hard and leaden, and the brown hills that had gleamed in the sun the day before looked dark and bare. The east wind, like a razor, stripped the trees, and the leaves, crackling and dry, shivered and scattered with the wind's blast. Nat stubbed the earth with his boot. It was frozen hard. He had never known a change so swift and sudden. Black winter had descended in a single night.

The children were awake now. Jill was chattering upstairs and young Johnny crying once again. Nat heard his wife's voice, soothing, comforting. Presently they came down. He had breakfast ready for them, and the routine of the day began.

"Did you drive away the birds?" asked Jill, restored to calm because of the kitchen fire, because of day, because of breakfast.

"Yes, they've all gone now," said Nat. "It was the east wind brought them in. They were frightened and lost. They wanted shelter."

"They tried to peck us," said Jill. "They went for Johnny's eyes."

"Fright made them do that," said Nat. "They didn't know where they were, in the dark bedroom."

"I hope they won't come again," said Jill. "Perhaps if we put bread for them outside the window they will eat that and fly away."

She finished her breakfast and then went for her coat and hood, her school books and her satchel. Nat said nothing, but his wife looked at him across the table. A silent message passed between them.

"I'll walk with her to the bus," he said. "I don't go to the farm today."

And while the child was washing in the scullery he said to his wife, "Keep all the windows closed, and the doors too. Just to be on the safe side. I'll go to the farm. Find out if they heard anything in the night." Then he walked with his small daughter up the lane. She seemed to have forgotten her experience of the night before. She danced ahead of him, chasing the leaves, her face whipped with the cold and rosy under the pixie hood.

"Is it going to snow, Dad?" she said. "It's cold enough."

He glanced up at the bleak sky, felt the wind tear at his shoulders.

"No," he said, "it's not going to snow. This is a black winter, not a white one."

All the while he searched the hedgerows for the birds, glanced over the top of them to the fields beyond, looked to the small wood above the farm where the rooks and jackdaws gathered. He saw none.

The other children waited by the bus stop, muffled, hooded like Jill, the faces white and pinched with cold.

Jill ran to them, waving. "My Dad says it won't snow," she called, "it's going to be a black winter."

She said nothing of the birds. She began to push and struggle with another little girl. The bus came ambling up the hill. Nat saw her on it, then turned and walked back towards the farm. It was not his day for work, but he wanted to satisfy himself that all was well. Jim, the cowman, was clattering in the yard.

"Boss around?" asked Nat.

"Gone to market," said Jim. "It's Tuesday, isn't it?"

He clumped off round the corner of a shed. He had no time for Nat. Nat was said to be superior. Read books, and the like. Nat had forgotten it was Tuesday. This showed how the events of the preceding night had shaken him. He went to the back door of the farmhouse and heard Mrs. Trigg singing in the kitchen, the wireless making a background to her song.

"Are you there, missus?" called out Nat.

She came to the door, beaming, broad, a good-tempered woman.

"Hullo, Mr. Hocken," she said. "Can you tell me where this cold is coming from? Is it Russia? I've never seen such a change. And it's going on, the wireless says. Something to do with the Arctic Circle."

"We didn't turn on the wireless this morning," said Nat. "Fact is, we had trouble in the night."

"Kiddies poorly?"

"No . . ." He hardly knew how to explain it. Now, in daylight, the battle of the birds would sound absurd.

He tried to tell Mrs. Trigg what had happened, but he could see from her eyes that she thought his story was the result of a nightmare.

"Sure they were real birds," she said, smiling, "with proper feathers and all? Not the funny-shaped kind, that the men see after closing hours on a Saturday night?"

"Mrs. Trigg," he said, "there are fifty dead birds, robins, wrens and such, lying low on the floor of the children's bedroom. They went for me; they tried to go for young Johnny's eyes."

Mrs. Trigg stared at him doubtfully.

"Well there, now," she answered, "I suppose the weather brought them. Once in the bedroom, they wouldn't know where they were to. Foreign birds maybe, from that Arctic Circle."

"No," said Nat, "they were the birds you see about here every day."

"Funny thing," said Mrs. Trigg, "no explaining it, really. You ought to write up and ask the *Guardian*. They'd have some answer for it. Well, I must be getting on."

She nodded, smiled, and went back into the kitchen.

Nat, dissatisfied, turned to the farm gate. Had it not been for those corpses on the bedroom floor, which he must now collect and bury somewhere, he would have considered the tale exaggeration too.

Jim was standing by the gate.

"Had any trouble with the birds?" asked Nat.

"Birds? What birds?"

"We got them up our place last night. Scores of them, came in the children's bedroom. Quite savage they were."

"Oh?" It took time for anything to penetrate Jim's head. "Never heard of birds acting savage," he said at length. "They get tame, like, sometimes. I've seen them come to the windows, for crumbs."

"These birds last night weren't tame."

"No? Cold maybe. Hungry. You put out some crumbs."

Jim was no more interested than Mrs. Trigg had been. It was,

Nat thought, like air raids in the war. No one down this end of the country knew what the Plymouth folk had seen and suffered. You had to endure something yourself before it touched you. He walked back along the lane and crossed the stile to his cottage. He found his wife in the kitchen with young Johnny.

"See anyone?" she asked.

"Mrs. Trigg and Jim," he answered. "I don't think they believed me. Anyway, nothing wrong up there."

"You might take the birds away," she said. "I daren't go into the room to make the beds until you do. I'm scared."

"Nothing to scare you now," said Nat. "They're dead, aren't they?"

He went up with a sack and dropped the stiff bodies into it, one by one. Yes, there were fifty of them, all told. Just the ordinary common birds of the hedgerow, nothing as large even as a thrush. It must have been fright that made them act the way they did. Blue tits, wrens, it was incredible to think of the power of their small beaks, jabbing at his face and hands the night before. He took the sack out into the garden and was faced now with a fresh problem. The ground was too hard to dig. It was frozen solid, yet no snow had fallen, nothing had happened in the past hours but the coming of the east wind. It was unnatural, queer. The weather prophets must be right. The change was something connected with the Arctic Circle.

The wind seemed to cut him to the bone as he stood there, uncertainly, holding the sack. He could see the whitecapped seas breaking down under in the bay. He decided to take the birds to the shore and bury them.

When he reached the beach below the headland he could scarcely stand, the force of the east wind was so strong. It hurt to draw breath, and his bare hands were blue. Never had he known such cold, not in all the bad winters he could remember. It was low tide. He crunched his way over the shingle to the softer sand and then, his back to the wind, ground a pit in the sand with his heel. He meant to drop the birds into it, but as he opened up the sack the force of the wind carried them, lifted them, as though in flight again, and they were blown away from him along the beach, tossed like feathers, spread and scattered, the bodies of the fifty frozen birds. There was something ugly in the sight. He did not like it. The dead birds were swept away from him by the wind.

"The tide will take them when it turns," he said to himself.

He looked out to sea and watched the crested breakers, combing green. They rose stiffly, curled, and broke again, and because it was ebb tide the roar was distant, more remote, lacking the sound and thunder of the flood.

Then he saw them. The gulls. Out there, riding the seas.

What he had thought at first to be the whitecaps of the waves were gulls. Hundreds, thousands, tens of thousands . . . They rose and fell in the trough of the seas, heads to the wind, like a mighty fleet at anchor, waiting on the tide. To eastward, and to the west, the gulls were there. They stretched as far as his eye could reach, in close formation, line upon line. Had the sea been still they would have covered the bay like a white cloud, head to head, body packed to body. Only the east wind, whipping the sea to breakers, hid them from the shore.

Nat turned, and leaving the beach climbed the steep path home. Someone should know of this. Someone should be told. Something was happening, because of the east wind and the weather, that he did not understand. He wondered if he should go to the call box by the bus stop and ring up the police. Yet what could they do? What could anyone do? Tens and thousands of gulls riding the sea there, in the bay, because of storm, because of hunger. The police would think him mad, or drunk, or take the statement from him with great calm. "Thank you. Yes, the matter has already been reported. The hard weather is driving the birds inland in great numbers." Nat looked about him. Still no sign of any other bird. Perhaps the cold had sent them all from up country? As he drew near to the cottage his wife came to meet him, at the door. She called to him, excited. "Nat," she said, "it's on the wireless. They've just read out a special news bulletin. I've written it down."

"What's on the wireless?" he said.

"About the birds," she said. "It's not only here, it's everywhere. In London, all over the country. Something has happened to the birds."

Together they went into the kitchen. He read the piece of paper lying on the table.

"Statement from the Home Office at 11 A.M. today. Reports from all over the country are coming in hourly about the vast quantity of birds flocking above towns, villages and outlying districts, causing obstruction and damage and even attacking individuals. It is thought that the Arctic air stream, at present covering the British Isles, is causing birds to migrate south in immense numbers, and that intense hunger may drive these birds to attack human beings. Householders are warned to see to their windows, doors and chimneys, and to take reasonable precautions for the safety of their children. A further statement will be issued later."

A kind of excitement seized Nat; he looked at his wife in triumph.

"There you are," he said, "let's hope they'll hear that at the farm. Mrs. Trigg will know it wasn't any story. It's true. All over the country. I've been telling myself all morning there's something wrong. And just now, down on the beach, I looked out to sea and there are gulls, thousands of them, tens of thousands, you couldn't put a pin between their heads, and they're all out there, riding on the sea, waiting."

"What are they waiting for, Nat?" she asked.

He stared at her, then looked down again at the piece of paper.

"I don't know," he said slowly. "It says here the birds are hungry."

He went over to the drawer where he kept his hammer and tools.

"What are you going to do, Nat?"

"See to the windows and the chimneys too, like they tell you."

"You think they would break in, with the windows shut? Those sparrows and robins and such? Why, how could they?"

He did not answer. He was not thinking of the robins and the sparrows. He was thinking of the gulls . . .

He went upstairs and worked there the rest of the morning, boarding the windows of the bedrooms, filling up the chimney bases. Good job it was his free day and he was not working at the farm. It reminded him of the old days, at the beginning of the war. He was not married then, and he had made all the blackout boards for his mother's house in Plymouth. Made the shelter too. Not that it had been of any use, when the moment came. He wondered if they would take these precautions up at the farm. He doubted it. Too easygoing, Harry Trigg and his missus. Maybe they'd laugh at the whole thing. Go off to a dance or a whist drive.

"Dinner's ready." She called him, from the kitchen.

"All right. Coming down."

He was pleased with his handiwork. The frames fitted nicely over the little panes and at the base of the chimneys.

When dinner was over and his wife was washing up, Nat switched on the one o'clock news. The same announcement was repeated, the one which she had taken down during the morning, but the news bulletin enlarged upon it. "The flocks of birds have caused dislocation in all areas," read the announcer, "and in London the sky was so dense at ten o'clock this morning that it seemed as if the city was covered by a vast black cloud.

"The birds settled on rooftops, on window ledges and on chimneys. The species included blackbird, thrush, the common house sparrow, and, as might be expected in the metropolis, a vast quantity of pigeons and starlings, and that frequenter of the London river, the black-headed gull. The sight has been so unusual that traffic came to a standstill in many thoroughfares, work was abandoned in shops and offices, and the streets and pavements were crowded with people standing about to watch the birds."

Various incidents were recounted, the suspected reason of cold and hunger stated again, and warnings to householders repeated. The announcer's voice was smooth and suave. Nat had the impression that this man, in particular, treated the whole business as he would an elaborate joke. There would be others like him, hundreds of them, who did not know what it was to struggle in darkness with a flock of birds. There would be parties tonight in London, like the ones they gave on election nights. People standing about, shouting and laughing, getting drunk. "Come and watch the birds!"

Nat switched off the wireless. He got up and started work on the kitchen windows. His wife watched him, young Johnny at her heels.

"What boards for down here too?" she said. "Why, I'll have to light up before three o'clock. I see no call for boards down here."

"Better be sure than sorry," answered Nat. "I'm not going to take any chances."

"What they ought to do," she said, "is to call the army out and shoot the birds. That would soon scare them off."

"Let them try," said Nat. "How'd they set about it?"

"They have the army to the docks," she answered, "when the dockers strike. The soldiers go down and unload the ships."

"Yes," said Nat, "and the population of London is eight million or more. Think of all the buildings, all the flats, and houses. Do you think they've enough soldiers to go round shooting birds from every roof?"

"I don't know. But something should be done. They ought to do something."

Nat thought to himself that "they" were no doubt considering the problem at that very moment, but whatever "they" decided to do in London and the big cities would not help the people here, three hundred miles away. Each householder must look after his own.

"How are we off for food?" he said.

"Now, Nat, whatever next?"

"Never mind. What have you got in the larder?"

"It's shopping day tomorrow, you know that. I don't keep uncooked food hanging about, it goes off. Butcher doesn't call till the day after. But I can bring back something when I go in tomorrow."

Nat did not want to scare her. He thought it possible that she might not go to town tomorrow. He looked in the larder for himself, and in the cupboard where she kept her tins. They would do, for a couple of days. Bread was low.

"What about the baker?"

"He comes tomorrow too."

He saw she had flour. If the baker did not call she had enough to bake one loaf.

"We'd be better off in the old days," he said, "when the women baked twice a week, and had pilchards salted, and there was food for a family to last a siege, if need be."

"I've tried the children with tinned fish, they don't like it," she said.

Nat went on hammering the boards across the kitchen windows. Candles. They were low in candles too. That must be another thing she meant to buy tomorrow. Well, it could not be helped. They must go early to bed tonight. That was, if . . .

He got up and went out of the back door and stood in the garden, looking down towards the sea. There had been no sun all day, and now, at barely three o'clock, a kind of darkness had already come, the sky sullen, heavy, colourless like salt. He could hear the vicious sea drumming on the rocks. He walked down the path, halfway to the beach, and then he stopped. He could see the tide had turned. The rock that had shown in midmorning was now covered, but it was not the sea that held his eyes. The gulls had risen. They were circling, hundreds of them, thousands of them, lifting their wings against the wind. It was the gulls that made the darkening of the sky. And they were silent. They made not a sound. They just went on soaring and circling, rising, falling, trying their strength against the wind.

Nat turned. He ran up the path, back to the cottage.

"I'm going for Jill," he said. "I'll wait for her, at the bus stop."

"What's the matter?" asked his wife. "You've gone quite white."

"Keep Johnny inside," he said. "Keep the door shut. Light up now, and draw the curtains."

"It's only just gone three," she said.

"Never mind. Do what I tell you."

He looked inside the toolshed, outside the back door. Nothing there of much use. A spade was too heavy, and a fork no good. He took the hoe. It was the only possible tool, and light enough to carry.

He started walking up the lane to the bus stop, and now and again glanced back over his shoulder.

The gulls had risen higher now, their circles were broader, wider, they were spreading out in huge formation across the sky.

He hurried on; although he knew the bus would not come to the top of the hill before four o'clock he had to hurry. He passed no one on the way. He was glad of this. No time to stop and chatter.

At the top of the hill he waited. He was much too soon. There was half an hour still to go. The east wind came whipping across the fields from the higher ground. He stamped his feet and blew upon his hands. In the distance he could see the clay hills, white and clean, against the heavy pallor of the sky. Something black rose from behind them, like a smudge at first, then widening, becoming deeper, and the smudge became a cloud, and the cloud divided again into five other clouds, spreading north, east, south and west, and they were not clouds at all; they were birds. He watched them travel across the sky, and as one section passed overhead, within two or three hundred feet of him, he knew, from their speed, they were bound inland, up country, they had no business with the people here on the peninsula. They were rooks, crows, jackdaws, magpies, jays, all birds that usually preyed upon the smaller species; but this afternoon they were bound on some other mission.

"They've been given the towns," thought Nat, "they know what they have to do. We don't matter so much here. The gulls will serve for us. The others go to the towns."

He went to the call box, stepped inside and lifted the receiver. The exchange would do. They would pass the message on.

"I'm speaking from Highway," he said, "by the bus stop. I want to report large formations of birds travelling up country. The gulls are also forming in the bay."

"All right," answered the voice, laconic, weary.

"You'll be sure and pass this message on to the proper quarter?"

"Yes . . . yes . . ." Impatient now, fed up. The buzzing note resumed.

"She's another," thought Nat, "she doesn't care. Maybe she's had to answer calls all day. She hopes to go to the pictures tonight. She'll squeeze some fellow's hand, and point up at the sky, and 'Look at all them birds!' She doesn't care."

The bus came lumbering up the hill. Jill climbed out and three or four other children. The bus went on towards the town.

"What's the hoe for, Dad?"

They crowded around him, laughing, pointing.

"I just brought it along," he said. "Come on now, let's get home. It's cold, no hanging about. Here, you. I'll watch you across the fields, see how fast you can run."

He was speaking to Jill's companions, who came from different families, living in the council houses. A short cut would take them to the cottages.

"We want to play a bit in the lane," said one of them.

"No, you don't. You go off home, or I'll tell your mammy."

They whispered to one another, round-eyed, then scuttled off across the fields. Jill stared at her father, her mouth sullen.

"We always play in the lane," she said.

"Not tonight, you don't," he said. "Come on now, no dawdling."

He could see the gulls now, circling the fields, coming in towards the land. Still silent. Still no sound.

"Look, Dad, look over there, look at all the gulls."

"Yes. Hurry, now."

"Where are they flying to? Where are they going?"

"Up country, I dare say. Where it's warmer."

He seized her hand and dragged her after him along the lane.

"Don't go so fast. I can't keep up."

The gulls were copying the rooks and crows. They were spreading out in formation across the sky. They headed, in bands of
thousands, to the four compass points.

"Dad, what is it? What are the gulls doing?"

They were not intent upon their flight, as the crows, as the jackdaws had been. They still circled overhead. Nor did they fly so
high. It was as though they waited upon some signal. As though
some decision had yet to be given. The order was not clear.

"Do you want me to carry you, Jill? Here, come pickaback."

This way he might put on speed; but he was wrong. Jill was
heavy. She kept slipping. And she was crying too. His sense of urgency, of fear, had communicated itself to the child.

"I wish the gulls would go away. I don't like them. They're
coming closer to the lane."

He put her down again. He started running, swinging Jill after
him. As they went past the farm turning he saw the farmer backing his car out of the garage. Nat called to him.

"Can you give us a lift?" he said.

"What's that?"

Mr. Trigg turned in the driving seat and stared at them. Then a
smile came to his cheerful, rubicund face.

"It looks as though we're in for some fun," he said. "Have you
seen the gulls? Jim and I are going to take a crack at them. Everyone's gone bird crazy, talking of nothing else. I hear you were
troubled in the night. Want a gun?"

Nat shook his head.

The small car was packed. There was just room for Jill, if she
crouched on top of petrol tins on the back seat.

"I don't want a gun," said Nat, "but I'd be obliged if you'd run
Jill home. She's scared of the birds."

He spoke briefly. He did not want to talk in front of Jill.

"O.K.," said the farmer, "I'll take her home. Why don't you
stop behind and join the shooting match? We'll make the feathers
fly."

Jill climbed in, and turning the car the driver sped up the lane.

Nat followed after. Trigg must be crazy. What use was a gun against a sky of birds?

Now Nat was not responsible for Jill he had time to look about him. The birds were circling still, above the fields. Mostly herring gull, but the black-backed gull amongst them. Usually they kept apart. Now they were united. Some bond had brought them together. It was the black-backed gull that attacked the smaller birds, and even newborn lambs, so he'd heard. He'd never seen it done. He remembered this now, though, looking above him in the sky. They were coming in towards the farm. They were circling lower in the sky, and the black-backed gulls were to the front, the black-backed gulls were leading. The farm, then, was their target. They were making for the farm.

Nat increased his pace towards his own cottage. He saw the farmer's car turn and come back along the lane. It drew up beside him with a jerk.

"The kid has run inside," said the farmer. "Your wife was watching for her. Well, what do you make of it? They're saying in town the Russians have done it. The Russians have poisoned the birds."

"How could they do that?" asked Nat.

"Don't ask me. You know how stories get around. Will you join my shooting match?"

"No, I'll get along home. The wife will be worried else."

"My missus says if you could eat gull, there'd be some sense in it," said Trigg, "we'd have roast gull, baked gull, and pickle 'em into the bargain. You wait until I let off a few barrels into the brutes. That'll scare 'em."

"Have you boarded your windows?" asked Nat.

"No. Lot of nonsense. They like to scare you on the wireless. I've had more to do today than to go round boarding up my windows."

"I'd board them now, if I were you."

"Garn. You're windy. Like to come to our place to sleep?"

"No, thanks all the same."

"All right. See you in the morning. Give you a gull breakfast."

The farmer grinned and turned his car to the farm entrance.

Nat hurried on. Past the little wood, past the old barn, and then across the stile to the remaining field.

As he jumped the stile he heard the whir of wings. A black-

backed gull dived down at him from the sky, missed, swerved in
flight, and rose to dive again. In a moment it was joined by others,
six, seven, a dozen, black-backed and herring mixed. Nat dropped
his hoe. The hoe was useless. Covering his head with his arms he
ran towards the cottage. They kept coming at him from the air, silent save for the beating wings. The terrible, fluttering wings. He
could feel the blood on his hands, his wrists, his neck. Each stab
of a swooping beak tore his flesh. If only he could keep them from
his eyes. Nothing else mattered. He must keep them from his eyes.
They had not learnt yet how to cling to a shoulder, how to rip
clothing, how to dive in mass upon the head, upon the body. But
with each dive, with each attack, they became bolder. And they
had no thought for themselves. When they dived low and missed,
they crashed, bruised and broken, on the ground. As Nat ran he
stumbled, kicking their spent bodies in front of him.

He found the door, he hammered upon it with his bleeding
hands. Because of the boarded windows no light shone. Everything was dark.

"Let me in," he shouted, "it's Nat. Let me in."

He shouted loud to make himself heard above the whirr of the
gull's wings.

Then he saw the gannet, poised for the dive, above him in the
sky. The gulls circled, retired, soared, one with another, against
the wind. Only the gannet remained. One single gannet, above
him in the sky. The wings folded suddenly to its body. It dropped,
like a stone. Nat screamed, and the door opened. He stumbled
across the threshold, and his wife threw her weight against the
door.

They heard the thud of the gannet as it fell.

His wife dressed his wounds. They were not deep. The backs
of his hands had suffered most, and his wrists. Had he not worn a
cap they would have reached his head. As to the gannet . . . the
gannet could have split his skull.

The children were crying, of course. They had seen the blood
on their father's hands.

"It's all right now," he told them. "I'm not hurt. Just a few
scratches. You play with Johnny, Jill. Mammy will wash these
cuts."

He half-shut the door to the scullery, so that they could not see. His wife was ashen. She began running water from the sink.

"I saw them overhead," she whispered. "They began collecting just as Jill ran in with Mr. Trigg. I shut the door fast, and it jammed. That's why I couldn't open it at once, when you came."

"Thank God they waited for me," he said. "Jill would have fallen at once. One bird alone would have done it."

Furtively, so as not to alarm the children, they whispered together, as she bandaged his hands and the back of his neck.

"They're flying inland," he said, "thousands of them. Rooks, crows, all the bigger birds. I saw them from the bus stop. They're making for the towns."

"But what can they do, Nat?"

"They'll attack. Go for everyone out in the streets. Then they'll try the windows, the chimneys."

"Why don't the authorities do something? Why don't they get the army, get machine guns, anything?"

"There's been no time. Nobody's prepared. We'll hear what they have to say on the six o'clock news."

Nat went back into the kitchen, followed by his wife. Johnny was playing quietly on the floor. Only Jill looked anxious.

"I can hear the birds," she said. "Listen, Dad."

Nat listened. Muffled sounds came from the windows, from the door. Wings brushing the surface, sliding, scraping, seeking a way of entry. The sound of many bodies, pressed together, shuffling on the sills. Now and again came a thud, a crash, as some bird dived and fell. "Some of them will kill themselves that way," he thought, "but not enough. Never enough."

"All right," he said aloud. "I've got boards over the windows, Jill. The birds can't get in."

He went and examined all the windows. His work had been thorough. Every gap was closed. He would make extra certain, however. He found wedges, pieces of old tin, strips of wood and metal and fastened them at the sides to reinforce the boards. His hammering helped to deafen the sound of the birds, the shuffling, the tapping, and more ominous—he did not want his wife or the children to hear it—the splinter of cracked glass.

"Turn on the wireless," he said, "let's have the wireless."

This would drown the sound also. He went upstairs to the bedrooms and reinforced the windows there. Now he could hear the birds on the roof, the scraping of claws, a sliding, jostling sound.

He decided they must sleep in the kitchen, keep up the fire, bring down the mattresses and lay them out on the floor. He was afraid of the bedroom chimneys. The boards he had placed at the chimney bases might give way. In the kitchen they would be safe, because of the fire. He would have to make a joke of it. Pretend to the children they were playing at camp. If the worst happened, and the birds forced an entry down the bedroom chimneys, it would be hours, days perhaps, before they could break down the doors. The birds would be imprisoned in the bedrooms. They could do no harm there. Crowded together, they would stifle and die.

He began to bring the mattresses downstairs. At sight of them his wife's eyes widened in apprehension. She thought the birds had already broken in upstairs.

"All right," he said cheerfully, "we'll all sleep together in the kitchen tonight. More cosy here by the fire. Then we shan't be worried by those silly old birds tapping at the windows."

He made the children help him rearrange the furniture, and he took the precaution of moving the dresser, with his wife's help, across the window. It fitted well. It was an added safeguard. The mattresses could now be lain, one beside the other, against the wall where the dresser had stood.

"We're safe enough now," he thought, "we're snug and tight, like an air-raid shelter. We can hold out. It's just the food that worries me. Food and coal for the fire. We've enough for two or three days, not more. By that time . . ."

No use thinking ahead as far as that. And they'd be giving directions on the wireless. People would be told what to do. And now, in the midst of many problems, he realised that it was dance music only coming over the air. Not Children's Hour, as it should have been. He glanced at the dial. Yes, they were on the Home Service all right. Dance records. He switched to the Light programme. He knew the reason. The usual programmes had been abandoned. This only happened at exceptional times. Elections, and such. He tried to remember if it had happened in the war, during the heavy raids on London. But of course. The B.B.C. was not stationed in London during the war. The programmes were broadcast from other, temporary quarters. "We're better off here," he thought, "we're better off here in the kitchen, with the windows and the doors boarded, than they are up in the towns. Thank God we're not in the towns."

At six o'clock the records ceased. The time signal was given. No matter if it scared the children, he must hear the news. There was a pause after the pips. Then the announcer spoke. His voice was solemn, grave. Quite different from midday.

"This is London," he said. "A National Emergency was proclaimed at four o'clock this afternoon. Measures are being taken to safeguard the lives and property of the population, but it must be understood that these are not easy to effect immediately, owing to the unforeseen and unparalleled nature of the present crisis. Every householder must take precautions to his own building, and where several people live together, as in flats and apartments, they must unite to do the utmost they can to prevent entry. It is absolutely imperative that every individual stays indoors tonight, and that no one at all remains on the streets, or roads, or anywhere without doors. The birds, in vast numbers, are attacking anyone on sight, and have already begun an assault upon buildings; but these, with due care, should be impenetrable. The population is asked to remain calm, and not to panic. Owing to the exceptional nature of the emergency, there will be no further transmission from any broadcasting station until 7 A.M. tomorrow."

They played the National Anthem. Nothing more happened. Nat switched off the set. He looked at his wife. She stared back at him.

"What's it mean?" said Jill. "What did the news say?"

"There won't be any more programmes tonight," said Nat. "There's been a breakdown at the B.B.C."

"Is it the birds?" asked Jill. "Have the birds done it?"

"No," said Nat, "it's just that everyone's very busy, and then of course they have to get rid of the birds, messing everything up, in the towns. Well, we can manage without the wireless for one evening."

"I wish we had a gramophone," said Jill. "That would be better than nothing."

She had her face turned to the dresser, backed against the windows. Try as they did to ignore it, they were all aware of the shuffling, the stabbing, the persistent beating and sweeping of wings.

"We'll have supper early," suggested Nat, "something for a treat. Ask Mammy. Toasted cheese, eh? Something we all like?"

He winked and nodded at his wife. He wanted the look of dread, of apprehension to go from Jill's face.

He helped with the supper, whistling, singing, making as much clatter as he could, and it seemed to him that the shuffling and the tapping were not so intense as they had been at first. Presently he went up to the bedrooms and listened, and he no longer heard the jostling for place upon the roof.

"They've got reasoning powers," he thought, "they know it's hard to break in here. They'll try elsewhere. They won't waste their time with us."

Supper passed without incident, and then, when they were clearing away, they heard a new sound, droning, familiar, a sound they all knew and understood.

His wife looked up at him, her face alight. "It's planes," she said, "they're sending out planes after the birds. That's what I said they ought to do, all along. That will get them. Isn't that gunfire? Can't you hear guns?"

It might be gunfire, out at sea. Nat could not tell. Big naval guns might have an effect upon the gulls out at sea, but the gulls were inland now. The guns couldn't shell the shore, because of the population.

"It's good, isn't it," said his wife, "to hear the planes?" And Jill, catching her enthusiasm, jumped up and down with Johnny. "The planes will get the birds. The planes will shoot them."

Just then they heard a crash two miles distant, followed by a second, then a third. The droning became more distant, passed away out to sea.

"What was that?" asked his wife. "Were they dropping bombs on the birds?"

"I don't know," answered Nat. "I don't think so."

He did not want to tell her that the sound they had heard was the crashing of aircraft. It was, he had no doubt, a venture on the part of the authorities to send out reconnaissance forces, but they might have known the venture was suicidal. What could aircraft do against birds that flung themselves to death against propeller and fuselage but hurtle to the ground themselves? This was being tried now, he supposed, over the whole country. And at a cost. Someone high up has lost his head.

"Where have the planes gone, Dad?" asked Jill.

"Back to base," he said. "Come on, now, time to tuck down for bed."

It kept his wife occupied, undressing the children before the fire, seeing to the bedding, one thing and another, while he went round the cottage again, making sure that nothing had worked loose. There was no further drone of aircraft, and the naval guns had ceased. "Waste of life and effort," Nat said to himself. "We can't destroy enough of them that way. Cost too heavy. There's always gas. Maybe they'll try spraying with gas, mustard gas. We'll be warned first, of course, if they do. There's one thing, the best brains of the country will be on to it tonight."

Somehow the thought reassured him. He had a picture of scientists, naturalists, technicians, and all those chaps they called the backroom boys, summoned to a council; they'd be working on the problem now. This was not a job for the government, for the chiefs of staff—they would merely carry out the orders of the scientists.

"They'll have to be ruthless," he thought. "Where the trouble's worst they'll have to risk more lives, if they use gas. All the livestock, too, and the soil—all contaminated. As long as everyone doesn't panic. That's the trouble. People panicking, losing their heads. The B.B.C. was right to warn us of that."

Upstairs in the bedrooms all was quiet. No further scraping and stabbing at the windows. A lull in battle. Forces regrouping. Wasn't that what they called it, in the old wartime bulletins? The wind hadn't dropped, though. He could still hear it, roaring in the chimneys. And the sea breaking down on the shore. Then he remembered the tide. The tide would be on the turn. Maybe the lull in battle was because of the tide. There was some law the birds obeyed, and it was all to do with the east wind and the tide.

He glanced at his watch. Nearly eight o'clock. It must have gone high water an hour ago. That explained the lull: the birds attacked with the flood tide. It might not work that way inland, up country, but it seemed as if it was so this way on the coast. He reckoned the time limit in his head. They had six hours to go, without attack. When the tide turned again, around one-twenty in the morning, the birds would come back . . .

There were two things he could do. The first to rest, with his wife and children, and all of them snatch what sleep they could, until the small hours. The second to go out, see how they were faring at the farm, see if the telephone was still working there, so that they might get news from the exchange.

He called softly to his wife, who had just settled the children. She came halfway up the stairs and he whispered to her.

"You're not to go," she said at once, "you're not to go and leave me alone with the children. I can't stand it."

Her voice rose hysterically. He hushed her, calmed her.

"All right," he said, "all right. I'll wait till morning. And we'll get the wireless bulletin then too, at seven. But in the morning, when the tide ebbs again, I'll try for the farm, and they may let us have bread and potatoes, and milk too."

His mind was busy again, planning against emergency. They would not have milked, of course, this evening. The cows would be standing by the gate, waiting in the yard, with the household inside, battened behind boards, as they were here at the cottage. That is, if they had had time to take precautions. He thought of the farmer, Trigg, smiling at him from the car. There would have been no shooting party, not tonight.

The children were asleep. His wife, still clothed, was sitting on her mattress. She watched him, her eyes nervous.

"What are you going to do?" she whispered.

He shook his head for silence. Softly, stealthily, he opened the back door and looked outside.

It was pitch dark. The wind was blowing harder than ever, coming in steady gusts, icy, from the sea. He kicked at the step outside the door. It was heaped with birds. There were dead birds everywhere. Under the windows, against the walls. These were the suicides, the divers, the ones with broken necks. Wherever he looked he saw dead birds. No trace of the living. The living had flown seaward with the turn of the tide. The gulls would be riding the seas now, as they had done in the forenoon.

In the far distance, on the hill where the tractor had been two days before, something was burning. One of the aircraft that had crashed; the fire, fanned by the wind, had set light to a stack.

He looked at the bodies of the birds, and he had a notion that if he heaped them, one upon the other, on the window sills they would make added protection for the next attack. Not much, perhaps, but something. The bodies would have to be clawed at, pecked, and dragged aside, before the living birds gained purchase on the sills and attacked the panes. He set to work in the darkness. It was queer; he hated touching them. The bodies were still warm and bloody. The blood matted their feathers. He felt his stomach turn, but he went on with his work. He noticed, grimly, that every windowpane was shattered. Only the boards had kept the birds from breaking in. He stuffed the cracked panes with the bleeding bodies of the birds.

When he had finished he went back into the cottage. He barricaded the kitchen door, made it doubly secure. He took off his bandages, sticky with the birds' blood, not with his own cuts, and put on fresh plaster.

His wife had made him cocoa and he drank it thirstily. He was very tired.

"All right," he said, smiling, "don't worry. We'll get through."

He lay down on his mattress and closed his eyes. He slept at once. He dreamt uneasily, because through his dreams there ran a thread of something forgotten. Some piece of work, neglected, that he should have done. Some precaution that he had known well but had not taken, and he could not put a name to it in his dreams. It was connected in some way with the burning aircraft and the stack upon the hill. He went on sleeping, though; he did not awake. It was his wife shaking his shoulder that awoke him finally.

"They've begun," she sobbed, "they've started this last hour, I can't listen to it any longer, alone. There's something smelling bad too, something burning."

Then he remembered. He had forgotten to make up the fire. It was smouldering, nearly out. He got up swiftly and lit the lamp. The hammering had started at the windows and the doors, but it was not that he minded now. It was the smell of singed feathers. The smell filled the kitchen. He knew at once what it was. The birds were coming down the chimney, squeezing their way down to the kitchen range.

He got sticks and paper and put them on the embers, then reached for the can of paraffin.

"Stand back," he shouted to his wife, "we've got to risk this."

He threw the paraffin onto the fire. The flame roared up the pipe, and down upon the fire fell the scorched, blackened bodies of the birds.

The children woke, crying. "What is it?" said Jill. "What's happened?"

Nat had no time to answer. He was raking the bodies from the chimney, clawing them out onto the floor. The flames still roared, and the danger of the chimney catching fire was one he had to take. The flames would send away the living birds from the chimney top. The lower joint was the difficulty, though. This was choked with the smouldering helpless bodies of the birds caught by fire. He scarcely heeded the attack on the windows and the door: let them beat their wings, break their beaks, lose their lives, in the attempt to force an entry into his home. They would not break in. He thanked God he had one of the old cottages, with small windows, stout walls. Not like the new council houses. Heaven help them up the lane, in the new council houses.

"Stop crying," he called to the children. "There's nothing to be afraid of, stop crying."

He went on raking at the burning, smouldering bodies as they fell into the fire.

"This'll fetch them," he said to himself, "the draught and the flames together. We're all right, as long as the chimney doesn't catch. I ought to be shot for this. It's all my fault. Last thing I should have made up the fire. I knew there was something."

Amid the scratching and tearing at the window boards came the sudden homely striking of the kitchen clock. Three A.M. A little more than four hours yet to go. He could not be sure of the exact time of high water. He reckoned it would not turn much before half-past seven, twenty to eight.

"Light up the Primus," he said to his wife. "Make us some tea, and the kids some cocoa. No use sitting around doing nothing."

That was the line. Keep her busy, and the children too. Move about, eat, drink; always best to be on the go.

He waited by the range. The flames were dying. But no more blackened bodies fell from the chimney. He thrust his poker up as far as it could go and found nothing. It was clear. The chimney was clear. He wiped the sweat from his forehead.

"Come on now, Jill," he said, "bring me some more sticks. We'll have a good fire going directly." She wouldn't come near him, though. She was staring at the heaped singed bodies of the birds.

"Never mind them," he said, "we'll put those in the passage when I've got the fire steady."

The danger of the chimney was over. It could not happen again, not if the fire was kept burning day and night.

"I'll have to get more fuel from the farm tomorrow," he thought. "This will never last. I'll manage, though. I can do all that with the ebb tide. It can be worked, fetching what we need, when the tide's turned. We've just got to adapt ourselves, that's all."

They drank tea and cocoa and ate slices of bread and Bovril. Only half a loaf left, Nat noticed. Never mind, though, they'd get by.

"Stop it," said young Johnny, pointing to the windows with his spoon, "stop it, you old birds."

"That's right," said Nat, smiling, "we don't want the old beggars, do we? Had enough of 'em."

They began to cheer when they heard the thud of the suicide birds.

"There's another, Dad," cried Jill, "he's done for."

"He's had it," said Nat, "there he goes, the blighter."

This was the way to face up to it. This was the spirit. If they could keep this up, hang on like this until seven, when the first news bulletin came through, they would not have done too badly.

"Give us a fag," he said to his wife. "A bit of a smoke will clear away the smell of the scorched feathers."

"There's only two left in the packet," she said. "I was going to buy you some from the Co-op."

"I'll have one," he said. "T'other will keep for a rainy day."

No sense trying to make the children rest. There was no rest to be got while the tapping and the scratching went on at the windows. He sat with one arm round his wife and the other round Jill, with Johnny on his mother's lap and the blankets heaped about them on the mattress.

"You can't help admiring the beggars," he said, "they've got persistence. You'd think they'd tire of the game, but not a bit of it."

Admiration was hard to sustain. The tapping went on and on and a new rasping note struck Nat's ear, as though a sharper beak than any hitherto had come to take over from its fellows. He tried to remember the names of birds, he tried to think which species would go for this particular job. It was not the tap of the wood-pecker. That would be light and frequent. This was more serious, because if it continued long the wood would splinter as the glass had done. Then he remembered the hawks. Could the hawks have taken over from the gulls? Were there buzzards now upon the sills, using talons as well as beaks? Hawks, buzzards, kestrels, fal-cons—he had forgotten the birds of prey. He had forgotten the gripping power of the birds of prey. Three hours to go, and while they waited, the sound of the splintering wood, the talons tearing at the wood.

Nat looked about him, seeing what furniture he could destroy to fortify the door. The windows were safe, because of the dresser. He was not certain of the door. He went upstairs, but when he reached the landing he paused and listened. There was a soft pat-ter on the floor of the children's bedroom. The birds had broken through . . . He put his ear to the door. No mistake. He could hear the rustle of wings, and the light patter as they searched the floor. The other bedroom was still clear. He went into it and began bringing out the furniture, to pile at the head of the stairs should the door of the children's bedroom go. It was a prepara-tion. It might never be needed. He could not stack the furniture against the door, because it opened inward. The only possible thing was to have it at the top of the stairs.

"Come down, Nat, what are you doing?" called his wife.

"I won't be long," he shouted. "Just making everything ship-shape up here."

He did not want her to come; he did not want her to hear the pattering of the feet in the children's bedroom, the brushing of those wings against the door.

At five-thirty he suggested breakfast, bacon and fried bread, if only to stop the growing look of panic in his wife's eyes and to calm the fretful children. She did not know about the birds up-stairs. The bedroom, luckily, was not over the kitchen. Had it been so she could not have failed to hear the sound of them, up there, tapping the boards. And the silly, senseless thud of the sui-cide birds, the death and glory boys, who flew into the bedroom, smashing their heads against the walls. He knew them of old, the herring gulls. They had no brains. The black-backs were differ-ent, they knew what they were doing. So did the buzzards, the hawks . . .

He found himself watching the clock, gazing at the hands that went so slowly round the dial. If his theory was not correct, if the attack did not cease with the turn of the tide, he knew they were beaten. They could not continue through the long day without air, without rest, without more fuel, without . . . his mind raced. He knew there were so many things they needed to withstand siege. They were not fully prepared. They were not ready. It might be that it would be safer in the towns after all. If he could get a message through, on the farm telephone, to his cousin, only a short journey by train up country, they might be able to hire a car. That would be quicker—hire a car between tides . . .

His wife's voice, calling his name, drove away the sudden, desperate desire for sleep.

"What is it? What now?" he said sharply.

"The wireless," said his wife. "I've been watching the clock. It's nearly seven."

"Don't twist the knob," he said, impatient for the first time, "it's on the Home where it is. They'll speak from the Home."

They waited. The kitchen clock struck seven. There was no sound. No chimes, no music. They waited until a quarter past, switching to the Light. The result was the same. No news bulletin came through.

"We've heard wrong," he said. "They won't be broadcasting until eight o'clock."

They left it switched on, and Nat thought of the battery, wondered how much power was left in it. It was generally recharged when his wife went shopping in the town. If the battery failed they would not hear the instructions.

"It's getting light," whispered his wife. "I can't see it, but I can feel it. And the birds aren't hammering so loud."

She was right. The rasping, tearing sound grew fainter every moment. So did the shuffling, the jostling for place upon the step, upon the sills. The tide was on the turn. By eight there was no sound at all. Only the wind. The children, lulled at last by the stillness, fell asleep. At half-past eight Nat switched the wireless off.

"What are you doing? We'll miss the news," said his wife.

"There isn't going to be any news," said Nat. "We've got to depend upon ourselves."

He went to the door and slowly pulled away the barricades. He drew the bolts, and kicking the bodies from the step outside the door breathed the cold air. He had six working hours before him, and he knew he must reserve his strength for the right things, not waste it in any way. Food, and light, and fuel; these were the necessary things. If he could get them in sufficiency, they could endure another night.

He stepped into the garden, and as he did so he saw the living birds. The gulls had gone to ride the sea, as they had done before; they sought sea food, and the buoyancy of the tide, before they returned to the attack. Not so the land birds. They waited and watched. Nat saw them, on the hedgerows, on the soil, crowded in the trees, outside in the field, line upon line of birds, all still, doing nothing.

He went to the end of his small garden. The birds did not move. They went on watching him.

"I've got to get food," said Nat to himself. "I've got to go to the farm to find food."

He went back to the cottage. He saw to the windows and the doors. He went upstairs and opened the children's bedroom. It was empty, except for the dead birds on the floor. The living were out there, in the garden, in the fields. He went downstairs.

"I'm going to the farm," he said.

His wife clung to him. She had seen the living birds from the open door.

"Take us with you," she begged. "We can't stay here alone. I'd rather die than stay here alone."

He considered the matter. He nodded.

"Come on, then," he said. "Bring baskets, and Johnny's pram. We can load up the pram."

They dressed against the biting wind, wore gloves and scarves. His wife put Johnny in the pram. Nat took Jill's hand.

"The birds," she whimpered, "they're all out there, in the fields."

"They won't hurt us," he said, "not in the light."

They started walking across the field towards the stile, and the birds did not move. They waited, their heads turned to the wind.

When they reached the turning to the farm, Nat stopped and told his wife to wait in the shelter of the hedge with the two children.

"But I want to see Mrs. Trigg," she protested. "There are lots of things we can borrow, if they went to market yesterday; not only bread, and . . ."

"Wait here," Nat interrupted. "I'll be back in a moment."

The cows were lowing, moving restlessly in the yard, and he could see a gap in the fence where the sheep had knocked their way through, to roam unchecked in the front garden before the farmhouse. No smoke came from the chimneys. He was filled with misgiving. He did not want his wife or the children to go down to the farm.

"Don't gib now," said Nat, harshly, "do what I say."

She withdrew with the pram into the hedge, screening herself and the children from the wind.

He went down alone to the farm. He pushed his way through the herd of bellowing cows, which turned this way and that, distressed, their udders full. He saw the car standing by the gate, not put away in the garage. The windows of the farmhouse were smashed. There were many dead gulls lying in the yard and around the house. The living birds perched on the group of trees behind the farm and on the roof of the house. They were quite still. They watched him.

Jim's body lay in the yard . . . what was left of it. When the birds had finished, the cows had trampled him. His gun was beside him. The door of the house was shut and bolted, but as the windows were smashed it was easy to lift them and climb through. Trigg's body was close to the telephone. He must have been trying to get through to the exchange when the birds came for him. The receiver was hanging loose, the instrument torn from the wall. No sign of Mrs. Trigg. She would be upstairs. Was it any use going up? Sickened, Nat knew what he would find.

"Thank God," he said to himself, "there were no children."

He forced himself to climb the stairs, but halfway he turned and descended again. He could see her legs, protruding from the open bedroom door. Beside her were the bodies of the black-backed gulls, and an umbrella, broken.

"It's no use," thought Nat, "doing anything. I've only got five hours, less than that. The Triggs would understand. I must load up with what I can find."

He tramped back to his wife and children.

"I'm going to fill up the car with stuff," he said. "I'll put coal in it, and paraffin for the Primus. We'll take it home and return for a fresh load."

"What about the Triggs?" asked his wife.

"They must have gone to friends," he said.

"Shall I come and help you, then?"

"No; there's a mess down there. Cows and sheep all over the place. Wait, I'll get the car. You can sit in it."

Clumsily he backed the car out of the yard and into the lane. His wife and the children could not see Jim's body from there.

"Stay here," he said, "never mind the pram. The pram can be fetched later. I'm going to load the car."

Her eyes watched his all the time. He believed she understood, otherwise she would have suggested helping him to find the bread and groceries.

They made three journeys altogether, backwards and forwards between their cottage and the farm, before he was satisfied they had everything they needed. It was surprising, once he started thinking, how many things were necessary. Almost the most important of all was planking for the windows. He had to go round searching for timber. He wanted to renew the boards on all the windows at the cottage. Candles, paraffin, nails, tinned stuff; the list was endless. Besides all that, he milked three of the cows. The rest, poor brutes, would have to go on bellowing.

On the final journey he drove the car to the bus stop, got out, and went to the telephone box. He waited a few minutes, jangling the receiver. No good, though. The line was dead. He climbed onto a bank and looked over the countryside, but there was no sign of life at all, nothing in the fields but the waiting, watching birds. Some of them slept—he could see the beaks tucked into the feathers.

"You'd think they'd be feeding," he said to himself, "not just standing in that way."

Then he remembered. They were gorged with food. They had eaten their fill during the night. That was why they did not move this morning . . .

No smoke came from the chimneys of the council houses. He thought of the children who had run across the fields the night before.

"I should have known," he thought. "I ought to have taken them home with me."

He lifted his face to the sky. It was colourless and grey. The bare trees on the landscape looked bent and blackened by the east wind. The cold did not affect the living birds, waiting out there in the fields.

"This is the time they ought to get them," said Nat, "they're a sitting target now. They must be doing this all over the country. Why don't our aircraft take off now and spray them with mustard gas? What are all our chaps doing? They must know, they must see for themselves."

He went back to the car and got into the driver's seat.

"Go quickly past that second gate," whispered his wife. "The postman's lying there. I don't want Jill to see."

He accelerated. The little Morris bumped and rattled along the lane. The children shrieked with laughter.

"Up-a-down, up-a-down," shouted young Johnny.

It was a quarter to one by the time they reached the cottage. Only an hour to go.

"Better have cold dinner," said Nat. "Hot up something for yourself and the children, some of that soup. I've no time to eat now. I've got to unload all this stuff."

He got everything inside the cottage. It could be sorted later. Give them all something to do during the long hours ahead. First he must see to the windows and the doors.

He went round the cottage methodically, testing every window, every door. He climbed onto the roof, also, and fixed boards across every chimney, except the kitchen. The cold was so intense he could hardly bear it, but the job had to be done. Now and again he would look up, searching the sky for aircraft. None came. As he worked he cursed the inefficiency of the authorities.

"It's always the same," he muttered, "they always let us down. Muddle, muddle, from the start. No plan, no real organisation. And we don't matter, down here. That's what it is. The people up country have priority. They're using gas up there, no doubt, and all the aircraft. We've got to wait and take what comes."

He paused, his work on the bedroom finished, and looked out to sea. Something was moving out there. Something grey and white amongst the breakers.

"Good old Navy," he said, "they never let us down. They're coming down channel, they're turning in the bay."

He waited, straining his eyes, watering in the wind, towards the sea. He was wrong, though. It was not ships. The Navy was not there. The gulls were rising from the sea. The massed flocks in the fields, with ruffled feathers, rose in formation from the ground, and wing to wing soared upwards to the sky.

The tide had turned again.

Nat climbed down the ladder and went inside the kitchen. The family were at dinner. It was a little after two. He bolted the door, put up the barricade, and lit the lamp.

"It's nighttime," said young Johnny.

His wife had switched on the wireless once again, but no sound came from it.

"I've been all round the dial," she said, "foreign stations, and that lot. I can't get anything."

"Maybe they have the same trouble," he said, "Maybe it's the same right through Europe."

She poured out a plateful of the Triggs' soup, cut him a large slice of the Triggs' bread, and spread their dripping upon it.

They ate in silence. A piece of the dripping ran down young Johnny's chin and fell onto the table.

"Manners, Johnny," said Jill, "you should learn to wipe your mouth."

The tapping began at the windows, at the door. The rustling, the jostling, the pushing for position on the sills. The first thud of the suicide gulls upon the step.

"Won't America do something?" said his wife. "They've always been our allies, haven't they? Surely America will do something?"

Nat did not answer. The boards were strong against the windows, and on the chimneys too. The cottage was filled with stores, with fuel, with all they needed for the next few days. When he had finished dinner he would put the stuff away, stack it neatly, get everything shipshape, handy-like. His wife could help him, and the children too. They'd tire themselves out, between now and a quarter to nine, when the tide would ebb; then he'd tuck them down on their mattresses, see that they slept good and sound until three in the morning.

He had a new scheme for the windows, which was to fix barbed wire in front of the boards. He had brought a great roll of it from the farm. The nuisance was, he'd have to work at this in the dark, when the lull came between nine and three. Pity he had not thought of it before. Still, as long as the wife slept, and the kids, that was the main thing.

The smaller birds were at the window now. He recognised the light tap-tapping of their beaks, and the soft brush of their wings. The hawks ignored the windows. They concentrated their attack upon the door. Nat listened to the tearing sound of splintering wood, and wondered how many million years of memory were stored in those little brains, behind the stabbing beaks, the piercing eyes, now giving them this instinct to destroy mankind with all the deft precision of machines.

"I'll smoke that last fag," he said to his wife. "Stupid of me, it was the one thing I forgot to bring back from the farm."

He reached for it, switched on the silent wireless. He threw the empty packet on the fire, and watched it burn.